Ellen Blackmar Maxwell

The bishop's Conversion

Ellen Blackmar Maxwell

The bishop's Conversion

ISBN/EAN: 9783743336865

Manufactured in Europe, USA, Canada, Australia, Japa

Cover: Foto ©Andreas Hilbeck / pixelio.de

Manufactured and distributed by brebook publishing software
(www.brebook.com)

Ellen Blackmar Maxwell

The bishop's Conversion

SIDNEY TEACHING SITARA.

BY

ELLEN BLACKMAR MAXWELL

WITH

AN INTRODUCTION

By JAMES M. THOBURN

Missionary Bishop for India and Malaysia

NEW YORK: HUNT & EATON

CINCINNATI · CRANSTON & CURTS

1893

6   CONTENTS.

INTRODUCTION.

IT has long been a cause of regret to missionaries in the foreign field that people at home seemed so prone to form incorrect ideas, both of their method of work and style of living. Many honest and earnest attempts have been made to correct the false impressions which have become current, both in England and America, but these have not always proved successful. The root of the difficulty is found in the fact that most persons measure all conditions of life and labor by the same standard without making allowance for the thousand points of difference which must prevail between people and countries so radically different as those found in the Oriental and Occidental worlds. To this must be added the fact that for two generations past a false ideal of missionary character and missionary work has been devoutly cherished both in England and America. The missionary is very much like other good men. His work is a very practical work, and all romantic ideals, or exaggerated ideas of angelic perfection, must be thrown to the winds by the practical observer who wishes to get a correct view of missionary life as it is.

Mrs. Maxwell has seen much and has served well in the missionary field, and has well earned a right to be

heard on the subject which she has chosen. Instead
of discussing in an abstract manner the various phases
of her subject, she has wisely chosen to bring it in a
more practical way before her readers by introducing
scenes from actual life, which illustrate the most important phases of missionary life as she has seen it.
Many of the incidents used in the course of her story
are recitals of actual occurrences, and are by no means
the creation of the imagination alone. Such a presentation of various views of missionary life and
labor can hardly fail to do much good, not only in
correcting false impressions, but in creating better
views and more healthy feelings among a large class
of good Christian people who are numbered among
the supporters of missions. Detached statements of
fact can never be made to impress the average mind
of reading people so vividly or forcibly as pictures
drawn from actual life, and especially when drawn by
one present at the scene of action.

Practical missionaries have nothing to fear and
much to hope from a truthful presentation of their
work to the Christian public. It is a work which
will bear inspection, or perhaps it would be more to
the point to say that it demands inspection. Christian people in America should make it a matter of
personal duty to acquaint themselves with everything
that pertains to this, the leading enterprise of the
coming century, the most sacred enterprise of all
centuries. The prosecution and completion of this
task is the supreme duty which our Saviour has in-
trusted to his people everywhere—a task which takes
precedence of every other, and must hold its precedence until the kingdoms and nations of earth shall

all have bowed to the scepter of our great Immanuel. All the Churches, the Church universal, are awaking, late, it is true, but none the less certainly, to a sense of a long-neglected duty and an appreciation of a long-rejected opportunity. In the new and brighter era just at hand no intelligent Christian will be able to afford to live in ignorance of the true character of the great missionary movement among the nations. Indeed, no such Christian can afford to live in ignorance of this movement in this closing decade of the nineteenth century, and the need of a copious and accurate missionary literature has never been greater than at the present hour.

It so happens that at the present time India is the most prominent of the great mission fields of the world, and it is therefore fitting that Mrs. Maxwell should have chosen that great empire as the field from which to draw her illustrations. In many important respects, however, these sketches will be found to represent faithfully scenes in China and other fields. All missions to non-Christian countries possess many important features in common. The missionary's problems in one country reappear in another, and hence all foreign missionaries are drawn together when they meet as if by the bonds of family relationship. To defend and help one is to hold up the weary arms of a hundred others. It may confidently be hoped, therefore, that Mrs. Maxwell's effort to speak a word for her fellow-workers in India will prove of great service to all workers in all lands who belong to the great and growing host of foreign missionaries.

THE BISHOP'S CONVERSION.

CHAPTER I.

THE PLAN.

IT was a cozy breakfast room, cozy as can be known only by those fortunate people who live where gleaming frost and snow out of doors make it possible to have bright fires, warm curtains, soft cushions, and thick carpets indoors. True, it was only October, but a fire, though not necessary, added to the creature comfort, and, as Mrs. Clinton said, "gave expression to a room." Perhaps the room had an expression without the fire; if it had, that expression was clearly elegance, modified by good taste and economy.

Harmonizing well with the room were Bishop Clinton, well-looking, portly, and comfortable, reading his foreign mail with his coffee, and Mrs. Clinton, a quick-thinking, slight, nervous, typical American woman, whose ambition outran her energy.

The Bishop looked across the white linen and dainty breakfast service and said, folding a London religious paper :

"My dear, this talk of luxury and ineffectual work among missionaries in India is really doing the cause much harm. I have half a mind to throw myself into the breach, and put a stop either to the talk or to the cause of it. I could go on to India after finishing the work in Europe."

"Yes; it might be a very good thing to do if traveling were not so very expensive," said she.

"Still, if I were to go part of the way very cheaply it might be feasible, and it would give me a chance to speak with authority to our people here. I might also be of great service to the missionaries themselves, for no doubt they are seriously at fault, though I do not credit all that is said. Certainly the heroic spirit has died out of missions, and there must be some bad management, some want of economy of time and money, else no one would dare make such assertions as are being made and printed everywhere. Even the secular papers, glad of the opportunity, are taking it up and making much of "the failure of missions," as they call it, through the mistakes and failures of missionaries."

Mrs. Clinton's eyes had a suspicious flash, and a wave of color went over her face as she said with some acrimony in her tones:

"What very stupid people the missionary secretaries must be to choose unfaithful and unwise men to send out on such important work! However, they must be wise in some lines, else they would not be able to live in luxury on the pitiful allowance they receive. I would be very glad to live a luxurious life on our allowance, which is many times greater than theirs, if I only knew how."

"Why, my dear, my dear!" said the Bishop, in mild astonishment, "it is not a case that calls for such strong feeling; and, besides, you underrate their allow-

ance, which is much better than many poor ministers
have in our own land."

"Allow me to say that I think it *is* a case that calls for
some feeling," she said, referring to the first part of his
remark; "for I have been tortured beyond endurance
during the last three months on this very line. The
letters of inquiry I have received as secretary of our
branch, and the questions I have had to answer in regard to this matter have worn my patience to shreds;
for instance: 'Is it true the missionaries' wives have
silk dresses?' 'Is it true they keep more than two servants?' 'Is it true that they have men stand about with
fans, fanning them when they are doing nothing?'
And allow me to say that I do not understate the
facts as to their allowance; when Em was here last
winter on the way to Michigan with her children she
made out a statement for me of their exact expenses.
Their allowance is, as you say, better than many a minister's; but out of it they pay first a large income tax
to the English government. Most of them keep up
some sort of life-insurance, as life is so uncertain they
do not know what day their families may be thrown
on their own resources, and the wife, with broken
health, is in no condition to earn a living; so that
leaves them still less. But first, before any of these
other items are taken out, they subtract a tenth.
There seems to be an unwritten law among missionaries that all shall give a tithe of their allowance to
the work; many of them give much more, but they
start with a tenth. Then they must send their children here to be educated, and the allowance for each
child is not enough to support it a year in school away
from home, whatever may be done by economical

people at home; you and I certainly understand that."

"Yes;" and the Bishop sighed as he thought of the sum that his two boys, who were in a good plain college and living plainly, were needing each month for books and clothing and board, etc.; "yes," he said, "it is impossible to do it without money. I suppose, however, the missionary, who is usually a man of education, might educate his own boys out there."

"I suggested this to Em, but she said there are not five undisturbed minutes in the day that the missionary or his wife can rely upon. Many have tried, in order not to be separated from their children, but it always has ended in their work being given up or in the utter failure of the little ones to learn anything. Besides, it is difficult for the children to keep in health after they are three or four years of age in that climate; and worse even than poor health was the disadvantage of bringing them up in a place where all manual labor, even by the poorest, is considered degrading. It leads them to form wrong estimates of life and unfits them for usefulness."

"Yes," said the Bishop, "wherever the cooly intervenes between the European and manual labor it is a great misfortune to the European, though it may be bread in the cooly's mouth. But if all this is true, what of Canon Taylor and his utterances, those scathing articles in *Truth*, this continual warfare in Hughes's paper, and these statements in the English papers by this returned missionary of the name of Lynn or Lion?"

"But," Mrs. Clinton asked, "how can Canon Taylor or the editor of *Truth* say in what manner missionaries ought to live? It must be much the same with them as with other people, though there seems to be some sort of an idea afloat that they might subsist on roots and herbs and be clothed with the grass of the field."

This was said with asperity.

"My dear," said the Bishop, with pronounced astonishment, "I am surprised to hear you speak in this manner. You really might be said to be—ah—nearly out of temper."

"Nearly? I am quite out of temper. I always hear much nonsense talked of missions, but I have heard so much more than usual in the last two months while you have been away that I have been out of temper several times. Only yesterday I asked Mrs. Long, who has thousands of dollars to spend on herself without ever giving an account to anyone, for a subscription for our Moradabad school work, and she said, 'I really think I cannot give anything this year. Nellie's bills at Long Branch and Jim's yacht have cost me so much, and I hear that the missionaries live like nawabs or nabobs or something of that sort, and of course luxury as well as charity should begin at home.' Think of that when she spends on one reception more than a missionary's whole allowance! And another, Mrs. Merrale, who has dozens of silk dresses, said, when I asked her for her usual subscription, 'Really I do not see much necessity for helping missionaries. The one who called here with you last winter had on a black silk dress far better than mine. I must say I do not feel like subscribing for silk gowns for missionaries.' Then I had to explain that I gave the dress to the lady she referred to (it was Em, you know), because she had no dress fit to make visits in; that she was my cousin; that if she had not been supporting two or three poor children and sending them to school in India she could have bought it herself with her own money, as she has a little; that I gave her a silk in preference to anything else because it would last longer and be more serviceable, and that her subscription was not to help missionaries, but to support mission work. I knew I was wasting my breath and getting hot and losing my temper all to no purpose. She had seen a silk dress on a missionary, and that was enough!"

Looking at the flushed face, as fair to him now as it had been twenty years before, the Bishop could easily believe the reference to losing her temper, and, though he made a practice of showing surprise when it did occur, he did not really mind it, because he noticed it was always when championing some other person's cause, and never for anything related to herself; for, after the custom of American men, he valued his wife as a partner in the councils of the family, and trusted her judgment, believing that there was never a cleverer or more sensible woman than she; and he was more justified in his opinion than men always are.

The Bishop finally broke the silence that had followed by saying:

"I really must see if I cannot extend my tour. A few weeks of extra travel would do it, and with a month in which to observe the various mission stations the trip would, I fancy, be altogether quite satisfactory; and I am necessarily away from you all so much of the time that it will be no added sacrifice."

Mrs. Clinton sighed in mock despair.

"I should like to have Em hear you say that. The one complaint when she talks of India, and the only one she ever makes, is that people—bishops and tourists interested in missions—only go there for the few months of cold weather, when the climate is really delightful. She said a native of India might as well try to judge of the rigor of a Vermont winter by spending the month of June in an apple orchard as for a tourist rushing through India in January to try to describe the climate of India. No; if you go, and wish really to be of service to the mission, you should stay a year, through all the changing seasons, and then you will be able to speak with authority, not only of the climate and the needs of the work, but of the work itself. What glorious missionary speeches one could make after a year of Indian life!"

The Bishop smiled. He often smiled at his wife's enthusiasms, and he had classed her missionary zeal and knowledge as among them, notwithstanding the fact that he found the latter useful for reference. He had no time himself to look really into mission work, though it had been an early dream of his to be a missionary in India. When, therefore, through indifferent health that idea had to be given up and relegated forever to the land of dreams, it was a great disappointment. But he had always kept up that dreamy way of looking at missions as though they were the romance of the church work, and not to be taken seriously or in a business way.

"I wish," he said, "you could go also, but I fear that is not to be thought of. The expense even for my tour will be an unheard-of extravagance, and as for remaining a year, it is Utopian in the extreme."

But Mrs. Clinton was thinking rapidly and to a purpose, and the beginning of her thought was this: "If missionaries can live on their allowance why cannot other people do the same?"

After a little silence she arose, and in a little excitement went around to her husband.

"If we three were to go, Lillian, you, and I, and live as missionaries for one year—that would be the only way to test the matter fairly—we could afford it easily, and perhaps it might be a matter of economy."

"Nonsense," was the answer. He had faith in her judgment, but not to that extent.

"Not nonsense at all. Bridget, with her wages and board, and what she breaks and loses, costs me my share of missionary allowance, and Tim and the horse cost your share to begin with. The clothes Lillian and I have now would do very well out there, whereas we should be obliged to have a new stock here. Then, you know, it would give Lillian the sea voyage that Dr. Hunter suggested for her the other day; and besides," dropping her voice a little, "we could have a chance of getting acquainted with each other again, for since you have had ecclesiastical honors I never really see you."

The Bishop rubbed his head thoughtfully. The statement that the missionary's family lived on what their one woman servant and her son, who looked after the cow and horse and garden, cost them, caught his attention, and he was revolving it in his mind. It struck him as being rather strange that he was going out to check the extravagance of people who were doing that. There was something wrong some-

where. Surely he and his family had never been
extravagant. In fact, they had lived much more simply than most of their friends, because they had been
obliged to do so. But if Bridget, Tim, and the horse
and cow were given up, and the house let for a year
to some friends who had only the day before asked
him to find a furnished house in that vicinity for
them, and Lillian's school bills saved, for she was in
a private day-school—surely, if this were all done, the
plan so suddenly thought of looked feasible; and besides there was a snug little bank account that could
be drawn on in case of necessity. Another thing, his
wife as well as Lillian would profit by the change,
and he looked at her rather remorsefully, for it struck
him all at once that though he had made many tours,
and had even crossed the Atlantic, she had never once
gone for a pleasure trip. She had been tied to the
children, who had required a great deal of care, to her
committee work, and her missionary meetings; but
now, as the two boys were at college, there was only
Lillian left at home, and she was not considered
strong, he thought, with a pang.

"Yes," he cried aloud, with almost boyish glee,
"yes, it can be done—that is, if the brethren make
no objections; and if the European work can be arranged with them, as I think it can, we will go as
soon after the holidays as possible."

Now, like a woman, Mrs. Clinton veered straight
around and was ready to back out of it all.

"I don't believe there is any good in going. I
know well enough that the missionaries are hard-
working, wise-planning, conscientious people, and I
don't believe the missionary secretaries are idiots, as

they certainly would be if they sent any other than hard-working and self-denying people, and it is their work to look into the matter, and not ours. And then besides, if India is so unhealthful as people say, it is no place to take Lillian."

The Bishop only answered the last objection:

"You know the doctor said that it is the severe winter here which is hard on Lillian, and that she would be better in a warm climate. My dear, I have settled it; we will go for our own sakes as well as for the missionary cause."

And he walked up and down the room with his hands behind him, humming,

"From Greenland's icy mountains,
From India's coral strand,"

as his heart swelled with the thought of pacing India's coral strand and sitting under the shade of the palm.

"Well, if I go there is one thing I want to stipulate—one thing which you must promise."

"What is it?" absently.

"That we in all things follow the custom of the missionaries, as far as expense is involved."

"Certainly, certainly! How else could we afford to go?"

"And as I have had a good deal of experience in the matter, and have acquired a great deal of information on the subject, you will not object to the suggestions I make in regard to finances, provided I can show you they are founded on my knowledge of facts."

"Of course not; why should I?" with a little unnecessary energy.

Mrs. Clinton repressed a smile as she turned away.

The first time she made a "suggestion founded on her knowledge of facts" was in regard to the selection of a steamer. The Bishop chose one of a favorite line as being the safest, quickest, and most comfortable; but his wife checked him.

"O, no!" she said, in surprise; "these points, of course, are to be considered, but we must find the cheapest. I see the one on which Mr. and Mrs. Milton sailed last year—you remember we went to see them off, and you said it was very comfortable indeed—sails just at the time we had decided on going."

"Yes, I remember," he said, dryly; "it was slow, and not very clean, and there were a lot of cattle on board. I am a bad sailor, and need as quick and comfortable a passage as possible."

"I know, but there were several bad sailors in the missionary party, and when I spoke of this I was told by some one in authority that it was much better than the old missionaries had who went around Cape Horn, and I ought to be thankful they had so good a way to go."

There was a quiver about her lips as she said this, and she turned her face away so that when her husband looked inquiringly at her he only saw the back of her head. He was not quite sure that he had not been that "some one in authority."

"However," she went on, "the missionaries themselves did not complain. In fact, Mr. Milton said he was glad to go as cheaply as possible, even if it were uncomfortable, as there would be so much more saved for the work."

"There is another reason why I wish to take a fast steamer. We must see London and Paris and Rome, and other places," he said, ignoring her remarks.

"But the missionaries are discouraged from doing this. It costs time and money to go sight-seeing. We must go straight to the field, for if we loiter on the way it will be a bad example for them, and you remember your promise."

I will not say that the Bishop regretted his promise, or that he regretted it far more before he landed in Liverpool, or that he absolutely hated the thought of it before he reached India. Let those who suffer from seasickness, and who know what the difference to them is between a clean ship, well-cooked and well-served food, and the exact opposite, say.

And as for Mrs. Clinton, who also was a bad sailor, it is on record that she considered it even a harder way of helping the missionary society than begging subscriptions from wealthy church members or holding bazars and fancy fairs.

CHAPTER II.

THE ARRIVAL AT LUCKNOW.

IT was about nine o'clock one February evening
when the train which brought the Bishop and Mrs.
Clinton and Lillian up from Bombay, slowly and de-
liberately, after the manner of Indian trains, moved
into Lucknow.

The station was well lighted, but the lights gleamed
coldly through the blue smoke which arose from
thousands of little fires around which half-clothed people were crouching in a vain attempt to keep warm.

Shivering coolies with their heads and shoulders
muffled in dirty white cotton sheets stood about waiting for a chance to carry luggage, and reminding Lillian, in their forgetfulness of their bare brown legs
and feet, of spring chickens on wintry mornings. The
wheels of small handcarts with their light weight of
luggage shrieked as loudly in moving over the stone-
paved floor as carts of ten times their dimensions
should. Railway clerks with papers in their dark
hands went about with as much manner as American
railway clerks, though without their briskness.

Parties of native ladies, preceded by a waft of perfume, their faces covered, and their hands firmly grasping untold lengths and fullness of silken skirts, jin-
gling many bangles and anklets, glided into waiting
coaches, followed by servants carrying silver pán

boxes, hookahs, and innumerable bundles tied in old rags.

Various and individual groups of people stood about, waiting for whomsoever the train might bring them. Here a cluster of callow subalterns, down to meet their colonel who had come on the same steamer as the Bishop; there a captain and his wife, the latter with a great bunch of cream and red roses in her hand, looking for her sister who was coming out with the colonel's wife for a winter in India, and whatever it might bring her in the way of amusement and matrimony. Farther down was the English millmaster, with a glow on his honest face as he caught sight of the tired wife and babies whom he had left in Manchester the year before, when he came out to try his fortunes in this strange land; beyond him was the Eurasian clerk still in his white drill hot-weather clothes, waiting for his wife's mother and big sisters and little brothers who were coming to visit him while his father-in-law was "temporarily out of employment." All these and many others, and yet the eyes of the Bishop's party went straight over them all and lighted on another group a little apart. Why, it would be difficult to say, for the members of it were doing exactly the same as all others on the platform, looking eagerly from window to window of each carriage of the slow-moving train, which finally stopped, leaving the carriage in which were the Americans opposite this very group. While waiting for the guard to unlock the door of their compartment Mrs. Clinton took observations.

First she at once noticed the absence of the discontented and vacant expression that she had seen on so many faces east of Port Said, though they had the appearance of being too hard worked to be merry or to care very much about the quality or style of their clothes, or in any way to think of the impression they were making. Two or three of the women had on broad gray felt hats, while all of the men wore the same, or cork helmets which gave them a grotesque appearance, heightened in the women by the cut of their clothes.

Mrs. Clinton could see at a glance that each one, though dressed very plainly, seemed to represent by the style of her dress a different epoch in the world of fashion.

One who looked a little younger than the rest, and whose clothes were a little fresher, had a dress and jacket in vogue three years before. Mrs. Clinton remembered this with exactness, because it was of the same style as one she had decided not to bring with her because of the ancientness of the cut, though the dress itself was fresh and new compared with the one before her. The other ladies each in turn represented preceding epochs, though in a cursory glance she could not tell the time chronologically.

"Certainly sometime," she said to herself, with a shudder—"sometime in the Middle Ages." Then to Lillian: "O, there is a dress exactly like the one Em wore when she came home, and I remember we wished we had hired a close carriage to take her from the steamer to the house, we were so ashamed. O"— with another quick drawing of her breath and grasping her husband's arm—"these are the Lucknow missionaries, and they have come to meet us. How stupid of us! We might have known!"

The Bishop, who had been looking thoughtfully all about, woke from his reverie, and said :

"I dare say. Certainly they have the appearance of veterans of some kind," and he stepped down, as the guard unlocked the door, to have both hands seized by a white-haired, white-bearded, hearty old gentleman, who said :

"I saw you in '72. Do you not remember Thompson, of Tippecanoe Conference?"

"Thompson, of course, but he was a young man" —in a bewildered way. This was greeted by a burst of quiet laughter, as it evidently touched a well-known sensitive point.

"A young man? Yes, he was and *is* a young man. I defy any one to say I am not."

"And do you remember me? I saw you in New York in '79," said Mr. Miller, a shy, delicate-looking man.

"And I saw you in Chicago in '80," said Mr. Mackenzie, another pale-faced, dark-bearded man, with a marked stoop in his shoulders, as though life's burdens were weighing all too heavily.

"But," he added, as he saw the Bishop's bewilderment in trying to talk to so many at once, and to introduce his wife, who had been seized by the women, "never mind all this; give me your receipts for your luggage in the van, and I will look after it, as you are to go with us;" and away he went with Thompson trotting after him.

"You must not overlook me because I am small," said a large, stout, jolly woman with tired eyes; "for I know you, though you do not know me."

Each and every one had a greeting for them that

made them feel as though they were mistaken in their
own identity and had come among their brothers and
sisters.   There was the stately superintendent of the
Lal Bagh school, the dark-eyed woman who had once
only gone from her native India, to cross the ocean
with the sick friend whom she left in its deep waters;
the wife of the dark-bearded man with the delicate
face; a short, stout woman with black eyes; the
Zenana teacher, who was so thin as to make one fear
her actual disappearance; and the scholarly teacher
of the college class in the Lal Bagh.   And when all
were done shaking hands, and the luggage was put on
a handcart, Mrs. Clinton found herself and Lillian on
the back seat and her husband and Mr. Mackenzie
on the front seat of a rather small carriage, behind a
small horse, both somewhat the worse for wear, going
over smooth, hard roads, past square houses with flat
roofs, their straight lines broken everywhere by trees
with round, thick dark foliage.   But Mrs. Clinton was
not thinking of what was about her.   An undefined
thought was in her mind struggling for clear expression.

"Lillian," she said, under cover of the men's talk
of the steamer and the journey up country, "did you
ever see any people like these before?   How did they
look to you?"

"Why, mamma, I thought they looked a little
sorry and"—hesitatingly—"a little glad too, as though
they had done something they liked to do; like those
men who went out when the ship was wrecked at
Nahant last summer.   They got lots of dead people,
but only one live man and one dear little baby.   But
they seemed so very glad they had tried, though they

were so awfully tired, and they were so wet and the water ran off of them, and they did not care about their clothes, or whether people knew they were wet. If we are missionaries will we have to not care about dresses and hats ?" she asked, anxiously. It was one of Lillian's little failings to care very much about " dresses and hats " for a girl of ten years.

Mrs. Clinton smiled and said :

" I suppose we will at least care about hats, for we will have to wear hats like those to protect us from the sun during the hot season."

" But it is cold now, and there is no sun in the night ; then why," she persisted, " do they wear them ?"

But Mrs. Clinton was thinking again, and did not answer. She felt things quickly and keenly, and she liked to follow out her impressions to see if there were any solid reason for them back of the misty cloud that reached her. Lillian had in her imperfect way expressed her own thought, but the picture these people recalled to her mind was different from that in Lillian's, yet similar. It came to her as an indistinct memory of more than twenty years before—a railway platform and some soldiers in worn and faded blue uniform ; their faces were pale and there were marks of pain on some, telling of unhealed wounds ; others had empty sleeves or walked with the aid of crutches; but over the evidence of suffering was the peace and calm which comes of earnest striving, mingled with the joy of victory, for they had had the most dangerous and exposed places and the longest forced marches, and finally had been personally commended by their commander-in-chief, who had said a great victory won had turned on their bravery and endurance. The tears rushed to Mrs. Clinton's eyes as she thought of the three groups of people— the life-saving crew, spent and exhausted, the soldiers, wasted, crippled, and weak, and this group of people on whom they had come to spy, and she said to herself:

"It is not romance, it is not imagination; they are one and the same in that they have risked all for what to them seems duty; that they all have counted not their lives dear if given for an object greater to them than their own welfare. Even Lillian saw it."

Then with a woman's tendency to turn to trifles she thought again and remorsefully of the dress that had not been good enough for a traveling dress, and of the fact of its being a better and fresher one than that of the best dressed of the group.

"I suppose you can do only half the work in this climate you could in America," she heard the Bishop say.

There was a sound of amusement in Mr. Mackenzie's voice as he answered:

"I work ten hours a day regularly, and twelve on extra occasions. I really have forgotten the limit in America."

"Well," said the Bishop, "we estimate seven hours for mental work and nine for mental and mechanical work combined. I suppose, however, you have little mental work. The simple-minded Hindoo—"

"My dear sir," interrupted Mackenzie, laughing, "allow me at once to destroy one preconceived notion. The 'simple-minded Hindoo' is the most complex and subtle of all individuals save and except his compatriot the 'simple-minded Mohammedan.' But here we are ; our long drive is ended, and we welcome you to our house. My wife is already here, I see, as she came with Miss Lowe, who has a better horse than ours."

"Now," said Mrs. Mackenzie, leading them at once to an inner room, " when you have taken off your wraps come out to the fire ; we have only one fireplace in the house. We will have some tea, and perhaps it will help us to get warm."

Mrs. Clinton threw off her wraps and went back to the fire in a hurry, for she did not want a minute alone with her husband. A hasty glimpse of the sitting room, or parlor, as she would have called it, had made her heart sink with fear and dread.

"Was she to lose her cause at the outset? If so, and if she had been mistaken and the missionaries were after all living like ' nabobs or nawabs ' or rajahs, she could never bear it. She would almost feel as though she had spent her life in vain—what would she or what could she do ?" and she sank down in an easy chair by the fire, where she was joined by the others ; and then came a servant in white turban and waistband, or kamarband, and silently held a tray on which were cups of tea, with milk and sugar, and a plate with slices of bread and butter. She took a cup with the sense of doing the man a favor. As she did so she gave a furtive glance at the Bishop, expecting and seeing the expression which always appeared on his face when the conclusion of an argument satisfied him that he had been right in his premises. Mr. and Mrs. Mackenzie hastily drank the tea, then the former said :

" If you will excuse my wife and me for a half-hour.

while you are getting warm, we will be glad, as we have a little proof for our paper to be read before we go to bed;" and they hurried away.

The sound of the word "proof" was to the Bishop like the smoke of battle to an old war-horse. All his spare moments, his vacations, and his holidays had been snatched for writing, and through all the heavy and absorbing duties of ecclesiastical life there had been a secret longing for a life devoted to literary work.

"Here is, perhaps," he said, tentatively, "a missionary who is devoting his life to literature instead of legitimate mission work. Certainly the first impressions," and he glanced up at the lofty ceiling, "are not of self-denying asceticism, at least."

It is strange that people who in their own environments are cautious in forming opinions, deliberate in drawing conclusions, and hesitating in expressing them, will, when in a foreign country, take the most startling leaps and make the most desperate attempts to bridge impossible chasms and most utterly lose their footing. It is as though they felt that wisdom was embodied and would die in their own native land, as though they were the apostles of that wisdom, and through them, and them only, could it be disseminated.

His wife was busy with her thoughts, and made no answer. The large, lofty room which at the first glance had seemed so stately and well furnished was being examined more closely, and her heart, which had fallen at the first sight, was now assuming its wonted cheerfulness, and there was a curious smile on her face. It was clear to her now that she would not be beaten at the outset, at least, and she did not much fear it later.

3

The room was large and lofty, there could be no
denying it; she had heard this was necessary; but
as to its being well furnished, she smiled as with a
woman's quickness she "speered" into one after
another of the simple devices to give the room a
comfortable and homelike appearance—simple, she
saw, both as regards time and money; yet even she
did not grasp the situation fully, not knowing the
prices of the various things used. Feeling chills
creeping over her she rose and stood with her back
to the fire, saying :

"I could almost believe this fire a pretense, I get so
little warmth from it."

The Bishop followed her example.

"It is because of the size of the room," he said, with
a little triumph in his tone; for no matter how good
and earnest men are, they do enjoy a triumph, and
there is no dearer privilege to the best of them than
of saying to their wives, "I told you so."

"It is because of the size of the room," he repeated, "for this is certainly a larger and loftier room
than we ever had in our house, or I may say than I
have ever seen in any minister's house in America."

"Yes," said Mrs. Clinton, looking across the room
that was filled with the same smoke that had softened
the landscape but which dulled the light of the lamp
and gave an inexpressibly dreary aspect to everything;
"yes," she said, meditatively, "my father's barn was
a very much larger structure than our house, yet I
never heard anyone express a desire to exchange our
cosy little home for it."

"Ah," said the Bishop, for he was honest to the
core, "ah, yes, that is really of what I was reminded :

it is rather barny, is it not? But still there are many very handsome things in it."

Just then Mrs. Mackenzie came in, shivering, with a shawl wrapped around her.

"How I wish," she said, brightly, " I could get warm once more. We live in extremes here; broiled in the long hot season, stewed and steamed in the wet hot season, and chilled to the marrow in the cold season. The fire looks warm, and that's one comfort; but this room is so big it is impossible to warm the air in it."

"But why have the rooms so large, if you do not like them and cannot be comfortable?" asked Mrs. Clinton, eager to begin the contest.

Mrs. Mackenzie gave a quick look, first at Mrs. Clinton and then at the Bishop, and she smiled as she remembered with what pain she also, when she first landed, had seen the large houses, for she had had a vague idea of living in grass huts.

"O," she said, "we have our houses, like everything, not for pleasure or comfort, but of necessity. They are built for the hot weather, and with the object of inclosing as many square inches of oxygen as possible; for when you are shut up in a house many hours every day for six months, with the thermometer at one hundred and seventy degrees outside, your life depends on oxygen, and to procure this we must shiver through our three months of cold weather."

"But I am sure a big stove such as we had when we lived in the country would warm this room," said the Bishop.

"Stoves!" exclaimed Mrs. Mackenzie; "do not begin to talk of luxuries like stoves. People here, some

3

people, do have them, but mission log cannot afford them."

"Well"—dryly looking about him—"I confess I have heard pictures and bric-a-brac called luxuries, though stoves are not usually put down in the same category."

"Supposing, however, one's bric-a-brac cost one nothing, and would bring next to nothing if sold, and one makes the pictures in moments when too weary for anything useful, would they still be counted as luxuries? And suppose a stove, even a small one, would cost as much as nearly everything else in the room, and if it were not necessary, then would not the order be reversed?"

"Of course it would," said Mrs. Clinton, sympathetically; "and even if it would not I know of no law, moral or otherwise, to prevent a missionary's wife from having a pretty room, if it should cost a little, though my eyes are keen enough to see that yours did not cost much."

"And you do not think Bishop A. was right when he reported my carpet to be Brussels?" asked Mrs. Mackenzie, with a laugh.

"Hardly—but what is it? It looks nice even to one who might see more clearly than the good Bishop."

"It is called färsh, and is a coarse sail-like cloth, dyed and then stamped by hand in the bazar, and costs the extravagant sum of ten cents a yard, inclusive of sewing and putting down."

The Bishop's mouth was open in a most unclerical way. Did he not remember his wife's saying something of getting a carpet that was "such a bargain" at three dollars a yard? He must be dreaming.

"And you will not say that I have expensive terra cotta vases filled with costly plants, I know; but for fear you might not understand let me say that those ' terra cotta' vases," pointing to some oval pots on the floor, "are the ordinary pots for carrying water, and cost three cents apiece, filled with wild jungle-grass."

It was Mrs. Clinton's turn to gasp with astonishment and delight and exclaim:

"They are perfectly lovely, and I shall take home a dozen of them."

"You might find them an extravagance, even at three cents apiece, if you attempt to take home a dozen. But I see you enter into the merits of the case, and will not if I give you green pease in the winter eat them with a relish, as one did, and then complain at home that missionaries could have green pease in February, when people who supported them could not afford it."

Mrs. Mackenzie's eyes danced, and she added:

"If he had only said we would have given ten times as much for them in July as in February perhaps it would have left a different impression on the minds of those who hear it."

"No, I certainly would not do that; but he must have been unkind as well as stupid not to have understood it without explanation."

"He is not the first nor the only one who has been entertained by us at much inconvenience and sacrifice, and enjoyed all we could give, and gone away to say we live too well."

"I wish," said Mrs. Clinton, with apparent irrelevance, "I could lay the ghost of the herbivorous missionary."

Mrs. Mackenzie laughed. Had she not wished the same many a time? But the matter-of-fact Bishop turned a startled glance toward her as though he feared some mental aberration.

"What?" he asked in explanation.

"The typical herbivorous missionary who wanders about, eating what he can pick up, and who is always sitting under palm trees, surrounded by an eager multitude who are begging him to read the Bible to them. He is a ghost that exists only in the brains of romantic people who never have anything to do with mission work practically."

"Certainly you cannot say that Dr. Moffat and Mr. and Mrs. Judson and others of their day were imaginary characters. Surely they wandered, and there were times when they were glad of roots and berries or anything else they could pick up. We shall never have better missionaries. These of the present day may well take example from them."

"Yes; but," said Mrs. Mackenzie, sweetly, "because Asbury rode a horse with saddle-bags all over the West, and ate with the Indians, do the Bishops of the present day think it necessary to do so or advisable not to make use of the railway?"

This was a clincher from the meek-looking woman, from whom he had hardly expected the *argumentum ad hominem.*

"No; for though the methods of those early days were good and efficacious for the times, yet with the size and importance of our present church they would be impossible. Time and strength would be wasted."

"Exactly," said Mrs. Mackenzie; "and may I ask

you to remember that progress touches even a mission?"

"There was a picture," said Mrs. Clinton, slowly, and smiling a little, "that hung in my mother's bedroom; in fact, there were two pictures, framed in solemn black, of a flying angel in the sky, and a lot of hands lifted up from a dusky crowd of people reaching for the Bible the angel held. There was a background of palm trees and mosques of unknown architecture, and on the lower half of one sheet was a certificate in my mother's name of life-membership of the Missionary Society. The other was of her mother; and when my aunt died there was another brought, and the three were somehow associated with the awfulness of my mother's room, where we were never found unless there was a necessity for a course of discipline; and they are somehow mixed up in my mind with missionaries and mission work."

There was a gravity on the Bishop's face that was only one remove from displeasure.

"But," she went on with an audacious smile, determined at least to make his face relax, "perhaps it was because I was always puzzled over the picture, wondering how people could hold up their hands and feet too; for there were so many and they seemed so mixed up that I thought some must have put up feet."

The Bishop did smile, but he said:

"I do not see what this has to do with the 'imaginary missionary.'"

"I do. My impressions of a vague, romantic, and unreal person began there. I say *my* impressions began there, but so did those of hundreds of other people; and impressions are often as tenacious as convictions. I hope mine end with entering the house of live flesh-and-bone missionaries."

Mr. Mackenzie had entered in time to catch the main part of this, and a bright look of appreciation of the fun, and relief at finding unexpected sympathy, lightened a face that had a settled weariness.

"Ah, then you at least will not be disappointed if you do not find the typical missionary?" he said.

"No, I shall not; for I do not believe he exists, with one exception, and he is a giant who scales mountains and traverses seas, and digs wells in the deadly sun, and lives on nothing if he happens to have it, regardless of the limitations of time and space and nutrition which bind other men."

"If there is only one how can you say he is typical?" asked the Bishop, with visible patience with the vagaries of the weaker vessel.

"He is typical only of the image that is called up in people's minds at the sound of the word 'missionary.'"

"Yes," said Mr. Mackenzie, "he is a pioneer and a grand one, but while it is necessary for a pioneer in any new country to fell trees and burn underbrush and turn up the soil the process would be of very little use if others did not follow—patient, plodding men who can plant and sow. This has been proved where he has done pioneer work that was not followed quickly by the steady plodders; it vanished like the dew before the sun. It is the steady, hard, well-organized work that tells. It cannot be brilliant work, for men who do it are rarely heard of out of their immediate circle. Permanent success is simply

a matter of time and patience and perseverance
through all kinds of difficulties and discouragements.
No meteoric showers of Bibles and tracts and sermons will ever effect any solid work, though they
may open the way for the plodders."

"Yes," said the Bishop, thoughtfully; "yes," he
repeated. There was something in those words that
caught his attention.

"Our Church in America," Mackenzie went on,
" is founded on broad business principles. Emotion
is allowed no part in its government and its plan for
extension. What is the result? The mightiest and
most sweeping advance the world has ever seen in a
Church ; but when she comes to missions you might
almost say they are her little recreation. She allows
her imagination to play, and will give, on impulse,
the most to the field that can tell the most thrilling
tales. She loves the 'herbivorous missionary,' as your
wife calls him; but it is time that she wakes up to
the situation and learns that the idea of one lone man
wandering through the jungle is mere child's play to
the work she has on hand. And the very first thing
she needs a clearer view of is the missionary himself.
Not only the Church, but the people at large, will
never understand mission work until, because we give
up our coats, they cease to demand of us that we give
up our cloaks also."

"I confess I do not understand your last remark,"
was the stiff rejoinder of his listener.

"I will make it more plain. We give up home
and friends, a friendly climate, our worldly ambitions—for even we have legitimate ambitions—and
come to a deadly climate, to a narrowing life, and one

that stunts all mental and checks moral development, and they try to demand that we give up also the necessaries of life."

"Not quite so bad. Allow me to say that statement is an exaggeration. No one would ever think of going so far."

"They would not mean to go so far, yet if one followed out their plans literally it would amount to deprivation of the things that are actually necessary to life. But you will allow this one statement to be true: the necessities of life in one country may be luxuries in another, as we have proved in the matter of stoves. It is so also in the matter of servants, and in that of food and clothing. Now, as a practical example, were my wife to attempt to do the cooking for the family for one month in the hot weather it would not only take up all her time, but would probably take her life also; so a cook is one of the necessaries of life here, whereas there might be places where he would be a luxury; and one of her luxuries now and then in the cold weather is to take a little time to prepare for the table some dish that we used to have in the home land. Look at that dish of pink roses, and these palms, that give such an air of luxuriance to the room, chiefly because roses and palms in February are associated with luxurious living. We, however, would give them all for a stalk of golden-rod or a handful of buttercups from the river pasture-land."

Mrs. Clinton broke in, exclaiming:

"Is it true? Would you give those delicious roses all, and the palms too, for a sprig of golden-rod?"

"Yes," said Mrs. Mackenzie, as her eyes filled with

homesick tears, " I would quickly. I am often reminded of myself by a pine tree that is back of this bungalow. It is so stunted and dreary-looking, and so homesick for its own natural surroundings that it never grows, and some day will die from sheer inability to become adjusted to the unfamiliar growths about it."

Mrs. Clinton took her hand and gave it a sympathetic squeeze as the Bishop said to Mackenzie:

" You have scored a point there, on the necessities of one country being the luxuries of another, I grant you, and a strong point which I shall consider and perhaps use in some future time; but you ignore the fact that missionaries are supported—ah—not exactly by charity, but what is in a way considered charity, and are not expected to demand what the other ministers do."

" But wherein has a Church a right to set apart one class of her servants, and say they are the objects of charity, as you are pleased to term them, while others, paid from the same subscriptions, and perhaps doing the same kind of work in their own land, surrounded by friends and a friendly climate, are put quite in another division of the Church? Say, for instance, that a man is a missionary in a foreign land. He goes home and administers mission money at three times the salary; he straightway is taken off the charity list and becomes a regular church servant. Who creates this difference?"

"The matter of fact is, for the responsible positions at home we must have superior, clear-headed men of ability, and we cannot get them on what you are allowed here."

"But we must have the same kind of men here. That we do have the same kind is proven by the fact that our men, when for various reasons they do go home to live, fill these same places. Now allow me to say that there is a mistake in the attitude of the Church, in which, if individuals were set right, there would be a different sentiment, and one that would enforce a little more economy at home under favorable climate, and not so much abroad, where it would be disastrous to all work. You see it is as though the Church, which is large and wealthy, with a large revenue, when she decided to plant a large branch of it in a foreign country, said as she called for volunteers: 'There is to be a great war; we ask you to take the difficult and dangerous posts. In order that you may be well equipped for this we should like you to have the best of food and plenty of it, the houses best calculated to protect you from the ravages of sun, heat, and disease incident to a tropical climate; we should like to give you the books you need to keep your minds fitted for your work, and conveyances to take you about, that you may not lose precious time and strength; but there is a sentiment in favor of an ascetic life' (which, let me say in passing, means death), 'and we cannot do it. There is no sentiment against well paying our servants who stay comfortably at home, but *you* are another class.'"

The Bishop looked perplexed. He could not agree with all this, but he did not seem to catch any point where he could disagree, or any point of which he could take hold.

"Well, of course," he said, lamely, "missionaries *are* another class."

"In what way?"

"They are especially consecrated to a life of devotion, and more is demanded of them."

"By whom? The same bishop ordains us all, we all serve God, whom we love, and we all live to propagate the Gospel of our Lord Jesus Christ. Do not misunderstand me. I have never suffered, and the authorities will never see us suffer for anything we need. It is only that the sentiment at large needs cultivating; but *we* have no time to stop and cultivate it or change it. We have hardly time to stop and say what shape or plan our houses shall be or how we shall live. The necessities of each day are all we want, and we cannot spend precious time over things unimportant in themselves. But I see Lillian is wishing for an opportunity to close her blue eyes, and your wife is hoping we will postpone the remainder of this discussion until to-morrow."

Lillian smiled sleepily, and Mrs. Clinton said as she rose, yawning, "You have divined my thoughts exactly;" and soon all was silent in the bungalow.

CHAPTER III.

JUGGLER AND SHAWL MERCHANT.

THE next morning the three travelers were up early and out exploring their surroundings with a Crusoe-like eagerness.

Lillian, with the quickness of childhood, caught a glimpse of a little girl at the end of the garden and flew away to join her, guessing she was the Katie of whom Mrs. Mackenzie had told her the night before.

It was a beautiful morning, with a strange fascination not found where there is a rustling of leaves, a whir of many wings, a twitter of birds, a general stir of men and animals glad and anxious to be about the business of the day. It was all so quiet. If the day was advancing it was doing so imperceptibly and with an infinite stillness. The sunny sides of the long-trunked Millingtonia trees, of the square-topped whitewashed bungalows, of the dust-covered foliage surrounding the bungalows, and the blue-gray cactus hedge were of a deep bright yellow; but the dark side of the trees, the bungalows, the hedge, and all the landscape that had not the high lights of the fiery sun, had a blue haze over them not unlike smoke, while the sky was a pale dull blue mingled with yellow.

Native people were sauntering by with no evidence of hurry, wrapped in dirty white or brown blankets. In sharp contrast to them were now and then English-

A NATIVE WATER-DRAWER.

men in "sola topis," or helmets, and gray business suits
who drove their dog-carts sharply past, startling the
sleepy natives just in time for them to wake up and
save themselves from being run over.

It was all strange and picturesque, from the creak-
ing pulley of the well (by which the bihisti with red
dripping drapery was drawing up a pigskin bursting
with water, showing in a most absurd way the head,
legs, and entire shape of the defunct animal from
which it had been robbed), and the sweepers with their
bundles of twigs sweeping the road clear of dead
leaves, to the garden with its roses and heliotrope and
the servants' houses of mud, with the happy brown
children playing before them.

"It is not the India of my dreams," said Mrs. Clinton, as she turned to greet Mr. and Mrs. Mackenzie,
who joined them, followed by a man with a tray of
tea and dry toast, who put it on a table in the middle
of the veranda and hurried away.

"No," said Mrs. Mackenzie, as she poured out the
tea; "the India of one's dream is a fanciful India, and
exists, as far as I have seen, only in visions and poets'
fancies. Yet there may be a realization of it somewhere in this vast empire, for there are no two towns
alike, and the customs in different parts of the country
vary as greatly as in the towns;" and then she added,
"It is cold here for our little breakfast, but it is colder
in the house. This veranda collects all the heat there
is going, and though you need your overcoats you
would need them much more in the house."

A man came just then with a basket of mail, which
Mr. Mackenzie took and began sorting.

"You will see by this mail that I have three vari-

4

eties of work under my charge. This," touching the largest heap, " forms the daily allowance for the publishing house, and these," indicating another pile, " are treasury letters, but I shall soon pass all that part of my work over to Dr. Wall, and these," handing another lot to his wife, " I have as editor of a young people's illustrated paper, and which I pass on to the subeditor."

" Your duties seem to be varied," remarked the Bishop; " I do not see just where you can find time for legitimate mission work."

" What is legitimate mission work ? "

" Preaching the Gospel to the heathen with all your might, mind, and strength," was the firm answer.

" That is just what I am doing ; I preach to many thousands every day. If you will come with me after breakfast I will show you my method of doing it; but now tell me what plans you have for sight-seeing. Of course, like other globe-trotters, your main effort will be to see Lucknow, including a glimpse of mission work, in a day and a half, leaving the latter half of the second day for taking the train to Cawnpoor and ' doing ' that place."

His only answer was a laugh from Mrs. Clinton.

" Or are you going to give the unprecedented time of three days to Lucknow alone ? "

Mrs. Clinton laughed again and said: " I see the sight-seeing fiend has been here and corrupted your minds ; but we will inaugurate a new era ; we are going to see India, and we are going to try to *know* India, and not simply rush about like mad people."

Mrs. Clinton did not care to avow their real plans, and the Bishop, strange to say, felt a hesitation, in the

face of the warm welcome he had received from all,
to explain that he had come as a spy. He finally
said, with a visible effort:

"I expect to make my home in Lucknow for one
year, and with it as a vantage-ground study India
thoroughly from the missionary point of view."

"Seriously?" said Mackenzie, setting down his cup,
and turning quickly and looking at the Bishop with
an absurd amount of incredulity on his face.

"Certainly," with dignity; "why not?"

"And you also?" to Mrs. Clinton, who was enjoying his surprise.

"Yes, as my husband says, 'why not?' You certainly do not think we should be qualified to speak on
India or on mission work in any shorter time? And
in order to do this in the best and most thorough way
we are going to be missionaries, live on missionary
allowance, and work as they do, without swerving."

Mrs. Clinton was rather careful to keep this latter
point before her husband, for now and then he
showed a tendency to ignore it.

Mr. Mackenzie turned to his wife in a helpless
way, as though he expected her to express his feelings for him, but she returned his look in silence, and
there was a pause, broken only by the hoarse cawing
of the crows that were flying about hoping for a
stray bit of toast. Finally Mrs. Mackenzie whimsi-
cally said to her husband:

"Will you kindly look out and see if the sky is
falling?"

There was a laugh all around, and then Mr. Mackenzie said:

"This is so nearly what we have wished, and so far

from what we ever supposed could be, that you will pardon us if our surprise is tempered with incredulity. If you can do it—observe that I say *if*—it will be the best thing that has happened for many a day."

"We do not care how strong an emphasis you put on the word 'if,' and we intend to prove our good faith by looking for a house this very day in which to begin our missionary career."

"See here," said Mr. Mackenzie, "Thompson leaves to-night to take his wife, whose health has failed, to America, and his house will be empty, and available to-morrow. If you are a missionary you must live in a mission house, though of course we hope you will remain with us as long as possible."

"And I will help you settle, for that is really the hardest part of the coming to India," said Mrs. Mackenzie.

"Do missionaries' wives usually help each other to settle?"

"No, indeed; we all help ourselves," answered Mrs. Mackenzie; "but you are different."

"Not at all. I do not mean or wish to be different. I will help myself when I can, and when I cannot if you will allow me to come to you for advice I shall be very glad. We wish in every sense to be treated as one of you."

"Then," said Mr. Mackenzie, rising, with a smile, "I will begin at once and say as I would if you were one of us, that I must go to work; I have lingered too long already."

"And I too," said his wife, taking up the letters and packages; "I must read and answer these letters, examine these manuscripts, and correct proofs steadily all day. But it seems rather rude to leave you quite to your own devices the first day of your stay here."

"O, do not mind us! We have letters to write that will keep us busy."

The Bishop was opening an *Indian Review* that his host had handed him, and made no answer. Just as Mrs. Mackenzie was vanishing through the door she heard the familiar sound of the little tom-tom with which the jugglers always announce their coming.

"O," said she, with a sigh of despair, "how the whole city can find out in one night that the 'Lord Bishop Sahib' has come is more than I have ever been able to discover. This man is only a forerunner of the visitors you will have to-day and every day for a week."

"What is it?" said the Bishop, laying down his book.

"Only a man with a performing monkey, a cobra, and a mongoose. The mongoose will kill the snake, and the man will swallow marbles and yards of cloth and twine, and you will find them floating in the air, besides doing other things too numerous to mention. Will you see him? If you have not time for him I will send him away."

The Bishop hesitated, said he must write letters, looked at the man, who sat down on the ground drawing various curious things out of a bag—and was lost. An Indian juggler reads a face as an open book, and he knew that the new Sahib was longing to see what he could do, and consequently hurried his operations. Lillian and Katie came running from the garden at the, to Katie, well-known sound of the tom-tom.

"Ah, I suppose one really must see the Indian

jugglers in order to judge of the customs of the people," he said, in lame excuse of his desire to see a támáshâ.

And he, as well as his wife, was soon absorbed in watching the sleight-of-hand of a second-rate juggler. First the man pulled out of his bag, by the tail, a cobra, a hideous, slimy, creepy cobra, that proceeded to make a spiral coil of the latter half of himself, while the former and bigger part he raised up in a straight, swaying column, with the vile hooded head turning viciously about. The children retreated with a scream behind Mrs. Clinton, from whence they peeped out fascinated in spite of their fear. Then the mongoose came out with his mouth covered with red powder, and followed the snake, which quietly and indifferently moved off, but finding itself in a corner at the end of the step turned and made a lunge at its enemy, who darted on it, setting its teeth sharply in the sleazy hood. The cobra struggled a little, and then fell down flat, apparently dead, and the mongoose ran behind the basket the man had and began eating something tossed to him by his master.

Hearing a sigh of relief, Mrs. Clinton turned to find Lillian pale and shaking with terror and Katie drawing a long breath.

"O," said Katie, "how I *don't* like to see the snake!"

They all laughed at her way of putting it, but felt that it expressed their feelings exactly.

"Mother," whispered Lillian, shivering. "Katie says that her mother found a snake like this in the house one night, only it was much bigger."

"Never mind, darling, we will try not to find any while we are here." But Lillian was still quivering with fear.

"Mamma, it is so horrible! I should die if I saw one in our room."

"Katie," said Mrs. Clinton, "when your mother found the cobra was she afraid of it, or was it afraid of her?"

Katie laughed. "I think both of them were afraid, for mamma ran to get a servant to kill it, and the snake ran away also. They both ran, so they were both afraid."

"Do you see, Lillian, the snake would be afraid of us as much as we of him. But look at the juggler; see what he is doing!"

First he beat the little tom-tom, then he drew out a monkey's skull, put it before him with a tender care, and said to it in Urdu, "Take care of my luck." Seeing the Bishop about to turn away he hastily held up a mango seed. That never failed to hold a newcomer.

"This," he said in Urdu, "will be planted, will sprout, and will bring forth fruit before the Lord Sahib's eyes, if he will wait to see."

Katie glibly translated this, and the Bishop sat down, saying as the man dug up the dry earth:

"That, indeed, will be worth seeing."

After having planted the seed the man covered it up with a large, tall basket, then he patted the monkey's skull, called on the monkey god Hanuman, who is the presiding deity of all jugglers, to see that it grew fast, because the great and wonderful Sahib, whose fame had traveled the world over, was waiting

to see what he could do.   While it was growing the
two monkeys were brought around and fought as
man and wife, quarreled, then made up and kissed,
the wife slyly rubbing the kisses off when her lord
was not observing.   Once more beating the tom-tom,
once more patting the monkey's skull, and naming
Hanuman, the man with a great flourish lifted the
basket and cried:

"Dekho!" ("Behold!")

Then the Bishop beheld and marveled, for there
was a mango sprout three inches high.   The basket
went over it again, and this time the man began swal-
lowing various things and pulling them out of ear
and nose and mouth.   He first opened his mouth
so that it could be seen plainly that a ball of ribbon
actually went down his throat, and then pulled it out
from his nose, reeling it off by the yard.   Then, his
mouth full of paper shavings, he spurted fire from his
nostrils.

After this the ball trick came in order, and he
threw up a dozen balls, catching them regularly and
throwing them up again; then a row of cups, and
the disappearance of rupees which were found under
the cups, where the Bishop declared they could not be.

Now he took a cup of water and watered the plant
under the basket, then did the trick of balls again and
again.   After this more tricks with the monkeys; then,
with the same call to Hanuman and the tap on the
monkey's skull, he lifted the basket, crying:

"Dekho!"

There *was* a tree, O, unbelieving Bishop and Mrs.
Bishop, growing before your eyes, thriving and promising, and this juggler smiled a smile, for there was

enough wonder and delight on the good Bishop's face
almost to repay him for his trouble, and even the
skeptical **wife** thought that this was one of the "more
things **than were** dreamed of in Horatio's philosophy."

Now the Bishop began to think of his letters, and
gave **the man** some pice, who went out just as a
swarm of other men came in at the gate—men in dirty
white with great bundles on their heads, followed by
other men in clean clothes, wearing dark blue and gray
pugris, dark woolen coat and white trousers, and
with sticks in their hands. Katie explained that they
were cloth merchants with beautiful shawls and rugs
and gold and silver embroideries from Cashmere.

"They sell them cheap, very cheap," the child
said, translating literally. "And they have risen
up early and come at once because the great name
of the Lord Bishop Sahib had gone abroad through
the land and reached them ; and because they wished
him to see good things, well made and cheap, and
also because they feared other merchants, who were
thieves and rascals, would impose on his good heart,
for this they had hurried and come."

"Ah," murmured the Bishop, "very kind and
considerate, but quite unnecessary, as we do not wish
to buy. Tell him so, little girl."

"But no, did not the Lord Bishop wish to buy ?
That was nothing. It would be more pleasure to
show these beautiful things to so great and good
a man, whose fame had traveled so far against even
the wind, than to *sell* to people of lower caste ; and
also to the great Sahib's honored wife, her who knew
so well the value of all the beautiful things of the

East; her appreciation of his things would quite repay his trouble." As he talked he unrolled soft white shawls, glittering gold and beetle-wing embroidery, gauzy draperies, dull, soft, silky-looking rugs of exquisite colors, tiger and leopard skins, black curly astrakhan skins, and those less curly and smaller, taken from the goat at its birth, and watched the admiring looks cast on them and heard the expressions of admiration with concealed triumph, for Mrs. Clinton could not forbear sighs and exclamations of delight even had she known that the wily merchant was taking stock of them and adding five rupees for every sigh and ten for every exclamation to the price he intended to ask. The veranda soon looked like a shop, and there was not a place where one could put one's foot on the floor without treading on beautiful things.

The moments fled, and Mrs. Clinton decided she must have a few things for her house, for even missionaries must have curtains and table-covers, and she began pricing things, and found to her surprise that these "exquisite, lovely, transcendent" things would cost only what she had paid for ugly, hideous, inartistic things of Western manufacture, and she wondered how she had ever endured them. The merchant, now that Katie and Lillian had disappeared in the garden, developed a very good use of the English tongue, and told her that he was only asking half that a Mem Sahib in the next house had paid him, because he had heard of her great kindness to the poor. So she selected a half dozen things, laid them out, and was about to pay for them, when Mrs. Mackenzie appeared on the scene and with a gasp stopped her. The merchants did not look happy at her coming. What they like and gloat over is a raw, untried "globe-trotter" without any of those mean people who have lived a long time in the country and understand things. Mrs. Mackenzie asked quickly what she was going to pay, and turned sharply, saying to the man in Hindoostanee:

"Why have you come to my house to rob my friends? Do you expect I will ever buy from you or allow you to come into my house again?"

"Pardon, pardon, Mem Sahib," and his hands came together in the usual form of supplication; "I, as is our custom, told her the first price, which is, as you know, and also all wise Mem Sahibs like you, only the talking price. But she, not waiting to ask the true price, said she would pay it. There was, of course, nothing for me to do. It would ill become me, a poor man and a humble, to correct so great a Mem Sahib, who should know far more than I."

Mrs. Mackenzie laughed as she translated to her friends, who laughed also, but not with full enjoyment. The person lives not who likes to be thoroughly "done" in a bargain.

"Now," said Mrs. Mackenzie, turning to the head merchant, "tell me exactly the right price, or I will not allow you to come here again. Remember, the truth, and nothing but the truth."

"Certainly, Mem Sahib. Of course, if she had asked for the truth I would have told her, as I now tell you at once on your own asking. For all these fine things, the table-cover, the tea-cozy, the curtains, I ask her the true price, and Allah be my witness that I say true words;" and he named just half he had asked Mrs. Clinton.

"O, you rascal!" she exclaimed, in exasperation, "how could you have had the heart to cheat me so?"

He heard as one who hears not, but Mrs. Mackenzie said: "She will give you two thirds of your *selling* price, not one pice more. Remember, I know what these things are worth."

"No, no;" and the man shook his head angrily; "I am a poor man, and now it is you that wish to rob me. I have spent my morning for nothing, and I will go;" and he began hurriedly to gather up the things and roll them together with a great show of indignation. Mrs. Clinton was ashamed, and she, as well as her husband, thought Mrs. Mackenzie had been a little hard on the man, but she smiled at them, and, when his back was turned, pointed to the things which he had put aside in a little heap while he packed the remainder of his goods. Then he begged for the price he had named, said he was giving them away even at that price; that they had wasted his morning, and, as a last plea, he was "a poor man with many children, whose stomachs were always empty, and always crying for food."

And again her guests wondered at Mrs. Mackenzie's hard-heartedness, wished there had been nothing said, and that they had paid his price without any parley. The man took the things in his hand with a sour face, put them in his pack, salaamed to all, and went off. There was a silence on the veranda, the Bishop visibly disgusted, Mrs. Clinton half inclined to call the man back, and Mrs. Mackenzie tranquil.

When half way to the gate the merchant turned, came back smiling, and begged the great Mem Sahib to take them at her own price, saying that he well knew that Mrs. Mackenzie was of a hard nature and would never pay more than was right.

"And O, brother," said she, in Hindoostanee, "do I ever pay less, or even try to make you take less than is just?"

"Never. The Mem Sahib is just, and I shall ever intercede with Allah for her long life."

They all had a laugh when she translated, and the Bishop said, looking at his watch:

"Where is the morning gone? I have not written my letters."

He was hurrying away when Mackenzie entered, and Mrs. Mackenzie said:

"We have been waiting breakfast for you as usual."

"Yes, but a man came that wanted two thousand tracts, and I had to help select them, and I had to finish an editorial and go to the bank for treasury money, as Clark has been worrying me for his allowance in advance. There is so much sickness in a native Christian village near him that he wants his own allowance to lend to them in installments."

"And how will he live?" asked Mrs. Clinton.

"On his good name, and trust to getting his money back; the latter, however, is not so certain as the former. But let us have breakfast, for I have five men up there now waiting for me."

"Are these men Christian inquirers?"

"No, indeed; *I* 'serve the tables and carry the money bag.' I have to leave the pleasanter work of the mission to those who cannot do this and can do that; for, strange to say, I have no time for personal mission work."

The Bishop looked and felt severe. There was something wrong when a missionary had no time for personal work.

"But," Mr. Mackenzie went on, "I console myself for not doing the pleasantest work by the fact that other people could not do it either were I not doing what I am. I make it possible for them to do a good deal of personal work through the *Kaukab-i-Hind*, the *Rafif-i-Niswan*, and all the other monthly and weekly papers we publish ; I myself speak to a large number through the paper which I edit; so perhaps after all I do a little personal work, though I always think of my paper as my recreation and not my work, as I do most of it in the evening, after the day is well over."

CHAPTER IV.

A MISSIONARY PRINTING PRESS.

AFTER a plain breakfast of cracked wheat, mutton chops, potatoes, and fruit Mr. Mackenzie persuaded the Bishop to leave his letters and go up to the mission publishing house with him.

"It is only a short walk, so you can spend a half-hour there and still have time for your letters," he said, taking up his white-covered umbrella, and also a white-covered cork hat, looking dubiously the while at the soft felt which the Bishop as usual put on his head.

"I beg your pardon; have you no umbrella?"

"Yes, but I do not need it, for certainly there is no indication of rain," answered the Bishop, looking up at the cloudless sky.

"Hardly," with a smile, "and there will not be until we have longed for it many and many a weary day; but you require an umbrella to protect you from the sun."

"You cannot be in earnest, for I feel really cold, and I would be glad of a warmer sun than this."

"For your feet and legs it might be well to have a warmer sun, but not for your head," Mackenzie answered decidedly, "and I have another umbrella, which I will get for you."

"No," waving his hand, "I do not require it."

"Then let me get you a sola topi like mine," indicating his ugly pith hat.

"No, no," impatiently, "let us proceed; we are wasting time."

Mr. Mackenzie looked troubled, but opened his umbrella and moved on.

"The native of this country, I have observed," remarked the Bishop, "goes without other covering than a little embroidered cap, and if foreigners would accustom themselves to the sun gradually no doubt they would be stronger and would more quickly become acclimated; and as the walk is short it is a good moment for me to begin my acclimatization."

Mr. Mackenzie said nothing. It was not the first time he had had the philosophy of the Indian climate explained and advice given to him in regard to it by people who were new to it, nor, he knew, would it be the last; and the Bishop was not the first man who had been given over to the tender mercies of experience. His host could only hope these same tender mercies would not be cruel.

The walk was not long, and when they arrived at the back entrance of the Publishing House they were in no way conscious of heat, but the veins on the Bishop's forehead stood out, and there was a flush on his face and a peculiar brightness in his eyes that told a well-known story. He was conscious of a confusion of head, and a curious faint feeling which he could not explain, and had never before experienced, but he was not in the least heated, and was rather loath to leave the bright sunshine for the damp, cold printing house. They passed through a high gate, which was unlocked by an obsequious, weather-beaten looking native who was night and day watchman, and one of whose duties was to search every man who passed out, to see if he were carrying off type, or books, or papers to sell in the bazar.

"This is shocking," cried the Bishop; "do you expect to make Christians of men when on the face of it you show you do not trust them? I must say I cannot approve of your policy in this."

"If I give it up will you promise to present us with a new outfit of type in six months?" asked Mackenzie, dryly.

"Yes," was the decided answer, "I will do so, for I have not so low an estimate of human nature that I cannot think it better to put men on their honor."

"Very well, I will not begin the experiment until you have been here two months; then if you still advise it, agreeing to give us new type if we need it, I will try your plan for six months."

It may be said, by the way, that when the time had expired he did not advise the change, and the matter was never referred to again.

At one side of the large yard were many lithographic stones drying in the sun; back of them was a pile of wood for firing the little engine; near the door a cart drawn by two white oxen, from which were being unloaded huge parcels of paper just brought from the paper mill. Through the open door could be seen the engine, and a native engineer in English dress. Entering, they saw a long dim room full of dusky figures busy setting type and printing from small hand-presses. One or two men were at work at the little steam press, rolling off weekly papers, one of which

5

was presented to the Bishop with a low salaam, by a half-naked man ; another, with the ink still fresh from a lithographic hand-press, was also presented to him in the same manner. Mr. Mackenzie informed him that they had as yet no type for the Urdu language in the Persian character, though there was plenty of Roman Urdu printed; and he pointed to a man sitting on the floor writing Urdu on a stone, with a pen made from the hard stalk of kusi grass.

On a little platform before them all sat the English manager of the printing department, surrounded by proof readers, who, by virtue of English education, were sitting on chairs.

"The strangest thing about these typesetters," said Mackenzie, " is that they can read neither English nor their own language, but can set type equally well in both."

"Surprising; and they are heathen?"

"Most are what you would call heathen; the remainder are Mohammedans and Christians."

"And the Christians, of course, do better work than the Hindoos and Mohammedans?"

Mackenzie smiled. "The truth is best; among educated Christians they do, but among printers, with a few exceptions, they do not, but not because they are Christians. There are several reasons," he said, after introducing the manager, Mr. Board, and the proof readers to the Bishop, "why Christian printers give less satisfaction than the others. The driftwood of the Christian community comes here. I take many of them in, not because they do good work, but because they are Christians; and there are various kinds of Christians among these people, as in other

countries. But will you look at our stereotyping room?" and he pointed to a closet where a man stood with a stick patiently pounding the stereotyping paper over the form. Then he took a dish of melted lead, put the form into a little hand-machine, poured the lead into it, and presto! one page was stereotyped.

"This is going back to the Middle Ages, Bishop."

"Altogether too much so. You must get out a modern electrotyping outfit from New York. I am surprised that you can tolerate this kind of work."

"I am only too glad to hear you say so. All we lack is money to pay for it. But look at our bookbinding department, and see what you think of that," he said, turning to the left and entering a large, long room at one end of which a dozen men were sitting on the floor with common table-knives, pastepots, and balls of fine twine binding books.

Mackenzie picked up some very neat-looking books. "Not bad-looking work, considering the means."

"I could not have believed they would have looked so well. They are a clever lot of men, though they do not have exactly that appearance," said the Bishop; "but it is too slow, too primitive. We must have all this changed at once."

"They ought to do them well, for they have done ten thousand of these same books this year," said Mackenzie, ignoring his guest's criticism.

At the other end little half-dressed boys were folding periodicals fresh from the press. As they passed these all rose and salaamed, for they too had heard of the Băra Sahib's coming, and hoped in a vague way for some advantage from his presence. Then to the packing room, where three or four men were putting up cases of tracts and schoolbooks, Bibles and weekly and monthly papers for missionaries in out districts.

"They are sent from one end of India to the other. These two cases," looking at the address, said Mackenzie, "go to two earnest, hard-working men two thousand miles apart; one eight days' march in the interior of the Himalaya Mountains, and the other south of Madras. This," pointing to another, "will go to Kurrachi, and that to Rangoon—I am afraid to say how many miles apart—at least three thousand by water. Not only so many miles apart, but they will do a work among people as widely different in their habits and customs as any two peoples you know. These parcels of tracts go here and there all over India. It is rather an unpretending place, but we send out more parcels and packages than any other business house in Lucknow. We preach to thousands and thousands every week, and when I think of that, think that we are the only ones that can or ever will reach thousands of people whose need is so great that they are unconscious of any need, I am content to do my work though there are trials and worries enough connected with it to drive a man nearly mad. Now," he said, as he led the Bishop straight through a large room with several clerks in native dress sitting at desks, "let us look at the shop, and then we will come back and talk over these things after I have dispersed these men," indicating a dozen men who stood around a desk shivering in their cotton clothes.

The front shop was lined with bookcases filled with

books, chiefly English stories, travels, biographies, and history. The tables in the center of the room were covered with books in Urdu, Hindi, and Bengalee, and some showcases had Christmas and Scripture cards, inkstands, and all the usual stationery found in bookstores.

"The sales of this room pay for a number of the clerks," said Mackenzie, "besides having a distinct work of their own to do; for when I have put a good book in a man's hand I believe I have done him a great and lasting favor."

"Yes," said the Bishop; "I agree with you on that;" but there was a commercial look and sound to much of this that he did not like, though he did not say so. He was not quite ready to formulate his opinion.

"Now here," said Mackenzie, as they went back to the large desk in the inner room, "is my workshop, and here I spend the greater part of my waking hours. Here is a report," handing him a pamphlet, "which will tell you that last year we sent out twenty-four millions of pages, and two hundred thousand of them free, besides a good many things in it which you may find interesting."

"Now, Chunga Nath, what is it?" he said to the man nearest him.

"Your honor, I must have more pay for binding your books, else I will give up the job."

"Did you not sign a contract for just what you are now getting?"

"Yes, your honor, but I am a poor man with a large family, and I must have more."

"Am I not paying you more than you could get at any other place?"

"Your honor, I am a poor man, and my children must have bread."

"Answer my question, brother; am I or am I not paying you more than you could get at any other place?"

"Yes, your honor," sulkily.

"And are you not coming now to ask for more because you know that the books are very much needed, and not because it is just or right?"

No answer, but the man stood first on one foot and then on the other.

"Answer me, if you can; if not, go about your work and give me no more trouble. I have the written contract, and can compel you to do your work well and in time." Then Mackenzie translated this to the Bishop, and the man slunk off, one end of his dirty kamarband trailing on the ground, and his dirty pugri having a discouraged look that rather appealed to the man who was having his ideas of mission work so upset and overhauled by what he was seeing that he was not sure he was the same man that had preached missionary sermons, portraying graphically the sufferings of the imaginary missionary; but surely he had never thought for a minute that dealing with dishonest contractors was one of their trials.

"Now, Charn Lal, what can I do for you?"

"Preserver of the Poor, I am sick and cannot work."

Mackenzie looked at him sharply, felt his pulse, put his hand on his forehead, then said, "What is the matter?"

"I have fever, your honor, and I will go to my home and lie in my bed."

Mackenzie opened a drawer, took out a clinical thermometer, put it under the man's tongue, bade him keep his mouth shut, and turned to his head clerk, who had brought a handful of letters and bills; he took them from him, read them rapidly over, signed some, returned two or three for correction, and then looked at the thermometer.

"Charn Lal, you have been telling a jhuth bat. You have no fever. Now tell me the truth. Why did you want to go away from your work when you know in what great need we are to have it done quickly? The truth now, brother;" and he smiled at him in a genial way.

The hands came together.

"Pardon me, Protector of the Poor. My brother is making his wedding to-day, and my heart bids me go."

"Why did not your heart bid you tell the truth? No, you cannot go. You have been away already this month so many days that your family will suffer for bread. If it were only you that would suffer I would let you go. Now, David, what do you want?" This was said in English.

"Sir, I in debt. The man come take my cooking vessels, and I beg you to give me nine rupees that I pay him, for if I have not the cooking vessels how can the woman cook?"

"Why are you in debt?"

"Sir, I make my marriage, and I a very poor man, and I get much in debt of necessity when I make marriage; and my wife is now all fool, and I am not advantaged by her, and all time men come and take away clothes for debt."

"This is bad, but you may go now, and I will look into the matter."

"David is a Christian, and one of the 'weak brothers,'" said Mackenzie to his visitor. "We will never make much of him, but he may be better than if he had been left to himself."

"And here is Brown again," he said, looking at a dark man in English dress. "How are you getting on with your work?"

"Not very well, sir. The people will not come to buy of me, but I am hoping much, as my prospects are a little brighter, sir. There is a very respectable soldier who wishes to marry one of my daughters, and that will be a great reduction of expense. I have come to ask you for a little advance, which I will try to return next week."

Mr. Mackenzie's brow contracted. He was not pleased.

"You may wait outside, and I will give you an answer soon. Here, Bishop, give me the benefit of your wisdom. This man is a leper."

"What?" said the Bishop, in undisguised horror.

"Yes, he is a leper. Did you not see that one hand was gone? Before it was known, he had a position as bookkeeper, at three hundred rupees per month. He was discharged because of this disease, and after that no one would employ him. I, with the help of some good friends, set him up in the coal business; but he says people will not buy. I fancy, however, that he has not energy enough to make it go. Now, the question is whether to give the man an advance and put him in debt to me, or, as I have given him a good chance to help himself, let him know once

for all that I cannot support him. Tell me what to
do."

The Bishop had heard little; he had, unnoticed,
half risen at the word "leper," and then sank back
into his seat. His head, confused by the heat of the
sun, refused to think clearly.

"Leprosy, and I exposed to it! It is all very well
if Mackenzie chooses to help a creature whose presence may be worse than death, but he ought not to
expose others to it."

"Mackenzie," he said, and his voice was a little
hoarse, "what right have you to expose yourself to
such a disease? You should consider your family if
you do not care for yourself."

The Bishop was laboring under a heavy amount of
excitement, Mackenzie saw, to his surprise. Risking
contagion in one way or another was so much a part
of his general work that he hardly thought of it, and
this sharp rebuke, wrung from the man who was wip-
ing the perspiration from a pale face that had been
flushed a moment before, hurt him like a blow, and,
it must be confessed, stirred his contempt a little.

"My dear Bishop," he said, before he had time to
think, "if you are to be a missionary, as you have
said, will you pick and choose? Will you run at the
first signal of danger?"

There was silence, and the face that had paled
at the thought of contagion so horrible, now was
flushed.

"I beg your pardon," Mackenzie said, "but you
did not tell me what to do. The man says he needs
money badly; I have the certain conviction that if I
begin advancing money I shall have to keep it up, for

he is of the kind that likes to be supported, or refuse
him at some future time. The question is, shall I refuse him now, or after he had drained the last bit of
charity money I have?"

The Bishop took out his purse.

"Here are ten rupees—give them to him; but can
you not hereafter send to him, write to him, anything
but have him come where you are?"

"I will give him five and keep the other five for
another time of need, if you do not mind;" and he
went out, gave the man some advice as to trying
harder, and told him he must try to pay back the loan
next week.

"Seriously, when you can send to a man like that
why bring him here among all these people, exposing
them as well as yourself?" persisted the Bishop.

"Well, it is difficult to manage, and lepers are
everywhere about the city. As a matter of fact, I do
try to go to see him myself once a week, though when
he gets hard up he comes to see me. But if you
think one can do much work for the people, and dodge
all disagreeable things and all dangers, you are mistaken. I suppose there is not a day in the cold weather
that I am not exposed to smallpox. Even to-day it
is probable that among the one hundred and seventy
men employed here at least one man comes with
smallpox infection about him, and I feel glad if no
one comes with the actual disease upon him, for it
often happens. Then, in the hot season, we have
cholera for a change. Do you see there?" and he
opened a little drawer, showing a dozen or more bottles labeled "Cholera Mixture." "I used and gave to
the men for their families during the last hot season

four dozen of these bottles, and even in the cold weather a man now and then comes or sends to me for it."

" And you expose yourself and take home infection to your family, then, every day in the year?"

Mackenzie's face grew grave and his voice was solemn with the weight of deep feeling:

" I confess to you that when I think of my family in this connection I do not find it pleasant or easy to bear, but I can only trust them as I trust myself to God's tender care. I have given myself and them into his hands, and the result is with him."

His questioner was rebuked, and as he reached over and grasped the hand of the man before him, who spoke so simply of these terrors, the old missionary spirit which had been in him as a young man rose and sang again a song of triumph; for he knew Christ's kingdom must come when such a spirit as this was an everyday matter. He well knew that while a man may, in moments of great danger, easily give his life once for all; while he may gladly suffer even martyrdom, which is over when the fire at the stake dies out, yet the same man may be utterly incapable of an hourly giving up or of living cheerfully or joyfully through constant and never-ending danger. He knew, too, that to suffer martyrdom does not require the entire and perfect consecration that is needed to work through constant depression and discouragement for people who often are unworthy, often ungrateful, and always incapable of comprehending the greatness of the nature that gives itself for them. But what was this sentence haunting him?

" While I do not for a moment credit all that has

been said of their faults and deficiencies, there is no doubt in my mind that the heroic spirit has died out of missions and missionaries."

He had said it in the pulpit, and he had written it where it had been published. It had sounded well, but he would now give much if he could blot out the remembrance of it from the mind of everyone who had heard or read the sentence, and there seemed a sorrowful voice in his heart, saying, "Inasmuch as ye did it unto them, ye have done it unto me." What had he done to them? He had condemned them unheard; he had criticised them in ignorance; he had not in any case rendered them their just dues of honor and sympathy, and if Christ's words meant anything they meant at least that he had denied Him love and sympathy, honor and justice.

CHAPTER V.

IN THE BAZAR.

MRS. CLINTON decided to open her housekeeping as quickly as possible. Mrs. Mackenzie's cook, who was a Christian, had promised to send her one of his friends, who was likewise a good cook and a Christian. Her first need after this was china for the table.

So at four o'clock the shabby little carriage and the scraggy little pony took them slowly down through the English and Eurasian quarter, past the Eurasian and native quarter, and then on to the business portion of the town, where they entered a long, long street, lined with little shops on either side, with now and then a temple or mosque, beside which grew the inevitable and sacred pipal tree. Mrs. Clinton had said as they started out:

"Now we will have a nice cozy talk of housekeeping, and you can enlighten me on many points."

But in a moment her attention was distracted by a group at the wayside well.

A man with a musical instrument somewhat like an elongated banjo, another with one of the shape and appearance of a small, dirty beer-barrel, and still another with a reed pipe were sitting under a tamarind tree in the midst of a group of friends, who listened, entranced, to a medley of wailing sounds that Mrs. Clinton thought the opposite of musical.

6

"The thing in the Indian people," said Mrs. Mackenzie, "that delights me more than anything else is their inconsequent way. They do not stop to begin, as we of an older civilization do. Now, these men are as happy, dropping down by the roadside and calling the first musicians that happen to be passing, as the European who builds an opera house or concert hall, hires his singers months ahead, prints programs and tickets, and then demands an elaborately dressed audience. Then here, see these two men. One wishes for a barber. He goes along on his journey until he meets one, and they sit down under the tree, perfectly oblivious to all passers-by, and the barber does his work thoroughly, even to cutting finger and toe nails and shaving the head, if his customer is in mourning."

"They are political economists of the first rank, I should say. No force or time is lost," answered Mrs. Clinton.

"Yes, indeed. Now here is another instance: that man nearly naked, passing along with a wet strip of cloth held over his head, flying behind him, is going home from his work. He has just stopped a few minutes by the well, washed his outer garment, which is usually wrapped around him like a shawl, and he easily holds it in the wind as he goes singing on his way. When it is dry he will again wrap it about him, and little or no time will have been lost."

Mrs. Clinton laughed.

"I like saving time quite as well as anyone, but I do not think I would like their way of doing it for myself."

"That is because we are so artificial. Now, he did all that as easily and naturally as a bird dips himself in

the river and flashes his feathers in the sunlight as he
goes singing up into the sky. It is perfectly fascinating to me. I am never tired of seeing how many
beginnings and endings they cut off from life. They
are not the products of an effete civilization, as we are.
Here is another example: see that man under the
banyan tree, with toys and some pieces of print and
a few boxes of thread spread out on old strips of
cloth on the ground above him. He needs no elaborately planned shop, no plate-glass windows, no carpets, no electric light, and no chamber of commerce to
interfere. He has got hold of ten rupees, honestly or
otherwise, and in one day has set up his shop, from
the proceeds of which he will give an offering to
Lāchmi, the goddess of plenty, if at the end of the
year he makes as much as we spend in a week, even
when we are economical."

"It is wonderful, but forgive me, the most wonderful part of it all is that it seems so dirty."

Mrs. Mackenzie laughed.

"There was a time when I too thought of that, but
I have learned that they are the cleanest people in the
world. In judging of the cleanliness of any nation
you must consider, not the rich, but the poorest and
lowest classes, and I know of no other poor people who
bathe every day. The Mohammedans, too, invariably
wash before eating, and even the lowest cooly
cleans his teeth the first thing in the morning. But
here is our shop," as they stopped before a stall where
was heaped up coarse china of various kinds. As
Mrs. Mackenzie alighted, she said, "We might almost
call this missionary china, for most missionaries have
it, though not from choice, I can assure you."

The whole street on both sides, Mrs. Clinton saw while waiting, was a succession of stalls, their fronts opening directly on the street, with one door from the back leading to the family rooms, but no doors or windows at the sides.

In the one next to the china shop cotton goods of all shades and colors were stacked up around the three sides of the stall, all mixed together without regard to dazzling the eye, or perhaps with that very object. Next to this was the gáráh wala shop, with its tiers of fresh-baked terra cotta waterpots, of all sizes, their lovely oval shapes as well as their rich color attracting the attention. The little space in the shop that was not filled with these æsthetic water jars, dear at three cents apiece, was festooned with stems of hookahs, wound in bright rainbow colors, varied by lines of hookah stands of a coarse sort of majolica, of brass and of silver.

Beyond this was a man sitting on the floor of his shop making jaunty little caps of thin embroidered muslin. They looked about big enough for an English baby, but they were on the heads of most of the men that were passing.

On the opposite side of the street was a shop that quickly caught and held Mrs. Clinton's color-loving eyes. There were dark low tables, on which were shallow baskets heaped up with scarlet, gold, crimson, and purple powders, and bronze, green, and orange resins, the pale straw of the baskets bringing out these masses of color from the deep purple shadows in the back of the shops, where the shopkeeper, as though to help in the harmony, sat clothed in dull light brown from head to foot, his hookah of burnished brass being the only thing near him that caught the light. Farther down was a shop with the same straw-colored baskets, only larger and filled and heaped up with salmon-colored dál, all shades of olive and olive-green in bájra and millet, the polished black seeds of the koda by the dull gold of the wheat, and in the center, lounging on a rug on the floor, the handsome, graceful-limbed, olive-faced young bunnia, or store-keeper, dressed in terra cotta color with a gold-embroidered turban, pulling at his silver hookah. The bunnia was a dude, and that is a thing not expected of a bunnia, but a bicycle leaning against the steps explained that he was of modern India, probably had his master of arts degree, and knew that his gods Ram, Siva, and Vishnu did not reside on the tops of the snowy peaks of the Himalayas.

"What," asked Mrs. Clinton of herself, "is not possible to a people whose very shopkeepers do themselves and their shops up in such harmony of color? Probably," she said to herself, "he has also chosen his occupation from its æsthetic fitness to himself."

Had she been longer in India she would have known that to have been impossible, for his occupation was chosen for him by his ancestors hundreds of years before his birth. There was to her an inexhaustible interest in all these shops, but the street was filling so fast with people that they shut out the view. She saw the shadows deepening and felt the chill of the night that was coming on, and just as she began to wish Mrs. Mackenzie would hurry up the man and conclude her bargain the latter came out of the shop, saying:

"Shopping is the most tiresome thing I have to do, I think. It is simply impossible to do it quickly,

even though they know just what I will pay. Now
we will go down by the river."

But they had to pass slowly through the crowded
streets that were kaleidoscopic in their moving color.
Most of the people were foot passengers, but now and
then there was a palki gari, through the closed blinds
of which one caught a glimpse of color and the flash
of the dark eyes of some begum out for an airing;
now and then a dhooly with a richly dressed native
gentleman inside stretched on his back, the monoto-
nous song of the coolies carrying it uniting with the
cries of the sweet venders and shrieks of the palki
gari drivers. The pony shied viciously at an elephant
who came slowly trundling along, carrying half a dozen
soldiers, but passed a string of camels unnoticed, and
soon took them out of it all where the air was fresh
enough to allow them to breathe freely again.

The sky in the west was a clear pale lemon, deepened into orange at the horizon, against which the
clock tower and the old imambaras and mosques lifted
themselves in dull purple excepting the domes, corners, and golden balls which still caught a strong light
from the warm sky, though the sunset call to prayers
had long since died away. Over the intervening
space the blue smoke was beginning to arise from the
evening fires, and the river—the sacred river Gumti,
which flows into the more sacred river Ganges—reflected every tree and bungalow on its shores and
every boat on its surface with mirror-like exactness.
It was difficult to tell which was the most beautiful,
the landscape above or below the water. Even the
old Chutter Munzil, surmounted by its golden umbrella, peeped out below the surface, and the red brick

bridge, with the evening lamps lighted, already gleamed sharply out just where one expected brown shadows in the water.

"The Chutter Munsil," said Mrs. Mackenzie, after a little silence in which they had enjoyed the scene, "was the zenana palace where the old King of Onde kept the most favored of his thousand wives, but it is now used as a club for both civil and military people. There is a fine library in it to which I am always longing to subscribe."

"Is it so very expensive?"

"Not at all, though what I would pay for that would defray the cost of a girl's day school; but notwithstanding this I am sometimes tempted to do it, for I do not believe it quite right to neglect my mind even to improve the mind of others, only I have not time for it. Could I have the health I had in America I might find time for reading, but I am obliged to use all the strength I have to keep up my mission work, and trust to some future day to improve my mind."

"I think, if you do not mind my saying it, I would give up a servant or two and use what they are paid for the subscription, and then take time; for if you are like me you will soon have no mind to improve, living as you do, so cut off from the world."

Mrs. Mackenzie, ignoring the hint as to servants, said:

"I fancy you are not very different from the rest of humanity in regard to your mind. We never mean to allow our minds to shrink and fall away, but there is such a rush and demand for every bit there is in us of body and mind that no strength is left for acquiring anything new."

"That is the very reason why you need to be adding; the exhaustion is so perpetual you cannot surely do as good work after several years of this process, nor can your judgment be so good; and altogether you cannot be of so much use to the mission."

"True," was the answer, given a little sadly; "I have myself often gone over this same ground, especially when I have noticed some marked case of stunted growth or checked development in people who gave great promise; and to me it is the greatest sacrifice I make—that is, to resign myself to being an inferior person when there might be a possibility of being the opposite."

"But why not give up a servant or two and have the subscription to the library? I shall do it if I can."

"That last clause is well put—if you can. I did not want to begin the servant question, for I should fail to make myself understood. It is the one thing that people cannot forgive us. Whether or not they think we can be teaching one school and superintending half a dozen others, or visiting a hundred zenanas a week, and at the same time cooking a dinner, is more than my feeble mind can divine. However, as you are come to be a missionary I will ask you at the end of three months to give up one or two or three or four, and see what you will say."

"But tell me this at least. Is it not a great care to keep so many up to their work?"

"Care? Look at my hair and see how gray it is. I believe every man about the house brings me an added gray hair every day of my life."

"Then why do you have so many, for it certainly seems to me that you have altogether too many. Of course I know in a general way their caste prevents their doing various kinds of work; but as you have part Christian servants I suppose you find them willing to do anything."

" There is some difference, but custom is strong, and cannot be changed in a day."

" Now, your cook, for instance; he is a strong man and is a faithful Christian, you tell me. He should do all your work, and I should insist on his doing it."

" Try it, try it, and then we will compare experiences, and I assure you beforehand of my utmost sympathy."

Mrs. Clinton was becoming annoyed at the evasive answers to her questions. She could not see why they should not be answered, and her annoyance made her lose her caution.

" I will most certainly try it, for that is just what I am here for," with a little touch of anger in her voice.

There was a dead silence; then, in a voice strained to appear indifferent, Mrs. Mackenzie said:

" You mean that you, knowing nothing of the country and the language and customs of the people, expect to be able to teach us who have been here for years how to live economically?"

" Yes, if you choose to put it that way."

" And that you came as a spy, if I choose to put it so?"

" Yes," was the short answer. She made this short answer because in a way it was the truth, and she felt too irritated to explain that it was not the whole truth—that she had come as a sympathetic spy, anxious to prove that the missionaries were right. She felt that Mrs. Mackenzie should know that without explanation, while Mrs. Mackenzie felt that her guest was conceited and mistaken and unkind to a degree that she could not express, though there were some things in her mind that she could hardly keep from saying; but having plenty of self-control she sat silent until they were back home and met by their husbands and a Mr. Rokewood, who were all more than ready for their dinner.

While these two good women had been manufacturing trouble for themselves out of nothing, the Bishop, having finished his visit to the publishing house, went on an exploring tour about the city, dropping in at several mission houses for a few minutes and then wandering on through the bazar.

He loitered longest in the manufacturing streets, where in all the little open stalls sat men with rude tools fashioning things for the use of the world. There was a fascination to him in seeing the interior working of the city exposed in this manner. It was like having the heart and lungs of a live man under glass, where the public could see every inhalation, every throb of vein and artery. The publicity of everything—the finding all stores, tailor shops, banks, restaurants, manufactories of gold and silver, in fact, everything that had to be made and bought and sold, within half a foot of the garis and foot passengers— was a genuine surprise; for, having had the privacy of family life in India so firmly fixed in his mind, he had ascribed to these people great delicacy of sentiment and feeling, which sentiment vanished forever when he saw children eight, nine, and even ten years old, quite, and grown men half naked; and as he went about poking his cane into idol manufactories, into seeds and grains, into stonecutters' shops, he revolved in his mind a grand governmental scheme for clothing the people.

He lingered longest over the potter who, as he turned his wheel evolving an etruscan-shaped water jar, also evolved a whole sermon out of the Bishop's mind; and the two women in blue and red drapery turning the heavy millstone gave him another sermon, or rather vivified an old one, on two women grinding at a mill—"one shall be taken and the other left." Leaving these at last, he found himself away from the bazar, and in trying to return to it he got into a park which formed the inner court of an old palace. He sauntered through this, listening now and then to the talk of young native men in a semi-native dress consisting of a round smoking-cap, tight-fitting long coat, and patent-leather shoes, who were constantly passing. He was surprised to find so many of them talking in English, and good English, though generally with a very strong Hindoostanee accent.

A number seeing that he was idling about said "Good even" with hand lifted to the forehead. This gesture, called "salaaming," was extremely pleasant to the Bishop; it was at once so graceful, so respectful, and also so self-respectful, for only a native gentleman who thoroughly respects himself can give a perfect salaam.

He finally joined a group and asked them about the park and the old palace.

One after another of the men who were passing joined them to find out of what so big and fine a looking sahib could be talking.

Then one man came who knew of him, and he told

the others in Hindoostanee that this was the Lord Sahib of the Christians who ruled over all the ordinary
padris, or ministers. This led them to questions,
which led to talk on religion, and almost before he
knew it he was speaking to a good audience, and conscious of a thrill of joy when he realized that he was
actually, as he had dreamed of doing, standing up as
a missionary preaching to heathen.

These men were gentle, intelligent, and refined, and,
it seemed to the new missionary, exceedingly simple
and susceptible, but he had no means by which to
gauge them.

The coming man, or you might say, the "Young
America" of India, is in a transition stage. He has
left off the old ways, but has not arrived at a settled
stage of new things. He is fearful that he may go
back to the old ignorant worship and more fearful of
going forward to new beliefs. He sneers at the ignorant superstition of his mother, and less at those of his
wife, because she, also touched by the spirit of progress, has fewer at which he can sneer.

He feels the embryo of something new, of something better in himself, but he has not learned to
handle his astonishing superiority and the astonishing
amount of knowledge he has acquired. He may have
risen from the merchant class or the artisan class, or
even the servant class, to being a teacher or clerk, or
baboo, as they are called, but he has generally risen
too far or not far enough. He aspires to English
clothes, to swearing, to drinking wine, to philosophy,
but more than all these, to an umbrella. He is clever,
has good intentions, but he lacks ballast, and is an
anomaly, as all things in a transition stage must be.

He will, however, develop, and his grandchildren will be settled, sensible men, good citizens, and loyal to the government which he himself condemns because it does not furnish patent-leather shoes and unlimited "pensins" to all who have passed their B. A. examinations.

This is the kind of material on which the Bishop began his missionary work.

After telling simply the old story of the sin of the world, of the prophecy of the coming Power that should conquer sin, of the arrival in the world of that Power, and of the expiation of the sin of the world on the cross, he said:

"Is there anything in this message that the Light of the World brought for you? He came equally for all men, for you and for me. Remember this, he came for you"—looking into one beautiful face which had not been turned once from his while he was talking—"and will you not accept him?"

The earnest face was a little confused, and the graceful head was lowered as he said:

"I—I not spik Englis—I make learn from you—I not see other sahibs to talk kăro."

There was a shadow of a smile on some of the faces, and the Bishop said:

"I do not quite catch your meaning."

Then up spoke a brave baboo, who knew English full well:

"He says, sir, that he wants to learn English, and as he knows no sahibs he was listening to learn it of you."

The Bishop's heart fell. And so this was all this man and also the others wanted? He had thought his words were sinking in good soil, and he had only been giving the man a lesson in English! But another said:

"Sir, if you will allow me, I will ask a question."

"Certainly," said the Bishop, brightening.

"Did the divine Spirit descend upon Christ when he was baptized by John the Baptist?"

"Yes," said the Bishop.

"Then, sir, was not Jesus divine before that, or did his divinity begin with his baptism by an ordinary human? If this latter, then may not any one of us become divine by baptism?"

The Bishop was bewildered, not by the question so much, for he was sound on theology, but by its coming from such an unexpected source. He gave the answer lamely and in a way that he felt carried little meaning.

Then another said:

"If I may be allowed I will also one question ask. Judas committed a foreseen act. Should he have been punished for a foreseen act that was to make and bring to pass all the good of which you have told us?"

Ah, this answer would require time, and before he could frame an answer which would reach their hearts as well as their heads another gentle-faced man stepped forward and said:

"There was a law by which prophets were judged. Jesus, a Jew, was tried by a Jewish Sanhedrin and found guilty of blasphemy according to the Jewish law, and where was the wrong in his being punished?"

These were not new points, but coming from these gentle-eyed young men, asked in the most polite and deprecating manner, they were confusing in the extreme, beyond even his own comprehension, and the consciousness of answering them without force annoyed him and made his words still less satisfactory to himself. But as it was growing dark he knew he must leave them, and he shook hands warmly with each one, the number having dwindled, and invited them most cordially to visit him in his house, when he should be settled, and discuss these points at length, as they were not questions to be disposed of lightly.

His manner was kind, and as a handshake from a man in high position is ever irresistible, so his heart did what his head could not, and won them to a willingness to believe what he said, though no doubt some of them could have answered their own questions better than he did.

As he went on in the direction of Mackenzie's bungalow he saw on a street that led into the one on which he was a man carrying a heavy valise, and walking as though tired, while two coolies were following along by him, evidently begging for the privilege of carrying the bag. As the roads converged the man stopped and, putting out his hand, said:

"How do you do, Bishop Clinton? My name is Rokewood, and I am a missionary."

"I am glad you know me, for I was wishing I knew you."

"Why?" asked Rokewood, smiling; "but I need not ask. It was because I am the first white man you have seen carrying anything larger than an eyeglass since you came to India."

"You have guessed very near it," responded the

7

Bishop, laughing a little. "I should really like to know why a man should carry a heavy bag like that, when it would be a favor to these poor fellows to let them carry it for two cents. I see no reason for your doing it, for this air, though cool, takes all the power out of one for walking, to say nothing of carrying a heavy weight."

"Well, now, Bishop, you have struck a vital point with me at the beginning. I simply want to show these clerks and shopkeepers and all others the dignity of labor. They would not be seen doing it, but I let them see that a sahib is not ashamed to do it, and then, besides, I want to make myself one with these poor fellows, to show them that to save them I will come down to them."

"Ah, that is the right spirit; that is the spirit that will conquer India," said his hearer. "I had been hoping to see more of the same in the mission than I have seen."

"I am glad of that. I heard you had come to be a missionary for a year, and if you begin on those lines we can work together. I must say I do not find much sympathy from the missionaries, but I mean to carry out my plan, though. Now, any other man would have hired a gari to come from the station. It is a good three miles' walk, and it takes time, but I could not pay for one, as I am trying to live on the same amount as a native clerk would; so I must do as he would do, though of course he would not have carried his bag."

"But what about the cooly? Even though you do show him you are not above doing the same work he does, will he be impressed if he has to go hungry to bed to-night because of the lack of the two cents he might have earned?"

"Yes," was the answer, "there is that side of the question, and it often puzzles me, but I would rather give him the two cents than let him think I am above carrying a valise."

"But there, again, it can never be beneficial to give a man what he is able to earn; for when you do so you make a pauper of him, and that is a lasting injury."

"O, yes; that is what the other missionaries are always saying; but I am not responsible for the way they take it. I am only responsible for myself, and for carrying out my own convictions."

"That is poor reasoning. You are responsible for their salvation, and you do this to show them you have sympathy with them; then you say you are not responsible for their being hungry, or for making them paupers? Now, then, as to hiring a gari. After you have walked three miles and carried this valise you will be unfit for more work this evening."

He hoped he would be contradicted, but Rokewood assented.

"Yes," he said; "but I do not believe in missionaries riding when they can walk, or hiring work done when they can do it themselves."

"Not even if the mission gains in the end tenfold by their driving or by their hiring work done?" asked the Bishop, ironically. He liked people to be reasonable.

"But it's the example I am insisting on," answered Rokewood, doggedly.

They were at Mackenzie's bungalow, and Mackenzie himself, coming across from the back road, joined them at the steps, hearing the last remark.

"What example? though I need not ask. Rokewood is giving you his theories. He thinks it worth while for the mission to go to the expense of sending a man out here and of keeping him here to do coolies' work, which he cannot do as well as the cooly himself, and for the sake of doing it he will leave undone work which no one else can do, and which, worse still, if he does not do it, will be forever undone," said Mackenzie, gravely. "There are more coolies here than there is work already, and I do not see the need of adding myself to the number, even though Rokewood is anxious to place himself with them. For it amounts to that. It is work that Indians cannot do which will lift India up, and we have no right to waste precious strength which is necessary to the accomplishment of mental and spiritual work."

Mrs. Mackenzie and Mrs. Clinton came in just then, and during dinner the conversation was on these same lines, the Bishop siding with Rokewood, on general principles, but disagreeing in some particular instances; but neither of the ladies took any part in it, and that night Mrs. Clinton said to herself:

"This is the evening and the morning of the first day, and if I did not know to the contrary I would say it was the evening and the morning of the first month, I have seen and learned so much, and to-morrow I will begin to be a missionary and see for myself what can be done."

CHAPTER VI.

OPENING HOUSEKEEPING.

THE morning of the second day Mrs. Clinton announced that they would have breakfast under their own vine and fig-tree. The Bishop looked dubious, and the face of Mr. Miller, who had come to take him to see the boys' schools in the city, expressed astonishment enough to warrant the use of the term thunderstruck, but, as men do, he waited-till he got the Bishop alone to make inquiries.

Mr. Mackenzie remonstrated with Mrs. Clinton, begging her to stay with them and go back and forth between the two houses until she had settled her own and was sure the machinery would be in good working order; but Mrs. Mackenzie said nothing. She was deeply hurt, and a little indignant withal. She said to herself, though she would have liked to say it to her guest:

"They may take their own way. They have come, with insufferable conceit, thinking that they, with no experience of the country, can manage better than all the hundreds of men and women who have come and gone in the mission. Do they not suppose there might be a few clever women and good managers in all the number that are still in the field? Even among the New England women, so famous for economy and thrift, do they not think

one might have been found to simplify household
matters, if they *could* be simplified? Yet the missionaries' wives are all alike, groaning under the
bondage of caste and the exigencies of the country
that force them to have their household work distributed among so many." So much for that side of the
question. But the hurt was deeper than the resentment. They, coming in this way, represented the sentiment of the dear people in the dear home land.

In all the weariness of the hot weather and of
dangerous disease and separation from home and
friends and country the thought of the many who
had followed them with sympathy in their work had
again and again cheered their hearts when almost
ready to sink; and though not given to posing as a
heroine, the thought of being known as one leading
an heroic life, and honored for it, had been a stimulus
to her, just as the soldier at the outpost is upheld by
the honor of having the most hazardous place given
him, and knows if he falls doing a dangerous duty all
men will feel a thrill of sympathy which they would
not have felt had he died in the ordinary routine of
life. This sympathy had been much to her, and
much to all the missionaries, even from those who loved
all the good things of life, too much to give them up
themselves. While the missionaries had seen the unkind and absurd things said of them (for now the
regular weekly mail rarely came without bringing
letters or papers that showed more or less distrust of
missions), yet they had never given these criticisms
serious attention, for they would not believe they
were the expression of the Church. Sometimes they
would say they would answer such and such remarks

if they had time, and now and then they would laugh over some absurd thing, and now and then they would be indignant at some misrepresentation, but on the whole they had not been sorry for the criticism, because they said it might waken an interest that would in the end be beneficial, and they knew that whatever outside people might say they had the Church with them.

"Evidently now, this comfort," said Mrs. Mackenzie to herself, "must also be given up. We were mistaken; the Church must believe these things, else why should a bishop and his wife be sent to investigate?"

It was this that made her sad and silent. It was as though the Church actually distrusted not only the methods and plans of campaign, but the men and women she had ordained and sent out. If so it was a mistaken policy, for when did ever a general win a great victory by saying to his soldiers:

"Though I have given you the work requiring discretion and courageous self-sacrifice, and have commanded you to be ready to face death rather than defeat, I neither trust to the former nor will I believe you have the latter."

So the old feeling of glory in standing in the front of battle must be given up; but the work itself was worth inexpressibly more than glory, and needed not to be gilded by any false light, though it hurt—*how* it hurt!

And Mrs. Clinton was not happy, as she said, in deep self-condemnation, while packing her trunk:

"There is at least one woman who would never do as an ambassador or a diplomatist;" and she fervently hoped her husband would not chance to hear how foolish she had been. Foolish, because all missionaries ultimately know what one missionary knows, and when it was once generally known that they had come to spy and correct they would be at once shut out from the sympathy of the mission, and this would be fatal to their object. When she thought of trying to explain she knew it would be impossible, for though she had told the warped truth, the untrue truth, yet it was the truth, nevertheless.

"I am sorry," said Mrs. Mackenzie, as her guest was taking leave, "that I cannot go with you to help you, but there is an amount of proof for the paper to be corrected that is appalling, besides a roll proof of the annual reports of the woman's work, of which I am editor, and I have not finished the table of statistics for the same; but I will give you Katie as interpreter and general expositor. She can tell you everything about the house and the servants, and can interpret better than I can."

"O," said Mrs. Clinton, deprecatingly, "I would not think of taking you from your work. I must do as other missionaries do, help myself."

"There is one thing, however, that I can do, and that is to lend you anything you may need for a week or so, or until you can supply yourself. Just send me a list and be mild and moderate in your demands, for notwithstanding the luxury in which we are supposed to be rolling there are very narrow limitations to the stock of things we keep on hand."

This was said with a smile, and Mrs. Clinton replied with a smile which was rather forced, for she had no words, and then she drove away with her trunks on top of a hired wooden carriage, Lillian and Katie on the front seat chattering volubly.

There are several kinds of houses on the plains of India, but those used by Europeans are chiefly of two kinds, kothi and bungalow. The former is built of sun-dried and kiln-burnt brick, and has a square-topped roof, held together by wooden rafters, etc., or by railroad iron. The latter has a sloping roof, tiled or thatched with straw or grass, and is much cooler than the kothi, but not so clean and safe from leakage ; also it is not so free from snakes, scorpions, and centipedes, which have an abrupt way of dropping down on one that is neither conducive to comfort, to peace of mind, nor always to long life.

This particular mission house, wherein a year of experimental life was to be spent, was a bungalow with tiled roof, and furnished with the absolutely needful heavy furniture—that is, tables and chairs and beds, two or three cupboards, a bookcase, a desk, and a couch. All were made rather roughly, but of good wood ; and the beds consisted of a wooden frame, across which was stretched coarse hand-woven tape.

There were six rooms besides verandas and bath rooms ; the rectangular sitting room, back of that the dining room, both in the middle of the house, the former opening upon the front veranda and the latter on the back veranda, which commanded a view of the cookhouse. On the west side of these rooms were two of the same size, used for bedrooms ; on the east were two more, one used as study and office, and the other as a bedroom. This was the extent of the house, except two small rooms and bath rooms. The walls were roughly whitewashed, and the floors were sun-dried brick, plastered over with mud and lime. Windows there were none, but the upper part of each door was of glass and gave light enough for all purposes, except on very dark and cloudy days.

The three wandered through the house, the elder of them wondering how the great, dreary, desolate rooms were ever to be made habitable.

A woman, on entering a house in which she expects to live, as naturally goes straight to the kitchen as a pointer points game. But here Mrs. Clinton's instinct did not serve her, for she found nothing that even in a remote idea corresponded to it.

Calling Katie, she asked for the kitchen. Katie looked blank and finally said, falteringly, that she did not know what "kitchen" meant. Lillian was amazed, and Mrs. Clinton smiled.

"Where is the stove for cooking?"

Katie grew positively red with shame. She had been born in India and had never heard the word before.

"Well, my dear, I see you do not know what 'stove' means either; but can you tell me where our breakfast will be cooked?"

Katie's face brightened:

"Of course I know the bawarchi khana," she laughed; "I like going there, but it is locked, though the cook is coming," she added, pointing to a man who was hurrying toward the cookhouse, followed by a half-naked cooly with a large shallow basket on his head. Another like him with another large flat basket on his head came on behind, and beyond him was still another straggling across the compound. The coolies came straight to the veranda, put their baskets at

Mrs. Clinton's feet, salaamed, and said something which Katie translated as asking for payment for bringing the baskets.

Mrs. Clinton took out her purse and asked Katie how much she must pay them. They, with eyes quick to see that Mrs. Clinton was new to their country, asked four times the right price. Katie laughed and said something to them at which they too laughed. Then catching up her hat she ran to the cookhouse, asked the cook the right price, and came back saying each was to have two annas, or about five cents. She helped Mrs. Clinton count it out and gave it to the men, telling them next time they came to be careful and tell no lies. They grinned with admiration at her cleverness, and went off with their baskets turned over their heads like bonnets.

"Why did not the cook bring this basket?" asked Mrs. Clinton of Katie, pointing to one filled with vegetables and meat, evidently the purchases of the cook.

Katie looked surprised, and said :

"O, it is only the coolies who bring things on their heads. Cooks are not coolies, and they do not bring things on their heads."

"They might have another kind of basket and bring it in their hands."

"Yes," said Katie, doubtfully, "if it were very small. Sometimes cooks bring things tied in a jharan in their hands, but never on their heads."

The cook laid out the things he had bought. There was a thin, scraggy-looking quarter of mutton, and a piece for chops, some carrots, pease, cauliflower, a little rice, a little pepper, a little salt in big lumps, a little cinnamon, a few cloves, some fresh ginger root, all tied up in bits of dirty rags; a paper bag of sugar, besides a little flour, and a little something that looked like lard, but which Katie said was "ghi," or melted butter, and a few small potatoes. After looking them over Mrs. Clinton concluded she did not want any breakfast, but told Katie to tell him to prepare what he could, and as quickly as possible.

They all followed him out to the cookhouse, to his evident consternation. When Mrs. Clinton saw the mud range built up at one side of the mud hut, saw the round, strange-looking cooking-pots, saw the absence of a chimney for the smoke to escape, and saw the cook's strange process of building a fire, she at once and forever abandoned any slight idea of doing the cooking herself. She felt rather relieved that one point was settled—that it was not within the range of possibilities for one not to the manor born to do cooking in India, even in cold weather. She could have gone as easily into a shop and made American cooking utensils as she could have cooked in an Indian cookhouse on an Indian fireplace. Going out quickly, with eyes streaming from the smoke, she surveyed the compound. In a distant corner under a clump of bananas was the well, and a man slowly pulling up a leathern skin full of water.

"Here at least is one chance of cutting down the list; the cook shall draw the water. If he only cooks for three people he will have time enough," she said.

Just then Lillian came around the corner of the house and said :

"There is a lady here to see you, and Katie says it is Miss Whitlow."

Miss Whitlow's name had long been a familiar one to Mrs. Clinton, and she hurried into the sitting room, where she saw a tall, strong woman with a broad felt hat on her head and a look of pain on her face, who said:

"I did not meet you at the station last night, as I had a headache. I could do no work this morning, so I thought I would come and see you."

Mrs. Clinton smiled at her candid suggestion that she would not have come if she could have worked; and she went on:

"I went down to the Mackenzies' bungalow, and you can, or rather you cannot, imagine my amazement at finding you had come to stay and to be missionaries, and were already in your own house. Perhaps you do not know that if you do things so suddenly in India you will make our heads swim and give yourselves sunstroke, or something worse."

Mrs. Clinton laughed.

"You must remember that we are Americans, and accustomed to be in a hurry."

"Well, be gentle in your movements, in mercy to us who have lived many years in a land where the motto is, 'Never do to-day what you can put off till to-morrow.' But, seriously, I am alive with curiosity. Have you really come as a spy—not to spy out the nakedness of the land, but the opulence and the extravagance, the bad management and idleness of the missionaries—and to be a sort of Moses to lead us into a land of better things?"

Mrs. Clinton's face had flushed, and she looked thoroughly annoyed:

"Who has said such an absurd thing? Did Mrs. Mackenzie? Surely she was not justified—"

"Mrs. Mackenzie said nothing of you but what was kind and complimentary. She said casually that you were going to try to live just as economically as possible, and if I could give you any hints as to the best manner of so doing she was sure you would be glad. But as I know a bishop's family cannot be in very straitened circumstances there must be some reason for this strange resolution, and there has been so much criticism on us at home for daring to claim the right of living like ordinary mortals, I just guessed it. I assure you we will all give you our hearty sympathy. If you can find any cheaper or more comfortable way of living, provided your plan will not interfere with our work or our health, we will be glad indeed; for you know that most of us put all the money we can save into schools and Bible women, and it will simply mean more schools and more work; and let me tell you, there is absolutely no limit to our work except the limits made by the lack of workers and money, to support the workers. But on what line are you going to begin?"

"The first thing that struck me was the number of men employed to do the housework. Tell me exactly how many you consider necessary;" and she took out her pocket notebook.

"First, a cook, and if you have a large family he will insist on having a boy to wash dishes."

Mrs. Clinton wrote "Cook," and said, "I grant the cook, for I see that he is absolutely indispensable, but not the boy."

"No; your family is small, and though he will ask for one it is not necessary. Next, a 'khidmatgar,' or table servant. He will wait at the table, make the tea and toast in the morning, which all have to have before going to work, and help the cook generally."

"Why cannot the cook make the tea and toast and wait on the table and 'help the cook generally?'"

"He must go to the bazar every morning early, if you want to get good meat and vegetables. If he waits to make the tea and toast you will not get good food, and let me emphasize one thing: it is not safe in India to eat any but good meat and the best of everything else you can get."

"Could I not make the tea and toast myself?"

"Yes, during this month and next, perhaps, if you have time; after that you must have something as soon as you are dressed, to keep your strength up during the day. Indeed, very many hard-working people take their tea before they rise, which to us, of course, seems a very indolent habit. Next on the list is a 'bearer,' who dusts the house twice a day, which is no small job, and he looks after the other servants. A really good and trusty man will save you an immense amount of care and anxiety, but many people who have small families combine bearer and khidmatgar. Mrs. Mackenzie has kept but one man for both kinds of work, but it insures a good deal of trouble, for it is impossible or next to impossible to have the work done well and the house kept clean with only one, and then the bearer will see that the others do not steal too much from you."

"Steal!" exclaimed Lillian, with wide-open eyes full of fear. "Are they all thieves?"

"No, my dear, no; there is really only one professional thief in each house."

Mrs. Clinton's eyes now matched Lillian's. Vague

thoughts of the horrors of the mutiny were passing through her mind, for the word thief seems always to have other crimes grouped around it in people's minds.

Miss Whitlow laughed.

"Your night-watchman, otherwise the chaukedar, is of the thief caste, and as long as he stalks up and down your compound, pouring forth a volley of unearthly yells, or even if he sleeps the whole night through, you may be sure no thieves will come about your place. Then there is the sweeper and the water-carrier, the man to wash your clothes, the man to sew, and the man to pull the punkah, and the two men for your horse."

"Two men!" exclaimed Mrs. Clinton, fairly bewildered; "this is indeed going beyond reason; two men for one little horse! Surely one man can be made to do the work, can he not?"

"Yes, with a good deal of trouble it can be done, but it costs just as much to buy your grass as to keep a man to cut it, and is very inconvenient. The first man has charge of the horse, harness, and gari; keeps them clean and oiled, gets the latter mended, superintends the shoeing of the horse, buys the feed, and drives when you have not a conveyance which you can drive yourself. The second man goes out early to the jungle, miles away, cuts a day's allowance of grass, and brings it home on his head. After he has cleaned the horse and stable he is free to go on errands or carry messages; you will find it very necessary to have such a man. People who have much work and different kinds keep a man whose sole duty is to carry messages and notes."

"Do you find it absolutely necessary to have a horse and conveyance?" Mrs. Clinton asked, in rather a despairing tone. She was beginning to feel that if she were able to keep house in India, to say nothing of doing any mission work, she would have her hands full.

"Yes, if we wish to do any mission work it is indispensable unless we have school work in the same house or very near. Usually the different parts of the work are so far apart that walking is an utter impossibility. In that case we would have to hire a gari every time we went out, which would not pay. In the hot weather people must have a gari in which to go out and get the air in the evenings or die. So your economies will not be able to touch any of these."

"But you spoke of the extra man for washing. Surely among so many the washing might be done without an especial man. It is simply an absurdity to call in a man for that."

"Well, in a way it is, but in another way it is not. In the first place, your servants and their wives do not even know how to do their own washing and ironing, so how could they do yours?" she added, persuasively. "In the second place, tubs and soap and starch and fire would cost more, far more, even if you did your washing with your own hands, than you pay the man that takes your clothes down to the river, bleaches them on the sands in the hot sun, irons them in his own house, and brings them home spick and span, barring the loss of buttons."

Mrs. Clinton wrote "laundryman" on her paper with a sigh of relief. The washing at home had been the one trial of her life. She hated the smell of suds and

8

the sloppy way the best of washerwomen would do the work in her neat wash room. She had always hated it all, and when she had not been well she had sent it away from the house to be done, though her heart had always condemned her for extravagance in doing so.

"Washing, starching, and ironing will cost for three of you only about fifty cents a week, and you know that the appliances and coal would cost that much."

Miss Whitlow said this in a persuasive manner, for, as Mrs. Clinton sat silent, she was sure she was not pleased.

"O," said she, "I am only too glad to find that it is economy to have it done away from the house, and if I could send a battalion of these men to America to relieve my fellow-bondslaves there from wash day I would be glad indeed."

After a little more talk on servants Miss Whitlow rose to go, as Katie came in saying the cook wanted to know if the Mem Sahib had a tablecloth.

"Yes, I am glad to say I have, for I brought table and bed linen and forks and spoons in the bottom of my trunk."

"Mrs. Mackenzie asked me to bring Katie back with me if you did not need her," said Miss Whitlow. "Come, Katie, are you ready? O, I have stayed so long that my principal errand has been forgotten. I came to ask you to come to the station meeting at my house Saturday night at seven;" and she was gone before Mrs. Clinton could ask what the "station meeting" was.

The Bishop soon came home filled with delight over

IN THE COOK HOUSE.

the four boys' day schools he had visited in the heart
of the native city. He was so interested in telling of
the brightness of the boys, of the wonder he had at seeing them so well informed and so well able to repeat
psalms, hymns, and portions of the Bible, and was so
generally enthusiastic that he was not very critical as
to their breakfast; nor did he seem to be very interested in her plans for economy. After prayers, to
which the cook was called, and who sat on the floor
like a tailor during the reading of the psalm, only
bowing his head during prayer, the Bishop went off
again with Mr. Miller to see more schools. Then
Mrs. Clinton called the cook to her and said:

"I intend to arrange my house so it will cost as
little as possible. This I wish to do that I may help
the mission which has done so much and is doing so
much for you and your brothers and friends, and I
wish you to help me."

The man salaamed.

"Now, for three of us there can be very little
work. I shall do some of it myself, and you will do
the remainder, for you will be the only man about the
place until a horse is bought."

The man looked troubled. He thought he understood what she had said; he knew she was the wife of
the Bāra Padri Sahib; so she could hardly be out of
her head or have a weak mind, but his English was
imperfect and he waited for further developments.
The native of India does not often lose his case by
being in too much of a hurry.

"It is the custom here, I am told, to have a man to
draw the water from the well and bring it to the
house; you certainly can do this yourself. In my

country the cook brings the water as well as cooks the food."

"But, Mem Sahib, well very deep, take long, long time to bring water, things all burn in cookhouse, and it not custom here. Me not make bihisti's work."

"But if I ask you to do so will you not try it for two days?"

"Yes, Mem Sahib, if it please you I make an arrangement for two days."

"One victory," thought she, "and very easily gained, for if he can do it for two days he will not dare refuse to do it afterward."

Had she understood the limitless elasticity of the word "arrangement" she could hardly have been so exultant.

"Now, everybody has a bearer and khidmatgar. I shall not have these. You must wait on the table and I will dust and care for the house. You can cook the food, put it in the dishes, and then put on a clean coat and bring the food in."

"Yes, your honor;" but his voice was lifeless, and even his pugri, which was so big and overpowering, seemed to lose some of its starched smartness and to wither and droop over his face.

"This is all right," thought Mrs. Clinton, "he will not mind after a few days;" so she was encouraged to go on.

"In my country, which is a great and powerful country, my cook sweeps my floors. It is always done when only one servant is kept. Can you not also do the sweeping?"

A look of horror had been gradually stealing over the dark face. The new Mem Sahibs were always

funny when they first came out, and said and did many
funny things, over which he and his fellow-servants
had often made merry around the hookah; but this
surpassed everything; to be bearer and khidmatgar
was bad enough, though it might be done; but to be
water-carrier, and, worst of all and beyond all belief,
to be asked to be sweeper! The new Mem Sahib's husband was undoubtedly a great and wise man, but she
was insane beyond all doubt. A sweeper! To do the
work of one of those depised outcasts! Why, even
his fellow-Christians would not eat or drink with him
if he did such an awful thing as that!

"No, Mem Sahib! No! It never done. I not
sweeper. I—I not make cooking for you;" and he
fled in fear and dismay from the room.

Mrs. Clinton saw the man's unaffected horror; she
was almost sure she had seen his face grow pale, and
he had trembled like a leaf in the wind. Pondering
on it she decided she must give this up also, and
write down "sweeper" under "cook" and keep on in
her service Dr. Thompson's sweeper, whom she had
seen about the compound.

She referred to her paper and found it would only
add a dollar and a half per month to her expenses, so
she went out on the veranda and called to the cook,
but he was nowhere to be seen. She went on to the
cookhouse, found the key in the door, but no signs of
the cook. She came back to the house, her head swim-
ming and having a strange sick feeling that made her
wish to lie down, but she stood in the door a moment
trying to think what she ought to do next. She certainly could not go to Mrs. Mackenzie and ask her to
get another cook; pride forbade that, and Mrs. Clinton

had her share of this unregenerate commodity. But how to do otherwise she did not know, unless she asked Miss Whitlow, and in any case one could not be had in a day. They might be without food for a day or two, and perhaps longer. Mrs. Mackenzie had said that good cooks were very scarce at that time of the year, though three months later there would be plenty, and as to finding another Christian cook, it would probably take a long time, and much of her hope of fairly trying her experiment lay in having a Christian. While she stood thus she heard a gari, and looking in its direction she saw one of the usual hired carriages, with its wretched, thin, scraggy little ponies and its shabby harness pieced out by bits of rope. The gari had on its top the usual roll of bed and bedding, done up in a bit of striped yarn carpet, the turkey-red quilts showing at each end, and the cabin trunk, and the cane lunch basket, which are the distinguishing marks of the missionary's luggage when he travels.

The occupant of the gari was looking eagerly about, and the instant the horses stopped was out with an energetic spring that told at least of health. He was in the house and then out, and coming across the compound, taking a visiting-card out of a notebook as he came, and looking for a servant to present it for him. Seeing none, he advanced toward Mrs. Clinton, who met him with outstretched hand, sure of a friend and almost sure of a future neighbor.

"I am Carnton; I have come to fill my appointment at the Christian College, and also, I am very glad to hear, to be a neighbor of yours."

"Yes," said Mrs. Clinton, leading the way to the sitting room; "my husband told me of you. He said he knew you. But you were expected before, though no one knew just when you were coming."

"I did not know myself when I could get off. There are so many people to see and so many last things to do in leaving one station for another that it is impossible to do it quickly; and just as I was about to start, ten days ago, a man came from a village not far away and asked me to go and baptize him and his family. I went and stayed until I baptized the whole village; then I had to arrange for a preacher to be left in the village to take charge of them and keep them instructed, as my successor had not then arrived."

Noting the gladness on his face, Mrs. Clinton answered, sympathetically :

"It was well worth being detained. Were you far from here ? "

"Yes, far in more ways than one. I was quite away from any English or Americans, and months sometimes passed without seeing a white face. Five days' march in the mountains from anywhere would about express the situation."

"You will like this better," she said, looking at the handsome, earnest face, thinking that he belonged with society and with friends.

"No," smiling; "I confess to you that I do not, but I am under orders, and what I am given to do I try to do with my might, 'heartily as unto the Lord, and not as unto men,' myself among the latter."

"How could it be possible that you do not like this better ? I can see that you might be willing to stay there, but how could you like it ? "

There was a smile rather to himself than to her.

"If I took time to tell you I should miss an engagement that I must keep, as it is with a native Christian; but if you will allow me I will explain when I have time enough to convince you I am in earnest. Now I am in difficulty as to my housekeeping, and have come to throw myself on your mercy."

Mrs. Clinton looked and felt alarmed. The only thing that was presented to her mind was a vision of her fleeing cook, his white coat-tail waving in the wind as he ran from her.

Carnton saw her hesitation and hastened to explain:

"I have my cook with me, but no cooking utensils nor anything for the table. I had hoped you would let me come and have my breakfast and dinners with you; my cook would assist, and it would really be no trouble to anyone." Then he laughed, such a cheery, happy laugh. "Hear me force myself upon you, and then say that Americans have no cheek. But we are so accustomed to considering ourselves as one family that I forgot you might not understand our encroaching ways."

At the mention of his cook the brow of his listener cleared at once, and a burden as heavy as that carried by Atlas rolled off her shoulders. She would now be saved the necessity of an explanation with Mrs. Mackenzie, and she only just now knew how much she had dreaded to go to her and explain.

"O, it is not that," she hastened to say, "but I have as yet made no arrangements for myself, and I have no cook; otherwise we would be delighted to have you with us."

"Ah, but perhaps you would not mind letting my cook officiate until you can do better."

"I shall be very glad indeed. I really did not know what to do, but this will solve the problem," she said, with a sigh of relief.

"How have you managed? Perhaps your bearer can cook."

"I have no bearer; I had a cook this morning, but he has departed, not to return."

Carnton looked the inquiry he did not speak.

"I might as well tell him if he is to be with us," thought she.

"The cook left because I told him I intended to do as we did in America—keep only one person to do the work; that he must carry the water and sweep the floors."

"What?" cried Carnton aghast, "you do not mean it."

"Certainly; why not? If he is a Christian he cannot be bound by caste."

"Not by caste, but by custom, and I hardly need tell you that it is utterly impossible. There is not a cook in India that will draw and bring the water and sweep your floors; and, what is still more serious, I fear you will, when the man once spreads his story, be entirely unable to get anyone at all, even if you now concede these points. I beg your pardon if I am speaking too plainly. I fear we missionaries become rather brusque from our close associations and the uncomfortable way we have of speaking the truth to each other, especially if it be disagreeable; but I will go and send my man over at once."

The arrangement was made, and Carnton came regularly to his meals, and the cook stayed on, and a water-carrier and sweeper did the work expected of them, and peace reigned for a space.

CHAPTER VII.

VISITING MISSIONARIES.

THE national practice of reversing the proverb in regard to doing things to-day and not to-morrow prevents any great expedition in settling a house.

The American, who generally overdoes the matter in trying to do a week's work in one day, finds his practice of rushing and pushing and hurrying as much out of place in India as his furnaces and warm carpets. A whole nation moving in opposite lines to his custom and habits is, at first, trying beyond expression, and the chances are that his gentle and peaceful disposition, which was the admiration of his friends, disappears, and he becomes nervous, irritable, and perhaps bad-tempered. No doubt if a person could come to India with plenty of money, and without the slightest interest under the sun in having anything accomplished, he would be in harmony with his environment and all would be well.

But no one comes under these circumstances, and the only way to save one's time and temper is to have many things brewing at once and possess the soul in patience.

For instance, a table is sent to the carpenter's shop to be repaired. The carpenter promises faithfully to have it done "kăl," that is, to-morrow. You send for it, the shop is locked and the man away somewhere taking other work to be done the following kăl. You wait two days and send again. It is not done, but will be kăl. You wait a week, because some other things besides sending for the table must be done, and then send again and again. After a month it comes home, only to be returned, because imperfectly repaired. Again, a sewing man, or dirzi, promises to come kăl, and sit cross-legged on your veranda and make the white suits the Sahib needs so much. Days go on, and when you have partially engaged another man he presents himself one day when you have a meeting on hand, and cannot measure out the cloth for him, so you will not know if he takes any for his own use, or, worse still, when you cannot give him directions in order that he may not spoil it all.

Another man promises to come kăl and bring glass and putty to mend the doors which the men broke when they were taking down the punkah poles. You are in a hurry to have it done. It ought to have been done months ago, but now the hot winds are beginning to blow, and the house must be hermetically closed. Days pass, and then when you send to inquire you are told he has gone to another station, or that he is very ill. The latter excuse may mean that he has more lucrative work on hand. You engage another, and he also promises to come kăl, and you are uncommonly lucky if your work is done after five or six days. These are only examples; the whole round of life is the same, and reminds one of the remark on jam by "Alice in Wonderland : "

"We always have jam to-morrow or yesterday, but never to-day."

This is made more applicable to the case by the fact

that the word "kăl" means both to-morrow and yesterday, and shows the utter indifference of the Hindoo to time.

The house in which the Clintons were domiciled had been left hurriedly by the Thompsons, and there was much to be done—plaster to be patched, nails to be driven, new matting to be put down, a chair or two to be repaired, and some general cleaning and whitewashing which had not been done at the close of the hot season, the usual time for repairs, because of the illness of Mrs. Thompson. When Mrs. Clinton consulted Mr. Carnton that first evening at dinner he said he would tell the cook to call the men to the house who would make the repairs. They would come and do it while she was making calls or seeing mission work if she would first show the cook what she wanted done, as it must be supervised by some one. It was really the bearer's work, and she must not expect it would be done properly without a bearer to supervise, as the cook did not understand it, and he would be in the cookhouse and could not answer for the safety of things in the rooms where the men would work.

Then she said she would stay at home and have work done only in two rooms at once, and Lillian could watch them in one room and she in another, which to Carnton seemed a great waste of time. At any rate, he advised her not to stay at home the first day, but go and make calls with him. He further explained that it was the duty of every new person coming to a place to make the first calls on all the English and Americans living in the station, and if they were pleased with him they returned his calls; if not, the calls were ignored. He had just two days in which to settle his house, make his calls, then would come Sunday, and on Monday his work would begin in the college. He did not like to make calls, and was glad he had no more time; but there were a few places he must go to, and he begged her to go with him. The Bishop was deep in mission work, and utterly refused to go, though he insisted, like many another missionary, on his wife doing duty for both.

So a gari was hired, and they started out early in the morning to visit the missionaries and see their work. It is not too much to say that Mrs. Clinton loathed hired garis, because they were dirty and rattled, and because the drivers beat the poor horses that always looked ready to drop with overwork and lack of food. She would have walked had the distance permitted; and she was pleased to see that it would cost them more to hire a conveyance than it would to buy a comfortable little phaeton and a decent horse.

There was another drawback to her going out besides hiring garis. She had been advised by Mrs. Mackenzie not to leave Lillian alone with the servants, but to hire a native Christian woman to stay with her while she was out; but as she meant to be out every day it would add another to the list of people she was having to do her work, and she was not ready to do that yet, though she much wanted Lillian to go on with her lessons, which she could not do if she always went with her mother. However, she had to take her this time. They went first to the High School and Christian College.

The building in which this was held was well built and commodious and set in the center of a large compound in which were growing many young trees. Across the road was another building in its first stages, which would be still larger and which would be for the college solely. At one side were long rows of houses where boys slept and ate; the missionary's bungalow was also in the same compound.

The Bishop had preceded them with Mr. Miller. They found the boys coming in for morning prayers as they arrived, and Mrs. Clinton watched them with great interest as they came quietly and gently into the room, salaaming to her as they passed, their embroidered caps and coats of various colors and materials bringing out the exquisite olive tint of their skins and the soft brilliance of their dark eyes in a most pleasing way and in pleasant contrast to the English dress which many of the Christians had on. While she was watching them and thinking of the many sides of mission work the Bishop was interviewing Mr. Miller. He asked questions like a school inspector as to the number and grade of the students, and learned that of the four hundred boys enrolled one fourth of the number were Christians, as also were one fourth of the members of the college class, besides many other things which he stored away for future pondering.

"Now," he said, after eliciting this information, "I should like to know the real essence of the school —what has it done, what can it do, and what do you expect it will do more than the other and secular schools of the country?"

Mr. Miller hesitated a little, and then said:

"These three divisions of your question will have to be taken as one in my answer, for they are inseparable. It has not done all it can do, nor all we expect it to do, for it is still in the formative process; but the need of this, as well as other schools which you will see, comes from the fact that we have an organized Church here, a body that has members that articulate with each other and are necessary to the exertion of its full powers. A fourth of these boys are Christians; some of them Christians, as perhaps your or my boys are, because their parents are so; others genuine Christians with a comprehension of what Christ's life means to his followers. Now, would you be willing to put either of these classes into a school where they would be taught that Ingersoll's ideas and Spencer's philosophy were true, which of course means that Christianity is false?"

"It is unnecessary to answer such a question."

"Very well; then I do not need to explain that Christian boys require a separate school. That in itself, then, is enough excuse for the school; but the other side of the same question is still stronger. The positive benefit from being in a Christian school is in the daily study and exposition of the Bible as one of the regular lessons, prayers in the morning, the weekly prayer meetings, in Christian society and the association together of those of the same belief. Many of them will go from here to our theological school at Bareilly, and I need not say to you that they will be much better prepared for that than had they been under Mohammedan or heathen influence."

"I grant this, but it after all must preclude much evangelistic work. You and Carnton here will give up your time to the dreary round of teaching, perhaps

9

mathematics, when you might be going forth sowing beside all waters."

Miller looked perplexed.

"Well," he said, "if your plan in building up a Church is to have only evangelists and evangelical work, of course then that closes the subject at once, but you surely do not expect to depend for the bone and sinew of any Church on evangelists. They have their place, and a noble place it is, too; but our own Church at home would hardly have assumed its present proportions had it had only evangelical work. Now, simply to put a point on this, tell me how much do you depend on them at home, small or great, known or unknown, in the real permanent building up of the Church?"

"Not very much," was the dry answer. This was a home thrust, for this particular Bishop had had particular trials with those wandering stars who flash here and flash there, exerting a sudden and strong influence that is sometimes as fleeting as strong, leaving the pastors of the churches they had helped or hindered to the toil of gathering up the fragments, to the educating and upbuilding of the converts they have made, only to find in many cases that the converts have been to the evangelist, and not to God.

"Very well; is it not reasonable to suppose that people who have always lived under the deadening and dwarfing influence of heathen superstition require more teaching and more steady drill, and better grounding, than those that have heard the truth from their childhood up?"

"I must answer yes to this, of course."

"Then let me leave this point until you see how much of a church we have here already, how much of an organized body, and then let me ask you if you wish us all to be evangelists. We must have some who do this work alone, and it is a glorious work to do, a stimulating, exciting hand-to-hand war; but we cannot choose our work. Some have a fitness for that, and some must do the drudgery;" and he sighed a little.

"There is another point that, I nearly forgot," he added. "We also do in these schools a great deal of evangelical work. The Christian students and teachers turn out on Sunday to teach and preach, and many of the students who come here with an aversion to Christianity are baptized and become among our best workers, because their understandings are converted as well as their hearts."

Carnton was talking with some of the boys when the silence-bell rang, and Mr. Miller, after introducing the Bishop, also introduced Carnton to the boys as the new vice-principal. They rose quietly, with their beautiful black eyes only moderately curious.

"One Sahib is apparently the same as another to them," said Mrs. Clinton, noticing the lack of interest on their faces. This was a mistake. The fact was the new missionary teacher had been thoroughly discussed among them, and they knew him well even before they had seen him, knew his antecedents, his qualifications, his friends, and, above all, his disposition and temperament, better, perhaps, than any of his own friends did.

Every native, whether he be gentleman or cooly, has two faces—two characters: one which he turns only to the English or American, and one which the people of his own nation see. They are not alike, they possess no resemblance to each other in any respect, and yet we cannot say that one is true and the other false. Perhaps it is safe to say the face that his coun trymen see is truer, for it is doubtful if ever the con queror sees the conquered in a true light ; so it did not mean that because these young men appeared indif ferent they were so.

After the Bishop had spoken to them in English, and asked some questions as to their purposes and plans, and sat down with beaming face, Mr. Miller translating for the benefit of those who did not under stand English, Mrs. Clinton was presented, and Mr. Miller asked her to " say a few words."

She rose and, looking at the sea of faces before her, on which interest, curiosity, and surprise were blended, though in a very moderate degree, said :

" In olden times a guest was allowed to make a re quest. I should like to make two this morning. You can grant two, I think, because of the great distance I have come, can you not ? "

Mr. Miller smiled as he asked them to respond, and every hand went up.

" First, when you marry that each will try to give his wife as much of the instruction he has received here as is possible."

The principal paused, before he translated, to say to her that the majority of the non-Christians were already married, the absurdity of which statement struck his visitors with far more force when looking at the youthful faces than when reading it in a mis sion report.

There were smiles all around at her request, and a hearty promise of the perfect fulfillment of which Mr. Miller had doubts in his heart.

Pleased with her success, she made the second request, that "when you have obtained the position for which this education will fit you you will always remember kindly the school in which you have received it and give something to help others to the same blessing you are now enjoying."

This was promptly promised by the Christian lads, who formed about one fourth of the number, and less readily by most of the remainder; by some half-heartedly, and a few made no response at all.

After prayer the boys were soon dismissed, and Mrs. Clinton, Lillian, and Mr. Carnton left Mr. Miller, who was always ready to utilize everybody, making arrangements with the Bishop for a course of lectures on the Authenticity of the Holy Scriptures, the Divinity of Christ, and some other kindred subjects in which he was known to be strong, and got into the gari and drove to the Girls' High School, which was in the same compound as the Zenana Home and a mile from the Christian College.

This school is composed of a few English, but mostly Eurasian and native girls, numbering in all about a hundred and forty. They were taken by Miss Dillon, the superintendent of the school, through the dormitory, where they saw the plain little rooms with simple charpais or native beds, saw the flat cakes called chappaties being prepared by the hundred for their breakfast, saw the garden where the girls could walk or play, and then went on to the schoolhouse, a short distance from the dormitory.

The different grades were busy under different teachers, mostly in separate rooms, and they all satisfied Mrs. Clinton's ideas of propriety by sitting on benches. Several of the teachers were from this very school and seemed to be teaching earnestly and well, and proud to show the progress of their pupils.

They finally stopped in a room filled with the more advanced pupils, who were having their Scripture lesson.

"This one," said Miss Dillon, pointing to a well-grown girl, "will go into the college class next year, and this one will enter the Lady Dufferin Medical College at Agra, and this one will take up regular mission work under Miss Lowe."

"And do they not wish to marry early, as their friends do?" asked Mrs. Clinton.

"Sometimes, though in many cases here marriage does not interfere with their occupations. I will tell you more of this another time. Will you kindly question the class a little? It is good for them, and please ask them difficult questions."

So she asked the first one to give her a list of the miracles. This was done promptly and chronologically, with a description of the places and events which called them forth. Then she asked for the parables, and they were given equally well, and, as Mr. Carnton said, better than nine tenths of the theological students in America could. A few other questions were answered promptly and with pleasure, some speaking in Hindoostanee, which Miss Dillon translated, but most in good English. After expressing themselves as extremely well pleased with everything, they left a message for Miss Lowe, who with her assistants was out in the zenanas, and was about to take her leave when Miss Dillon, noting the looks of interest from the girls toward Lillian, asked her mother to leave her at the school for the day, saying she would bring her back at night. Mrs. Clinton gladly acceded to her request, and she and Carnton were soon out on the street going toward the Home for the Homeless.

"They are pushing things to the utmost in the school now, as we do everywhere in the mission during the short cold weather, hoping things may acquire enough momentum to carry themselves on during the great heat that will soon be here. There is already a lessening of the bracing quality of the air to-day, and I have not begun my work," Carnton said, a little anxiously.

"I see no difference between to-day and the other days I have been here."

"I suppose not, but you do see there is a wind?"

"Yes, and it is getting stronger."

"Very well, that is the beginning of the "lu," which I shall not describe to you, for I cannot. I suppose you noticed what a fine property the ladies' society has here. It was bought at a great bargain, and belonged to one of the members of the court of one of the old kings of Oude, as did the tomb where we are going also did."

"What a pity Miss Whitlow could not have found a better place for her women! I do not like to think of one of our missionaries living in a tomb," said Mrs. Clinton.

Carnton laughed and said:

"Wait till you have seen it. There are tombs and tombs."

It was a great rambling structure with a large dome in the center, and there was a pleasant garden in front of it.

"It is not a very *grave*-looking place for a tomb, after all, is it?" said Carnton.

She had time only to smile, when they were met by Miss Whitlow on the veranda. The rooms were large and divided by Saracenic arches. It had been built by a Mohammedan gentleman for his own tomb, and he had actually been buried in the large central room under the dome.

"What a fine place for exercising one's taste, and how I should like to drape it and decorate it! One's fancy could run riot here, and still there would never be too much ornamentation. How can you resist it?" as she looked around and saw how bare and unadorned it was. Only a few chairs and tables scattered like oases in a desert and a few pictures on the wall.

"There are two trifling obstacles to letting my æsthetic tendencies come to the front—that is, time and money."

"But I saw so many pretty pieces of cotton in the bazar, and Mrs. Mackenzie told me they are only a few cents a yard, and so very pretty, and, put here and there, they would make these rooms so restful for you when your work is over."

"After my work is over I shall want a smaller tomb than this," was the quiet answer. "And another obstacle," she went on in a lighter tone, "when my women want new dresses and chuddars, if I did not have money to buy them I would take down my draperies one by one, and the marks in the plaster of the nails would be there to reproach me for my extravagance. But will you come now, Mrs. Clinton, and see the women? I cannot ask you to come, Mr. Carnton, much as I should like to do so."

"Very well, I will walk on home then, and get some writing done before breakfast;" and he was off.

They went through the large central room, past the grave of the old Mohammedan whose spirit must have revolted at the sound of the hymn,

> " There is no name so sweet on earth,
> No name so dear in heaven,"

sung in his own language and floating about and above his grave, but it was fitting and right, and thus will it be until time is no more; the hymns of the true must ever float above the graves of the false.

The women in plain dark skirts and white chuddars rose and salaamed and sat down again on the floor, with smiling faces, for they were pleased that this the wife of the great Sahib from that great vague land across the great misty water should come so soon to see them.

They had heard of her from Pulmoni, who had represented her as sweet and pleasant in her disposition and of infinite charity. This they could easily believe, for was she not small and thin? and for what else but a pleasant disposition would so great and powerful a Sahib have allowed her to have the honor of being his wife?

"Some of the women speak a little English and understand more than they can speak," said Miss Whitlow, in warning. "You observe Pulmoni is smiling, and for the first time. Her heart seems bowed down with sorrow. I must say you are beginning your mission work quickly and well. Where did you find her?"

"O, I deserve no credit for finding her. Just before dark last night she came in at the door and stood before me with her baby in her arms. I looked at her closely, for her face expressed the most hopeless woe I have ever seen on any human being. As I said nothing she sat down at my feet and touched them with her forehead. My heart ached for her, and as I could not speak to her I put my arms around her. Perhaps it was not wise, but I could not help it, and she sat quite quiet, as though at rest. I called the cook and told him to go and ask Mr. Carnton to come and see what she wanted me to do for her, for it was plain she expected something, and I knew she was not a beggar. He came and questioned her, and though she turned her back toward him and stood trembling with her face covered with her chuddar, yet she answered, he said, very straightforwardly, that a pundit had told some people when they were sitting at the village well in Paripur of a strange people who were called Christians, of how they preached a salvation for women as well as men, and how they were kind and helpful to all. He was not telling her—she was a widow, and beneath any one's notice—but she was in the clump of bananas behind the well and heard, and then she rose early in the morning and came all the way, twenty-five miles, I think. I said at once that she must be sent to you, and I would be responsible for her support if you had no other means."

"She told me a little more, which I will tell you later," said Miss Whitlow.

After a Bible lesson from the Hindoostanee translation, and a prayer in the same language, in which the women nearly all joined, they began their lessons.

"Some of these women are low caste and some are high caste, but nearly all were utterly without education when they came, not being able to read or write one word; and yet now several of them can read and write three languages, taking them all along at once and without the least difficulty."

"And yet they do not look so very clever or bright; I can hardly credit what you say."

"Of course it is not true of all. Some are dull and do not interest themselves in their lessons; these I train for ayahs or nurses. Several of these latter are now in good places and putting aside money for their old age or for their marriage, who were perfectly without resource except the very last and worst a woman can have."

"But why should such women learn more than one language? It does not seem necessary."

"Then things are not as they seem in this case, as in many others. They are preparing to be Bible women, and to make efficient ones they must be ready to read the Bible and explain it in Hindi and Urdu or Bengalee. The population is so mixed that we never know what language we will need in the zenanas. Of their own accord they try to pick up English—why I hardly know, unless it is because they wish in everything to be like us."

"Then I suppose they would not mind sitting on chairs. Certainly that would be the first thing I would teach them. Civilize them first, and I am sure you could Christianize them much more quickly."

"Ah," said Miss Whitlow, with a sigh, "you have

struck the edge of one of our most difficult problems. If you will come out here in the shade of this tamarind tree," she said, bringing a chair, and then going back for another one, " I will explain my meaning."

They were facing the women, and could see some busy with slates and pencils writing out translations; others learning letters, swaying back and forth and repeating them in a drowsy monotone, and still others knitting or sewing. The hum of bees in the yellow balls of the babūl tree at the side of the house added to the women's voices, the little children rolling about on the ground in the sun, laughing merrily, the men in the street outside the high wall calling out the prices of fruit and vegetables in the baskets on their heads, now and then camels or elephants passing in processions, the mosque at the corner, the various domes and the flat roofs of the whitewashed houses which reflected the sun in a blaze, and the peacock's shriek mingled with the street cries—all told Mrs. Clinton of a different life from any she had ever known. How entirely different she could not comprehend, for even those who live years in it, until they too become a part of the strangeness, often see only the surface, and none save those with the second sight given to people who love humanity as Christ loved it ever see below the surface, and none to the bottom. It is not given to the Western nature to comprehend the Oriental. None can do it save and except the Oriental himself, and it is doubtful whether even he ever comprehends his own life.

" This is not America," Mrs. Clinton said half to herself, " though it is not exactly the India I expected to see. I have said this before to Mrs. Mackenzie, and I say it to myself every hour of the day."

"The India we expected to see exists only in America," said Miss Whitlow. "Before I came to India I used to wonder at Moore's genius in writing 'Lalla Rookh' without ever having been here, but now I think his genius would have been greater had he written it after being here."

Mrs. Clinton laughed.

"You evidently do not take a romantic view of India."

"No; though still there is a strongly picturesque side to it, even if it is not all marble fountains and poetry and soft, low music. All our civilization detracts from the picturesque in their life. The English dress and the English manner do not mix with those of India any better than oil and water. But what was I going to talk to you about? O, yes, Pulmoni's story and the question of chairs.

"When she came last night she said her husband had died and left her to the care of his brother, but with no separate provision for her support. She had lived on in the house as a slave, bereft of her few fine clothes and her few jewels. Her two children, both girls, had married some distant cousins and had gone far away into the Punjab. Eight years had passed, and in all the household only one was kind to her and that was her husband's brother. I need not tell you the result of that kindness in her sad and lonely life. When she had to tell her mother-in-law and her sister-in-law they demanded that she should kill the child about to be born, and thus the family shame would not be known; but she refused, even though they talked to her in a way that in her own words 'killed her.' Then they beat her cruelly, but still she refused to either commit murder or allow it to be committed. Then they turned her out and told her they would beat her to death if she ever came back. She wandered away from village to village, until a not entirely hard-hearted woman took her in for a day or two until her child was born, and then, while she was still weak, told her to go on. 'She had lowered her head and now she must take the consequences.' So on she went, getting a little food, now and then by begging, until one day she heard the pundit at the well tell of the Christian's God, who, he said, forgave the worst of sins, even of women, and she believed it all, though the pundit said he did not believe it and it could not be true ; that women were not made for heaven, and very few even of the best would ever have a place there ; and so she came, as she felt it was true. She is bright, and I think will turn out well, and you will not be sorry you sent her."

"It is a pitiful story," Mrs. Clinton said, with tears in her eyes.

"Yes, it is, and, sadder still, it is not an uncommon story. Now about the question of chairs."

"Yes," said Mrs. Clinton, "I really think the 'ladies at home' would regret very much to hear that you did not insist on the women sitting in chairs. Surely it would increase their self-respect."

"I have not the least doubt in the world of the truth of both of your assertions. As to the latter, I find the self-respect of the women increases in a ratio that I find impossible to keep up with, as far as new wants and new habits and new things altogether go.

That is the very point. I was one of the 'ladies at home' myself and held very decided opinions in regard to all these things, but my opinion has changed with the change in my point of view."

"That is to be expected; but what possible objection can there be to chairs? Surely no moral principle is involved."

"As much as eating with knives and forks off of plates, instead of eating out of the degchi, and wearing hats like ours, or coats like the sahibs, or collars and cuffs. All these and a hundred other things do not seem to have a moral bearing; yet if a native Christian cannot afford to buy all these things, and he and his family are unhappy because they cannot have them, or led to give up work in the mission where he is needed in order that he may get larger wages and supply himself with luxuries—for they are to him neither more nor less than luxuries—then the whole thing has a moral phase."

"Yes," was the decided answer; "it is true, but it is a novel light in which to regard chairs and knives and forks."

"Now some of these women here will," Miss Whitlow went on, "marry Christian men who earn four or five dollars a month, or even less. If they get accustomed to chairs and knives and forks and clothes such as we wear they will never be so happy as they would without them. If they can provide themselves honestly with the first luxuries they have habitually it will put a different light on the whole matter. As to women copying our dress, it has still another moral bearing. Their chuddars are a shelter and protection to them, and they are not prepared to give them up and go about without them. They would lose their modesty and seem to us more or less bold. Laying it aside to them is what laying aside our bonnets or hats and even part of our dress would be to us; it would be unnatural, and therefore would do us harm, as also giving up their chuddars would be unnatural to them and do them harm; and besides, anyone with artistic feeling could hardly wish them to do so, for, so far as actual beauty goes, their dress far exceeds ours."

"I agree with you perfectly as to that; I never knew how ugly our dress is until I saw theirs. But I must hurry home to breakfast"—looking at her watch; "I shall be late as it is."

"Fancy putting a hat on this child, and see what a guy it would make her, compared to what she is. Come here, Sitara," she said as a pretty little girl-woman came out of the house wrapped from head to foot in a soft scarlet sari with gold-colored border, and carrying a shining brass lota in her hand from which the rays of the sun were reflected in sharp lines to their eyes. She came shy and trembling and put a little hand in Mrs. Clinton's and looked up with half-merry curiosity in her large dark eyes, made more brilliant by the scarlet and gold about her face. Dimples and white teeth showed quickly in answer to the smile Mrs. Clinton gave her, and when she put her arms around her the child nestled in them with ready love.

"You darling!" exclaimed Mrs. Clinton, kissing her.

Sitara looked and felt happy. She knew at once without an intelligible word that the great Mem Sahib was truly pleased with her.

SITARA.

" Sitara has been a brave and a good girl, and she has a good husband."

"This child!" cried Mrs. Clinton.

Miss Whitlow said something to the girl in Hindoostance, and she gently, with a look full of love, lifted her hand to her forehead and bowed to each of the ladies and glided quietly away toward the schoolroom.

"It is an interesting story, this of Sitara and her husband, and if you come early to the station meeting to-morrow night I will tell you all about her. I assure you she is not uncommonly young for a wife."

As she got into the gari Mrs. Clinton felt a giddy sensation and nearly fell.

"What is coming to me?" she said to herself, half alarmed; "this constant confusion of head and this disagreeable sensation of not being sure of keeping my feet! I wonder if it is anything that I have eaten."

At the breakfast table she spoke of it, and the Bishop confessed to the same sensation, varied by a constant and intense dull ache at the back of his neck, and before they had finished he was obliged to go to his room and lie down. Then followed a bad hour or two of sharp pain in his head and vomiting. He was not able to get up for lunch, but his wife told Carnton he was much better. Had he not been better she would have sent for a doctor.

"He has just escaped sunstroke," said Carnton, after she had detailed the symptoms of his attack," and you will be obliged to do as we do, wear ugly sola topis, or have still worse trouble.

"But the sun is not uncomfortably hot," argued she; "in fact, it is only comfortably warm. How can it hurt us?"

" I do not know how, but I know that it does, and there is no possible way of acclimatization for us. I tried it and was ill. Most of us like to try it for ourselves, but in the case of Nilton, of Agra, he carried his experiment too far, and died in the prime of his life from sunstroke."

Carnton said no more, but he observed that three sola topis appeared in the house the next day, and thereafter there was no complaint of headache and giddiness.

And that was the first bit of experience that cost them something, but not the last.

CHAPTER VIII.

MAKING CALLS.

THE government of India is a vague, illusory thing in the minds of the masses of the Indian people. There is a shadowy superstition of a sort of fairyland where the head fairy is an indefinite Buri Rani, called Victoria, who is something after the style of Lăchmi, their own goddess of plenty, who sits aloft in the clouds on a lotus flower and regards the sufferings of the world with uninterrupted placidity.

They have an unlimited idea of the great sea, and the fact that the empress lives beyond it separates her from them as completely as though she were in heaven.

The Lord Sahib, or the Viceroy, comes a little nearer. They have a consciousness of him when their especial "talukdár" raises their taxes to supply entertainments and fêtes à la Arabian Nights for him when he is on his annual visit. But the only real governmental providence they comprehend is the lieutenant-governor of the particular province or presidency in which they live, who has his court on the plains in the cold season, and in the mountains in the hot season, and swings pendulum-like between his two or three governmental seats.

All who are received by him and his family at Government House are respectable and "in society," even if not "of society;" and the first duty of every self-respecting European not in trade, on arriving at a place where there is a government house, is to present himself in all that is correct in clothes and cards and smiles, and have the invisible label and stamp put on him, which will make it safe for seedy colonels, red-faced majors, and bankrupt lieutenants to return his bow or receive an apology for being thrown against him in a railway collision. This is an advantage to the missionary in many ways. He needs government backing and he gets it, for the government, wise in its generation, sees that the missionary is not only law-abiding himself, but that he makes law-abiding citizens of his converts; that his schools and homes and churches do what no other power, however strong, can do; and grants of land and money are given freely when well-known and long-standing missions ask for them. So calling at Government House is encouraged—that is, missionaries encourage each other to call, but it is only the obliging new ones that really go, and just as they are starting they find they are asked to register the names of all the other missionaries of the place in the visitors' book, which takes the place of a call; they also find that the normal missionary hates calling at Government House, and all other merely conventional calls, as badly as merely conventional people hate to see him coming.

Carnton, on being told it was his duty to call, begged Mrs. Clinton to go with him, and she acquiesced, as she had been told it was her duty to do so. They drove in through a rather imposing entrance, beyond which passers-by could catch a glimpse of smooth-

shaven green lawns, of well-grouped trees, and through
their openings gleaming pillars, bits of verandas, and
scarlet and gold-liveried servants.

One of these latter, salaaming low, ushered them
into a magnificent room at the end of which were
two young ladies, the nieces of the lieutenant-governor, Sir Mayland Wild.

"They are pretty and well dressed, for English
women," thought Mrs. Clinton, with the impulse of
natural antipathy fostered by many Fourths of July.
They received the missionaries with respect, first,
because the word Bishop on Mrs. Clinton's husband's
card, which she had brought in lieu of being able to
persuade him to accompany her, had caught their eyes,
and Carnton carried his own welcome with him in his
fine figure and handsome face and an unconscious air
of being perfectly at home and at ease in any circumstances.

Then, too, the words "American Mission" on Carnton's card had given them a hint of something interesting, and they had visibly brightened, for they
were tired and bored. It was, of course, their regular receiving day, and shoals of women had come and
gone; senior subalterns' wives, many; captains' wives,
some; colonels' wives, a few; but not only not one
person of distinction, but, what was worse to them,
no interesting men. Lady Huff and Lady Puff would
not kotow to girls who were officially at the head of
society only from the accident of their uncle being a
bachelor or widower, one or the other, or both. Society did not seem quite sure under which category he
came, and it is possible that he himself was not sure.
So altogether the young ladies had not had so satis-

factory a day as might have been expected. A bishop's wife was not to be despised, and one, the eldest, looking at Carnton as he advanced, said under her breath :

" Ah, if I could only tame him ! What a handsome 'bow-wow' he would make, even if he is a missionary."

And the other thought, with a flush on her fair face :

" I will find out about these horrid American girls, if he can talk of anything but converting the heathen."

Carnton fell to her share.

" You belong to the American Mission ; I suppose you are very enthusiastic in regard to the natives ? "

The one trace of the world that lingered around Carnton was his manner to women ; not of the wicked world, but essentially of the world—half-deferential, half-amused, as though talking to pretty children, and wholly fascinating, though unconsciously so.

He smiled, bending a little toward her.

" That depends somewhat on what you mean by enthusiasm ; and may I ask why it is a foregone conclusion that I am enthusiastic ? "

Her face lighted—she was not going to be bored, for at any rate he could talk.

" For two reasons: missionaries are always—not fanatical, but very excitable and hopeful, and Americans are always enthusiastic. You know Colonel Sellers in Mark Twain's book ; he is a typical American."

" Really ! " answered Carnton, with a gentle look of derision. " I had not thought Colonel Sellers a typi-

cal American. It is rather difficult to say exactly
what a typical American is. In fact, the only one I
ever thought to be so proved to be an Englishman
born and bred. But if as a missionary I were con-
victed of enthusiasm, it would mean—" and he
stopped with a gleam of amusement in his eyes that
gave her an unaccountable feeling of shyness.

"O, it would mean that you were sure of converting
all the natives very soon, and that they were to be instantly respectable, truth-telling people. But I assure
you frankly it cannot be done; it is wasted time and
strength."

"Why?"

"My uncle, who favors missions, had a chaprassi
who said he was a Christian, and he stole a lot of
money—hundreds of rupees—and fled, and we have
never seen him since. I am perfectly sure that they
are naturally dishonest and nothing will cure them."

"Such a strange thing as a dishonest servant is, I
suppose, never known in England?"

"O, yes, plenty of them."

"But I suppose they were not professed Christians."

"All we ever had were, for mother would have
none other."

"And yet you did not think there was no Christianity in England because one of your servants was
not honest."

"True enough," frankly and with a slight confusion; "I had not looked at it in that way. But I want
to ask you a question—about American girls. What is
it that makes them so fascinating? Are they so much
prettier than English girls?" she asked, earnestly.

"I really cannot say; I have seen so few English

girls. Perhaps Mrs. Clinton can tell us," noticing that the other Miss Wild had stopped talking in order to listen.

Turning to Mrs. Clinton she repeated her question. The fair face was flushed and eager, and Mrs. Clinton, looking at her, said, gently:

" I do not really see how they can be prettier than some English girls I have seen."

The questioner drew back a little, and said, with a conscious increase of color:

" What is it then? In London the best men run after them and forget others. Every place they go to they are surrounded by men, and we sit about and look on."

" Perhaps it may be their dollars," said Carnton, lightly; " I have heard that given as the reason."

" No; this girl was poor—ah—" catching herself, " I mean I saw one girl who was known to be poor, and she was not prettier than—than many girls there, and yet men one did not expect it of left others to talk to her the whole evening."

Surely there was more than personal pique in this. " Men one did not expect it of" meant one particular man that she had not expected it of. There was no answer, and she went on:

" And she did not seem to care one bit for them, and liked to talk to women just as well, and the strange part of it all was that we all liked her."

" I think," said Carnton, gravely, rising as Mrs. Clinton rose to take her leave, " I think you have explained the reason in your last remark better than we could;" and they were soon out in the open air, leaving the perplexed questioner to ponder.

Mrs. Clinton laughed a little as she said:

"I was interviewed as well as you on Americans. The elder sister told me she was surprised to find us using good English, and that this girl in London, of whom her sister was speaking, also used good English; but when she mentioned it to her, and told her that she did not talk a bit like Mark Twain or Artemus Ward, the girl had said that she could really take no credit to herself, for an English missionary had lived near her father's hut, and she had learned from him. When I smiled and said, 'Indeed!' she went on to say that when she explained it to her Cousin Jack, who had been in America and seen her father's 'hut' on Fifth Avenue, in New York, he rolled on the floor and laughed, and said she was chaffing me. She said 'chawfing.'"

Carnton laughed.

"That is really good; in fact, it goes beyond anything in my experience, though I have been asked funny questions without number. Colonel Jones told me plainly that we had no writers or books in America, and when I timidly mentioned Irving as being used for the standard English in the schools of India, and Emerson, whom I knew he read, and Longfellow, whom everybody reads, he declared indignantly that they were English, and it was absurd for Americans to claim them. I said nothing whatever, as I felt I was not adequate to the occasion. But of course such men as he are no more representative Englishmen than Colonel Sellers is a representative American."

They were now driving in at the entrance of a zenana mission.

"Yesterday we were visiting missionaries in a tomb, and to-day we find them in a palace."

"Really that sounds very much like ' From the Log-cabin to the White House.' Whom, I beg of you, shall we find in the palace ?"

"Miss Mellen, though every one calls her 'Sidney,' the zenana missionary of the other society, and her assistants. She lives in this old palace which was given to their mission, and was built by one of the old kings of Oude for his vazir, or prime minister. But how is this, that *I* am giving *you* information?"

"Of course I have heard often of them, but I have never seen them. I have been too busy, and when in Lucknow for a few days I have always had mission work on hand. Where have you seen them?"

"Miss Mellen was calling on Mrs. Mackenzie the first day we were here, and she is simply lovely. But I thought she cared too much for the fit of her dresses and is too pretty to be a good missionary."

"Well," said Carnton, laughing, "you surely cannot say that of Miss—some of the other missionaries," catching himself before he had uttered a name.

"Hardly," was the answer.

The gateway through which they came, like most gateways in India, had no gate, but was only an entrance to a large compound filled with shrubs, clumps of roses, and pots of ferns and palms, beyond which the old palace loomed, so big and so irregular that, looking up, when fairly before it, they could only see one part of it. There was a veranda, below and above this an open terrace, and from this came the sound of shuffling native shoes, and an ayah looked down over the railing and disappeared. Then a bearer came with a salaam, and " Miss Sahib hai," and taking their cards disappeared. They followed, as the word salaam indicated that they would be received.

They went up a short flight of stairs, a turn, up a long flight, across a landing, across a terrace, and into a plainly furnished sitting room. Here were the same Saracenic arches that so often in Lucknow stirred Mrs. Clinton's æsthetic sensibilities. There were various devices to shut off the draughts caused by these same arches, but nothing ornamental, nothing but rude screens and plain chairs.

Mrs. Clinton said, with a mock sigh, to Carnton:

" I have a great mind to be a missionary to the missionaries and live to drape their houses and make them pretty; to remodel their bonnets and make them respectable; to show them that they have no right to deprive themselves of the help a little beauty would be to them, and live as they do on the plain bare facts."

" But this would hardly agree with your avowed purpose in India. How is this?"

Mrs. Clinton laughed and was about to reply, when Miss Mellen and Miss Harris came in. After twenty minutes passed they were out again in the carriage. Carnton was silent. With her usual instinct of penetration Mrs. Clinton felt that Carnton was not the same man that had gone in with her. There was a change, subtle and undefined, a something gained or a something lost; and she reviewed the twenty minutes spent in the shabby room.

Both ladies were in plain working-dresses, as they had just come in from the zenanas, and had that wearied look that is on the faces of those who have worked hard but happily, which is entirely different from the weariness of boredom, or weariness coming from uncongenial burdens.

Miss Harris looked as tidy as when she had gone out in the morning, but Miss Mellen's hair hung in little brown rings and curls about her forehead, and the large braid that crowned her head was decidedly tumbled. Her cheeks, naturally a wild-rose red, were deepened by the sun into almost a purplish tint, and her mouth drooped wearily. Carnton had sat in a seat near her, and they had talked. What of? Mrs. Clinton did not know; she was engaged with Miss Harris, who was telling her of a disappointment in her work. A Mohammedan's wife and daughter had been about to become Christians with his consent, when suddenly he had removed them out of the city and she could find no trace of them. While she was listening to this story she had still seen that the other two were absorbed in each other.

She was not romantic, but she knew some things, and she wondered if she had been seeing the very beginning of a love story. She felt awed by the thought. Love was not a trifle to her; not something to be treated with amusement or in any way lightly. It involved too much; it was too great, too terrible to be regarded otherwise than solemnly and sacredly. So she sat silent, and the driver whipped his thin little ponies, and the wind blew the dust all about them as they drove around corners, and went down narrow streets. Finally Carnton said:

"What do you say to our going home, and leaving the other mission houses for another day?"

Mrs. Clinton assented, nearly convinced that something serious had happened.

CHAPTER IX.

THE STORY OF SITARA.

SITARA and her husband, Shew Pershad, had lived in separate villages until their marriage, and then she came to live in the same house in which he had always lived and was his little playmate and his mother's assistant in preparing the food for their simple meals.

They had been married a year or two when it first dawned on Shew Pershad that there was a great world worth seeing and knowing, and that they, in the secluded little village, were ignorant and simple compared with others who traveled on railways, worked in offices, and studied the language of the sahibs who ruled the country.

True, there was a little school in the village, but he had already learned all that was taught there, and had been looked up to with great admiration by those who could not read, and who had never been to school; for the school was a modern affair and not known when his parents were young. He helped his mother in the little shop by which she had been able always to be comfortable, and which had been, in unusual liberality and kindness, left to her by her husband when he died.

Some cousins of his, also sons of widows, had been to a mission school and came back full of the wonderful things they had learned. When they had convinced him that the world was round and not flat, and did not rest on the back of a turtle, and was not bounded by seas full of serpents and dragons, that trees, however sacred, could not control destiny, that even mud images could do nothing for human beings, that smallpox and other diseases could not be driven away by sacrifices and music, and that many other things of like nature in which he had believed were untrue, he was bewildered and excited and indignant at his teachers and his mother for teaching him falsehoods, and angry with himself for having believed them.

Many days, sitting in the little shop when his mother thought him half asleep, he pondered these things. What did it all mean? He had firmly believed all the things that he now found untrue; but more disturbing than this was the fact that he had also heard of a God whom these great and powerful people, the sahibs, worshiped, who was pure and good, and who demanded of his worshipers that they also should be pure and upright and truthful and honest. But, while his cousins were content to take the surface of things and accept the facts with a sneer for those who did not know as much as they, Shew Pershad determined to go below all the facts and see what it meant, and for this end he resolved to learn it from the teachers at first hand. One day, after his cousin had helped him with the accounts of the shop so quickly and so cleverly that his mother was filled with admiration, he said:

"Mother, I am neither foolish nor mad, and can learn as well as this boy, my cousin. I, too, will go to Lucknow to school."

The mother objected, but the son was the head of the house and had his way and went to school with his cousins. They all boarded with a connection of the family, and went together as day students. All that his cousins took as a matter of course astounded him, and nothing so much as the Christian religion. It was wonderful and beautiful. Not a bowing down to imperfect, vindictive, and sensual gods, but to a glorious Being in whom was all truth and all love, and in whose worship he would also come to a higher and better life; who regarded the souls, and not bodies, and in whose sight his loved and loving playmate, Sitara, was as good as himself. This latter was to his head the most difficult of all, though his heart accepted it with joy. Finally, after months of teaching and of faithful study, he presented himself to Mr. Miller for baptism. After thoroughly catechising him in regard to his reasons for the request and with regard to his understanding and belief, he promised the boy baptism. Mr. Miller also advised him to at once acquaint all his friends, and especially his mother, with his determination.

There was great trouble when this was done, and his mother and all the members of the family and the caste were angry, and declared him no longer one of them, but out of caste, and that he might go his own way. Word was even brought to him that his wife would refuse to see his face again if he did not turn from his evil ways. He was saddened, but so simple and earnest was his belief that he only looked upon it as the result of their ignorance and superstition, and believed that they in their hearts still loved him. More, he *knew* that Sitara did, and he determined

11

that at least she should be free from the awful darkness in which his mother lived. There was a troublesome thought now and then that he too, perhaps, might die early, as his father had done, and Sitara might be left to struggle against all the temptations and trials of early widowhood.

When he thought of this he was more determined than ever to free her, but he knew it would not be safe for him to go openly to bring her away. He had some money of his own, and he wrote her letters which he sent by a man selling jelabies and other sweets. The man was to stay about the house until he could give them into her own hand. He had taught her to read a little, and he only wrote very, very short letters. First, "My heart runs back to Gopal Gunge to make its salaams to you;" another time, "You are still dear to me;" and then another on a great fête day, "My heart says that you still love me. If so, send me the hár of jasmine that you wear around your neck to-day;" and she sent it.

After receiving this he wrote again: "I am a Christian, but I know you will come to me. There is a school here where you can live and be cared for, and I can see you at least each Sunday in the Christian worship-house, though I may not speak to you. Then, when I have finished school, we will have a house of our own, of which you will be sole mistress. If you will come to me at the well in the mango grove by the old temple outside the village at nine o'clock one week from to-day send me the coral necklace I bought for you at the Ajudiya mela."

The necklace came, and the jelabi man, who had been faithful to his trust, was dismissed with enough

rupees to enable him to give a dinner to his relatives.
Then he got leave from school for a few days on the
plea of seeing his wife, and met her at the well.
There was a room in the old temple where he and his
cousins had spent many a pleasant day, and to this he
took her and there explained all he wished her to do.
She agreed readily, for had he not always been kinder
to her than anyone else, and was he not wise and
great, having traveled so far and read so many books,
and did she not love him better than his old mother,
who was often so fierce with her when matters did
not go well in the shop? He had brought food
enough in his pockets for the next day, and he would
remain there all the day and the next night. She
was to bring all that belonged to her and join him,
and they would go away into that wonderful world
that lay far beyond the little village and its sleepy inhabitants.

When he presented his wife to Mr. Miller the good
man was much surprised, and hardly knew what to
say, and so sent her to Miss Whitlow for a short time
until arrangements could be made to place her in
some school.

This is the story Miss Whitlow told Mrs. Clinton
as they sat in the gathering dusk waiting for the
missionaries to come in for the station meeting.

This latter was a time-honored institution, and was
of a nondescript type of monthly assembling together
for mutual help and encouragement. There was a
president to preside and secretary to keep record, and
in this record could be traced the circumstantial history of most of the work done by this mission in the
place.

To-night there was added interest in the meeting, for it was understood there was a " chiel amang them takin' notes," and whether or not he meant " to prent them " they were all anxious that the notes might be favorable, as much of the future of the mission might be endangered if they were unfavorable. Each and every one was sure that if the Bishop could see his own particular work in all its bearings he could not fail to be more interested in it than in any other, and consequently give his time to help in that direction.

After the reading of the minutes of the last meeting Miss Lowe was called on for her report. She began :

" We have had an unusually good month. The heads of several good Mohammedan families have sent, asking us to come and see their women. When there are promising new families ready to be taught anything we wish to teach them we drop out the old places which seem less hopeful, for we have so many more places than we can visit that we must make a selection. I see a marked growth of interest in the Bible in many places, and especially in the villages near Lucknow. The ground is new in the villages, the women more simple, and they receive the word more gladly, and we are giving our time chiefly to village work. I must tell you of one pitiful little scene in a zenana yesterday. I was hurrying up a lane over at Hosainabad when an old woman, evidently a servant, came out of a door in a wall and said :

" ' Miss Sahib, will you come and see my mistress. She is very ill, and my heart tells me that she will soon die, perhaps even to-day ; and the tears rolled down her face as she spoke.

I was late, but I thought I must go, and I followed her through the door into a court which was filled with palms and marigolds and saw that I was in the house of one of the better class of Hindoos. The woman motioned me to go quietly. On the veranda I saw a charpai and a heap of bright color on it. As I went closer I saw that a girl wrapped in a red and green quilt was lying on a bed with her eyes closed, and even then I could see that the face was as sad as the voice in which she was murmuring the words, 'My baby, O, my baby!' She looked like a little girl, and yet I concluded she must be the woman's mistress and a wife and mother. I motioned to the woman to tell her that I had come, and I stood a little back, where she could not see me. Her eyes opened quickly, and with a start she raised herself up on her elbow, but sank back at once, as though too weak to support her head. Her eyes looked so big and mournful, and even the surprise of seeing me did not take the heart-broken expression out of them. Pretty soon her face changed and a very bright look of recognition came into them, and she said, joyfully:

"'O, it is my Miss Sahib! It is my Miss Sahib! Janki,' she gasped to the woman, 'how often I have told you of her!'

"I bent over her and took her hand and said:

"'I am very glad you know me. Where did you see me?'

"'Do you not know? In a little school in Ghasira Mundi. I went a little while only, but it was sweet and good.'

"She was very weak, and her breath came quickly, and to let her rest I spoke to the woman and asked about her mistress's sickness. She told me first that the child's husband was old and cared chiefly for his shop. She had been ill six months, ever since her baby died; and as she said this the tears came fast from her eyes, but the poor little mother lay quite quiet until her servant had finished, and then she said so sadly, so very sadly:

" 'And O, Miss Sahib, he was such a beautiful baby, so strong and so glad always, and his father was so proud of him! He went, and soon I shall go, but not where he is; for into the body of some wild animal he will go, and who will care for him?'

" I shall never forget the sad hopelessness of that gasping cry. I knelt by her and took her tiny hands in mine, and I said: 'Do you not know what Jesus Christ our Lord said—"Suffer little children to come unto me, and forbid them not, for of such is the kingdom of heaven?" It is true, and your beautiful child is safe with him, where you too can join him. *It is true.*' I said it in a way that convinced her, for I felt there was no time to lose.

" 'How can I go?' she asked, eagerly; 'women have no place in heaven. It is only men who have a right there.'

" 'Then,' I said, 'you must believe all my words, for they are true. "God so loved the world that he gave his only begotten Son, that *whosoever* believeth on him should not perish, but have everlasting life." '

" 'O,' she said, 'I learned that in the school, and I have said it many times since, but my little boy's father said it was not true. Is it true?' and her eyes held mine as though she would force the truth from me.

"I said, 'It is true, and if you believe it and ask God to forgive you and take you to him and to your dear baby he will do it.' I wish I could tell you how joyful her poor pale face was; then she closed her eyes, and while praying sank into a gentle sleep. I came away, telling the old woman to get nourishing things for her, though I had not much hope that she would need them long. I was so glad she had been in the school even for a few days, otherwise I fear she was too weak to have understood my words. This morning I went, and she had gone to meet her beautiful baby."

There was a little silence; then Miss Dillon said:

"The school has gone on as usual. One or two new ones came, and I had one or two applications for scholarship, but as I had no more I was obliged to refuse. The girls' prayer meeting has been especially good of late. There seems to be a new interest in it. Two girls that have been perfectly incorrigible have taken an earnest stand and professed a personal experience of the salvation of Christ, and have told me they hope to devote their lives to mission work. I have looked for a change in their daily lives, and have not been disappointed. The effect has been felt all through the school, and I hope much from them. They will be baptized soon, as their parents have made no objection, though they are not decided Christians themselves.

"I find my greatest difficulty in keeping the girls to their native habits of dress, and find more need than ever to simplify my own dress and habits of life."

Miss Whitlow came next:

"That latter point of Miss Dillon's is one with

which I can sympathize. There seems something in woman nature all over the world that delights in adorning itself with what it considers beautiful, and it is often a great question to know where innocent pleasure ends and vanity begins. I have learned at least one thing in my fifteen years in India, to be more strict with myself in my dress and not so strict with them. I have found it easier to discard every sign or suggestion of trimming or frilling or ornament in my own dress than to explain to them why my dresses should have it and not theirs.

"Two new women have entered the Home this month, of one of which Mrs. Clinton can tell you; and one has left because she preferred to go back to her old ways of sin. Three women are ready for baptism, and will present themselves for it next Sunday if all is well."

Then Mr. Mackenzie gave his report:

"The papers have gone on as usual, but I have had difficulty with the bookbinder. He demands more than I will give him, as he knows we have promised books that are not ready. Otherwise from this I have had no unusual trouble. Bishop Wilbur's tracts are in great demand, and the call for moral essays and all that kind of books is steadily increasing. Several prominent Hindoos have sent for handsomely bound Bibles, and the general tide seems to be toward reading English books of any kind if they are only cheap. This shows me more than ever the great need of good and suitable books and the necessity of setting apart a missionary whose sole work will be to select things for translation and also write in the vernaculars. There is so much bad cheap literature floating about that something, and something very strong and wide-spread, is needed to counteract its influence, and also to take its place, and any English books that can be widely advertised as being cheaper than this vile trash that is read will easily supersede it."

Mr. Miller said there was nothing new in the school; Mrs. Miller, Miss May, of the college class, and Mrs. Mackenzie all said they had been working hard, but had nothing to tell, as it was only in the ordinary routine of their work, and Mr. Carnton told of the coming over of the whole village of Belai to Christianity.

Mr. Train, of the English Church, said his work was going on as usual. The Epworth League, modeled on the plan in America, was increasing in interest and was uniting the young people and creating a sentiment which was especially needed. He reported several conversions among Eurasians, and said they would be on probation and under instruction and baptized on proof of their stability. The native pastor was not present, and Mr. Miller reported for him that he was faithful in his work, earnest in preaching, and generally popular among his people. That one of the things in which native Christians needed especial training was the holy keeping of the Sabbath and in the regular attendance at church. It was difficult for them to understand that it could be required of them to go twice a day to hear sermons as well as once a day to Sunday school on every seventh day. The natural conclusion was that one sermon a day was enough and all they could remember and understand. He thought there was a general missionary feeling in the Church, a feeling of responsibility for the conversion of their neighbors and friends; they supported one large Sunday school in the city, and they always give liberally to missionary collections and to support their own pastor.

"What do you mean by liberally?" said the Bishop.

"When we speak of the native being liberal it does not mean what it would were I to say I was liberal, as their salaries range from two dollars a month upward to thirty, with very few above this, and when a man keeps a family on two or three dollars per month he has not much left for giving."

Mrs. Clinton was asked for her report in rather a jocular way, as though not expecting any, and all were a little surprised when she gave an account of what she had done in the way of settling her house and making calls, and also the story of Pulmoni, and there was a vigorous clapping of hands when she closed. It is hardly necessary to say that she omitted her experience with her cook, for some things had already shown her the absurdity of part of her plan, and she regretted that she had not waited a few weeks before she began her experiment.

As her report was so full and extended the Bishop was asked to give his, and, perhaps unwisely, also asked to give his impressions of mission work.

"I have been in this place nearly a week," he said. "I have seen all of the missionaries of our own mission, and some of those of other missions; I have seen jugglers and shawl-merchants; I have seen coolies and Brahmans; I have seen Mohammedans, Hindoos, and Christians; I have seen boys' day schools, the boys' boarding school and college, and the girls' boarding school; I have seen the publishing house, the Central Native Church and the English-speaking Church, and the Home of the Homeless. I have given a superficial attention to each one of these, as in the short time I could not give more; I have been amazed, I have been pleased and displeased; I have been surprised at the strength and disappointed at the weakness of the work. I have seen men and women depriving themselves of comforts in order to provide schools and distribute books and tracts, and yet indulging in luxuries; I have seen methods wise and methods as unwise in the conducting of various parts of good work. I would say there is great need of many changes and much perfecting of plans and much correction of methods in a work whose size and extent is amazing to me. I beg you to remember that I was asked to give my impressions, and I have done so, but it is only fair to say that I shall give them to no one else until they have hardened into opinions. I will not now go into details, but simply say that I am open to conviction in regard to the points on which I differ from you and in which I believe you are making mistakes. But I am sure of one thing at least, we want less working on organic lines, less of looking to the health and comfort and respectability, and more of the old-time enthusiastic evangelical work, more stir, more rush, more abandon, and, if need be as a consequence, more missionary graves in India."

This was a bomb in the midst of this quiet circle, and after its explosion there was silence. It is possible that the Bishop thought his episcopal authority extended to India and warranted him in his attitude

toward the missionaries. Certainly he did not understand the fact that he was dealing with men who were
practically bishops themselves in their own territories,
and looked upon him simply as a visitor without any
authority. It was noticed that he did not mention
his humiliating defeat by the sun, though he could
not have forgotten it, for his head was still aching and
his eyes bloodshot.

The president said, gravely : " Your report has the
merit of being frank, at least. As you wisely say,
you are only giving impressions. I shall ask the secretary to make this evident as she records your words.
At the end of the year you propose spending here we
shall hope to record your judgment, and allow me to
say that I sincerely hope some of your words will not
be recorded the second time."

The formal meeting was closed with prayer, and
then tea was served and conversation became general.
Mrs. Clinton regretted her husband's plain speaking,
for she did not see how it could fail to intensify the
antagonism in the mission which she was sure was
there, for she did not see how it could fail to be there.
But, however, there was apparently little attention
paid to his remarks; in fact, no one spoke to him on
the subject except Mrs. Miller, to ask with asperity,
" If he was willing to set the example in regard to *all*
he was advising ?" but he ignored the question, and
argued with Dr. Wall, who had come up from Allahabad to take over the treasury work from Mackenzie.
Dr. Wall was trying to show him that already the
evangelical work had outstripped the organic work,
and that a man was in no position to judge until he
had seen all the mission stations. The subject on

which all were talking, and which seemed to elicit a good deal of amusement, was a circular letter which each had received from some one in authority asking, in consideration of various reports which were being circulated at home, that each missionary should give a detailed account of his manner of living and send a photograph of his home. The point involved that seemed to afford amusement was the modest request for a photograph.

Mrs. Miller said : " He, at least, must believe we are extravagant, else he would not have asked us to do so extravagant a thing as have our houses photographed. We cannot even afford our own photographs to send to our friends. I have wanted one for years to send to my father, and could not find any money with which to pay for it. I have half a mind to send a letter saying we should like to have a photograph of his house and an account of the way he lives. We have as much right to ask it of him as he of us, for he is supported by missionary money as well as we are."

There was a laugh at this sally ; then Miss Whitlow said : " The cost of a photograph would just support the school that I have been obliged to give up for the one year, so I cannot send one, and I cannot find time to write letters now at any rate."

" I mean to do it," said Mrs. Mackenzie ; " not the photograph, of course, but the description. I shall not say my house looks well and is quite all I want, but I shall describe the dry-goods boxes I use for tables ; and also the fact that I have not one curtain in my house would make a good point."

Then some one spoke of the approaching festivities

in honor of the visit of the future King of England,
and some one else asked Carnton if he registered the
names of all the missionaries of the station in the visitors' book at Government House.

"O," laughed Carnton, "this is why you all insisted
on the necessity of my calling there."

"Yes," answered Miller; "and why not? The
newcomers usually are sure of something respectable
in which to appear. We did duty when we first came,
now it is your turn."

"And if we did not get our names on the visitors'
book we would not be invited to meet the prince,"
said his wife.

"Would that be an irreparable loss?" asked Mrs.
Clinton, a little scornfully.

"Perhaps not," said Mackenzie; "but we must appear to show our loyalty."

"And you forget the Fourth of July and all that
sort of thing," said Miss May, who was also one of the
new missionaries.

"No; but one of the first steps in making men better and stronger is to teach them to be good citizens
and loyal to the government that protects them."

"A very just sentiment," remarked the Bishop.
"We certainly have enough of the opposite to this in
people coming to America and working against all
law and all who execute law."

"Well," said Mackenzie, "I am willing to be loyal,
but I am not sure it goes to the extent of buying a
new hat, as I shall be obliged to do if I appear on this
occasion."

"I also," said Miss Lowe.

"I likewise," said Miss Whitlow.

"And I," said Mrs. Mackenzie, amid the general laugh.

After the large square cards came requesting the honor of their presence to meet his royal highness at a garden party in the park some of the new hats were bought and some were not. Those that bought them reflected that if they did not buy them then they would have it to do the following year; those that did not buy them reflected that next year they would be fresh.

CHAPTER X.

THE VISIT OF THE PRINCE.

THE prince came, of course. On the morning of his arrival there was great stir and rush and commotion in the European quarter of Lucknow, and even the native part felt a thrill of expectation, and poured out its inhabitants in their best dress to throng the streets and add color and movement to the scene.

Arches of welcome lifted themselves bravely on the roads the royal visitor was expected to pass, and the roads themselves were outlined by fences of lattice-work which was to support the chirags for the illuminations. All society was on the terraced tops of the principal hotels waiting impatiently; for at seven in the morning, even in February, the sun is too penetrating when straw hats and unlined parasols are the only barrier between its rays and the head of the European.

All not of society waited in the streets on foot, in shabby garis, and sometimes in smart carriages. The soldiers forming the guard that extended from Government House to the railway, station gazed with stolid eyes on the procession of elephants and camels, in their best scarlet and gold drapery, as they lumbered down toward the station to pay their respects and lumbered back again behind and before the plainly dressed youth who sat erect in his carriage looking very tired and almost sad because of all the attention he was receiving.

The program of his visit at Lucknow was as follows: The public reception at the railway station; bath and change of dress, and tea at Government House; the opening of the Female Hospital erected under the auspices of the association organized by that wise and gracious lady, the Countess of Dufferin; breakfast; a drive to the ruins of the Residency and Dil Kusha; a garden party; a dinner and a reception by the native princes, with a private departure the following morning. That the prince's speech at the opening of the hospital was not a marvel of eloquence, and that his words were halting and shyly given was not so strange as disappointing to those who wished the English government to appear at its best.

Following the breakfast, at which were only the *crème de la crème*, was the drive. Following this the garden party in Wingfield Park, to which the whole of the government list was asked.

This park is beautiful with all that nature, shaped and guided by art, can do for a plot of ground. Grand old trees of banyan, tamarind, and pipal, their round dark masses of foliage contrasting well with the straight tall palms and the gray, undecided-looking eucalyptus, through the openings in whose foliage were views of arch and dome and minaret.

The central part, free from many large trees, was brilliant in all of color that flaming begonias, bougainvillias, beds of roses, crimson, pink, yellow, white, could give to a place. Through it all wound the smooth dull red roads, cutting softly into close-cropped green sward and joined by small bridges

12

thrown across nullas ending in fine perspective at marble shrine or pavilion.

To-day the roses bloomed their best, and both roses and heliotrope greeted each newcomer with a breath so soft and sweet that it was a delight simply to live and inhale it. When Mrs. Clinton and Lillian, with Mrs. Mackenzie, arrived, the park was alive with beautiful women in fresh costumes and men looking shy and self-conscious in unaccustomed black.

Along with these, but clearly not of them, were native princes in all the glory of priceless shawls or brilliantly colored gold-embroidered chapkans. There was more than the buying of new hats to make the mission lög dread the garden party. They are so generally buried in their work that they are annoyed with anything that is not work and do not know how to manage it.

Now and then kind-hearted people go out of their way to ask them to garden parties or dinners, but those who receive the invitation are often sorry and those who give it, nearly always sorry; for when the latter have actually got a missionary on their hands they do not know what to do with him. He is heavy and often sad, he is stern and pays no compliments and tells no stories; he steps on the ladies' trains and wishes himself home in bed gathering strength in order that he may put two days' work into one. So it is with a sigh of relief on both sides that he bids his hostess good night, and it will be many a long day before he is invited again; and he burrows in his work and forgets the social amenities of life. When the viceroy comes on his annual tour, or some royal highness happens along, then comes the request,

otherwise command, to be present at a ball or garden party or reception. The first always calls up a smile and the latter are laid on the table with the thought that they ought to be accepted, and, if there is time that can be snatched, the missionary and his wife emerge for an hour or two and look on what is to them another world. Though it brightens them up they feel so little lot and part in it all that they go back happy to their work and their native friends.

There was an unusual number of missionaries present to show their respect to the prince. They came at different times and were of different missions, but they gravitated toward each other and stood quietly about, interested in the new costumes, fresh from Paris for the occasion, chatted with occasional acquaintances among the native princes, or sat under the "shamiana" quietly observing the scene and wishing it were over. The Bishop came late with Carnton, both having worked up to the last moment. It was not long before the latter stood by Sidney, who was in the marble pavilion, with Lillian at her side, looking at the jewels placed there in securely locked glass cases for general inspection. The wild rose color was a little deeper in her cheeks than usual, for the others had been remarking on the fact of her having both a new dress and a new hat for the occasion, and Mrs. Clinton said, laughingly, that it might be a good thing to suggest to the "ladies at home" to make an especial appropriation for one new dress and one bonnet for all the single lady missionaries each year.

"Yes, indeed," said Lillian, so earnestly that all laughed.

"Lillian's judgment is sound," said Carnton, watching the color deepen in Sidney's cheeks. Sidney turned away and bent over the case of jewels next to her. It was all very well for the others, but from him, her new friend, for she claimed him as such, she could not bear that kind of talk.

"O, Miss Mellen, look!" cried Lillian. "The mark on this coat is forty thousand rupees! Is it not perfectly lovely?"

"What?—the mark?" said Carnton, teasingly, as he glanced indifferently at a purple velvet coat, embroidered heavily with gold, and thickly sown with pearls, large and small.

"And this," said Lillian, oblivious to any remark, and giving Sidney a pull, "isn't this a darling?" pointing to a necklace of pearls; "and this," indicating one of diamonds; "and this," dragging her friend along. Then there were more necklaces of pearls, then a huge one of topazes, with long pendants of the same, then a case of opals and moonstones, and next to that one of sapphires and turquoises.

Lillian had a passion for stones strange in a child. Their color and brilliancy delighted her beyond measure, and here she found a feast.

Others looked at the prince and watched Sir Mayland's struggles with him, but she had eyes only for the treasures before her. Carnton had introduced a nawab, who could speak English, to the Bishop, and then felt free to do whatever he liked, which seemed to be to look at Sidney and talk to her.

"Sir Mayland looks worried," he said, lightly, as the prince came near, "as though he feared his lion might slip his leash, escape his keepers, and be at large in a defenseless crowd."

"Certainly; whether or not he is afraid, his eyes never for an instant leave his royal guest. Some one who knows him well says that his hair is perceptibly grayer than it was yesterday morning. Of course, I suppose it is something of a responsibility to make the visit a success all around—native princes and all."

"Yes, indeed, and I do not envy him in the least; but what do you think of him—not Sir Mayland, but our future sovereign? This is the proper thing to say to-day, and leave the weather to some less fortunate day."

"What do you think of him?" Sidney replied, asking another question.

"I am profoundly sorry for him. Traveling night and day, constantly assisting at functions and making speeches, and attending fêtes and dinners and balls and receptions, until his soul must loathe the land of India. It is new and strange, and the strangest part of all must be his sudden coming to the front in this way, for he has been kept as a boy at home."

"By the way, our native Christian gathering was a failure this morning."

"How was that?"

"There was something wrong in the management or the program, and it turned out a muddle, and disappointing to those who had taken the trouble to come. If we had gone in for a little more shán-o-shaukat we might have succeeded in getting the commissioner's attention, or had it been the prince's most august grandmother it might have been a different matter. Speaking of her reminds me of the last exploit of our tamasha wala missionary. Did you hear what he did?"

"Mr. Creed? No, but something funny, I am sure."

"Of course. He tried first to get an audience with the prince in order to solicit his subscription for the *Gawahi-i-Hind*, but he was barred out. Then he wrote the prince a most grandiloquent letter begging a subscription, which was answered by the private secretary, who sent the price of two copies of the paper for a year. Then Creed wrote a letter of profuse thanks, and sent his salaams to 'the respected grandmother,' and begged the prince on his arrival at Windsor to solicit her subscription for the paper."

"The most annoying part of it all is that he is not given credit for zeal, but is simply taken as a specimen of Yankee cheek. Colonel Reed, who told me, said as he finished, 'Creed is a genuine American.' I must say one gets rather tired of 'the genuine and typical American' after having him so often pointed out."

They found themselves alone in the Baradari, the people, like a lot of children with a hand organ, having followed in the wake of the prince, who had been taken down one of the walks between the pansy beds to see a fight between a cobra and a mongoose.

"I need hardly ask you if you have been in the fernery," Carnton said, leading the way down the steps toward it, "for I hear you never go to any place but to your work."

"My presence here to-day confutes that statement."

"To-day does not count. Everybody must come to-day—that is, if asked, but the time to see the park is at daybreak. I have been down twice this week at that time. I get the exercise I need, and have a book of history which I have to teach in my pocket, and prepare the lesson as I walk. You would enjoy the walk."

"I dare say, but we are on our way to the zenanas at that time, or will be after this week. It is getting a little hot already in the middle of the day."

"Yes, the hot winds have fairly begun now," as they entered the fern house; "is not this worth coming to see?"

"Yes, surely," answered Sidney. Ferns and ferns and ferns, small and fine as lace up to those large and coarse as palms. Palms as fine as ferns, canes glossy and luxuriant, crotons with splashes of scarlet and pale yellow and emerald green; orchids that would have made the fortune of an American florist, and many strange, uncanny plants that Sidney did not recognize. There was a delight in being there for which she hardly could account, and was it the sunlight filtering down through the palms and huge ferns and on the gleaming goldfish in the basin of the small fountain, or the band in the distance playing one of Schumann's most dangerously sweet melodies, or the soft fragrance in the air about them that made life so bright to Carnton just then? Or was it the brown eyes so full of earnestness and truth lifted to meet his? Or, after all, was it the consciousness, which he had had from the first moment he had seen her, of a nature perfectly sympathetic with his own?

They talked a little of the plants about them, and then went back again to their own individual work and the special incidents of the week; but what did the subject matter when both felt the joy two natures of a generous mold feel in meeting?

What curious creatures we human beings are! What is our best strength but weakness? We may live lives that are noble, and such as our whole natures, guided by a reason that is in subjection to a higher power, approve, and yet in the details of that living we falter and grope and stumble and are far from sure that we are right unless we have the approval of other beings equally faulty, equally fallible, and as likely to be wrong as ourselves. And when we find a nature that, apart from volition or will, is so constituted that it is in entire sympathy with us, then comes a sense of rest and peace that is like a benediction.

It was thus that Carnton felt; Sidney was a benediction to the highest and best of his nature. And he so little knew what it meant that he would have been surprised had others not felt the same. So sure was he that her superiority was apparent to all, he would have been surprised had anyone criticised her, and he would have taken the criticism only as an evidence of the person's own degeneracy.

Others came into the fernery, and they moved away in a happy dual silence that can only come where there is perfect sympathy.

Carnton was essentially a modern missionary. Had he been born fifty years earlier he would have been a pioneer, who would have broken new ground and led exploring parties and planted missions in new countries. In fact, his work in the remote mission station in the mountains had been much of that type. He had had foundation work to do in a comparatively new place—primary schools to organize, native preachers to train and advise and reprimand, accounts to keep, and, what he liked better than all, evangelistic work in villages.

It was a great trial to give it up and come to the college and do the routine work of teaching; yet the very pioneer work which he had done made him willing and anxious to have a chance to train men to be helpers; for he had been so hindered, had so often been foiled in his plans by the lack of trained intelligent assistants, so often disappointed in the power of his native preachers to grasp fully the truth they taught, and to convey to others, even when it was intelligible to themselves, that he was ready to spend years in training minds and developing character. People who have around them and have had back of them for ages a Christian civilization can have simply no conception whatever of the deadening effect of priesthood and image-worship, whether of the Roman Catholic Church or of the Hindoo form of religion on the hearts and minds of a people; for the narrowness of outlook, the lack of comprehensiveness or grasp of mind it engenders is appalling, and to counteract these tendencies requires patient, unwearying teaching.

Though the heart of man always, when quickened by the Holy Spirit, grasps the truths of the Gospel of Christ gratefully, the mind inactive or dormant lags behind, and needs food and training and up-building.

Carnton, though he knew he had faults, felt he had a character and a plan for work and for making men nobler and better that he was willing to impress on other young men. He was strong physically, mentally, and morally, and he did his work heartily, as unto God, and not unto man. There was nothing ascetic in his plan, for he said he was a follower of Christ, who, while preaching a self-denying, self-sacrificing life, had no asceticism, and preached none. He walked and talked as though life were full of interest, as though every hour were worth living, and as though, through the grace of God, he was not only master of his work but also of himself. He had never been in love. When a strong feeling of admiration had come for this or that woman he had put it down or ignored it or kept away from the person that inspired it, believing that discretion in such matters was the better part of valor, as he had no wish to hamper his life-work by marrying. Of course, like other men, he had, down out of sight in his heart, an ideal woman whom he should meet some day and on whom he would pour out the strength of a heart that he knew might be full of a strong and worthy and enduring love when the sweet fair unknown should dawn on his life. But not in India was she going to be found. Not any strong-minded lady doctor or superintendent of a girls' school, or zenana teacher, who had control of as much and as important work as a man, and who had an office and a desk where she transacted mission business and interviewed assistants and planned and organized. O, no; but a sweet, shy, household goddess, who was to find her whole happy sphere in her home and the simple round of home duties.

· Of course, he had the highest respect for the women, both married and single, who were doing a work that no one else could do, and without whom the work would progress but slowly, and he understood that the husbands of the married lady missionaries were making the greatest possible sacrifice in allowing their wives to give their whole minds and strength, growing old before their time, to mission work ; but it was not his plan, for some way it had never seemed quite right to him, though he was at a loss to say just where it was wrong.

No, not in India was the home of his heart to begin ; but some day he too, like others, would be worn out and need a change, and then he would go back home and find some sweet woman who would complete his life and give him in exchange love for love, full measure and shaken down.

This interest in Sidney only struck him as a very common, natural sort of thing. He felt that if he must go out it was a great relief to have one so sympathetic with whom to spend the time, and beyond this he would not or did not reflect, and did not see what Mrs. Clinton saw—that he had been strangely silent out of Sidney's presence since the first day he had seen her.

The long shadows of the tamarinds stretched farther and farther across the green sward, the fronds of the palms back of the flat-roofed Baradari against the sunset sky began to look soft and gray and more feathery ; the statues half hidden by dark green shrubs had a cold look, and flushes died away from the cheeks that had glowed under the fervid sun, and perhaps under other glances as fervid.

All began to remember that the day was not half done, and still the prince stayed. The missionary parties began to melt away imperceptibly, for it was not etiquette to leave openly before his royal highness. Probably Mrs. Clinton left the most willingly of all.

She did not like all this—that is, she liked it well enough for herself, for it was quite right and proper that she should see all there was to see; but a garden party in the afternoon and a reception in the evening of the same day were too much for missionaries. It looked too much like the ordinary life of ministers at home; and if it went on this way the whole year what material would she have with which to make missionary speeches?

True, there was nothing very frivolous in groups of missionaries dividing into twos and threes and wandering about in this gay scene in their rusty browns and blacks, like an unobtrusive minor melody through the symphony of color.

She had also found that they were like Christian in *Pilgrim's Progress ;* they always carried their packs on their backs, for when she joined different groups here and there they were invariably talking of work, of new schools or of old scholars, of appointments; and there seemed a general disposition to get each other's opinions that surprised her, for she had been saying to herself—not to her husband, you may be sure—that the missionaries were self-sufficient, opinionated, and altogether too well satisfied that they were right. She also said that they were too lively; there was too much of a tendency to look at the absurd and humorous side of life, to tell funny anecdotes, and to seem to seek occasion to laugh and be amused.

She did not discover that this resentment toward them began with her little disagreement with Mrs. Mackenzie, and was intensified every time she made a suggestion to anyone that was shown to be absurd, and every time she hit the wrong nail on the head.

and every time she had to acknowledge herself beaten, as in the case of the cook and in regard to the wearing pith hats. She had a distinct feeling of being out of it all that was a constant irritation.

The strange part of it was that she had always thought and her friends had said of her that she cared nothing for position and deference and having a leadership. But as she had always had all these, who could tell how much she cared for them until she was deprived of them? It is said we are each made up of a trinity of characters—that is, what others think we are, what we think we are, and what we really are. It is a curious study to see the transition from the person made up of the two first, to the nakedness of the last, and nowhere can it be seen more clearly than in the flitting of a person from one civilization to another. It seems sometimes to involve an utter change of nature, though in reality it is only a sloughing off of the character ascribed to them—it is only the tadpole, that would have remained forever a tadpole, smothered by the environment of position and convention, emerging into the full-grown frog; and the patience that the missionaries show with the mistakes made by those " fresh in the field " leads the thoughtful to suppose that their own tadpole experience is not far enough removed for forgetfulness. If when Mrs. Clinton was watching the missionaries for weak places, for a lack of heroic endurance, and for unnecessary self-indulgences, if ever a remote suggestion was made to her consciousness that she was getting to be a different person, a person that she did not like as well as the Mrs. Clinton who had been amiable and popular and wise in America, she dismissed it at once, saying it was the country that was different; like the old Indian lost in the woods : "Injun not lost, wigwam lost. Injun here," slapping himself on his breast.

However, as time went on she was less sure about the "Injun," though she lamented the loss of the wigwam. Her resentment toward Mrs. Mackenzie was also a curious thing, and only to be explained by the fact that it is easier to forgive people anything else than the injuries, either in thought or deed, that we do them. But she kept it well under, and it amounted only to a feeling that made her a little unhappy, but did not prevent her being on friendly terms with Mrs. Mackenzie and going with her any place she wished to take her; and so after the garden party they went away together to a native Christian women's prayer meeting held by Mrs. Mackenzie.

The Bishop had found several native gentlemen who could speak English and one or two who, though not speaking it very well, could understand it and stood by interested while he conversed with those who spoke more fluently. He was loading himself with information, and was loath to go when Carnton came and reminded him that he had promised to be present at the college students' weekly prayer meeting.

Sidney also had hurried off to meet her Bible women and prepare the Bible lesson for the next day's teaching in the zenanas. Each and every one of the mission log had some especial duty, and rushed away feeling he must work all the harder for the brief idleness. Just as the Bishop and Carnton were getting into the latter's cart Mr. Miller came and asked them to drive to Nola Gange and see Shew Pershad, the boy-husband of Sitara, who was ill, and had sent for him to

come and see him; but he had a class of students in English which he could not well postpone, and would ask them to go in his place. So they drove away as fast as the pony could take them, down the one English business street, past the ruins of the old Residency, the tower of which showed darkly against the afterglow still in the sky, though the old cannon of mutiny fame at its base was lost in purple shadows.

Talking of the horrors of that dreadful time and of the chances of its ever being repeated, they were soon at the beginning of a street so narrow they were obliged to leave the cart and walk down streets where three could not walk abreast, around square corners, past tanks and drains of green and black water that made them hold their breath, and past many high mud walls in which were small wooden doors. At last they stopped before one of the latter, and Carnton, rapping, called out the usual question: "Koi hai?"

It was quickly opened by a female servant, who asked what was wanted.

"It is I, the teacher of Shew Pershad, come to inquire of his health and well-being."

The woman salaamed low and led them quickly across one corner of the small court around three sides of which the house was built and showed them into a small room, empty save for the bed on which the boy lay and a brass lamp in a niche in the wall. The inexpressible dreariness of the Indian home never struck Carnton more forcibly than now as he took Shew Pershad's hand in his and said,

"What is it, brother, that is making you so ill?"

"Nothing, only fever. I am very glad you have come; I knew you would, and I want Sitara and my mother."

This was said feebly and with the hesitating utterance that told Carnton the fever was high, even before he placed his hand on the hot forehead and felt the heavy throb of the pulse.

"What has the doctor said?—of course you have a doctor?" The last was said anxiously, for he well knew the native dislike to any road to recovery.

"I wanted the doctor of the hospital, but the people here in the house said no, but to have one of their witchcraft men to come and practice charms, and I had neither."

An exclamation of impatient disapproval escaped Carnton, and he said,

"I will see your cousins," and went out quickly.

The Bishop had stood silently in the shadow beyond the reach of the dull light of the little lamp, but he came forward and took the boy's hot hand in his, and after a word or two of greeting—for he was acquainted with his history—knelt on the mud floor by the rude bed and prayed earnestly in his deep and solemn voice for the recovery of health and for peace of mind and joy of heart to come to the poor sufferer before him, and then closed with the holy benediction, which fell with a calming force on the troubled heart. Though Shew Pershad's knowledge of English was imperfect, the strength and power of the vigorous Christian man by his bedside impressed itself and his heart grasped what his head, dulled with fever, failed to comprehend.

"May God give you the blessing of perfect faith

in him, and in his Son Jesus Christ!" Carnton, who had come in quickly, translated, as Shew Pershad did not quite understand.

"He has given it to me. We will be saved from sin and from transmigration, both I and Sitara, and afterward my mother perhaps. The great Sacrifice saves us."

"Amen," said the Bishop, and "Amen" said Carnton in his heart. Then aloud:

"I have told these people that you must have a doctor, and I am going to bring him at once, that there may be no mistake;" and beckoning to the Bishop they went out.

When they were outside Carnton said:

"The boy is very ill, and unless he is looked after at once he will be gone almost before we know it. The careless way the natives live, their utter disregard of the laws of health, their indifference to contagion, and the absence of animal food, make them swift and easy prey to any disease that comes along. I will drive to Miss Whitlow's and ask her to take the boy's wife down there; for at least she will be some company for him, and can get him water and see that his food is brought at the proper time. If you will take entire charge of the prayer meeting, I shall be greatly obliged. Field will help you."

The Bishop promised, and the doctor came, as did also Sitara. Miss Whitlow brought some corn flour and arrowroot, as she knew that probably nothing had been given him but curry and other things impossible for an invalid.

The doctor's opinion was not given, as he said he must wait and see him again.

CHAPTER XI.

THE TALUKDAR'S RECEPTION.

IN the old days after the Mohammedan conquest of Hindostan, when Delhi was the capital and the center of the power and magnificence of the Mogul empire, Oude was one of the twelve "sūbas," or districts, into which the conquered territory was divided by the Emperor Akbar. From being simply a "sūba," with a governor appointed by the emperor, it was gradually transformed by the energy and ambition of its governors into something like a state, with a nawab wazir at its head. Later on the nawabs became kings, and Lucknow their capital, where they had a court renowned even in the Orient for its extravagance and splendor. Different kings built palaces for themselves, and the locality where the principal palaces are congregated is called "Kaiser Bagh," from the fact that one of the kings said he would form a dynasty after the plan of the Cæsars, but which should rival theirs. Now only old palaces used for various government offices, for club libraries and museums, and the name "kaiser"—a corruption of Cæsar—remain to tell of his foiled hopes and ambitions. The largest of all, the old zenana palace, built by Wazid Ali Shah, the last reigning king, for his thousand wives, is a huge structure extending originally around four sides of a park in which were pleasure-houses, pavilions, fountains, shrines, and a small lake over which was thrown a bridge. It is indeed a huge palace, but a large one was necessary, that each woman could have a suite of rooms for herself and servants.

When Wazid Ali Shah was transferred to Calcutta, Oude taken from him and annexed to the British territory, the women were scattered far and wide, and now part of the palace is empty and part rented to various people who choose to live there, and the principal pleasure-house in the inclosed park, owned by the Maharani of Balrampore, has come to be the place where the native princes, or "talukdars," give their receptions. This is called the White Baradari, and consists of a house with several large rooms built well up from the ground. The large, lofty central room is supported by pillars; around this are side rooms, and if more space is needed the wide arched verandas, which are arrived at by flights of steps, are inclosed. The building has the appearance of being of white marble, though only the finishings are of this, and when lighted and filled with people it has a most splendid appearance.

As the Bishop, Mrs. Clinton, Miss Whitlow, and Miss May drove in at one of the great gates the park was a blaze of light, and the roads and walks were one mass of moving humanity.

Miss May, the Bishop, and his wife were all going to this reception for the same reason—that is, because they had never been; and Miss Whitlow was going because she had been before, and Mrs. Clinton preferred having some one with her who knew the etiquette of the place; but most of the missionaries had found it impossible to come from one reason or another.

The sides of the zenana palace had been covered with bamboo lattice-work, the driveways were fenced with the same about three feet high, and in the corner of each square formed by the intersecting bamboo was a little terra cotta cup with about an ounce of oil and a lighted wick.

Over the gateway opposite to the one used as an entrance lights formed words which blazed a welcome. The trees and shrines were hung with colored lanterns, and the walks and drives were filled with natives and some Europeans, baboos, teachers and merchants and clerks; in fact, all the great mass of the population were out to see the Walayati prince that they thought might in the years to come bring them weal or woe, but whose death knell has since sounded around the whole world, which thrilled with sympathy for the grief-stricken mother; to see also their own princes in all the glory of their richest clothes, and last and least the bold Mem Sahibs who came with uncovered heads and—it was reported—uncovered necks and shoulders. Policemen in their red pugris cleared the way before them, and, leaving their wraps in the carriage and showing their cards of invitation to the sergeant stationed at the foot of the stairs, they went up the red carpeted steps between two rows of soldiers standing as stiff and straight as statues, the light pouring through the open doors gleaming on the bayonets at their sides.

Mrs. Clinton's party had come early, hoping to get away a little earlier by so doing, and they selected a seat where they could observe well without seeming unduly curious. Few English were yet present, but many of the native swells had arrived; only princes, of course—not a princess in all the number could appear. They, the princesses and native ladies, were already asleep at home dreaming of the glories their lords were seeing, and hoping for a full description of the festivity when they should once more have left Lucknow and entered their elephant howdahs or their bullock-carts for their palaces in the various parts of Oude, and when the tediousness of the journey should be relieved by hearing what had happened in their visit to Lucknow. The princes were dressed much as they were at the garden party—velvet and gold, diamonds, rubies, and emeralds, and the light blazing from the chandeliers was reflected from all this, and blazed and bragged of the wealth of the small principalities represented. They talked little, but stood about watching others come—now and then a party of English, now and then some natives; but soon the stream of people became continuous—here a matron, well satisfied that the daughters following her were all one could wish, from fair hair banged low over their foreheads to evening dresses made by native men; behind them a rajah with his fingers covered with flashing jewels which were repeated and multiplied on his turban and on his belt, or kamarband; then the handsome face and figure of the wife of the general commanding the division, followed by the fair-haired wife of the commissioner, and the homely face of the surgeon general's wife; then a party of missionaries with their high-necked, long-sleeved dresses, looking very foreign and out of place among the bare arms and shoulders of the other women. They were followed by Lady Huff and Lady Puff, and colonels and captains and judges without number, and their wives.

Then the band struck up, and there was a rattle of arms, a general movement, and a Government House party appeared, the prince walking with the governor, who looked perfectly fagged, and only kept up by the knowledge that this was the last "tamasha" on the list, and a few more hours would see the end of the ticklish business he had on hand.

The prince only looked a little more tired than ever, doubtfully watching his keeper as to plan of procedure.   The usual address was given by the talukdars and responded to briefly, and then the fireworks began with their customary rush and fuss and explosions.

The native of India loves fireworks.   Their light, their flash, and their cheapness suit him; he revels in them and cheerfully goes without food, tightens his kamarband to make up for the loss, and is happy in watching them as they flash for a moment and are gone.

The prince and his party were in a draped balcony, and those who were not near him tried to get near some one that was near him.

Again Carnton, who had done all possible for Shew Pershad, is near Sidney.   She is unthinking, he is unthinking, but both are elated and happy.   He begins to be sure it is a good thing for a missionary to leave his work and go out now and then among people; it brightens him up so much.   He had no habit of introspection, else he would have tracked this feeling to its source.   But his healthy, hearty, strong nature let him live and move and have his being without hunting down all his feelings and sensations.   Herein, however, lay danger to his plan for his life-work. So they talked, standing near Mrs. Clinton and the Bishop and Miss Whitlow, the Bishop moralizing on various things, asking how the money for the entertainment was provided, who kept up the park, to whom the old palace and the Baradari belonged, all of which Miss Whitlow answered, drawing Sidney into the conversation. Then Carnton wandered away. There was a nawab he wished to see, whose opinion he wanted on some question the Bishop had asked, and he mingled with the rajahs and nawabs in order to find him. Standing here and there in the semi-darkness he overheard bits of conversation pertaining to the prince—like this:

"When the queen dies, then her son will come to the throne; but he is ill, and if this prince becomes interested in us it will pay us for all."

From another group:

"It is costing too much; the price is very heavy. Once the viceroy comes, as he leaves India, and we give him a tamasha; once the new viceroy comes, as he enters India, and we give him a tamasha. Now the prince comes and we give him a tamasha, all in one year. It is too heavy."

"True, true, but what will you do? They must come."

Then below this he heard the soft, deep voice of his friend Syed Mohammed Khan, "Yes, yes, they are different;" and then a voice from a shorter, younger figure, whom a flash of rocket showed to be his son, still a boy, but Carnton remembered having been bidden to his wedding, which was to come off next month.

"But the English—they wish our women to be like theirs. The Miss Sahib who comes to teach mother and my sisters tells them of many things that English women do; they go about alone, and are never afraid. If our women learn to read and write will they also want to put away their chuddars and go about with uncovered heads in their carriages like these women to-night, and also uncovered shoulders ? "

" No, you do not understand, my son. The Miss Sahib is here, but she is not like these. The mission people, did you not see, are covered. I do not myself understand all their ways. In the blessed time when the King Wazid Ali was still here and glory was everywhere present I thought them bad and dangerous. I feared our women seeing them would be less amenable to our authority, and would go about the streets and talk with other men than their husbands, but not so. I have now these many years known the mission people, and they make our women better. They give them something to do and make them less like children."

" But to-day even the Miss Mellen Sahib, she walks about among all the people with our Carnton Sahib, and talks and smiles. She also teaches our women in the zenanas, but it can never be that we allow our women thus to talk to men."

" They are different, and with different customs, and among them it is allowed that they converse often with each other when they are to marry. It is a good way, for then they know each the mind and disposition of the other. and can more easily be happy together."

Carnton came forward quickly.

" Forgive me, Nawab Sahib, I have been hearing what you have said to your son. I am glad you see so clearly. Were all your people as clear-sighted, the Hindoos would not now have outstripped you in the matter of education and government positions."

"True words, Padri Carnton, but there is a better time coming for us. When our women can teach their sons something besides ghost stories and old women's tales there is hope for us, for the Mussulman is ever a cleverer man than the Hindoo. The children of this my son will see it and partake of it, for has not the good Miss Lowe Sahib taught his future wife for many years? and she is bright and quick to see and think. You will not forget that you are to come to his wedding next month?"

"O, no; I could not forget it, my friend. If I am well I shall surely be there, and if you would not mind I would like to bring the Bāra Padri Sahib and his wife, who have come from America to see India and her people. He is very interested in all your national customs."

"By all means; we shall be very happy indeed."

Carnton bid him good-night and followed the stream of people who were entering the side rooms, where tables were spread with refreshments, soda-water, lemonade, coffee, tea, cakes, jellies, sweets, and, Carnton saw with a pang, wines. The aversion with which he had always looked on the use of wine in India amounted to extreme intolerance. Joining the Bishop, who was having a cup of coffee in a small room with the other missionaries, he said in fierce indignation:

"We show them a better religion and a higher civilization, and then men and women calling themselves Christians practice things that a good Mussul-

man thinks beneath him. He would die before he
would allow his wife or daughters to be seen dressed
as some women here are dressed, and he would consider himself unworthy of the religion of Mohammed
if he drank wine."

"Yes," said the Bishop, "it is one of the serious
drawbacks."

"Drawbacks! It is worse, it is almost hopeless to
try to teach them Christ when they think they must
do these things if they become followers of his. A
Mohammedan said once to me: 'Is your religion better? I think not. I see every day Christians reeling
through the bazars. Shall we also have to drink wine
when you have converted us?' Of course it was
said in derision."

"The Hindoos, I believe, have no objection to
wine?"

"No, though they also connect wine-drinking with
Christianity. A young Hindoo, bright and keen,
came to me one day and said:

"'I am English. Give me work.'

"'English?' I said, 'how is that? I would not
have taken you to be English.'

"'Look at my clothes, are they not English? I
drink wine, and I say "damn."'" Sometimes I feel as
though I cannot restrain my indignation; I think I
have seen all there is to be seen, and I will go, for I
have had enough of this side of life;" and with a
hasty good night to all he left and went home to
think.

He had ignored the nawab's remark on his attention to Sidney, but that did not mean he had not
heard and understood, nor did it mean that he did

not feel as though he had had a small shock of earth-
quake.

He told himself that he had been careless in forgetting that all he did was of great interest to his native
friends; that they, with their civilization, could not
comprehend the motives that underlay the actions of
a European; that of course they could not understand
that although he did not wish to marry in India he
craved friends, and it would be hard indeed if he
could not have such a sweet friend as Miss Mellen
simply because they could not understand there might
be friendship between men and women. He told
himself this and much more of the same kind, but it
did not prevent him from being unconsciously joyful
at the thought of a possibility of her caring for him,
at the thought of their names being connected in that
way, and he began to wonder if the nawab had seen
anything in her face or manner to lead him to the
startling conclusion at which he had arrived, which
was a decided wandering from the point on which he
wished to think. That point was how, without injury
to her, to disabuse the minds of his native friends of
the thought of anything serious between him and Sidney; but some way he could not keep his mind where he
wanted it. It would dwell on the varying color in her
face, of her devotion to her work, of the difference
between her and all other women he knew, and even
on such trifles as the color of her bonnet, and her interest in and love of flowers. He wondered if he
might not now and then send her some as a friend,
which was a decided step in the wrong direction, if he
wished to remain in single-eyed devotion to his work.

There was a group of servants outside the cookhouse, with their pugris off and sitting, so to speak, in slippers and shirt-sleeves, which for a native means a good deal more, or rather a good deal less. The hookah was being passed around, and in a little way off were two or three others gathered listening to some one playing on a sitár.

Their voices were perfectly distinct to Carnton as he lay on his bed in the room above them, but he paid no attention until his own name was mentioned.

"Yes, Carnton Sahib is good enough, since one must have a sahib, but then you see he has his gods also, as we do, which accounts for his pleasant disposition" (kush mezagh).

Carnton raised his head in astonishment and wondered if he had heard aright.

"On, Bala Ram, do you think we are babies that you tell us this? No sahibs have their gods as we do. They are followers of Jesus Christ."

"But I tell you," said Bala Ram with conviction, "he has. There is one, Shnton, whose house is on the mantel, and there is another, Omer, who wrote one of Carnton Sahib's sacred books. He also sits over the fire. It is that they perhaps are the gods of fire, only Shnton is the American god and not the English."

Carnton was shaking his bed. Washington and Homer come to be the gods of fire, along with Agni! It was so funny that he could hardly stop to listen.

"It may be true, but the English and the Americans—who can tell, with all their mad ways?—who can tell what they worship? There is this thing at least that is true, the mission people all worship chairs, for do they not always, when at their morning puja, kneel to their chairs, their faces lifted toward them? And also our people, when they become Christians, do they not at once purchase chairs and put them in their houses that they also may kneel to them? And you see how much kinder and better these sahibs are who have chair-worship than the soldier people who never have any gods. Your words are true, and it is far better to have service with such as are rational and have gods as we do."

There was a silence then, broken only by the sound of the water in the basin of the hookah, and the sickening odor of the smoke filled the air while Carnton marveled anew at the power of the native mind to draw original and startling conclusions from the simplest and most ordinary acts, and he resolved that before another sun set "Shuton" and "Omer" should alike be broken in a thousand pieces; and with this was mingled a little indignation that Bala Ram, who had been with him for two years, should so misunderstand him.

He was just falling to sleep when Rokewood's name floated up.

"Yes, Rokewood Sahib is quite out of his mind; though they are all out of their minds, as far as that goes, and Rokewood Sahib is only a little queerer than the rest."

"That is as I said, brother. It is all one, and he is a good sahib, though he is of low caste and without the proper respect a sahib should have. It is, of a surety, that he is of the carpenter or sweeper caste."

"Hear the words of our brother the wise," said Dabe Din, in derision. "He, without doubt, has been to the sahib's country, and hence can tell of what caste the sahib people are."

14

"But no—" a little abashed at the laugh which followed the last speech ; "but even the blind can see that he is of low caste, else why did not the Lord Sahib call him to-day to the tamasha to see the son of the great queen? and, also, why does he have a sweeper cook, and why should he carry his own bag, and why will not the other sahibs allow him to ride in their garis? Though they will let him put his bag in the gari, Rokewood Sahib himself is not allowed, he is of such low degree."

"True," said Dabe; "but now the sweeper cook is a Christian. Still, who can tell what all these strange men mean? Not I, surely."

When Carnton, before going to work the next day, made a pretense of clearing his room, and cleared out old newspapers and various other things that accumulate in a bachelor's room, and also threw those marble busts far out toward the cookhouse so energetically that they broke in many pieces, he found out that they all trembled with fear, saying,

"For once our pleasant-natured sahib must be angry, O, very angry indeed, when he thus would smash and destroy his gods." And for days they did their work with care and fear and trembling.

Then was his soul for a time filled with despair. The utter impossibility of their ever coming to any understanding of the truth seemed to come over him like a wave of the sea—of the impossibility of men of such low intelligence ever being brought out into light; and he had to recall, in order to cheer himself up, some of the marvelous instances of those that had increased in intelligence after being converted, and he could name among them hundreds of

A NATIVE PREACHER.

"AYAH," OR NATIVE NURSE.

YOUNG BOY.

NATIVE WOMAN.

men he was glad and proud to know were called Christians.

Not sleeping well, he rose early and again took the doctor down to Shew Pershad. Just why he felt uneasy and troubled about his young friend he could not say; but there was no doubt that he was decidedly uneasy, for all through the festivities of the night before, and even through these startling thoughts of Sidney, every now and again the fever-bright eyes and pinched face of the boy rose before him.

It takes about a minute and a half to form a lasting friendship with any of the people of India, provided the conditions are right, and the conditions had been in favor of Carnton and Shew Pershad being friends, for Carnton had heard of the Lochinvar-like raid the boy had made when determined to have his wife removed from the narrowing influences which surrounded her, and was ready to give him warm-hearted sympathy. This was repaid with something like adoration from Shew Pershad, to whom the tall, vigorous frame, the fair hair and eyes, the genial, magnetic presence of Carnton were almost godlike, and from knowing him he said he could better see how Jesus Christ, who was strong and powerful, could care for each and every one; for if he, a human being, could be so good, how much more was it possible for a divine being, for Carnton was, after all, only human, and not divine.

Most people liked Shew Pershad. He had a brave, simple way of meeting the truth gladly; in fact, he seemed sometimes to divine it where others would only see a mist of falsehood. It was a sharp blow to Carnton when the doctor said that there was little chance of recovery unless some unexpected turn of the fever came soon. Still, though it was a shock, yet some way it was not unexpected. He was not so much surprised as filled with sorrow.

Remaining a while to look after him, he learned from Sitara that the witchcraft man had been there, unknown to the patient, and had gone through his performances and tried the quality of his various charms, but ascribed their ineffectiveness, as did also their priest, to the fact of his having become a Christian, the gods being too angry at this to relent.

When the people in the house, who were distant relations and not at all fond of the boy, saw he was sure to die, they wanted, after the usual custom, to take up the bed and carry it down by the Gumti and let him die there by the sacred river. But his cousins said they would have no such thing done; it belonged to the old days of ignorance and barbarism, and they hinted that the doctor, who was a good Hindoo, would have something to say about it, and would probably make trouble if they persisted, for he had studied under an English doctor, and, besides, got his pay from the English government. The people did not like it; these new days and new ways were not for them; it was unlucky to have a person die in the house, and much more unlucky for a wretched Christian, who was now suffering from the anger of their god. Their family priest, a fat, well-fed old fellow, and well paid by the family, which was not poor, tried to force them, and there was much discussion; but the cousins held firm and said they would report to the judge; so poor Shew Pershad was allowed to die in peace, and Sitara, hardly knowing the meaning of death or bereavement, wept as she saw her mother-in-law and her mother, who had arrived, weeping. It had been a sore trial to them when their son and son-in-law became a Christian, and this was the thing they might have expected, and the priest strengthened this belief by repeating many proverbs and quoting from old traditions. When the priest governs the family, whether he be Hindoo, guru, or Roman Catholic padre, superstition is the whip by which he controls, and, strange to say, women, who are always credited with such correct instincts and intuitions, are easily led where the superior judgment of men rebels.

Both Carnton and Miller visited Shew Pershad, and gave him words of comfort, and he brightened much as the end drew near. He told Carnton of the plan he had had to go back to his village and teach them the Gospel of Christ, and with this also to teach them civilization, better ways to till their ground, to provide against famine, and better ways of building their houses; he had thought of it all, and it was hard to give it up; but Sitara, she was so quick, so intelligent, so gentle, she might go if she were trained. It was his wish for her to stay in some mission school until she had learned much, and then go back and tell them from him all the truth. He was too weak to think or to be spoken to about all the difficulties in the way; but Carnton promised to see Miss Whitlow and have all done as he wished, if possible. He then asked that he might be buried as a Christian, and the next night the gentle spirit passed away. It was sad, yet Carnton felt glad he had known him, glad that he himself was there to help just such rare simple natures, and it gave him more hope than ever for the people he loved.

When he spoke of Shew Pershad's wishes the cousins told him it would be impossible. The mother was satisfied to consider him back in caste, as ceremonies had been performed over him, unknown to him, before his death. The family would not hear of it, and declared they would appeal to the law, as the mother was perfectly rabid already, and there would only be a disgraceful hand-to-hand encounter if the Christians persisted; and so it came that a straggling procession in the old Hindoo style followed the body wrapped in a new white sheet and placed on a litter. There were in the procession all the relations and many of their caste, and there were a loud drum and cymbals and a horn or two, and much wild wailing of voices crying, "Rām, Rām, ki jai."

As Miss Whitlow watched them pass by her house, the hot wind whirling clouds of dust about them, the dreariness of it all came over her anew, dreary from the sound, dreary from its being forced, and most dreary of all because of the entire mockery it was in being done for one who, had he been alive, would have repudiated it all.

Though it was a long way to the burning ghat by the Gumti their voices did not tire, but mingled with the wail of the wind as it rushed madly down the hot, partially dry river-bed, over the square-built funeral pyre that stood stolidly waiting for its burden of clay that so short time ago was quick with the precious spirit now far from beyond all power of ignorance and superstition. And even though the body had to be subjected to the usual rites by the priest, and by the nearest male relative, who lighted the fire that reduced it to a charred and blackened torso which was tossed into the river, what did it really matter when it was so well, so very well, with the spirit?

And Sitara? Miss Whitlow went at once to bring her away according to Shew Pershad's wish, but the little door in the wall was shut and locked, and all was still. No answer was made to her question, "Koi hai?" and she looked at the door as though she would question it in lieu of anyone appearing. She felt that the hot wind, driving the sand against the door, knew as much as she did, or perhaps ever would, of Sitara's whereabouts, so perfectly helpless is the European when the Hindoo shuts the door of his castle against him.

Other days, haunted by the remembrance of her bright face and by the remembrance of Shew Pershad's simple, faithful life, she would go there, but the door was always locked, and there was no appearance of it being inhabited. The cousin had found another place in which to stay, and could not or would not tell what had become of the poor little child-widow, swallowed up by the dark surging sea of native life.

CHAPTER XII.

HOUSEKEEPING CARES.

THERE was a consultation in the Clinton household one morning. The Bishop had been over to the college, where he spent much of his time, and Mrs. Clinton and Lillian had been to the annual prize distribution to the pupils of the girls' day schools of the mission. Both she and Lillian had enjoyed it very much. It was held in the native church, the door having had a covered way improvised so that zenana women could get out of their dhoolies and ekkas and garis without being seen by any chance passers-by, every man employed about the place being first sent off. The room was nearly full, chiefly of Mohammedan women and girls, though there were some Hindoos, and all in their best silks and jewels and embroideries. Each recited selections from the Bible hymns and the Ten Commandments. One from each school read an essay or recited poetry, and one read the history of the schools and spoke in a commendatory and grateful way of each lady missionary who had superintended them. The government inspector of the schools, a clever and capable Eurasian lady, who had been educated in mission school sat at Mrs. Clinton's side and translated.

It was all very hopeful and interesting, and it was with the greatest pleasure that Mrs. Clinton, with

Lillian's help, awarded the prizes, most of which had been sent out by children's mission bands at home. Lillian felt a new interest in these same children's bands, and secretly resolved to work harder when she returned to America. Then they had gone home in the usual hired gari to breakfast, which was late, and a late breakfast in a treacherous climate means great exhaustion and a chance of other and worse things ; so the family consulted.

The days were all so full that they hardly had time to talk unless time was taken. The Bishop was in great and constant demand, and Mrs. Clinton in no less. They seemed, as Miss Whitlow said, to supply a long-felt want, for there was always a little help needed; some extra impulse to be given to especial or new lines of work, and then they were always glad of help in the regular services in the two churches. So much and so important was the work each day that the housekeeping, and even Lillian, was left rather in the lurch; but for a few days things had been too bad and called for a halt.

There were three points to be considered. First, it was plain that if Mrs. Clinton was to be out doing schools and meetings and other things twice or three times a day she could do absolutely nothing else. Was she to do mission work or housework ?

"Mission work, of course," decided the Bishop.

"Very well, that means another man to do the dusting, watch the house, and make tea while the cook goes out in the morning."

"Very well, then, let it be another man, and let us hope we may have things in time and be relieved from the annoyance of having the house uncared for," said the Bishop; and the first point was settled.

The next point was Lillian. She could not go everywhere with her mother, as it was exhausting the child, and was for many reasons not wise. But she must go with her or have a woman to stay with her at home. There was no other way.

"Very well," said the Bishop, "if there is no other way, then of course there *is* no other way, and the woman must come; for I also can see that it will not do for Lillian to go about all day. She is already looking the worse for it."

Now the third point. They were paying out more each day than the cost of owning a horse and gari, losing time and risking infection, and getting fleas and other things in the hired gari. It had been clearly shown them sometime earlier that where there was a necessity of going to all parts of a city spread over thirty-six square miles walking was out of the question, even would the hot winds and sun permit, which they did not.

The Bishop disposed of this third point by saying he had already made inquiries and got Mackenzie to do so, for a second-hand gari and a serviceable horse. And then they sat down to their tardy breakfast.

Do not for a moment suppose that Mrs. Clinton had given up her struggle or that she did not still feel a little "out" with Mrs. Mackenzie, or that Mrs. Mackenzie forgot. O, no; but there was so much to be done that things which were not of the very first importance got crowded out or driven aside, though she meant ultimately to go to the bottom of everything, and while she yielded the points of two more persons who were to do the work she had the feeling that the battle was not yet lost. These two, the khidmatgar and the woman to stay with Lillian, were only two, and her number was still less than Mrs. Mackenzie's, and she meant to keep it so. There were other points about which she felt sure she could prove Mrs. Mackenzie in the wrong, points enough to give her a comfortable, self-satisfied feeling.

The Bishop seemed so absorbed in the work he had on hand that it was difficult to interest him in the very things in which she had expected to have difficulty in restraining his condemnation, and she felt aggrieved a little to think she after all was having to do what *he* had come to do.

The Bishop was not asleep or indifferent. He had a mind that did not occupy itself with details, but took things largely, catching the salient points of a scheme slowly, perhaps, but rather surely. The size and extent and foundation of each department of the work engaged his full attention, and it was impossible that his mind could dwell on unimportant and petty ways and means; and he felt some little impatience at his wife's insisting on appealing to him with regard to every change she made. But she was too wise to make all these changes and advances without getting his sanction and having him understand they were necessary, as she knew there would come a time in the future for summing up experiences.

Not the least of a housekeeper's trials in India is the grappling with a foreign language. The men among whom her work is divided all know more or less of her language, while she does not understand one word of theirs. This is enough to keep her from starving, but it also places her more effectually in their hands and leaves her more perfectly at their mercy.

Mrs. Clinton soon found that she must learn the names of some things at least for which there were no English equivalents. So, without intending to study the language, she got a Roman Urdu and English dictionary, and finding the nouns unexpectedly easy she learned a long list of them, as well as some easy sentences, and then began. She told a man to bring her a large fine house when she only wanted an ounce of butter; she asked for a child to lay on top of a bed of coals when she wanted wood; she told her husband she saw the girls at the Lal Bagh school eating grass houses when she meant the round flat cakes which are their common food; she complained to the cook that the bread was an "old man" when she only meant it was not fresh; and she asked the butcher what "time it was by the calf's hat," when she wished to know the price of a calf's head. This latter she would never acknowledge even though Carnton was coming up the steps and heard the bargaining with the man at the end of the veranda.

There was never a smile from those gentle, dark-eyed people, and even the man with the calf's head understood, which proves two things: First, that they are a superior race of people, and, second, that they have had much practice in understanding strange and curious forms of their own language as used by English-speaking people.

If when congenial friends and caste brethren are smoking the hookah together, the stories of their Mem Sahibs' efforts at Hindoostanee furnish food for much derision, and their Punch and Judy shows are formed on the Sahib's mistakes and his treatment of the servants, what then? It is a very small and harmless recompense to them, for all they must suffer in keeping their faces grave and solemn when they would give half their wages to be able to laugh.

When Mrs. Clinton first arrived in India she felt happy in seeing the soft-voiced, white-robed servants moving quietly about, cleaning and putting the house in order, decorating the table with flowers, bringing the food already cooked to the house, and then at night, after every thing was done, closing the doors softly and vanishing to their own houses, there to cook their own food, or to eat it after their wives had cooked it.

It seemed to her that at last she had found the paradise for woman—a place where she could be in harmony with her environments, a place where she could bid carking household cares begone. and, with her mind and body free, do whatever seemed best. What books might be read and even written! what old accomplishments might be raked up! and the mission work that could be done seemed to stretch in alluring endless perspective before her, if only she had not come on a mission of reform, and if she could only settle down with the accepted number of men that most people had. Then, after all her wearisome and unsuccessful attempts to reduce the number, she finally had to surrender, backed by episcopal authority, and had nearly the usual number. She even then found that things in India, as elsewhere, are not what they seem. In succumbing to the usual number she hoped to find relief and to be able to do

much mission work and much visiting and **write**
many cheering, interesting **letters to** the **elect** ladies
in America interested in missions.   She had been a
good housekeeper **at** home, **using her quick** brain to
simplify work, and **to** do the most in **a given** time
with a given amount of strength ; but it was **a** wearing existence, and one which she had often wished
could **be less** so, and **yet** she **knew** of no woman of
any social position in her own land, and with children,
who had a **less** harassing life.   But she thought when
she first saw the Indian households that here, with
the same money she spent **on** her home in America,
on furnishing, repairs, on table and servants, she
might have an ideal home—beautiful, comfortable,
and all arranged and **kept up with the** noiseless, **fric-**
tionless, turbaned, salaaming, and respectful servants
of Hindostan.

Vain dream !   There **is no such paradise for**
women on the round earth.   Their lot **is far** removed
from paradise, **and** nowhere **is it farther** than when
served by these same respectful, soft-eyed **Pir Buxes**
and Baba Lals.   **Not** that, considering everything,
they are not in their way remarkably good servants.
Not that Mrs. Clinton did not acknowledge that each
one, when once understood, was less trying **in him-**
self than Bridget or Tom, but there were so many,
and each one's work depended on others, and the in-
fluence of climate, and one thing and another, **were so**
adverse, that to feel comfort and rest was impossible.
The mind was always braced for some disaster, some
failure of carrying out orders, some broken dish **or**
ruined treasure, some lack of coming up in time, so
that her nerves began to be in a very strange **state,**

and she could agree with an old missionary who told her that if she went on with the same anxiety for her house and housekeeping much longer she would "lose her religion."

Her anxiety on this score was as much for her husband as for herself, for they both loved order and regularity and promptness, and the one reason of her unusual success as a housekeeper at home and of the great amount of literary work her husband had done was their habits of regularity and promptness; so this irregularity was telling on him too.

"I really believe," he said one day as he had looked at his watch twenty times in a half-hour, "I really believe that I shall be tempted to chastise that cook if he does not bring breakfast more promptly."

Mrs. Clinton regarded him with horror. Was her husband losing his mind! Surely sometimes she had felt as though she was going mad, but her calm, unemotional husband—a bishop of the Church—beating a fellow-being!

He smiled a little at her look, and said: "I hope you do not think I would do it in anger, but what can we do? My morning's work is quite ruined by this delay. I cannot resort to the usual method and keep back part of his pay, for you say his wife is ill, and so he especially needs what little he gets."

His wife did not lose her shocked expression.

"Do you not see," he said, "they are like children, and should be punished as children. There is not the least excuse for Nǎbi Bux having breakfast an hour late. Now see;" and he opened the door, which was closed as usual to keep out the hot wind, and went on the veranda and lifted the heavy canvas that was also

15

there to bar the wind and dust. "Balek," he called at the top of his voice to the khidmatgar, and an echo of a voice was heard above the howling of the wind:

"Your honor?"

"Is breakfast ready?"

"I have brought it, your honor," and the Bishop stepped back, dropping the canvas and closing the door, and sat down with a confused swaying of blood in his head.

"His answer is nearly the first Hindoostanee word I learned. You know Welton, that old white-haired saint? I heard him call for his breakfast one day, and the answer was, as usual, 'Liya'—that is, 'I have brought it.'

"'Liar,' said Welton, laughing; 'of course you need not tell me that. I am reminded of the fact about fifty times a day.'

"He explained then that 'liya,' which sounded very much like 'liar,' meaning 'it is brought,' is the politest possible answer a servant can give when you call for anything, and politeness in their idea of faithful service always comes before truthfulness. He said he never heard it without being tempted to give them the word in return that sounded the nearest like it."

Then they waited and waited, and finally, faint and half exhausted and patience all gone, Balek came, bringing the usual dish of cracked wheat and jug of milk, the milk a trifle sour.

"Why is this milk sour?"

"I do not know, your honor."

"Did you boil it?"

"Yes, your honor, but the day is very warm. Perhaps this is the reason."

"If that were the reason it would be sour every day. No, Balek," Mrs. Clinton added, "you are taking bad milk, and keeping the money which I give you for good milk for yourself. But you will get no pay for it when it is sour."

"As it pleases your honor."

"No, it is not as it pleases me. I do not do it because it pleases me, but because we cannot starve, and we cannot use such milk as this."

While they were eating the cracked wheat with sugar alone Balek brought the red pottery surahi, or bottle, with drinking-water, and poured it out into the glasses with a gurgle that sounded cool, though it was not.

Taking up the glass to drink, the Bishop stopped short of putting it to his lips.

"Balek, what does this mean?" he said, sternly. "Look now, look well. Do you wish us all to die?"

Balek took it with apparent surprise and held it up to the dim light from the glass in the door. Even his face fell a little, for there were twenty or more of the larvæ of the mosquito wriggling around in the water. Mrs. Clinton then examined her glass with the same result.

"Have I not told you over and over again to look sharply after the filter? Was this water boiled?"

"Yes, your honor, with my own hands."

"Did you put new charcoal in the filter?"

"Yesterday I did, Mem Sahib."

"Did I not tell you that you must bring me two pice every time I found anything in the water like this?"

" Yes, your honor," sullenly.

" Well, you are disobeying constantly, and I can
overlook some things ; but when you, by carelessness,
endanger our lives, what can I do ? I must punish
you in some way ; therefore you may go and get two
pice and give them to me."

Balek stood silent and sullen a moment, then said :
" No, Mem Sahib, I won't-do-it ; " the last three words
pronounced as one.

Mrs. Clinton, without looking at her husband, rose
and picked up his light bamboo cane which stood by
his hat and umbrella, and quietly gave the man a tap
on his bare calf with it.

" Now will you go ?" she asked, quietly, but firmly.

" Yes, Mem Sahib, I will," and he fled.

Mrs. Clinton looked up at her husband, who was
regarding her with a gaze she could feel before she
encountered it.

" I am acting on your suggestion that they should
be treated like children," she said, with a demure
smile, even though her face was flushed. " I never
allowed a child to disobey me, and it had to be dealt
with at once."

" Yes," doubtfully ; " still, if told by the servants,
it would have a strange sound to people, especially at
home."

" I know, but I have temporized too long with these
men. Many women tell me they scold and storm, and
in that way make them obey, but I cannot and will
not do that, so I must do what I can do, even if it
means using a stick now and then."

The Bishop sighed. It was all true. He had seen
gentlewomen get into a perfect rage and excuse it by

saying it was the only way they could get anything done, and most women in India had fallen into at least a garrulous tone when expostulating with them. It was to be deplored, but the Bishop thought, in the language of the people, " Kya karega "—" What can you do ? "

Balek returned quickly with the piee, and was most assiduous and deft-handed in his attention.

But after prayers he presented himself to the Bishop in his study and said :

" I will go. I not stay. It was never known that the Mem Sahib beat me. The Sahib will always, if he please, beat, but not the Mem Sahib."

" Does the Mem Sahib ever give you trouble if you do your work? Is she not always kind to you ? "

" Much, Sahib, much."

" Very well, you may stay or go; but if you give her trouble she shall beat you when she likes."

He did stay, and there was a general brightening up and coming to time all around. The cook was told the same was in store for him if he did not have breakfast and dinner at the appointed hour. And that was the last and only time Mrs. Clinton was obliged to punish a man other than by a few piee cut from his wages now and then; but she never told Mrs. Mackenzie how she conquered her unruly household.

This does not mean that it ended the cook's attempts to take double the right prices from her. How was she to know just how many annas a fowl ought to cost, whether five or ten, and she could not dispute the price of beef when she was not quite sure what was the right price. The sort of continual struggle that is involved in trying to pay the correct value of the daily purchases for the table is, to a conscientious person of limited income, nothing short of maddening. Purchases of fruit, vegetables, and meat must be made each day, and as these prices vary with the season, and still more according to the income and social position of the consumers, it is impossible not to be cheated a certain amount each day. And when a new Mem Sahib comes to the place all in the bazar conspire to keep her from knowing the correct prices.

The person living in the house immediately preceding her may have had a large income or have been regardless of expenditure. Very well; the incoming Mem Sahib is expected to pay the same prices, even though, having a large family and a small income, she may try to pay just the right price and no more. She finds herself avoided, and she feels it in the air that she is regarded with dislike and aversion by all the men who come to bring her bread and milk, meat and fruit, by her servants and all she has to do with. Perhaps, if she persists long enough in a straightforward, kind, consistent way, she may after a while inspire confidence, and they may come to understand that she is just and will not take advantage of them, and this they really prefer to a large profit one day and a beating down and loss another.

It was annoying, bewildering, and harassing to Mrs. Clinton, who especially wished to bring her expenditure within a certain limit, and each day she felt that some way, with all her care and anxiety, she was going beyond the line. Each day she knew, in spite of all her efforts, the food on the table was not what it ought to be, and each night she went to bed with the unsatisfied feeling that the day had been, in some sense, a failure.

The most harassing thing of all was the knowledge that they were not always getting food that was wholesome or even safe to eat. First, there was the milk. It was—even if not sour—thin, watery, blue, and smelled of smoke from a fire built of cow manure, and there was always a sediment of sand at the bottom of the cup. Lucknow was a noted place for enteric fever, and the fever commission appointed to investigate the cause had decided that infection was communicated through cows being badly fed; at any rate, through milk. So she insisted on the cow being brought to the door that she might have it milked before her into one of her own clean copper cooking vessels. The milk was better then, but if she were not there to see each morning, and watching sharply, she could not be sure the man would not add old milk which he brought in a bottle concealed in his clothes. Then the cook found her a cow he wished her to buy, and said he would look after it himself, and it could then be no trouble to her. This would be better. She could then be sure it was fed with good grass and other necessary food, and she could see the Bishop drink a glass of unboiled milk without shuddering, for though he had been persistently warned that it was unsafe to drink uncooked milk, yet he could not drink it after cooking, and he had always had a glass of milk in the morning.

So the cow was bought, costing five rupees for every seer of milk it was warranted to give a day. The man who sold it said it would give eight seers, or quarts, a day. This was so unusually large a yield that she did not wholly credit it, but paid him only for five seers a day—that is, twenty-five rupees; but she found after two weeks' trial that it gave two quarts in the morning and two quarts in the evening, and she then knew she had paid five rupees too much.

Having the cow allowed her to have the butter made at home, and lessened one anxiety and trouble. At least she thought it would, for the man had only to boil the milk, set it, skim the cream off the next morning, and, putting it in a large glass bottle, shake it until the butter came. This was done every morning before she was up.

But while their chances of infection were lessened, and while the number of men coming to the house to be dealt with was lessened by two, imagine her surprise to find a strange man milking the cow.

"Who is he?" she asked of the cook.

"This man? O, he is the man who cares for the cow, gives her food and water and grass."

"But who pays him?"

"Your honor, when he has done your honor's work your honor will of a surety pay him."

"But who employed him?"

"Your slave. Your honor told me to make arrangement for cow; I have done so."

"Why do you not feed her and milk her? I cannot afford this nonsense. There is plenty of grass here, and she needs no care except her food in the morning." And her tones were sharp and her brow contracted.

"I, Mem Sahib?" in shocked surprise. "You are my mother and father, and hence I could not refuse to do your commands; but it is not custom to cooks, and they never, never do it."

"There are the two men for the house; surely they can do it?"

"Yes, Mem Sahib," doubtfully.

"Call them at once."

"Protector of the poor, the grass-cutter has gone to the jungle to cut grass, and the other man has gone with the Bissip Sahib to the bazar. Always at time of taking milk the grass-cut has gone to jungle, and many times the driver gone with Bissip Sahib or Mem Sahib, and they not do it; it not the custom."

"But the bihisti, he has goats and he milks them and feeds them. Why can he not do it?"

"He knows goats, he not know cow, and he not do it; it is not the custom."

"The sweeper, then?" doubtfully.

"Mem Sahib, no one drink milk that sweeper bring. I not cook with it," was the answer, with indignant emphasis.

Exhausted and angry she turned to go into the house. It was useless to beat her head against the solid wall of caste and custom. Turning back she asked impatiently what such a man must be paid, and was told four rupees, or a dollar and sixty cents, per month.

She went in and sat down in indignation. She thought of Bridget and Tom, and she would in that moment of unsanctified wrath and disgust and exhaustion have been glad to have sent all the white-robed, soft-voiced, barefooted servants into their mother Ganges could she have seen Bridget's honest face about her house.

Another source of possible infection and certain trouble Mrs. Clinton found in the meat supply. During the cold weather beef, mutton, fowls, and fish were to be had; in the hot weather only mutton and fowls. The fowls were bazar-fed, and that means fed on anything—refuse or nothing, varied by a little good food now and then—and were naturally very thin and scraggy.

Mrs. Clinton felt tempted to try to keep fowls, but fearing another man would be required she contented herself by buying a dozen or two small ones and paying for grain to feed them. But many of them disappeared, "eaten by jackals," the cook said, and so she found it rather expensive.

Then, even in the season for them, it was difficult to get good beef and good fish and good mutton. She found them nearly always poor, until it was suggested to her by Miss Whitlow that perhaps she was getting goat meat instead of mutton. Then she insisted on seeing the mutton every day before it was cooked. The cook looked injured and innocent, but the next morning brought the mutton wala up on the veranda, asked the Mem Sahib to come out and see the quarter of mutton in the man's own hand, and to also see the foot which had wool on it, and be convinced and doubt his honesty no more. The mutton wala also looked eager to prove his good intentions and immunity from such a culpable thing as selling goat meat for mutton.

Mrs. Clinton was ashamed. "How could these men ever be honest if they were continually and unjustly being suspected of such sly, underhand tricks? and for her part she was done with it;" and she lifted the foot of the sheep which was dangling by a ligament.

Ah, why did it come off so suddenly in her hand? Looking inquiringly into the face of the cook she saw the most shamefaced, the most guilty, the most humiliated man she had ever seen, and the mutton wala's face was a duplicate of it but less intense. *He* was not the Mem Sahib's servant, and could not be dismissed.

Not knowing what else to do, Năbi Bux picked up the foot, and looked at it helplessly. Mrs. Clinton took it from him and examined it. The end of the ligament was covered with glue.

"How many legs of goats has this been stuck on to deceive honest people, Năbi Bux?"

He hung his head in silent shame, and after a moment the cook and butcher both vanished around the corner of the house.

There seemed an attempt to do less of a business for himself on the part of Năbi Bux for a few days, and Mrs. Clinton thought perhaps this little episode might have had a permanent effect; but one thing was certain, she was paying for more eggs than were eaten, though with cheerful alacrity the cook would, when asked, give a strict account of each one, and in such a way that she was convinced in spite of her unbelief. But one morning when he had brought his purchases in to show her as usual he returned for something forgotten at the cookhouse, and while he was gone she took out her pencil and quickly made slight marks on the white surface of the dozen eggs before her. Three days after eight of that dozen were returned with four fresh ones when the cooly brought the market-basket with the cook's morning purchases.

The marks were very slight, but she slowly and

gravely picked out the eight and put them before him and looked him straight in the eye.

"There," said she, "I have paid you once for these."

Astonished and injured he said, "What, Mem Sahib?"

"You heard what I said. Now, remember, let this be the last time you do so contemptible an act as this. I have ways of telling some things that you do not know, and it will be necessary for you to be more honest."

Năbi Bux felt sad. This new Mem Sahib was very troublesome. A good Mussulman may cheat; but a *good* one is never found out; hence his sad and depressed countenance for the next few days.

These are only examples of the processes of the native servant. Each one has his own department, and each one knows exactly the best way to elude the vigilance of his mistress and cheat her out of enough to make a useful addition to his wages. The grass-cut puts stones and sticks in the bundle of grass he brings to make it weigh up to the full amount, the other man for the horse steals the grain with which he ought to feed the horse, and feeds his children. He breaks the harness and says he paid double the amount for having it mended that he really did; he declares he has used all the oil for the carriage, and you give him money to buy more, which he pockets and shows you the oil you bought a month before as a recent purchase. The water-carrier breaks the rope at the well, mends it himself, and tells you he got a man from the bazar, who charges eight annas, which you pay. The "kit" gets stale bread and sour milk cheap; you pay for good, and he pockets the difference. The cook has his regular percentage, often irregularly large, and the ayah and sweeper have their own individual sources of revenue, otherwise "perquisites," and the mistress lives in a continual warfare. The most that women with other work than housekeeping can do is to restrain·this stealing, and the most that women who give their whole time to housekeeping can do is to restrain it a little more, but both have the consciousness of dealing with forces that will inevitably conquer.

CHAPTER XIII.

THE MAHABIR MELA.

THE hot winds wailed louder each day about the corners of the house, the hours that one could remain outdoors during the middle of the day grew less, and yet the mission work went on with a steady swing. There was a busy hum in many schoolrooms where boys and girls who would form the future Church were learning to live; there was a noise of printing presses turning out books and papers filled with words that were to be life to a dying people; there were, each day, many doors in zenanas opened to receive gladly welcomed visitors who taught the love of Christ; there were faces of preachers, both white and dark, seen in and out of the business streets as they pursued their calling; there were voices daily lifted in the market places and wherever a group of people stood, preaching the forgiveness of sins and judgment to come.

The plan for each department of work was complete and independent in itself, but all plans united, articulated, and formed a strong power, imperceptible to many, perhaps, but none the less strong for that, in its onward sweep. And this busy working force and effects were repeated and duplicated in every town of importance in India; in some places with much greater and in others with less success.

One morning a few weeks after the death of Shew Pershad there was an unusual stir in the mission houses conseqnent on the breaking of the steady routine of work. The garis were ready at an early hour, and, filled with missionaries, with Bible readers, and with some of the older boys of the school, all well provided with Bibles, hymn books, illustrated papers and leaflets, were proceeding at dawn out of Lucknow to a village in the suburban jungle. The large mission tent had been sent the night before, and was pitched near the temple of Hanuman, the center of attraction which was drawing people here for the annual religious festival.

The Bishop and Mrs. Clinton were not far behind the other missionaries, for since the hot weather had come on they made a practice of rising at four, as this was the custom in the mission. It will not do to say the Bishop always found this agreeable, or to say that after a night, sleepless because of heat, mosquitoes, sleepy punkah coolies, fleas, and so forth, he did not think it would be better to temper zeal with wisdom and remain in bed until a reasonable hour. Never before had he risen before six or seven, and yet he had been counted as an uncommonly hard-working and energetic man.

As they drove slowly down the long road they saw the pilgrims of various kinds proceeding by the fair by many different ways; but those who expected to receive much benefit from a pilgrimage on this day, or had to fulfill vows, were dragging themselves along on the ground.

It was not a pleasant thing to see these dark, nearly naked bodies measuring themselves on the white sand.

marking a place ahead of them as far as they could
reach, drawing up their bodies and placing their feet
at the mark, and then stretching out again like huge
measuring worms. Some were fresh and untired,
having evidently just joined the pilgrims. These
looked about at the passers-by with an air that said:
"Do you see how devout I am? Surely you must believe there will be a great reward for such a one as I."
Others appeared weary, exhausted, and their eyes
were full of pain, whether mental or physical Mrs.
Clinton wished she knew. Certainly their devotion
was bringing them anything but peace.

"Perhaps," said Mrs. Clinton, "it is the sin they
are trying to expiate that gives them this agonized
expression."

"Hardly," answered her husband; "I fancy it is
entirely physical. They must be in great pain from
the unaccustomed strain on their muscles after traveling in this way for days with little food or water,
as some of them do."

A little farther on they came to a man who lay on
the ground with his arm outstretched to measure a
new length, overcome with either exhaustion and
faintness or with sleep, it was difficult to tell which,
as his whole body, as well as his face, was covered with
dust and clay. The others were so busy in crawling
that they had no time to stop for this one of their
number that had fainted by the way. They only
turned their heads at the strange spectacle of a Băra
Sahib noticing a fakir.

A pundit who was passing stopped by the man
and said in English, salaaming to the Bishop as he
spoke:

"This man, is he dead?"

"No, I think he is only fainting," answered the Bishop. "What can we do for him?"

"Not anything, Padri Sahib. It is this way that they want nothing done."

"But give him some water at least. I am sure he is fainting."

"No, Sahib, I not do this thing; behold this," and he pointed to a dirty string extending around the prostrate body and up over one shoulder. "He is Brahman and I am not Brahman."

"Then call a water-carrier, or some one who is a Brahman," he answered sternly, hoping to see a bihisti with a bag of water as he looked about.

"There is no one," said the pundit; "and he would die before he would take it from me."

"This is a dreadful religion," the Bishop said, hotly; "horrible! How can you believe a creed that makes you so cruel and indifferent to each other's sufferings?"

The pundit lifted his shoulders, and with the common gesture of the land, a putting out of both hands, turning the palms outward, which is Hindoostanee for "What can I do?" That is, "It is the custom, and how can I, only an atom, put myself in opposition to a custom which is as old as the hills themselves, and almost as firm?"

"But how is it that you who have read and studied can continue to hold to an absurd thing like this? You know that this poor fellow will gain nothing but suffering and perhaps death, and that there could really be no harm in his taking water from your hand; that it is all a lie and based on a lie."

16

"Yes, sir," the pundit answered, with a troubled countenance.

"The religion of Christ"—and here the Bishop's voice grew reverent—"teaches the high to serve the low. He said, 'Whosoever will be great, let him be a minister,' that is, let him be a helper; 'and if any would be greatest of all, let him serve.'"

"Very good word, Padri Sahib; I know the words of Christ; they are true and good."

"And you really believe them?" asked the Bishop, eagerly.

"Yes, I believe them, Padri Sahib," he said, provisionally; "they are good words, very good words for *you*."

"But if they are true are they not good words for all? If they are true other religions cannot be true," said the Bishop.

"They are very good words. I know them all, I read them when nothing to do, but they are for the Sahib lōg. My religion is better for me."

"And do you mean to say that if you were fainting and dying it would be right for a Brahman not to give you water?"

"Why not? It is the custom."

"And would you die rather than take water from a person of no caste—a sweeper?"

"Certainly, yes—why not—er—unless I had many rupees, and I could buy my caste back again."

Mrs. Clinton was getting impatient for something to be done for the man. People as they passed gazed curiously at the tall form of the Bishop, at the pundit, and at the prostrate fakir whose pilgrimage seemed so nearly at an end. As the Bishop turned in perplexity he asked another man who had half halted and said "Good morn," to display his English,

"What can we do for this creature?"

"God knows."

"Shall we leave him here to die?"

"If it be God's will. Where could he die better? He would be sure of eternal life dying while in so noble pilgrimage."

The Bishop got into his gari blazing with indignation, but with a sad heart.

"Never, never did I before realize what a degraded thing human nature is without Christ. He is the only teacher who has ever taught humanity to really feel for others," he said to his wife.

They were now leaving the main road, which was hard and smooth, and the horse went slowly and heavily in the white sand which had been loosened by the feet of hundreds of pilgrims already at their destination. The road each side was lined thicker and thicker with dusty crawling humanity, and others who were walking or riding in gayly draped carts with fat white bullocks, or in natty ekkas likewise drawn by ponies decorated by great necklaces of turquoises. All were in their best clothes, the women in red or purple or blue chuddars, with bright-colored skirts, the men in gold-embroidered caps and soft white muslin clothes.

There were many family groups of father, mother, and children, with brothers and sisters and their children, cooking their morning meals; for though the mela was local, still many had come from many miles the other side of Lucknow the night before, and were now settled and grouped as though for an artist.

Near them the bullock cart with its wide, thick, heavy, unpolished wheels, its scarlet and white covering, the luxurious-looking pearl-white, gentle-eyed bullocks standing near the women in their gay clothes at work pounding the golden huldi for curries or scouring their bright brass vase-shaped cooking vessels, making them so bright they mirrored the colors about them, and the fires, with the blue smoke rising, all formed another of the picturesque bits that Mrs. Clinton could never forget.

Later on, when the sun was well up, blazing down on the surging, moving mass, exaggerating the color so that it dazzled the eyes, she came upon a group of mission workers under a tamarind tree, though even there it was hot enough to make her head feel dull and heavy. In the center of a group of women was Miss Lowe, and near her one or two Bible women. As Mrs. Clinton stopped before them they finished singing the hymn,

"Uth Musafir kar taiyari ab to kuch din nahin hai."

When it was finished Miss Lowe, in her sweet, soft voice, began talking of the hymn. The women had liked the hymn, and they listened with interest to the explanations and the comments, especially when she said :

"We are, as the hymn says, all travelers, and our days are nearly spent. Soon the sun will go down and the night of death will come on, and how dire will be our extremity if we have made no preparation! and, poor mortals that we are, what preparation for that dark hour can we make?"

"None, none," said the women, shaking their heads.

"But there is One who has made preparation for us. Christ has done it all, and in his kingdom all will be saved who believe on him."

"Is this true, Miss Sahib?" asked one woman in plain white clothing, who had kept in the background— "true for all widows also?"

"Yes; in God's sight all are equal. He looks not at the body or at the condition, but only at the heart. A woman's soul, even if she be a widow, is the same as a man's, and if she believe and obey and the man does not believe and obey, then she will be saved, while he will be lost and punished."

"And are women, then, in your heaven not punished for the death of their husbands?"

"No, O, no. God is just, and would not punish a poor woman for what she was not responsible."

"Ah, wonderful and sweet, and my heart tells me it is true!"

"But," said another, the well-dressed, happy mother of sons, drawing up her golden-embroidered chuddar impatiently, "surely there can be no place where widows are equal with wives! How can that be?"

"Where," murmured the widow, "can I find him? Has he a temple here, that I may worship him?"

Then Miss Lowe began with the story of the wise men journeying until they found the Babe in the manger, and while she talked others came and joined the group until she was surrounded by as many as could get within the sound of her voice, all listening, eager-eyed and silent. Now and then a man passing saw the mission log and stopped to listen.

Finally, when she had finished, the women making

comments as they rattled their bangles and toe-rings and rearranged their chuddars, one of the men, a Hindoo in the finest of embroidered muslin and a gold-embroidered cap, with a handsome, clever face, stepped forward a little and said,

"Miss Sahiba, this is not true."

It was said respectfully and quietly, but firmly.

"O, yes," she said, with equal quietness, "it is true."

"No, Miss Sahiba, I have known many Europeans, and not one have I known that was not sinful, many of them very sinful, doing things of which even a poor Hindoo"— and there was an indescribably proud tone as he pronounced these words—"even a poor Hindoo would be incapable, and not one have I known that was saved from sin. If this story of Christ were true would not all who believed it hasten to be saved from the bondage of sin? When you can show me one, only one, who is freed from this curse, I will believe; until then do not preach."

Miss Lowe's face looked sad, and her large dark eyes were more pathetic than ever, and her lips quivered.

How true this was, how sadly true, of herself among the rest! But as she hesitated Elizabeth Uma, the eldest of the Bible women, stepped a little forward in her majestic way.

"Ah," she said, "if we were preaching ourselves then you would do well to say you would not believe until one perfect preached to you; but we preach Christ, who was perfect, and on him, because he was perfect, you can believe. We are poor weak creatures, full of faults and ever stumbling and falling, and if it were in our own merits we ask you to believe, then you might challenge us, but we challenge you to find one single thing wrong or imperfect in the life of Christ. If you do find it, then continue to worship your gods that are blind and deaf and dumb; if not, then accept him who was called Jesus, because he can and will save his people from their sins."

"These are wise words," said Puran Mul, for this was his name, while a shadow fell on his face, a shadow cast by ages of darkness and superstition, and he salaamed and went his way, still thinking of the wise words of Elizabeth, thinking that they might be true and all this mummery of worship to his gods would then be nothing, as he had often suspected. Ah! if only there might be a sure and perfect provision in this life against which all the terrors of Yama would be as the laughter of a child, then indeed would life be robbed of its sting, and instead of grim despair ruling his heart there might be sweet rest. What would he not sacrifice for rest from the capricious power of the mischievous gods that could be relied upon only to do their worst for man?

With this still in his mind he found himself in a group of men who were listening to a tall, fine-looking man speaking in English, which was translated by another tall man with fair hair and beard, who spoke his language with an accent that attracted him at once.

There were many young men listening in order to improve their English, and the majority of those standing about were intelligent and of the better class of clerks and students, though some were of the peasant or field laborer caste.

Puran Mul glided in among them and came upon his brother and some friends.

"Who are these sahibs, and of what are they talking?" he asked.

"Hush, it is the high priest of the Christians and the new master at the Christian College. See what fine big men they are—quite devils in size."

"Yes, yes; but of what are they talking?"

"Listen with your ears: mine are my own."

And Puran Mul listened only to find it was the same wonderful story he had just been hearing, "The forgiveness of sin through repentance and a life of faith on Jesus Christ, who was the atonement. No expiation by the sinner possible, no cleansing of vile hearts by washing in sacred rivers, neither by laborious pilgrimages nor by cutting the flesh; nothing at all gained by works; Christ had once for all made the only expiation possible."

When the speaker finished some young men from the college sang a hymn, the burden of which was that Christ was a wonderful Saviour, and through him all gloom and terror were dispersed because his was a heart full of love.

Then Carnton asked in his clear, kindly voice if any there accepted this as the truth and would be baptized into the faith and ever afterward be known as Christ's disciples.

"Come," said Puran Mul to his brother, "come; my heart speaks strongly and tells me that all this is true and that it is for us."

"Are you mad?" cried his brother. "What will you do but bring disgrace on us all?" for they were of a good caste. "Those sahibs practice witchcraft; I have often heard of men falling under the power of their words and being mad ever afterward."

"Nonsense; it is only the ignorant chatter of the bazar. You and I, who have read and studied, should know better. We can judge of a thing for ourselves whether it be true or false"—shaking himself loose from his brother's detaining hand—"and I can find rest in these words and in the worship of a God who is pure and true and all-powerful."

He moved forward with a dozen others to the tent where Carnton, with the Bishop beside him, drew them for quiet conversation. A number had been pondering the matter for years, having got their first knowledge of Christ from leaflets scattered by unknown hands. To others it was new, but to nearly all it had come home to their hearts with a force not alone of the speaker and his words, but of the Spirit which teaches all men when they "will to know of the doctrine."

And when he put the final searching question, "Do you believe, and will you renounce all your idols, give up all your sins and all worldly prospects, if need be, and cling to Christ, being baptized as a sign and seal of your belief?" there was a ready response from ten, Puran Mul among the first, notwithstanding the persistent protest of his brother and friends who stood back of him, hoping still to dissuade him.

The simple but impressive ceremony of baptism was soon performed and the names and addresses of the men recorded. They were told in return the names of the native preacher or missionary nearest to them, and arrangements were made for future meetings and books and papers for their instruction.

It was well into the afternoon when the missionaries with their assistants, English, Eurasian, and ceremony, but they were liking him better than at first. He was less self-assertive with his preconceived ideas and notions; he was amenable to reason; he wore a cork hat and carried a white-covered umbrella; he had given up inviting sunstroke by reckless walks in the sun, and, more than all else, actually had the good of the work at heart, and helped in any way and every way possible.

"Then," said the Bishop, in answer to Mackenzie's remark, "I would suggest putting on an 'extra' or two, and let there be less hurry. The best work can never be done in a hurry."

"Send along your extras, and we will be only too glad to use them. There is not a mission station where one more man, and in some places three more men, are not needed to prevent dangerous risks—dangerous, I assure you, not only to the health of the workers, but to the best interests of the work. But let us go out; it is not so hot now, and I want you to see the whole of this religious festival; for when you have seen this you will have a very good idea of others which are held here and there all over India, and in which much evangelical work is done. The native people look forward all the year to them, for various reasons: the women chiefly because it gives them a chance for change and amusement; the men the same, and because they can make bargains, arrange marriages and fulfill vows, and enter into negotiations with their gods for children and for prosperity in business. Here is the temple, and if we stand here on the upper veranda of this empty house we can cover the whole ground."

As they mounted the stairs a stream of people was

ceremony, but they were liking him better than at
first.   He was less self-assertive with his preconceived
ideas and notions; he was amenable to reason; he
wore a cork hat and carried a white-covered umbrella;
he had given up inviting sunstroke by reckless walks
in the sun, and, more than all else, actually had the
good of the work at heart, and helped in any way and
every way possible.

"Then," said the Bishop, in answer to Mackenzie's
remark, "I would suggest putting on an 'extra' or
two, and let there be less hurry.   The best work can
never be done in a hurry."

"Send along your extras, and we will be only too
glad to use them.   There is not a mission station
where one more man, and in some places three more
men, are not needed to prevent dangerous risks—dangerous, I assure you, not only to the health of the
workers, but to the best interests of the work.   But
let us go out; it is not so hot now, and I want you to
see the whole of this religious festival; for when you
have seen this you will have a very good idea of
others which are held here and there all over India,
and in which much evangelical work is done.   The
native people look forward all the year to them, for
various reasons: the women chiefly because it gives
them a chance for change and amusement; the men
the same, and because they can make bargains, arrange
marriages and fulfill vows, and enter into negotiations
with their gods for children and for prosperity in
business.   Here is the temple, and if we stand here
on the upper veranda of this empty house we can
cover the whole ground."

As they mounted the stairs a stream of people was

pouring toward the temple. Many with cups of Ganges water, brought by pilgrims and sold at a good price, which they placed at the feet of the god; others with garlands of white, sweet-scented flowers which they hung near or threw down before the hideous image; still others deposited money and grain. Over beyond the temple were a group of fakirs, all with their pilgrims' wooden bowls that served to receive money or food, and from which they ate—the only property they had except a dirty cloth about their loins. Their long, dirty hair hung in tangled masses down over their shoulders, and their bodies were smeared with mud. Some there were whose vocation was to lie flat on their backs, never rising but twice a day for food and water; others with holes cut in their flesh through which pieces of wood were thrust; still others in cramped and unnatural positions doing penance for sins. Near them were deformities of various kinds which were here to be worshiped—cows with five legs, calves with two heads, a sheep with a double head, a cat with a rabbit's stump tail, men without apparently any bones in their bodies tying their legs and arms in knots, and other grotesque creatures equally interesting to these strange, childish people.

Out away from the temple they could see the crowds broken up by little eddies of people that were circling around various centers.

"Here," said Mackenzie, pointing to one whirlpool, "is a sort of 'Punch and Judy' show, only Punch is a burlesque Englishman and Judy is a native servant; and not far from them is an English mission tent, and over there is the tent of the ladies of our mission; beyond them, the center of interest, is a merry-go-round. At the left is another English mission, and beyond them are the ladies of their mission at work; and here comes Rokewood, later, as usual, than necessary, for he has walked, sacrificing a third of the day for the price of a gari."

"What a strange, strange scene!" mused the Bishop —"this huge kaleidoscope of color; this sea of dark faces with perhaps a dozen white ones among them; and in this dozen people the goodness, the truth, the civilization and intelligence are centered—the thousands of others do not together aggregate as much. They remind one of swarms of gnats circling round and round in a meaningless way; and really what does it all mean, this swarm of humanity left so long without Christian civilization?"

"I cannot tell. I myself feel almost overcome with the portent of life, with the puzzle of humanity when I see a huge beehive like this. It seems to be too great for the mind to ponder, for it is only as a drop in the ocean of uncivilized, un-Christianized humanity. That these millions should be born, grow up, live, and die with no more spiritual life than your gnats, presents a greater problem than I can solve, or ever try to solve. But look! over there near where Miller is preaching an Arya Somaj man is warning the people not to leave their old customs, and not to dare come within the sound of the voices of these Padri Sahibs who are emissaries of the evil one—that there is enchantment in their words that brings evil on all who listen; not only on them, but on all they hold dear."

"Yes," said the Bishop, "I saw one of them this morning, near one of the other missionaries, trying to counteract his words; but what I was going to say is

this: while the task is so great, while the immensity
of it strikes me to-day as never before, I have also
to-day seen more of the work I can especially com-
mend than ever before.   To-night one hundred men
will go to sleep with the name of God on their lips
who rose with that of Hanuman, because you have
to-day gathered all your forces and for a time left
the plodding work of making books, of teaching
geography and the other machinery that takes your
time.   What could be accomplished if you were all
to leave it altogether and fulfill our ideas of mission
work is almost more than I dare think when so
many have in so short a time been converted!"

"As *I* reckon time it has not been so very short;
about thirty years would cover the time it has taken
to effect what we have seemed to do to-day.   Thirty
years ago we had no schools, no printing-presses, no
native preachers, no Bible women, no zenana teachers,
no books or tracts or papers.   Nowhere is it shown
to me plainer than in this very work that the organic
work of the mission must come first, and it is so evident to me that I hardly know how to prove it to
you.   The printing which you want to put aside is
responsible for some of the best of our converts to-
day.   One man from a remote village in the country,
for instance, was given the gospel of St. John, in
Urdu, fourteen years ago by an English official.   He
has been reading it to his friends and pondering it for
years.   Happening—if we can say 'happen' in regard
to these things—on a visit to some friends who were
coming here, he came with them and was ready to
hear and understand the truth, which otherwise
probably he would have not comprehended, or would

17

not have been interested in. He will be well supplied with books and papers when he returns, and in six months from now, when we can send a preacher, probably the whole village will be baptized. Another, a priest who found the gospel of Matthew in the road, has been teaching his people the precepts of Christ for years, and they have prayed the Lord's Prayer, though they still kept up their idol worship in a desultory way, because it was the blind leading the blind. To-day he received the truth gladly, and there will be another village soon that will all come over. So much do I believe in the power of printed words for these people that if I could I would fairly flood this great empire with religious and moral books and papers. It is a transition period with the people, and hence an impressionable one. They have begun to read, and to counteract the works of such writers as Zola, Ouida, or Ingersoll, and others equally pernicious which are sold here cheap, we must have good and attractive cheap books and papers, and plenty of them; and right here I want to say that if you will endow the publishing work, even in a very small way, you will do away with much of the commercial flavor that is about it, and to which you have objected."

"There is one thing," said the Bishop, "that always strikes me: whatever the subject in hand you people generally get back to the point you start from—more money to enlarge a work that will still require more money to keep it going."

"Of course; but when people are so poor as the great mass of the people here, even though self-support is taught and encouraged among them, it cannot for years amount to much. What can a man who earns three dollars a month do toward building a church after he has paid the living expenses of his family?"

"Surely not much. Consequently I do not see where the support is to come from when you have a Church of ten times the present number."

"Chiefly from themselves, for as they grow in intelligence they command higher wages. Some of the older churches are not only supporting their pastor, but supporting other work; and then we are taking more to native methods of work, and thus are cheapening it. But what I started on was to show you that the organic work to which you object is the backbone of the structure, and it would be a useless affair without it, even if it would be in existence enough to call it an affair. You would have to cut out to-day all the Bibles, all the native preachers, all the helpers that have been in schools, all the leaflets, all the hymn books, all the illustrated papers, and you would then have nothing, or next to nothing. What could we do without a translation of the Bible from which to read or quote? What could we do without hymns translated and set to their own tunes, or sung in ours? What could we alone, Carnton, Miller, and I, and the lady missionaries, do without the Bible women and native preachers and Eurasian assistants? How could we have had them but for the educational work?"

"Of course, some of this is necessary, but you will agree that it should not be put first?"

"I deny that we put it first. It in a way has to be done before others, just as all the munitions of war have to be made, and soldiers drilled, before victory can be achieved; but no one would say that it was considered more important, even though it must come first; and I will say this also: where in schools the organic work becomes an end, as whenever more is thought of accouterments and drill and intrench-ments than the gaining the victory, there it is an evil. Otherwise you must grant that it is the only way."

"Could you not say it *has been* the only way? Is not that day passed? The Bibles and hymn-books are here, the workers are here; what more do we want?"

"We want more books, more papers, more preach-ers, and more teachers; for the baptisms are increas-ing in geometrical ratio to the other work, and the building up of workers requires time. Now, of these men that were baptized to-day fifteen are chumars, or leather workers, from one village. We want an edu-cated man to put at once in that village—educated to the extent of being able to read and write and do ac-counts, and to know the Bible sufficiently to teach it correctly, and to have been insulated in a Christian school from heathenism long enough to understand what it means to be a Christian; and I assure you, after all, that is the most important qualification in the man who is to teach new converts."

"You call them converts, and yet imply that they do not know what it means to be a Christian?"

"They have understood with their hearts but not with their heads. There is the beginning of spiritual life in them. Now, for instance, a baptized man may be found with two wives in his house. He cannot know it is a sin, for his old religion does not forbid it, and it has never occurred to him that it might be a sin.

There are other things that they will not understand they must leave off. There must be a man to teach them, and there seems to be none available, and yet he must be found or their last state will be worse than their first. The Christian community begun with these fifteen men, and with a teacher-preacher, as he is called, to lead them, will be doubled and perhaps quadrupled at the end of the year. There will be a mud house built, costing, perhaps, fifty dollars, used for a church on Sundays and a school room and a place for dispensing books and leaflets during the week. From this as a center other villages around will be reached."

"If they were left without a teacher do you mean to say they would go back to heathenism?"

"Think what it is in our own land to leave even converts who have lived all their lives surrounded by Christians and well knowing what a Christian should be; think how loath you are to leave them, even within the sound of a dozen church bells, without direct pastoral care, and then see what it means to baptize a man that has had one day's teaching, and, perhaps, has been previously only self-taught by reading or being read to by his sons or his neighbor's sons, and leave him among a lot of people who think he has done an act to bring down the wrath and vindictiveness of their gods on himself and on all that are anyway connected with him, and whose one aim is to reclaim him. He must be taught; he must be under pastoral care or he will go back to an unbelieving idolatry, which is worse for him, far worse, than his first state. Then his teacher is often so ignorant himself that books and papers must supplement the teaching—not many, for one illustrated paper will last an incredible time, and one book, if it be the right sort, will be sufficient, besides his Bible; but these, even at a nominal price, cost more than he can afford. There is another strong reason why they must not be left alone. Now, for instance, this Puran Mul, who is so promising. I cannot tell you, nor begin to tell you, what he will have to undergo here where men are so subservient to their parents. Long after an American would decide for himself they will yield to their parents. A case that has just happened near Madras will give you a little idea of what he may suffer. A young man, by name Appu Rao, was shut up for six weeks in a close, dungeon-like room and watched day and night. Enchantment and violent purgatives were resorted to in vain to drive out the Christian heresies imbibed; pepper and cloves sifted in his eyes did not enlighten them; lime-juice rubbed daily on a shaven crown did not induce wisdom after Brahman judgment; and though his Bibles were burned before his face, and the ashes mingled with his drink, his well-stored memory still gave out its riches of the words of God to cheer and sustain and to meet the subtle arguments of vakis and gurus and the temptings of both the loved and the vicious; for there are, I am sorry to say, methods resorted to in these cases much worse than keeping all food from them. Besides all this were the threats of powerful neighbors, among whom was the magistrate himself, who visited the house constantly to coax or threaten the man into apostasy. One night, his watchers being sick simultaneously, Appu Rao was left alone, and raising the door off its hinges it fell back, though still locked, and he escaped."

"This is terrible! Such things should not be allowed by the English government."

"What can the government do except the case be brought to court? The man does not complain. He is taught by our religion when he is reviled to revile not again. Wherever we can keep from appealing to the authority of the government we do so. It is not 'by might, nor by power,' that we expect to conquer.

"Now, there is another thing: if our schools were given up as you would suggest, where would our Christian children be educated?"

"Of course that is a point. They could not be put in schools where they would be taught the Vedas or the Koran."

"And where," urged Mackenzie, "would we find men—Christian teachers and preachers—and also where would we find wives for these men?"

"Let them be taught of the Spirit, as in the olden time."

"Would that work in our Church at home?"

"No; but that is somewhat different."

"O," sighed Mackenzie, "how tired one gets of those indefinite answers of good people! 'It is different.' 'It is another case.' 'It is not the same thing.' But perhaps you may, when you have been here longer, find that human beings are much the same, and the core of Christ's teaching is improvement and a going forward. Speaking to them and telling them to go forward is hardly necessary, for the religion of Christ impels forward. You cannot stop its impelling force. But what I want to do to-day is to put you to thinking in regard to what the Church is going to do with all these people that she has got and is getting on her hands. A thousand a month will not cover the converts made in our evangelical work alone. Now, the object of all this talk on my part is to point out to you a duty you have incurred by coming here where you can see things as they are—that is, to help make the Church see the responsibility she has for the care of these poor creatures to whom we are giving a little light. We can win them, convert them, but the Church is directly responsible for their care; and by the Church I mean each and every one who believes on the name of Christ. Each and every one has as much responsibility as he has influence and money that he might use; and it is this you must impress on the people at home. But let us go down; I must see to the men that are distributing books, and if you like you may help me with these leaflets;" and he gave him half of the package he held in his hand.

Mrs. Clinton had been taken about by Mrs. Mackenzie, both giving out leaflets as they went from group to group of the lady missionaries, finding them happy and busy singing or teaching the words of life. The leaflets were hymns and Scripture selections printed on bright-colored paper, and at once attracted the attention of the women, who sometimes took them hesitatingly from their hands, looking at the hats and dresses and faces of the givers with strange, unaccustomed eyes that told the ladies that they might be the first white women that had ever been near these shy creatures. Others evidently wanted the leaflets, but, fearing contamination by taking them from white hands, held out their chuddars, in which the ladies dropped the papers, being careful not to touch the garment. Still others motioned them to throw the papers on the ground, from which they would be picked up after the donors were far enough away, so that there might be no contamination from their shadows. Some there were, however, who would gather up their skirts and draw away with scornful glances and describe a half-circle around them, and would not touch even a paper from the hands of such dreadful people, sure that their sons would die or become mad, or that even their husbands might die if they more than looked at the bold Mem Sahibs who went about with their faces uncovered.

Mrs. Clinton liked distributing leaflets, and would have been happy to have gone on until dark, but she found herself ready to faint after two or three hours, and begged Mrs. Mackenzie to take her away. The latter was quite willing, as she had work to do on their paper, and also because Katie was far from well, and she could not free herself from anxiety about her, although Lillian was spending the day at the house, and she always felt happier when she did not have to leave her quite alone. So they asked Carnton to help find their gari for them and to bring the Bishop home with him when he came.

As they were about to get in Sidney Mellen passed them with Mary Harris, one of her assistants. Carnton lifted his sola topi gravely, and she acknowledged it distantly, while her greeting to the ladies was as cordial as usual.

Mrs. Clinton's brow contracted. Something was going wrong in this love story, in which from the beginning she had been interested, and she only half nodded in answer to the lifted eyebrows and inquiring look Mrs. Mackenzie directed toward Carnton's back.

"I thought so," said Mrs. Mackenzie, as they drove off, "and it would be a capital arrangement, for they seem just suited to each other."

"And it is so hard for a girl to be alone in a terrible country like this; it is too hard altogether," rejoined Mrs. Clinton.

"Yes, though it is about as hard with a husband and little children to be anxious about; still, it is something to have the support of constant love and sympathy that no freedom from anxiety can compensate. At any rate, whatever we think, if he wishes to marry her he probably will, for he impresses one as being able to carry out anything he undertakes. As I had not seen them together of late I thought probably there was nothing in it, though some way the native Christians seem to take it for granted."

Mrs. Clinton reflected. She too had not seen them together of late; in fact, not since the day of the prince's visit. From the distant greeting to-day, and that cold look on Sidney's face of hardly seeing Carnton, she inferred things could not be going right; she hoped Carnton would not have to suffer, for she was fond of him and thought of him already almost as a son. She had often said to her husband that she would almost be willing their sons, who were respectively nineteen and twenty-one years old, should be missionaries could they be so noble and strong and wise as he.

Now she could recall instances of Sidney's evident avoidance of him, and once of his being unaccountably away when Sidney had come to spend the evening with them, and while she talked with Mrs. Mackenzie she still wondered and pondered as women will.

But what did these two women mean? Were they in league against the society which had sent out Sidney, one of its brightest and sweetest *protégées*, and one from whom was expected so many years of unswerving devotion, simply because she had never seemed to care for any man in her life?—which latter fact, had they been wise, would have made them less instead of more sure of her.

Perhaps Mrs. Clinton thought if Carnton fell in love with one of another mission he would not and could not take one of the young ladies sent out from the society in which she was especially interested; so that no complaints of falling away caused by him could be presented to her ears.

Still, it might be simply that no woman is able to look coldly on a love story; that, whether young or old, it has a deep fascination for her. It may be a matter of wonder that this is true when they know well what a prosperous love story costs a woman. Perhaps they forget to count the cost, and perhaps it is as well for the success of the love story that they do.

When the two mothers hurried out of their gari and around to the back of the house—for the front was still closed—hurried as all mothers do in this uncertain land when they have been away from their children long, with the ever-present fear of some calamity falling in their absence, they heard sounds of a Hindoostanee translation of "Sweet By and By" being sung in the dining room. Mrs. Mackenzie signaled to Mrs. Clinton to step softly. Peeping through the shutters they saw Lillian, Katie, and Sarah, the native Christian woman who was always with Lillian when her mother was away, sitting on the floor at one end of the dining room, and the servants and their wives and children sitting about them, or, more correctly, the babies were rolling on the floor.

When they had finished the hymn Katie said, "Now, Lillian, you must read in the Bible;" but Lillian passed it on to Sarah, who took it willingly and read, swaying backward and forth, in a most wonderful intonation, a few verses on which Katie catechised them in what Mrs. Mackenzie recognized as an absurd parody of her own manner, and then they all fell on their faces in the true Mohammedan style, and Katie prayed in Hindoostanee part of her own evening prayer, and wound up with a petition that God would "make all present honest and truthful if he could;" which might have been considered somewhat personal.

Then Lillian began also with part of her evening prayer, adding petitions for the native people, and to her mother's surprise and almost terror she prayed that God would make her good enough when she grew up to be a missionary, like Miss Mellen, to the native women, to teach them about Christ.

She was followed by Kalan, the fat cook, who looked comical enough in his short ever-dirty cooking coat, and he in turn by Sarah; then with a repetition of "Sweet By and By," perhaps because Katie did not feel safe to try any other, the meeting closed, and the mothers, with smiles on their lips and tears in their eyes, came in at one door as the congregation, looking a little shamefaced, vanished through the other, Katie expediting their retreat by picking up the squirming babies and lugging them out on to the veranda, from which they rolled and tumbled to their own houses.

Mrs. Clinton said to herself in irony tinged with self-contempt:

"I have often urged upon young ladies the beauty and desirability of a life spent as a foreign missionary, and I have consoled their mothers by telling them that a mother could not have a greater blessing than a daughter noble enough to give up home, friends, and all that makes life attractive for the purpose of uplifting poor ignorant people who are nothing to her personally. O, yes, I have talked very well, and I thought I believed what I said, but when it comes to Lillian it is another thing; the beauty and desirability seem to wane, and I can only hope she will be less tenacious of this idea than she is of most plans she makes."

CHAPTER XIV.

IN THE ZENANAS.

THE days went on and Lucknow grew hotter and hotter, until there came a time when the earth, heated seven times, refused to do anything but to give viciously back the heat that was poured upon it; when the air, filled with burning sand, gave its help to the sun; when tall columns of dust marched up and down the streets, and when the sky, unsympathetic as burnished brass, gave no relief. The birds, with parched throats, panted their lives out on the dust-covered branches and dropped dead on the bare ground, excepting, of course, the fiendish "brain-fever" bird, which one hoped would die before his prodding, stabbing note had driven his hearers into the brain fever of which he was always shrieking, and his brother-fiend, the "blacksmith" bird, with his never-ceasing metallic note, that Mrs. Clinton could not distinguish sometimes from the heavy throbbing in her head; which proved that the two together, added to the heat, might do, in the way of producing brain trouble, what one could not alone.

The Clinton family, taken together, were giving the busy people of the mission no little anxiety.

First, Lillian began to look like a pale little ghost, then her mother turned into a companion ghost, with weary eyes and despairing face; not that she was unhappy, but the heat was taking her strength inch by inch, and she was fighting it with all the obstinacy born of a determination to prove herself not in the wrong. She had yielded every one of the points in which she had thought the missionaries mistaken but two, and they were punkahs and a vacation in the hills, unless one were ill.

Now, punkah is a generic term that includes all kinds of fans, even to the fire bellows, but when one speaks of punkahs usually he means the long plank or pole swung by ropes from the ceiling, to which is attached a wide flounce of white starched muslin. A rope tied to the center of the pole extends out on to the veranda, where a cooly sits and pulls this rope. From the middle of April to the middle of October these punkahs swing night and day in all European homes, and in many native homes. They are disagreeable, cumbersome, and add to the expense of the household and a great deal to the annoyance, for they knock off pugris and chuddars, they are a bar to all tidiness of hair, they blow papers and letters about when one tries to write, they destroy any pleasant or attractive appearance a room may have, and they are generally irritating to the temper.

However, there is one trifling redeeming quality: they are absolutely necessary to work and even life in India, and one becomes resigned to them after five or ten minutes of work in a room without them, and hurries back dripping with perspiration and with bursting head to sink exhausted on a couch under one of these swaying evils.

Mrs. Clinton had set her face against punkahs, especially because of the vague rumors which had gone about at home of missionaries "having men fan them while they did nothing." She had denied it indignantly many times when begging for missions, and she was now going to show the missionaries that punkahs were not necessary, for she did not know just how she could have the face to ask for all the money she meant to ask on her return if she were obliged to say that they had had a half-dozen men or more to do their work, and two merely to fan them, and, worse than all, often to fan when they themselves were doing nothing.

Mrs. Clinton had to acknowledge to doing nothing more hours in the day than she liked. They rose at four or five to get a little air that was fit for breathing purposes, and that they might work while moderation of heat made it possible; but after nine each day she lay on the cane couch, and Lillian lay on another, made of the stalks of kusi grass, in the sitting room, because that was the coolest room. This room, in order to keep out the hot air and the glare of the sun, was shut so close that it was impossible to read or work; but, even had it not been so, they were too stupid and weak and too overcome with the heat to do anything but lie quiet, sometimes in a sort of stupor, and sometimes asleep, until four o'clock, when they would drag themselves into their bath room, and, after a bath, dress while the perspiration poured off of them and while they felt almost too faint and giddy to stand.

If Mrs. Clinton ever ventured to lift the dark shade of the small window in her bath room—the only window in the house—and look out on the sun-baked earth, the dry trees, the birds panting like weary dogs

or fallen to the scorching sand beneath, saw the air
filled with clouds of dust, and the brave little ponies
drawing the rattling ekkas, their drivers sitting with
their dirty chuddars wrapped around their heads to
keep off the hot wind, she dropped it quickly, and
the tears rolled unchecked down her colorless face as
she tried in vain to believe that somewhere at that
very moment, somewhere there were orchards in
bloom, fresh green pastures, where cattle stood knee-
deep in moist grass; and there really were, somewhere
cool springs of water surrounded by fresh ferns under
the shade of dustless forest trees. It was not possible
to believe it; the whole world was only a dreary
burning furnace, which was peopled by men and
women who were living because they were too exhausted and tired to die!

The Bishop himself was feeling the climate to the
fullest extent of its power of making a person uncomfortable, though he was able to do more work
than his wife.

The waves of heat that went over his body to his
head, caused, perhaps, by his full, sanguine temperament and plethoric body, were partly robbed of their
deadly quality by prickly heat. People have a most
ungrateful way of dreading this disease, for its marks,
though disfiguring, are a sort of flag flying or an ex-
ponent indicating that there is none of the fatal and
insidious fever or not much danger of apoplexy.
It is simply a thick rash caused by profuse perspiration. Profuse perspiration has other evils besides
this. It makes cuffs and collars, as well as starched
linen, impossible, likewise dry clothes, unless a change
is made every hour of the day. "Rivers of water"

18

run down the face, dropping off of the various eaves
formed by the eyebrows, the ears, the nose, and the
chin, and one big river down the spinal column, fed
by tributaries from the table-lands of the shoulder-
blades, but, worst of all, every drop and every rivulet
leaves a train of nettle stings in its wake, and these
maddening stings are the first indication that prickly
heat has marked you for its own. Bad as it is, painful and uncomfortable as it undoubtedly is, this is not
the most aggravating phase of the disease. When
the usual question is put to you as to your health in
this trying season and your answer is "Miserable,"
your friend quickly, with the face of concern that the
suggestion of illness always brings in this terrible
time—for no one knows when it once begins where it
is going to fetch up—inquires what is the trouble.
But your answer, given in actual torment and distress,
"Prickly heat," only calls forth an indifferent, "O,
that is nothing; it is good for you."

Then you begin to feel the old aboriginal blood
stirring in you which would lead you to take the life
of your neighbor; but it is checked at once, and you
content yourself with a wish nearly as bad, but lawful:
you wish your friend to have this thing forever that
is so good for people, this stinging, irritating, tantaliz-
ing prickly heat.

The Bishop had it as bad as possible, and all those
to whom he spoke of it smiled with perhaps a touch
of malice; at least with amused satisfaction, feeling
it was a sort of poetic justice. Certainly any lingering resentment they may have had at the self-
sufficient attitude he had taken on his arrival in India vanished about this time. They may have felt

that two or three months of this especial affliction
would amply avenge any wrongs they had suffered at
his hands; and as for his wife, all, even Mrs. Mackenzie,
forgot everything but the fear they had that she was
carrying her experiment too far.

The Bishop felt the need of punkahs less than his
wife, perhaps, for he was often out till eleven in the
morning, sitting under a punkah in the college, where
he was giving some regular lectures in English, or at
the publishing house planning out tracts with Mackenzie, or here and there, and would come home to breakfast and fall asleep in his study quite overcome, or
perhaps, finding he could not successfully compete with
the power of the heat, would go off to his bed and sleep
two good hours. Even then he only got his usual
amount of sleep, for when a man begins work at
five and goes to bed at eleven or twelve it is not
strange that sleep, assisted by intense and oppressive
heat of a thoroughly foreign climate, overpowers
him.

This sly, insidious climate, which says, "I am not
so bad after all; you can live with me if you only try,"
is all the time gradually putting water in your veins
instead of good red blood, and turning your hair gray
in one season; but the rooms are dark and you do
not see it, nor would you care if you did, for, with
other things, it steals your care for, or interest in,
yourself. This vile climate—it taps you all over like
a hungry fly, and finally, finding the weak point in
your body, begins its silent work. Perhaps your
grandfather had consumption—the bad air, the great
lowering of the temperature from noon to midnight
at all times of the year, weakens and takes all strength

or fiber from the lungs; or there is a little defect of liver—it is made the most of; or there is a tendency to eat nothing or to indigestion—it is seized on, and then comes cholera and sweeps you off at once; or you are strong and stout, and there is congestion of the brain or apoplexy.

Knowing all these things, the members of the mission circle were anxious in regard to this family of self-appointed exiles. There was no imperative duty keeping them, and it was a time either to flee or to take the best personal care; the latter involved three things—willingness to do it, knowing how, and having the means with which to do it.

Finally, when Miss Whitlow was ordered to the mountains for a month by the doctor she told Mrs. Clinton that they all ought to come with her; but no, Mrs. Clinton said:

"We will do as others do. When the doctor tells us that it is necessary to the preservation of our lives to go, then we will go, but not otherwise," thinking in her heart that she would not go until Mrs. Mackenzie did, at least.

This sort of dull, obstinate despair is not uncommon to worn-out people in that weary land, for they get a settled conviction that no change will make things any better; they hope to hold out until the cooler weather comes; but it does not seem to matter much, for it is a notable fact that good judgment departs with the departure of red blood from the system.

Lucky are they if in this comatose state of strength and reason some good friend rises up and drives them, by various threatenings and scoldings, off to the home-land or to the mountains. They go, often angry and resentful of the interference, as they call it; but when once more returning, clothed in strength and in their right minds, they laugh at their own obstinacy while earnestly thanking their friend in need.

Too often—ah, how much too often!—no friend rises up to protect them from themselves; perhaps the temporary loss to the work is thought too great to permit the absence, and thus a great permanent loss to the work is risked once too often and there is another blank in the Conference roll, another sad-eyed woman in black is left to wonder why the demands of God's work are made so heavy, or some helpless little children are sent with a bewildered, grief-stricken father across the water to find home and care as best they may.

So Mackenzie, who did not mind saying anything that he thought right to say, told the Bishop that he was risking his own life and the lives of his wife and child by the course he was pursuing.

After some persuasion, and without saying that going without punkahs was none of his own doing, the Bishop ordered punkahs, and superintended their putting up, for it is doubtful whether Mrs. Clinton had strength enough left to oversee it herself, as the Bishop saw with alarm that she had none left to oppose it.

Then he arranged for ice to be sent every day, for some bitter waters, and twice a day the cook was ordered to bring them beef-tea. This was all at Mackenzie's suggestion, and there was a visible brightening all around. Then Lillian's winter clothes was got out and she was sent off with Miss Whitlow to Naini Tal, to the girls' school, where she was to be

eared for, but not allowed to study. This also Mrs.
Clinton did not oppose, for about this time news was
coming in of the havoc being made by the hot weather
in the ranks north and south.

News from Rangoon of a young strong man falling dead before his wife's face; from Bangalore of a
wife, under physician's orders for a home climate,
who had begged her husband to let her stay another
year that he might not be working alone, sinking
quickly under unexpected pressure of circumstances,
and now he was to be forever alone. From Cawnpoor the hands of another worker slipping unwill-
ingly off from work passionately loved, loved more,
perhaps, for the very fact that it had in four short
years bleached her black hair to a snow; and from
one and another station rumors of prostration and
fever. It was a time to look sharp, to go softly
and hope for better times, and it was now that the
Bishop thought the house, that had seemed so large,
too small and close; it was now that he would have
given much for vegetables and fruit; it was now
that the meat was as tender and palatable as boiled
leather, the milk three fourths water and perfectly
impossible as a drink; it was now that he had grave
thoughts of importing vegetables and fruit from England and America, and rashly invested in tinned vegetables, though they were said to be unsafe and many
cases of poisoning had been known.

And it was now Mrs. Clinton would have been glad
of something bright to look at in her dreary rooms—
some pictures of snow, or of green fields, or of flowers; of anything to relieve the blankness of it all;
anything to keep her mind on but the thought of

NAINI TAL. AMONG THE HILLS.

work she wished to do and could not; anything but the thought of other people who were overworking, sick, or even dying, for with all other people, as well as with them, life was going heavily.

All work went on with a great effort, and none more laboriously than the zenana work in which Mrs. Clinton had especially interested herself. She liked it; it was attractive work—in the two months of bearable weather—but after that each week she left more and more of the work to Georgiana, the Bible woman, with whom she always went.

Often, as the narrow lanes and byways and open sewers became more and more overpowering, when the hot, stifling little rooms made her gasp for breath, when some interesting child disappointed her, or some woman in whom she believed and of whom she had grown fond developed startling proclivities to evil— often Mrs. Clinton would compare her old romantic idea of zenana visiting with the reality and wonder how she could have been so mistaken. Sometimes she would blame the missionaries who had told of this life that they had left the shadows to the imagination.

But she forgot that the worst, the saddest, the most terrible things are those that from their very nature could not be told from a public platform, and even if they could would a good soldier ever tell of the difficulties? Hardly, for it is too much like sounding his own praises.

Perhaps she finally saw this, but she determined that when she saw zenana missionaries standing on platforms and telling of dearly bought victories as though they were a simple matter of course she would rise and tell the people to fill in between the lines all that imagination would allow them of details, of difficulties, of sickening odors, of constant contagion, of stifling air that brings a deadly faintness to the body, of vile lives whose details are so confused with the heat and the stench that one can hardly tell which it is that most fills one with loathing of life.

She would tell them this, and of the going through all this and more, upheld by the dire need of these people for something better, and by the certain indications that good was being done, until perhaps an unthinking, meaningless word arouses suspicion in these ever-suspicious minds, and the doors in these walls are closed and nothing can open them, and the zenana teacher is crushed by the thought that perhaps because of her own imperfect teaching those that she thought emerging into light have sunk back into darkness and obscurity.

It was something like this that was taking the color out of Sidney Mellen's face earlier than usual, and perhaps it was not all this, though as the heat grew fiercer and fiercer it was enough to blanch the face of anyone, young or old.

Perhaps Carnton had something to do with the fact that she was not standing the hot season quite as well as usual. Certainly the brightness and extra interest that her first acquaintance with him had thrown around her work had vanished, though she could hardly tell when the sympathetic friend she had found and claimed had disappeared, and only a man who rather disapproved of her and all she did was left in his place.

It was hard—she did not deny it was hard—and

she rebelled against many things, but first and fore-most against her sex, that would not permit her to go to him and say:

"Why are you disappointing me? Is friendship so common a thing that you can take it up gladly for a moment only to tire of it and throw it down the next?"

This was what she said to herself when daylight stared her in the face; but sometimes in the dead of night, when she was alone in the heavy darkness, did she tell herself the truth, or what, she would say with a face hot with waves of blood, might possibly be the truth:

"He is, for some inscrutable reason, afraid of caring too much, or perhaps—*perhaps* he might have thought that I would come to care too much."

Sometimes when this suggestion would present itself she would almost fear that in the morning it would be known—that all would have the second sight to see this terrible thought that had been in her mind; but the night and the swaying punkah and the sleepy punkah cooly told no tales, and the days went on and her strength did not seem quite up to the usual demands. Sleepless nights do not qualify one for days of furnace heat, and she went wearily in and out of the houses, haunted by a fear that some day she would reach the limit and would have no strength to get in and out of the gari, no will strong enough to urge her lagging steps up the stairs into her dreary, unsympathetic room; and then what would happen? Perhaps some of those merciful diseases with sudden terminations, which always stand waiting around the corner out of sight, would end it all quickly, and another lady would come out from the home land full of enthusiasm and strength. Perhaps she might do the work better, and perhaps Carnton might be pleased with her also, until he came to know how much she cared for friendship, and then she, too, might find his eyes unkind. But she hoped that she, this imaginary new zenana teacher, might not be young—"not young, for life looks too long in its dreary perspective without any friends for whom one really cares."

But not often did she allow herself the luxury of such fancies. She was there for work, and work she loved more than she loved herself or her own happiness; work, whose interest increased in proportion almost as its difficulties increased, and just now, in some respects, these seemed to be multiplying.

There was one house especially the inmates of which gave her much thought. From the first day she had been called to visit it, which had been recently, there seemed not only to herself, but to her assistants, an air of mystery about it that they did not like. One accustomed to constant dealing with Orientals comes to trust to impressions or instincts or whatever may be called that peculiar sense that detects the untrue, the unworthy, and the mysterious. This is a grateful sense and develops in proportion as it is trusted, even though it be trusted simply because there is nothing else to guide one. There are so many unexplored parts to an ordinary native's mind, so many secret drawers, so many false bottoms, that a European of a confiding nature and given to trusting surface appearances is apt to be led in dubious ways, and to often find himself in pits of the existence of which only experience could convince him.

In this house, concerning which Sidney was feeling a little uncertain and uncomfortable, were a woman called Moonia and her daughter Jumia, a girl quite beyond the age when girls are usually married. This circumstance the mother was careful to explain, saying that she was a widow and too poor to provide the marriage portion of her daughter; and yet some way, though they dressed plainly, they did not give, exactly, the impression of being poor. But the mother explained fully that they had lived in a little village where all the men cared more for money than beauty, and she had come to Lucknow in the hope of finding some one that would be satisfied with her child's beauty, and that alone.

"Now," she said, with much satisfaction, on the day of Sidney's first visit, "my efforts have been rewarded and a husband has been found both rich and intelligent who wishes his wife to be taught that she may also understand and be wise."

This sounded plausible; but there was something in the girl's pretty face that contradicted a part or the whole of the statement and warned Sidney to be cautious.

Then there was the lack of the usual shyness that was invariable with girls on meeting a woman with a white face for the first time; a lack of the usual curiosity in regard to her dress and habits that was puzzling; and equally puzzling was the fact of her being well taught for a village girl, though her mother said briefly that Jumia had taught herself, which was so palpable an untruth that Sidney did not credit it a moment; but the girl was so gentle and loving, so eager to learn, and so earnest in begging Sidney never to miss a day but always to come, that she went as often as possible.

One day when the mother, who had never before left them for a moment, went out into the courtyard Jumia said, quickly :

"Miss Sahib, I want to come and live with you. I suffer much. May I come ?"

Sidney was startled for a moment, but the mother returning immediately prevented her giving any answer, and afterward, on thinking it over, she concluded it was a mere impulse. During the next visit they were again alone for a few moments, and Jumia said, hurriedly and with great emotion :

"My dear Miss Sahib, I am a lie. My name is Sitara, and I was the wife of Shew Pershad, who died. Your Carnton Sahib knows me, and also Miss Whitlow Sahib, with whom I was in the Bewa Khana."

"How can this be ?" said Sidney, her head in a whirl.

She knew the story of Sitara, of the bright promise of Shew Pershad's life, and of his wife's disappearance after his death. Carnton himself had told her of the legacy of trust Shew Pershad had left him in regard to Sitara.

Watching Sidney's face as she saw her gradually comprehending the situation, she said, after waiting a moment,

"Now may I come to you ?"

"Why not go to Miss Whitlow ? She searched for you and longed to find you."

"Mother would find me there, because she knows I wanted to go back, and Miss Whitlow would have to give me up. They will not think I am with you, and

in that great old house in which you live there must
be a corner for me. Miss Whitlow and Carnton Sahib must not even know that I am here—that Sitara is
in Lucknow; for it is their way always to speak the
truth, and my mother would ask them. Only close in
your heart can the knowledge be of me, for even
walls have ears and eyes, and can speak of things that
are. You will let me come, because Shew Pershad
said I must be a Christian?"

Still Sidney was silent, for it was all too sudden and
too confusing. There was too much involved to be
able to answer quickly or even at all.

Then the girl, still with her eyes half on the door,
where she expected every moment to see her mother,
pleaded:

"You alone can help me. You *must* help me.
There is no one else. You are happy and free, and
your God cares for you and does not let dark
clouds of sorrow wrap you about. But see, I will
come to you and live with you, and your God, who
does not despise women, will also care for me."

This last was said as though reading it from the
Bible, as the mother was just coming in; and then
Sitara really began reading.

"My dear child is learning rapidly," said the
mother, with a smile that showed her teeth blackened
and her lips red with the pán she was chewing, and
she arranged her chuddar with a satisfied air. "She
is soon to make a great marriage. We are poor,
very poor, but Ram is good and has given her a
very handsome young and rich husband. She will
have silks and velvets and jewels until her heart is
full, and then every day curry and rice, with the best

of spices. Ah!" and she gave a sigh which was partly a groan of satisfaction.

"Does she—does she like this man?" asked Sidney.

She was going to say, "Does she love this man?" but knowing this would shock her prejudices she changed the word.

"Not now, but why will she not? It is not the custom to like much before marriage. It would not do, but she will be very fond when she has all these clothes and jewels."

"It is as useless," thought Sidney, "to tell her that clothes and jewels cannot bring happiness as it was to tell my own aunt at home, who wished me to marry a rich man. There is a similarity. Girls, whether in the Occident or Orient, are expected to fill their hearts with jewels and clothes."

"But, Moonia," she said, "you know that if he is not good her heart will be heavy even though she has a world full of silks and jewels."

"Tut," she said, looking with a warning glance toward the girl, "he is good, of course he is good. Why else should he give her all these things? Come, Jumia, you have a new chuddar to sew. Show the Miss Sahib how nicely you are sewing it."

The next day Sidney went for the lesson with anxious heart, but everything was as usual; the reading in Hindi and Urdu, and then the Bible lesson which Sitara always enjoyed, and through which her mother sat scowling and silent. She was, however, willing to permit it, for the sake of the other teaching, and trusted to the effect of her always telling Sitara, after Sidney had gone, that it was all a lie, a fable like the stories she had told her of talking tigers in

the jungles and of birds who cooked and ate men's
food.

When Sidney was leaving, Sitara brought the usual
offering of cardamom seeds and pán, and as she handed
Sidney the pán her back was toward her mother and
her lips framed the word "inside."

With a nervous hand, when once in her gari, Sidney opened the glossy green pán leaf, and instead of the
usual paste of betel nut, cardamom seeds, and lime, she
found a scrap of paper on which were the words in
Hindi, "I will come to you when the darkness
comes."

Sidney was much agitated, for she knew this taking
refuge with her might involve much trouble, though
how much she did not and could not guess. She
wished for advice, and she thought at once of Carnton. She had not seen him for many days, but she
knew that he had often been sad that he had not been
able to fulfill Shew Pershad's trust in him. Now he
would be glad and, perhaps, be grateful to her for
being able to do what he could not, and perhaps he
would once more give her his kindly approval, and
she was ready for a moment to do what would please
him, but only for a moment. In an instant she put
the thought aside, and also all thought of Carnton,
that she might not have her idea of duty warped.

But after all this was not necessary. It was really
taken out of her hands. Sitara had purposely arranged giving her the message so that she could not
refuse. Thinking it over again she saw this, and she
could only wait, not being able even to say she would
or would not receive her. She could only say:

"It is in God's hands now, and if she is true and
19

earnest he will care for her, as he has ever cared for his own."

When again the wind had gone down, when not a leaf moved and the twilight, heavy with the scent of jasmine and babūl, was over all, every person about the house seemed to have departed on one pretext or another, even the assistants having gone to evening service, and Sidney sat alone on the first of the steps that led to the front veranda.

She was anxious, and yet peace was in her heart. Watching the gateway she saw nothing, but suddenly there was a shaking of the pomegranate tree that reached down to where she sat, a tinkle of anklets and toe rings, a swish of silken garments, and Sitara was panting like a hunted deer in her arms.

She drew her quickly inside, then up the winding stairway and into an empty unused little back room which opened off of her rooms by a rude little door hung with a portière. She had not thought where she would put Sitara or what she could do with her, for it seemed too much like planning to take the child from her mother; but now that she had come of her own accord she would do the best she could for her. She brought what was needful into the room and then, having dropped the curtain and closed the little door, sat down on a low chair that she had brought for herself, and said:

"You said once you were in great danger; tell me all. Be very careful that you speak truly: that all you say is straight and right."

Sitara knelt by her side and laid her head on Sidney's shoulder, who, with one arm around her, listened.

"It is as I said on the day when my heart first stood

up to speak to my dear Miss Sahib. My mother and father gave me to Shew Pershad when I was six years old, and I went to live with his mother. He was a brother to me and I was his sister, for his mother was of a very bad disposition and was very unkind. Then Shew Pershad became a Christian after he had been to the mission school, and he brought me away that I might learn to be a Christian also, and we were to have a house when he had finished school and we were to be married in the church by the Padri Sahib as Christians. It was then I was with Miss Whitlow when he became sick, and he sent for me and told me I must stay with Miss Whitlow and be a Christian and learn to teach others to be so too. After he died his mother arranged with my mother and she took me away, pretending that she was going to take me to Miss Whitlow's Bewa Khana, but it was only here in another part of Lucknow that we came. Then she found this man, who is old and hideous, who will kill me if he finds out that he has been trapped into marrying a widow. When she told me that she had arranged for me to marry him I was very angry, but she said I must not tell him I was a widow, but marry him quietly, or she would do worse."

"What could be worse?"

Sitara hesitated, her head went down, and she whispered:

"She said she must have more money, for she loves money more than anything else, and she would sell me in the bazar to any one."

Sidney was appalled to think of this poor lamb left among wolves, and remorseful that she had thought for a moment of refusing to shelter her.

"I never meant to pretend to marry him, and he thought me stupid. So he said I must be taught, and you were called, and O, Miss Sahib, how glad I was! I had said I would kill myself, and I did not eat and I was as thin as paper; and there is a deep well back of the house that would have received me kindly had you not come. But my poor heart lifted itself up when you came, for I knew you were good because you are to marry Shew Pershad's Carnton Sahib."

"What!" was the startled exclamation.

"I knew Carnton Sahib, whom Shew Pershad said was so good, would not take you for his wife unless—"

"But who said—"

"The cousin of Shew Pershad, who is in the school, said it. O, it is well known, and he is a fine, handsome man, and of pleasant disposition," looking a little curiously at Sidney's agitated face.

After a pause Sitara went on :

"I knew you would let me come to you, and it would have been death to stay there. I think Mohun Lal suspects I have been married, for he came twice when he knew my mother was not in the house, and he was very unkind to me, and he has put off the marriage, though my mother was not pleased to do so, and they are talking of something else, of which they do not let me hear the words."

Sidney was weighing all this in her mind. The only thing that did not seem true was that they were poor. She finally asked :

"But if you are so poor how do you have all these jewels and this pretty silken dress?" for she was dressed as a rich woman dresses.

Sitara laughed the gleeful laugh of the child she was.

"I have not said we were poor. My mother says it. She says that to make people believe her when she tells them I am not married; otherwise people would have suspected at once that I am a widow. I did not mean to let her have these things. They are mine, and I love them. We are not at all poor. See!" And she lifted one skirt and showed another of gold-colored satin underneath. Under this was a purple velvet, and under this a silvery gauze heavily embroidered with gold.

"And in each pocket of each are my jewels," she added, gayly; and she drew out of one a huge nose ring, set with many large pearls, a necklace of gold set with turquoises and pearls, and toe rings and finger rings. "And they are all full," she said, patting the other skirts, which dragged in two or three places.

"And see!" and she lifted her skirt and showed the heavy anklets of gold on the little ankles, and the armlets of gold and pearls and turquoises and the bangles of silver and gold.

"O, my Sitara, what have you done! What have you done!" and Sidney wrung her hands. "Why did you bring them?"

The large soft eyes opened wider than ever in astonishment.

"Why not? They are mine. Father bought them for my wedding. I was the only daughter, and he had money. Shew Pershad's mother never knew how many I had. They are mine," she said, a little fiercely, "and I love them," touching them with a loving pat.

Sidney walked the floor. What should she do? She

saw it all at once. The story would go that the child had been kidnapped for her jewels. She would be advertised in the zenanas as the kidnapping zenana teacher, and not only she, but other zenana teachers would be maligned with a show of truth. She knew that already many such stories were told to the women in zenanas, but against constant love and kindness these stories had had little weight. Now they would be believed. Should she send her back and sacrifice one for the many? No, no. She would do what seemed right; for if she sent her back it would be only to a life of infamy, for even if there was a marriage it could not be aught but a pretense.

"Sitara, listen to me. Do you know that by bringing your fine clothes and jewels you have endangered what is worth more than life to me?"

The startled fawn-like look came again to her face, and she said, solemnly:

"My Miss Sahib, I would go away into the hell of life with that man before I would cause the wind to lift your hair. What have I done?"

"They will call me a thief, and say I have stolen you for your jewels."

Sitara knew enough of native ways of doing to need no proof of this.

"True, O true!" and she rocked herself back and forth. "I did not think, I did not know."

She rose sorrowfully and came and put her arms around Sidney, laying her head first on one shoulder, then on the other.

"Salaam," she said; "I must go quickly, and they will not know what I meant to do. They will kill me if they find it out;" and she was gliding out of the door before Sidney understood and caught her by the arm.

"What do you mean? Are you going back?"

"Yes, O, yes! It is better for me to go back than bring trouble on your head."

"Wait, Sitara, wait," she cried. "I must think. I cannot keep you with these jewels and clothes. Would you rather give them up and stay, or keep them and go back?"

"I will give them up, I will give them up; for if I go back there is only the old well back of the court-yard for me, and"—shuddering—"it is very deep and dark."

Sidney shuddered too, but she now knew Sitara was in earnest and understood what she was doing.

"Very well, then," she answered, "you shall stay; but let us gather these things up quickly; we have no time to lose; put the jewels all together in this while I am gone."

She went out, bolting the door at top and bottom, and hurried down stairs, stopping neither right nor left, though Mary Harris had come back from evening service and was waiting to speak to her. Out into one of the arms of the old palace she went to a native Christian woman.

"Matam Gini," she said, "I want a clean siah and chuddar at once, and mind, you are to tell no one I asked for them."

Matam Gini gave them quickly, showing no signs of astonishment, and soon Sidney was back in the little room and Sitara had them on, and her own clothes and jewels were tied in one compact bundle.

"Now I will get them out of the house as quickly

as possible," said Sidney, and went out to where the assistants were sitting in the dark, and asked Mary Harris, the oldest and most experienced of the girls, to come to her room.

"Now," she said, "I have something very difficult and dangerous for some one to do, but if it is done well it will be of great help to us and save us much trouble. This bundle must be put in Moonia's house at once. It will not do for you or any of the servants or anyone connected with the mission to take it, or even any native Christian, but you may know some one who is quite unconnected with us, and who is accustomed to going about in the native city, who can find the house without asking any questions, and, remember, the utmost haste is necessary. The girl you saw there, called Jumia, has come away from her friends and says she is determined to stay with us and be a Christian. But she has brought her jewels and rich clothes. You see they must be returned at once without anyone's knowledge. How can it be done?"

Mary Harris looked startled, for she saw even more clearly than Sidney did the full danger of this, but she said quietly:

"I can manage it, I think," and then added, "I will take Hannah Leach with me if you do not mind, and go home and arrange it from there."

"Certainly, but say nothing to anybody. I can trust you. I am so thankful that I can trust your wisdom and discretion;" and she kissed her. She could feel Sidney trembling as she returned the kiss, and she knew she alone must take the jewels home if harm was not to come out of it. Taking the bundle under a white shawl which she usually wore on evenings less hot than this, she started out with Hannah, and they were soon at their own home. After greeting her mother she went straight to her own room and opened a box and took out a dark cotton sari that had been given her by one of the rich high caste women she had visited. Folding it around her she brought it up over her head and looked in the glass. She was dark and regular-featured, and no one would suspect in any light that she was not a native in that dress. A pair of dark eyes and a sari will transform anyone into a high caste native lady. She went out the opposite side from the servants' houses and slipped through a hole in the wall, and then, with a swift rush through a dark narrow lane, she was in a native quarter; then another narrow lane, and she struck a broad street. This she had to cross. She did it fearfully, but saw no one, and passed on down another dark narrow lane and turned a corner, and was in still another. All along were natives half asleep on their charpais, with their sheets drawn quite over their heads. She had slipped on some old soft shoes that made little sound, and she glided along like a dark shadow. Sometimes a man turned on his bed, but she was out of sight before his sheet was pulled off, and on she went, her heart making to her startled ears more noise than her feet. And then she was at the house. Turning to the right she thought the lane would bring her to the side of the courtyard, where a wide-spreading pipal tree near the gate she had always entered would shade her, and between which and the wall she hoped to drop her burden quietly and unnoticed. But going on she was appalled to find she had miscalculated and was on the opposite side. Her heart stood still as she peered over the wall and saw people moving about hurriedly with chirags in their hands, and by their light exploring the corners of the courtyard, and then Sitara's mother and the servant passed out at the gate. Now she saw that she would surely have been discovered had she come out as she had intended.

When their footfalls quite died away she hurried around to the back of the house, raised herself on the wall, dropped the precious parcel close between the wall and tree, and then softly fled away, back through the dark lanes into her own room, unmissed and undiscovered. Here she sank on the floor, pulled off her sari, gasping with fright and loss of breath, and here her sister, wondering at her long absence, found her. As soon as possible she forced herself to go back, talk a little with her mother, and then on back to the old palace to relieve Sidney of her apprehensions.

CHAPTER XV.

SITARA.

AFTER Mary Harris had gone with the parcel Sidney took a chair and a palm-leaf fan and went out on the terrace where Lily Jahans, the other zenana teacher, was sitting in the murky darkness. They sat in silence, trying in vain to get cool and to rest; but every moment the air seemed closer and heavier. Finally Sidney said:

"Come, let us go up on the roof; it may not be quite so hot, and it is possible that there the air may be moving a little. We surely cannot sleep to-night unless we can get cooler; and no sleep means work so poorly done that it would better be left undone."

"Yes, Miss Mellen," which was the only answer this girl ever gave to any suggestion or request. Had Sidney told her to go up and throw herself off the roof she would have answered, "Yes, Miss Mellen," in the same soft, low tone, and, what is more, she would have done it. At least Sidney used sometimes to say this to herself a little impatiently. They went across the terrace, up a narrow, dark stairway, through a room open to the air on all sides, across another open terrace, then through a little door that led up another narrow little stairway which brought them out upon the flat roof of the palace. Sidney drew a long breath as she took one of the chairs always there.

"This is better," she said; "I always feel better here—nearer God; the great vile city is so far below and the stars seem so kindly; one can forget many troubles and disappointments up-here."

"Yes, Miss Mellen."

They stood a moment looking away across the round dark clumps of foliage, with the spire of the church breaking their monotony in the foreground, to the sky in the west, where was still a pale clear light against which the domes of the old tombs showed in grim dark masses. All was perfectly still; not a breath of air, not a leaf, not a twig moved; the darkness, so heavy and suffocating, seeming to transfix the trees beyond the power of anything but the mighty monsoons to stir them; but the time for these beneficent wet winds was not near, and people were hardly yet allowing themselves to long for them.

Then came a woman, saying:

"The Băra Sahib's gari has come and the Bări Mem asks if you will see her?"

"Of course. Give her my best salaams and ask her, if not too weary, to come here where it is less hot."

A few minutes later Mrs. Clinton came toiling up and sank exhausted into a chair. While fanning her and waiting for her to recover her breath Sidney saw with throbbing heart a tall form, too slight for the Bishop, emerge from the door and come toward them through the darkness. Carnton, for it was really he, took her hand as he asked the usual question:

"How are you standing this terrible heat?"

"Fairly well, I think, but there are so many other things to think of I can hardly tell; I have not time to stop and inquire of myself how I feel."

" Well, I can tell you," said Mrs. Clinton, languidly, " I saw Sunday evening at the church that some one must take you in hand and look after you, or soon there would be only a shadow left. Don't you know how thin you are growing?"

" Am I?" said Sidney, absently. She was trying to conjecture with confused head why he had come to see her after marked avoidance of her for months; and, more than this, why a return of the old, protecting, sympathetic manner—why?

" Yes," said Carnton, with more feeling apparent in his voice than he wanted, "yes, you are thin and careworn, and "—in a lower tone—" it cannot fail to make your friends anxious. Why "—half impatiently, as she made no answer—" will you bear everybody's burden and forget that your first duty is to yourself?"

Still Sidney said nothing. It was sweet, dangerously sweet, to be so chided by him, to know that he thought or cared, even though he might again relapse into coldness.

" If people really wish to commit suicide why do they not do it quickly, and not give their friends months of lingering anxiety?" said Mrs. Clinton. "This sounds shocking, but it seems to me that some of you really are determined to kill yourselves with work."

" There were some other people, not long ago, who gave their friends anxiety in that same line," said Carnton, with quiet meaning, "and now they not only have reformed, but are trying to reform others."

" Yes, I acknowledge it," said Mrs. Clinton, with a little laugh; "it was foolish, and I want other people to be wiser."

Sidney was wondering if it would not be possible
to get his opinion on the especial matter she had in
hand, whether he would think she had done wisely or
whether he would say she might have done differently.
The longing for his sympathy and approval was so
strong that she felt she must have it. Had it
been possible she would have confided the whole matter to him. But it occurred to her, happily, that
the topic assigned for the next missionary conference
had a bearing on this very point. The point to be
considered was the advisability of ordaining women
that they might baptize converts in the zenanas, but it
would cover much ground and many points that were
always arising in their work, and on which different
people held different opinions, and would be thoroughly discussed. She said, abruptly:

"The missionary conference comes on next week.
Are you both prepared to give decided opinions on
the question chosen for discussion?"

"What is it?" asked Mrs. Clinton.

"The ordination of women," answered Carnton,
quickly, "and I for one—"

"Yes, we know you 'for one,' or two or three, if
possible, object," said Mrs. Clinton. "We know you
object for two reasons, but the principal one is that
you dislike the idea of women usurping authority.
You would like all women to be household goddesses
and find their sphere of action in the home circle. I
agree with you in theory, but it makes me a radical
advocate of woman's rights to hear a man state my
belief for me, to lay down the law for us; so I always
try to anticipate him if possible, for I really do not
want to be forced to believe women should vote."

They laughed a little, and Carnton said:

"That is rather too complex for a dull brain to comprehend, but you forgot to state my other reasons. It seems a sort of interference in family life. Generally speaking, it must be best for the women to wait until they can be baptized openly; there can be few cases where it would be well to do anything to separate them from their families."

"But," said Sidney, "if a woman cannot live a Christian life in her own home, or if her life is in danger, and she of her own accord separates herself from her family, what can we do? Must we turn her back to death, or a life of moral death?"

"Never. In such a case there is only one thing to do, and that is to give help, as we must always when a human being comes to us for succor; I, of course, was not referring to a case of that kind."

"Even though it bring trouble and suspicion on ourselves should we shelter her?"

"What has that to do with it? If it is the right thing to do, then it is the only thing we *can* do, and the consequences are with God, and not with us."

She had her answer now, and if he should hear of her being unsuccessful in her work, or being talked about in the city, he would remember and know that what she did was not rashly done, but with an earnest wish to do the right.

"Well," said Mrs. Clinton, "I cannot see why these poor creatures should not always be encouraged to leave their wretched homes, where they are looked upon in the light of servants, or at the best as children, and at the worst beyond all imagination."

"There are many sides to the question," said Carnton, gravely; "it is not a good thing to interfere and break up families; there is nothing for the women to do and nowhere to put them, and it must in many cases be a better thing for them to learn to live a noble, unselfish life in the family, even though it be hard; but is it not time we were going? And will you kindly explain our errand to Miss Mellen?"

"Yes, I suppose we must go some time," rising; "I have got in the way of feeling as though I can never get up out of my chair when I have once sat down; but what was I going to say?—my memory seems as lazy as the rest of me. O, yes; I want you to come with us for a long drive to-morrow evening. We are going out to Bibiapur to see if we cannot find some air to breathe that is clean, even if it does come out of a baker's oven. I am going to take some sandwiches with me, so we will not have to hurry back, and you are not to say no."

"Air from a baker's oven" was the only expression Mrs. Clinton ever seemed to think conveyed any idea of the heat they were undergoing.

"I will not say no, for I shall like it very much indeed," said Sidney.

"My husband has a meeting," Mrs. Clinton went on, "for English-speaking natives, but Mr. Carnton will come with us. In fact, it was he who proposed it, and I am only going along for propriety."

Sidney had hardly said she would like to go when she remembered it would not be well to leave the house, unless she was obliged to do so, while nothing was settled about Sitara. To go away three or four hours would be unsafe at this time, and she hardly noticed what Mrs. Clinton was saying, except that

Carnton was also going, and the vision of this long drive with them and the quiet hour by the river was tempting and made her for a moment wish it could be arranged, and that she might leave Mary Harris in charge of the poor child down stairs. But instantly she knew it could not be, and she said in a voice made cold—or at least Carnton thought it cold and stern, by her disappointment:

"After all, I am afraid I cannot go, much as I would like it."

"Nonsense," said Mrs. Clinton, "you must go. You must get a little rest and change, otherwise you will have to give up altogether and go off to the mountains."

"No," she said, decidedly; "I cannot, and that ends the matter. The demands of my work will not allow it."

Mrs. Clinton was surprised at the cold and abrupt way she spoke. It was not like her, and she could not account for it, unless she wished Carnton to understand distinctly it was because he had planned the drive she would not go, and that she wished him to understand definitely that "the demands of her work" were more to her than his wishes or even his love.

"Well," said Mrs. Clinton, to cover his defeat, "then we must ask Helen May. She needs a little rest, and Kate Deane also."

Sidney went down with them, and Carnton's cold "good night" told her that he would return, as she feared, to his old unkind, distant manner, and she wondered impatiently what kind of person he could be, so full of moods; it was not like a man, and of all men least like him. She would have liked to

20

give them a hint of the particular demands of her work which would not allow her to go, but there was Lily Jahans sitting quietly in the dark, and, besides, the air of India is full of invisible telephone wires that carry all the smallest acts of the white people to the millions of ears ever open to hear the worst of the sahib lŏg.

Sidney stood looking regretfully an instant after them as they disappeared in the star-twilight, thinking what it might have been to her hungry heart to have that long evening near him, even if she only sat silent and listened to his voice. Then she turned away quickly and went down to Mary Harris, who was waiting for her.

"It is all right," said Mary, in a low tone, for the bearer was fastening the lower doors near them. " But, Miss Mellen, you must not be surprised if this leads to great trouble. I know these people, and we must be prepared for anything."

Sidney was startled by the seriousness of her tone. Her inexperience had assured her there could be nothing serious to fear if the girl had no valuables with her.

"Why should they make trouble? If the man comes I will simply tell him the facts of the case— that she has been married before, and rather than be a party to deceiving him she came to me of her own accord; that I did not suggest it to her; that I did not even know she was coming until that day she came; that I did not wish her to come, though I am glad now that she is away from them."

" Dear Miss Mellen, he will not believe you, and if he did he will pretend he does not, and the mother—

do you think she will easily give up a home for herself, which she will have if she can marry Sitara to this man, or the price she will get for her if she cannot marry her?"

"But what can we do?" asked Sidney. "I could not tell her to go back to that horrible life. When she came do you think I should have told her to go back?"

"No, indeed," was the answer. "It was right, I am sure, to give her shelter. What else are we working for but to help the oppressed and distressed?"

Mary Harris was one of the many helpful Eurasian girls educated in mission schools who have given devoted, earnest service to the mission work, and in whose judgment all have confidence. Sidney bade her good night and went away to her room. She had been longing to go before, but had waited, as she wanted no appearance of hurry to be perceptible, but to have everything go on as usual.

Passing through her own room quietly she lifted the purdah which hung over the little door and went in.

Sitara, sitting on the floor with her head on her arms and her arms on a chair, was sound asleep, like the child she was; her chuddar falling back revealed the pretty face and thick shining black hair; one little foot was extended from beneath her skirt, and on one ankle was a large round spot like a blister.

Sidney stood looking at her sweet, innocent face, and she said to herself, "Mary Harris and Mr. Carnton are right. We are here to help the helpless, and, no matter what comes, I am glad I can help her, and I will now rest on this thought and not swerve, no matter what disaster comes to me."

As she moved away Sitara started up in fright, staring at Sidney in bewilderment and fear; only for a moment, however, and then she rose and threw herself into the arms of her friend.

"O, Miss Sahib, I had forgotten where I was and what had happened, and I had great fear." Sidney could feel her heart beat, and she was trembling in her arms like a frightened bird.

"You need not fear; you are among friends who will care for you and not allow you to suffer harm."

"I know, I know. Did I not go to sleep without fear—the first time since my mother took me to Mohun Lal's house? Did I not know that my dear Miss Sahib would make all things right? But you will not let them take me back?" and again she trembled and fluttered in Sidney's arms.

"No, no; but "—trying to turn her attention from herself—"what is that sore on your foot? Did you hurt yourself?"

"No, no; Mohun Lal made it."

"Mohun Lal? How?" asked Sidney.

"With an iron."

"With an iron!" she repeated, in horror; "did he strike you?"

"No; the iron was hot."

"Look at me, Sitara. Tell me the truth."

The soft eyes looked into hers wonderingly.

"Why should I not tell the truth?" she said, simply. "He cannot find me here if you take care of me."

"Sitara, is this true? Did Mohun Lal take a hot iron and burn you, knowing what he was doing?"

"Surely? why not?"

"But why did he do this," asked Sidney, sternly. She was bewildered at the indifferent way the girl regarded the wound. It spoke of familiarity with worse things than burns.

Sitara drew the folds of her chuddar over her face, and her head went lower and lower, and she half whispered :

"He came when my mother was away—and—and—I did not please him, and because of his anger he made the iron hot to punish me."

Sidney was appalled. Then these things were true of which she was always hearing vague hints, and of which she now and then read accounts in the English papers, given in no vague terms, of men beating their child-wives, starving them, burning them with irons, and of their dying from all kinds of injuries. Of course, she had believed these accounts, but she had not realized what it really meant until she saw this pretty girl shivering and crouching with shame at the very thought of what she had undergone.

"And, Miss Sahib"—gaining courage as she felt Sidney's arms about her—"he told me he could kill me, that he would do so unless I obeyed him, and no one would know, as it was his own house we were in, and the deep, deep well by the house was also his and had no voice; and, Miss Sahib, I tell you, his eyes were red and glaring as the eyes of the tiger in the jungle." She was trembling so much with fear that she could hardly speak, but with great effort she went on : "He came always when my mother was gone, and the servant, who also feared my mother and this evil man, thought with me that my mother knew he came, that he had found out I was a widow and now would not marry me, but would buy me, and that my mother would allow the arrangement."

The last words were so low that her voice could just be heard and the words only guessed at, and then, except for her sobs, there was silence—a silence of fear and horror on her listener's part, fear for the girl and horror that a mother, a *mother* could do this hideous thing!

Suddenly the girl started up with a new fear, as Sidney made no answer, and throwing herself at her friend's feet she clasped them in her little trembling hands.

"O, my dear Miss Sahib, you will not let him come? You promised, *you promised!*" The last words were almost a shriek.

"Hush, my child, nothing shall harm you. Do not fear. God will care for you if you put your trust in him. Now lie down on this mattress and go to sleep, for I must go to sleep myself, and get strength for my work to-morrow; you will be alone, but you need not fear, as this room is a secret drawer; even I had forgotten it, and only thought to hide the ugly door and keep out draughts in the cold weather by a curtain; but"—turning back—"when have you had food?"

"Not for days. It was thus that I could make my mother fear, because if I died it was only that she would lose the money for me."

"Then I must get you something; will you eat our food?"

There was no answer. She did not like to be rude, and yet there was the old iron-bound caste to make her shrink.

"Did you never eat with the other women at Miss Whitlow's and with Shew Pershad? He was a Christian."

"Never; always alone at Miss Whitlow Sahib's, and after him when with Shew Pershad; it is not our custom to eat with men."

"But think a moment. Did he give you no sweets or any part of his food?"

"Sweets, yes, when we were on the railway train, and white English bread, but—that was different."

"No; if you took bread from his hand your caste was broken then, and now it will not matter."

Sitara was silent. It was a shock to her that no person of white skin can ever comprehend. Every instinct of her nature was against her eating with Christians, as with one of lower caste.

"I will bring you food, for if you die you well know they would tell it in all the zenanas that I killed you."

"Then I will eat," she said, simply.

Having brought her some bread and butter, the only thing she could get without being noticed, she kissed her and went away with a heavy yet thankful heart—thankful that she had not entirely refused to let the girl come, and thankful that the poor thing was out of the clutches of those people. She could only say over and over again to herself,

"What a mother! what a mother!"

The next day was a trying one. The heat was greater or her strength was less, but the zenanas all had to be visited just the same, only she intended, on Sitara's account, to make the visits shorter, though the child was quite happy in the little room with some bright bits of cloth and a doll, whose clothes were a never-ending source of interest.

Sidney found the doors of two houses closed, and no sound came when she knocked. It did not look as though all was right, for they were houses where she was regularly expected. A little anxious she went on to another, a favorite place, because the women there were more intelligent and the man, the head of the house, decidedly sensible and liberal in his opinions. The door was shut, but in answer to the usual "May I come?" a voice said:

"We are all sick and cannot see you to-day."

"But if you are sick I can at least read you good words, and I can also tell the Doctor Miss Sahib, and she will come and make you well."

She could not believe they did not wish to see her, for they had been so affectionate and bright and so earnest in their efforts to improve themselves and their homes.

"No, no," was the answer in lower tones; "we are forbidden to read any more;" and very low, with mouth near the door, "We are sorry! our hearts are fallen down with sorrow, but we are forbidden."

Sidney could echo her words; her heart, also, had "fallen down." The walls must have heard and told the air that a girl wished to become a Christian and had run away from her home. How else could these people, so far from Mohun Lal's house, know, and this was only the beginning of a bitter trial, she now knew; for if these people who loved her and had so much confidence in her would give her up because they had only heard idle rumors—and this must be all they could have heard—then others who cared less for her and for her teaching would also close their doors against her.

She went back to her wooden gari, the smell of its paint blistering and burning in the sun making her sick and faint. She got in with difficulty and swung the wooden doors to with a wish to shut out the whole world—the world of her work in which she had put her heart; the world that was for the first time showing its thorny side to her. The distance from the ground to her room seemed too long to be traversed, but she pulled herself up by the railing, and when in her room threw herself on the bed to rest a few moments before going to Sitara and to try to think; but her head was throbbing, and she could only rest. Soon rising, she went out and got more food, and, taking it to Sitara, found her tranquil and happy, having made two whole garments for the beloved doll.

That night about midnight a gari drove up, and Mary Harris, who slept in the arm of the old palace that stretched out to the native houses, heard the chaukedar say to some one in the gari:

"Go away, you rascals. We are not women-thieves. Why should you come here with such lie words?"

"But I tell you," was the answer, "you are rascals, and your fathers before you and your ancestors for all generations. The girl has been stolen, and we have eaten great offense."

Then the answer:

"Your ancestors were inhabitants of the jungle, and you will return to the jungle in the body of a jackal when you die, and I will waste no more time with you. Only that I may sleep now, when all people of honest disposition are sleeping, I will tell you again that the Miss Sahib comes and goes alone, shut up in her gari, and wants none of the low caste women of your house. All these days do I not sit at the gate and see who goes out and in, and would I not know if any outsiders came in? And none at all have come but sahib people, and even your arrogance would hardly declare that you were of the sahib caste."

This sort of conversation, called "giving gali," intensified a hundredfold, went on for some time. Finally the man in the gari said, as he drove away:

"I will go to the magistrate, and then with the paper from him I will find out whether or not you are the outcast servant of a woman-thief."

There was some conversation among the servants who had been aroused, and then all again was quiet.

Mary could only hope that Miss Mellen had not heard the noise and would know nothing of it until morning, at least; but she slept little, wondering what could be done, but perfectly sure that the man would return with a warrant.

The next morning, as Sidney was going out of the gate, two men in police uniform, with fierce-looking pugris on their heads, came with a paper from the magistrate, which was, as Sidney feared (for she had been warned by Mary of the man's threat), a summons for her to appear before the court and show that she had not stolen or abducted Sitara, the child of one Moonia.

Sidney felt the blood leave her face as she said briefly that she would be there at the required time.

Mrs. Clinton heard of this, for before many hours

it was all over the mission, and, indeed, well over Lucknow, and offered to go to court with her, which was a great comfort to Sidney. And all the mission people during the two days that intervened before she was to appear came with expressions of sympathy and offers of assistance. Carnton alone did not come, and she thought it cowardly of him, and hardened her heart against him.

The magistrate wished to make it as little embarrassing for her as possible, and perhaps shortened the inquiry that she might not be kept in suspense. But it was not pleasant; the dirty court room, the crowds of staring natives, the answering of questions, even though kindly and respectfully put.

She was cleared of any intent of abduction, but Sitara, poor little Sitara, was consigned to her mother's care, as she was under age, and was taken shrieking out of the court room, and the last glimpse of her Sidney had was just before the gari door closed on her, when she was sobbing too violently to see the loving, longing eyes resting on her; and thus the child went back into the impenetrable darkness and shadow of native life.

The magistrate, seeing Sidney's despairing face, said:

"It is the law, and I can only execute it, though I am firmly convinced in this case the law is not just, but," in the usual cry, "what can *I* do?"

Her work was almost stopped, as from the first day she had known it would be. It had been told from house to house, this story of abduction; it had been told at the bathing ghats as the women put the finishing touches to their toilets; and it was told at wedding feasts as a warning to foolish people who would trust the strange Miss Sahibs in their houses, and servants, as they chatted on the road with their babies out for an airing, or sat around their food at night, told it.

Though many men knew that Sitara had run away to escape from her mother and this man Mohun Lal, and also knew of their cruel treatment, it was not well to let the women think this was the reason of her flight; it was better to let them think the Miss Mellen Sahib, in her eagerness to make Christians, stole her, imprisoned her until she was starving, and then gave her food when she was too hungry to refuse, and thus broke her caste; also that she had used some sort of witchcraft by which she had cast a spell over her, and even though she had come back to her mother it was as one possessed of an evil spirit. Many a heart stopped beating from fear, many a mother vowed that never should the hateful Miss Sahibs bring their witchcraft into their houses again; so from one and another house Sidney went and found each one shut, and no response to her call for admittance. Now and then some of the women that had been visited for years would ask her in timidly, and perhaps shyly put forth questions which she was glad to hear, for it gave her a chance to explain. But perhaps the next time she went she would again be refused admittance, and the nervous and debilitated condition of her system and the great heat made all this even more crushing than it would have been had she been well. Mary Harris warned her to be careful, and begged her to stay away from her work or go away for a change of air, as it was quite possible that her life was not safe.

But Sidney replied, sadly :

"I am not here to save my life. I must go on as long as there is one house open, that I may prove that all they are saying is not true; but"—and the tears rolled down her cheeks—"I did not think there were so few of all the people for whom I have been spending all my life, and whom I thought loved me, so few who were true to me and who really trusted me. What could I have done but let that child stay with me? It has brought disaster on my work, but I am sure it was right. It must have been right."

She was not now burdened with work, nor were Matam Gini nor Hannah Leach nor Mary Harris and Lily Jahans. So they spent an hour each day talking over the best plans for work—whether it was best to teach in any house where they would not be allowed to teach the Bible, and whether it was worth while to spend time teaching the women to sew when there was enough Bible-teaching to fill up all the hours. And then they had long Bible lessons, bringing out new thoughts and new ways of presenting old truths. Sidney had often wished for this, but their time was so taken up with teaching that they could only have their lessons once a week, except, of course, the preparatory prayer and Bible lesson for the day's work.

Then they also went out to the villages near Lucknow, which had been heretofore unvisited. The distance was long and consequently exhausting, yet they were welcomed, and as the days went by they grew cheerful again, though Sidney could not get over the sense of wrong and injury because her native friends had given her up so readily. There was the worst sting possible in this to her—the hardest thing a conscientions person can have to bear—the feeling that her work must have been faulty and imperfect, else she would have had a stronger hold on them after giving up years of her life to serving them.

Then she had another thing to weigh on her. Carn: ton was distant and cool. She had felt sure of a little sympathy, but there was none, and she felt lost and alone and forlorn. She knew he loathed any publicity for women, and she knew he did not like, abstractly, the thought of any woman in whom he was interested to live alone, or to have a work of her own that made her in any way prominent, though he said he honored and revered the single ladies that were in mission work, and confessed that their work was even more important than his own.

Knowing this she only thought that he could not be friendly with a woman whose name was in the mouth of native and European alike throughout the whole city, and, in fact, throughout the Northwest. It was not noble in him; this she acknowledged, yet she could not find a harsh thought in her heart for him. She only felt it as an added burden, and wondered sometimes if there could be any other calamity in store for her, and, if there were, whether it could add anything to her suffering. Her pretty color had long ago faded, her mouth drooped in a pathetic way, and yet there was a courage and a patient endurance in her face which had never been there before, and which made Mrs. Clinton take her in her arms and say,

"My poor child, this is too much for you to bear."

"Yes, too much for me to bear alone," she answered, with quivering lips; "but I am not bearing it alone; I could not."

A CHURCH FOR ENGLISH-SPEAKING PEOPLE.

CHAPTER XVI.

DANGEROUS ENEMIES.

THE hostile tribes on the frontier of the English or American housewife are not many, nor are they strategic in their operations. They are known; their methods of attack are also known, and, though ever present, they yield to a persistent fire of brooms, dusters, and scrubbing-brushes, backed by a few accessories.

But in India, though the warfare may be long and the ground well contested, the housewife is ever on the losing side; and if she be wise she finally yields to opposing forces, both of nature and human nature, glad to save a remnant of the sweet temper and pleasant disposition upon which she had erst prided herself.

Mrs. Clinton arrived in the winter, but hardly had she stopped shivering in her big, empty house when the lû began to blow.

Now the lû is not a wind to be regarded lightly, either from its character or its effects. It is hot, dry, and dust-laden, and though it is not, as tradition has it, immediately fatal in its effects, it often amounts to the same thing in the end. It begins in the morning and howls steadily all day. While it is going all doors and windows are closed, and after a week or two corked, for it shrinks everything shrinkable. It

21

is so full of sand that even though doors are closed
and corked it is possible to write one's name on any
smooth surface an hour after the article in question
has been dusted.

Not only does it fill the house and every thing
therein with dust, but everybody seems permeated
with it. Eyelids grate on the eyeball as they wink;
nostrils are dry and parched; the throat feels as
though lined with sandpaper, and even the temper
seems to be so full of it that only a state of constant
irritation is possible. In the wake of this wind are
neuralgia, toothache, rheumatism, croup, fever, and
general leanness of soul.

Mrs. Clinton had put up the few draperies and
pictures that she had brought and bought, but they
were only very small oases in the dreary desert of her
whitewashed rooms, and sometimes she had been
tempted to wish the missionary allowance were a little larger, that she might be able to make the house a
little less bare; especially did she wish for carpets,
as the matting was not only very coarse, but it wore
out so very quickly that she saw there would not in
the end be much economy in having it. But after
the lū began to blow, her longing for more furniture,
except in the matter of carpets, ceased, for every extra
picture and drapery and curtain was only a trap for
dust and other and worse things. Her first disen-
chantment was brought about by the beautiful skin of
a peafowl that she had bought in a fit of extravagance. It was not very wild extravagance, as she
paid only one rupee for it, but she counted every
pice with a nervousness that she had never before in
her life experienced, for, no matter how well and

easily she thought she was going through the month, there were so many unexpected incidentals that she had found herself getting in debt. This was something that had never happened to her before in her life; and she did not mean to buy any unnecessary thing, but this peafowl's plumage was so beautiful that she could not resist it. It was simply the whole skin ready cured for stuffing. Driving in a nail she hung it in a bare side of the room where the light fell full on the brilliant iridescence of green and gold, and delighted her eyes many a day when she was too exhausted to read or think.

One morning, being up before the sweeper had swept, she saw on the matting underneath where the skin hung a little shower of feathers, and, with a sinking heart, examined it only to find it full of larvæ, and though she had it thoroughly cleaned and powdered with arsenic, yet she took no more pleasure in it, for there were apt to be bits of feathers now and then floating down from it. Finally it was removed and given to the servant's children, who built little gardens with the long feathers in the hot sand.

The next disappointment was in her steamer-rug. It was such a soft, pretty rug, and with it she had draped the old cane-seated couch which helped eke out the scanty supply of chairs in her parlor. She had been ill a week, and when coming around again as she dusted a little here and there she found it fairly filled with tiny black burs that eat at the rate of ten knots to the hour. Holding the rug up toward the door she was appalled to see daylight through it at a hundred points.

The third trial was a bit of gold and terra cotta

colored embroidery she bought while with Mrs. Mackenzie. She had draped it over an unsightly air hole between the dining room and parlor. It was of cotton, and she had no fears for it, but this too was riddled out by the shining slimy fish-moth, the *bête noire* of all good housewives.

Most moths are fairly respectable in their way, and have a choice of food, keeping strictly to one diet, but this creature is a perfect scavenger, taking wool, cotton, and linen, and especially does it delight in starched clothes, in which most people of India abound; but more than all the hatred and aversion lavished on these moths is that poured in spirit on the heads of the Indian crickets; not the big, brown, homely cricket that sits by the chimney-corner and sings, and inspires teakettles to sing also, but a little pale yellow creature, whose motto is,

> "The cricket who eats and hops away
> May live to eat and hop another day;"

and perhaps this may be the reason why he, more than all other foes of the housekeeper, is the most dreaded. Even an occasional cobra in the bath room, or many scorpions under the matting, or centipedes dropping from the ceiling, do not inspire the terror that the cricket does when one finds he is in the house to stay. He usually comes to stay when he does come, and when firmly established in a house nothing short of burning down the house will exterminate him, as he thrives brilliantly on carbolic acid, kerosene oil, and nitrate of silver. This is his first bad point, and his second is the rapidity of his work, which is in fact so summary that it permits no interference whatever.

The first of his handiwork Mrs. Clinton saw was on a new light-weight flannel coat of the Bishop's. He had had it made and sent home, and wore it one afternoon. Taking it up the next morning he found one sleeve and the back perforated.

The second specimen was rather a masterpiece in its way. Mrs. Clinton had found her kid boots covered with the green mold of ages one day after a month of the rains. On inquiry she was told that they should have been kept in a tin-lined box, but since they had once been covered with mildew if she wished to save them she would better have them blackened every other day until the close of the rains, even if she did not expect to wear them. So there was a row of boots and slippers to be blackened each day, and it was the bearer's work, when he could not get the sweeper to do it.

Looking at the kid boots and also a pair of Lillian's one morning, she thought her eyes must have been deceiving her; but no, they were the same boots, but every bit of the upper surface of the kid had been gnawed off, leaving fantastically mottled purple and white boots. She had no words sufficient to express her indignation, so she said nothing, but the loss was great, for she well knew that unless some miracle was performed they would have no more kid boots while they were missionaries.

When she showed them to her husband she thought —I only say she *thought*—she heard him mutter something about " miserable vermin." and she had a guilty sense of hoping it was true; for such remarks, even by proxy, have a power of relief not to be despised.

After Mrs. Clinton had found these crickets in her best Saratoga trunk, and was told that it would never be safe to put anything in it again, she offered a piece for every dead cricket brought to her. She gave out a good many piece, but as the crickets did not diminish in the rooms she began to examine the dead as they were brought, and judged by the dried and withered appearance she had been paying over and over again for the same old cricket.

However, she could not think of giving up her expensive and nearly new trunk, and she exposed it open to the sun when the thermometer stood at 170 degrees for days, then had the lining taken out, and paste made of flour mixed with two or three things said to be deadly to all the insect tribe, and new lining bought ; then a man came up from the bazar and worked two days and lined it fairly well. She congratulated herself on her economy and clever management until, thinking one day she would fill it with winter clothing she opened it and a half-dozen crickets hopped out, and she found the lining a tissue of rags. This was the straw that broke this housewife's back, but the Bishop, though he sighed sympathetically, was not entirely discouraged until he, too, had his Waterloo.

Dr. Thompson, who had been in the house before him, asked him the day he was leaving, which was the day before the Bishop entered the house, if he might put his books in his care. The Bishop was very glad indeed to have them, as he had felt it a great privation to be without books for a year, and one which he had contemplated with secret dismay.

This did not prevent him resenting Dr. Thompson's earnest request that they might be well cared for.

"Certainly," he said, a little dryly, "I really see no reason why I should not take good care of them. I have been accustomed to a fairly good library all my life, and understand that good books need care."

Dr. Thompson looked a little doubtfully at him, but said no more.

But when a boxwala one day offered him a book at about a quarter of its cost, and when he saw Dr. Thompson's name in the book, and saw that it was the third volume of the *History of England*, and that this boxwala had also one of Thompson's *Gibbon's Rome*, he remembered that doubtful look on the good man's face, and concluded that books in India require a kind of preserving care of which he knew nothing, and thereafter kept the bookcase locked, and carried the key in his pocket. It was a tiresome process, and he hated to have to unlock a door every time he wanted a book of reference.

After the lū began to blow he found that even though the bookcase was a good one the dust filtered through to an extent that made him dread to touch the books.

It was then that he and his wife succumbed to the necessity of having a boy to dust and look after the house generally; but even with all the time and care the bearer could give the Bishop found himself getting peevish at the dust. When the rain came on the books required much more care, for he found them mildewed inside and out, as though they were three hundred years old. The Bishop was sad, because he knew no one likes a musty, mildewed book, but every bright sunny day the bearer spread a rug out on the walk in the sun and placed the books open on it, and then sat by them until they were dry, to prevent the necessity of having to buy back any more from wandering box-walas or peddlers. Of course this process was bad for the books, but it stopped short of utter ruin.

One morning, as the three months' rainy season was about half over, the Bishop was called into his study by his wife.

"See here," she said, pointing to something on the wall over a water-color picture that looked like a huge spray of thin gray coral, " what do you suppose this is ?"

He came closer, climbed on a chair, touched one end of it with his finger, when some of it crumbled off, leaving a lot of little gray creatures running wildly about. Looking at the back of the picture he found it plastered over with mud. Then turning to the face again he saw the creatures at work under the glass.

"Ah," he said, after a moment's pause, "these must be the white ants of which we have heard so much, and we have here ready-made Sir John Lubbock's plan of watching them under glass. See them! They are organized like an army of sappers and miners; each one has his beat, and is relieved by the man who had his place before him."

She looked and saw them march back and forth across the white margin of bristol board, carrying away bits of the Whatman's paper on which the sketch was made. There was already a crescent-shaped hole in the middle of the sky of the picture.

" This is indeed curious, but we would better put a stop to it. Dr. Thompson will hardly like to have this picture spoiled." But just then, glancing from his post on the chair at the top of the bookcase, his face whitened, and he jumped down, tore open the bookcase, took out a book, and, opening it, sank down in a chair in despair. Fearing sudden illness his wife rushed to him, but he could say nothing, and only showed her the book in silent pain and disgust. He had respect for all books, and felt it for the sake of the books; besides, he had these books in trust, and he felt it much more from this fact.

His wife hastily took out book after book only to find them completely honeycombed with little canals, winding in and out without any apparent method, full of dust. Of course the books were completely ruined.

Again Mrs. Clinton thought she heard ecclesiastical anathemas pronounced, but this time it was on the "confounded country," and again she felt like saying, "Those are my sentiments; please say it again," but she did not dare.

There was some excuse for this good man. Within the last week he had been tortured beyond endurance by the various powers which seemed in league against him. First, he had found a karait coiled on the wire of the lantern kept burning in his bedroom. A light is always kept at night, as snakes are said never to come into a room where there is a light. The next morning there was a huge cobra in his bath room, which wandered out while he was hunting a stick with which to kill it. The advantage of being bitten by a karait instead of a cobra is somewhat, as the former is warranted to kill in twenty-eight minutes and the latter in a half-hour. He had been bitten nearly mad by mosquitoes, fleas, and kătmăls: he had been startled

by huge muskrats running across his feet as he sat at
his desk, making the cold chills creep up his back,
thinking that a cobra was at last about to finish him.
He had been worried in his bath by big ants; he had
had his tea flavored by little ants that were hidden
in the sugar, and his body had been the campagna for
a moving army of middle-sized ants. He had thrust
his bare foot into a slipper and been given a chill by
touching one of the numerous little toads that come
in droves into the house in wet weather; he had had
a big lizard fall across his mouth from the ceiling
with a thud just as he was having his first morning
yawn. He had found his new silk umbrella, bought
in London, riddled by mice, his new coat perforated
by crickets, his steamer-rug cut up by moths, his
writing-desk of teakwood, which he had bought with
the purpose of taking it home, inhabited by the grub
that spends its life in the wood and leaves the desk
worthless; his new Gladstone bag had happened to be
where the roof broke under the pressure of a pouring rain and had been soaked with muddy water and
its natty appearance completely destroyed; his new
fountain-pen was stolen—that is, it had disappeared
from the tray on his desk; and now this, and this was
really the worst!

Then as he thought of it all—of the horrible dust
and heat of the dry season, of the dreadful mildew and
steam and slimy dampness and prickly heat of the wet
season, of the cheating and stealing of the natives, of
the slowness of development of the native Church, of
the deadly infectious diseases lurking in every drain,
touching one in every breath, ready to snap the thread
of life in a moment—as he thought of all this and of

the languor and depression and confusion of mind and exhaustion of body, his face reddened, and he fairly threw the book across the room—across the room, mind you—and said aloud and with perfect conviction, "This is a *beastly* country!" And then his wife sat down and laughed till the tears came, for she knew this was a word he hated, and she was now sure of the other expressions, and they meant as much from him as many worse words would have meant from another man, and they sounded so strangely funny, for he had resolutely, as became a bishop, always abstained from anything but the most moderate of terms.

And in his exclamation and in her tears there was much homesickness and much longing for the old, quiet, reliable existence, and much loathing of a country whose climate and attributes and accessories permit safety to neither animate nor inanimate things.

The Bishop did not smile. He felt it all too much. But he arose and got the *Daily Pioneer* and looked at the shipping list for Liverpool, and then said:

"We could catch the *Souchong;* it sails on the 31st."

His wife stared. In answer to her evident amazement he said, firmly and boldly:

"I am quite satisfied with my experiment. I do not want to be a missionary to the missionaries any longer. They are quite welcome to any scrap of comfort they can snatch from the powers that militate against man in this awful country, and I have come to the conclusion that if I were a fixture here, and there was no other honorable way of escape, I would take the first good opportunity I could get of going to heaven. If people choose to stay here they may stay, and if they want it I will vote to double their allowance, but let *us* go."

His wife's face was bright with relief. She felt she could shout for joy; but then they would not be fulfilling their contract if they did this, and how people would laugh, and the missionaries, especially Mrs. Mackenzie, would actually chaff them, and with reason; and there was too much obstinacy in her nature to give up quickly. So she said, wearily:

"O, no, we cannot do that. The people at home know our plan and are expecting much from it; and we promised to do in all things as missionaries do, and you know *they* cannot throw up their appointments, and leave when they are tired and discouraged. We must stay, and then we can speak with authority."

"My dear, I can say all I will have time to, with all the authority I want, and more than will be listened to; and if I vote to double their allowance and to give them full power to use the plans that seem best to them, that will speak strongly enough."

"But it would not do to bring Lillian down into the heat, even for the week it would take us to get to Bombay; and there are the schools and your tracts and the Chandausi mela and the Conference; besides, you have been so tied to this work you have had no time to see the other mission stations. Of course we can now speak for the Lucknow work, but there are hundreds of people who want to know of Bareilly, Moradabad, Calcutta, and Bombay; and "—winding up with the remark—"you know, dear, you promised."

During two or three days following this conversation Mrs. Clinton learned how uncomfortable it is to live in the same house with a person who silently resents a position into which he has put himself but out of which he cannot take himself.

CHAPTER XVII.

ROKEWOOD'S ILLNESS.

IT was near the close of the rains, and the day had been a little more stifling than usual. It had required a little more of an effort to rise in the morning, a little more of an effort to dress, and a little more of self-persuasion to put one foot before the other when it seemed necessary to cross the room. There was a little less air that was fit for breathing and a little less strength to draw the breath; for what had been left from the ravages of the hot winds had been pilfered by the damp heat of the monsoons; what vigor had not been burned out in the dry weather had been steamed out in the wet.

Katie Mackenzie had been having fever for a week, when the doctor had ordered both her and her mother off to the mountains for a month, as they were very much reduced; and Mackenzie had just finished his lonely tea in the morning and was starting out to the publishing house, when Rokewood came wearily up the steps with his valise in his hand as usual and sank down in a chair, took off his topi, and fanned himself without speaking. Seeing he was ghastly pale, Mackenzie asked, anxiously:

"What is the matter? You look completely fagged."

"That is just it! I am fagged—exhausted; I did

not want to wait at the station for anything to eat, for in addition to the cost of breakfast I would have had to take a gari; for by the time I had eaten it would have been too hot to walk."

Mackenzie uttered an exclamation of impatience, went out quickly, and said to the servant:

"Here, bearer, bring a glass of milk at once for the Padri Sahib, and having done this prepare tea and toast at once, and mind that you bring it hot."

And taking the milk he strode back to Rokewood, who took it and drank it eagerly. Then Mackenzie, whose face was as stern as his voice, said:

"What do you mean by risking your life in this manner? Do you think it no sin to commit suicide?"

Rokewood smiled faintly.

"Of course I think it wrong, and even if I did not I would not do it; I love life too well."

"But if you take a course that your common sense tells you, or ought to tell you, is calculated to kill you, how do you differ from Sita Ram, who killed himself yesterday in the bazar with a knife? He did what he believed would kill him in a short time; you do what will kill you just as surely, though it may take a little longer to do it."

Mackenzie was apprehensive of resentment on Rokewood's part, but there was none. He only answered, meditatively:

"Something like that seemed to strike me for the first time as I came along. I suppose there is a limit to what we can stand, and I begin to think the limit is much sooner reached here than in any other country in the world; and God wants men to live, not to die, for him. There are not too many workers."

"Too many? They are counted by tens where they should be counted by hundreds, and whoever unnecessarily risks lessening the number sins!" This was said with indignant energy.

The tea was brought, and then Mackenzie asked:

"What are you going to do to-day? Tell me quickly, for I must be off."

"O, I hope to sell fifty rupees' worth of books. I am behind with my subscriptions for the Leper Asylum, and I must make it up. That was really why I did not take a gari."

"Well, I have this to say, Rokewood," said Mackenzie, firmly, "you shall not go out to-day through the heat unless you hire a gari; there is too much fever and cholera about. You are staying with me, and I will be no party to such absolute recklessness."

"Perhaps I will to-day, but you know I cannot do it often and live on my prescribed allowance. You men that take the full amount forget that we cannot do as you do."

"Nor could you, my dear fellow, live on your prescribed allowance if we did."

Rokewood looked surprised.

"I do not understand," he said, simply.

"You will pardon me, I know, for finally saying what I have kept back so long for fear of seeming inhospitable and rude. But when you urge us to try and live on what you are living, remember that if we were not prepared to give you good food when you are going from station to station you would exceed your allowance; that you are really not living on your income, but upon ours? Much of your work is done when you are staying with missionaries who could not give you entertainment if they tried to live on the miserable pittance you do, and when with us you do not live on native food, which makes it an unfair test also in regard to that; and when you say you live on native food and in native style, and thus save out of your allowance enough to educate a boy, you are not stating the truth."

Rokewood's face flushed and he looked ashamed and miserable.

"Upon my word, Mackenzie, I never thought of it that way. I hope you will believe me, but it is so much the custom for us to stay with each other—"

"Of course, and we want you to come, and do not want you to do anything else but come, and we like to help you carry out your theories, but you must state the truth and you must let us advise you now and then in return for it;" and added, as he got no answer, "I beg of you, dear Rokewood, don't look so hurt, and do be wise and sensible; get a gari and do your work, and, mind, you are to come back promptly at eleven for breakfast;" and he went off hurriedly, as he had talked longer than he had intended.

Mackenzie did not feel exactly happy as he went on. In fact, he felt much as he might had he given a friend a blow in the face.

"I did not mean to hurt Rokewood," he said to himself, "though I have always meant to tell him the facts of the case; but I lugged it in by the neck, and I did not say just what I meant to say, and it was a muddle, only it was the truth."

All the morning he was oppressed by this feeling as he went on with his work, and he hurried home, anxious to see Rokewood and remove the sting he knew his words had left.

However, he did not find him, and, after eating breakfast, he went over to the Bishop's bungalow, thinking he might be there.

"Where is Rokewood? Is he not here?" he asked, anxiously, as he saw only the Bishop, his wife, and Carnton at the breakfast table.

"No, was he coming here? I saw him in the bazar, but we were both driving fast, and I only gave him a nod, but did not speak."

"O, it is all right if he was in a gari. He did not seem well, and I urged him not to walk about the city to-day, but he did not promise;" and he hurried off.

"Well," said Carnton, as he ate his sūji and milk, "I am glad to see that Rokewood affects someone else as he does me. He is always on my mind, and he reproaches me without meaning it and exasperates me without knowing it."

"Why?" asked Mrs. Clinton, with interest. She was always interested in seeing how different people affected each other.

"Why, you know Rokewood and I are alike in that we are alone in this country, not only unmarried, but likely to remain so, and that we both are anxious to do the most for our fellow-creatures possible in the time that will be given us to live. He follows a course that my reason will not allow me to follow. I have tried it enough to know what would be the consequences—tried the native food and the native houses and the walking to and from work; but still when I see him persevering on that line I am always

22

conscious of a longing to do as he does and cast reason to the winds."

" I would say then you would better follow your feelings," said the Bishop. " We want more mission aries like Rokewood. I tell you plainly that he in terests me more than any other man here. I have watched him closely, and he is doing just what he ought, and I encourage him, whenever I see him, to keep on, and I wish there were more men willing to try it and thus popularize this way of doing mission work."

" It is useless to try to popularize his method, for people, excepting Rokewood, who have lived long in India are too wise to try it," answered Carnton ; " but perhaps there may be men in America willing to come out and set the example."

The Bishop looked sharply at Carnton. He was inclined to think there was an implied reproach in his words, and Mrs. Clinton laughed a little con sciously, but said nothing. As far as she was con cerned she was quite willing to forget that it had been part of her husband's idea originally, and, later on, her own, to set an example to missionaries, for anything requiring so much energy as an example was beyond her ; and, more, she had said something like this to Mrs. Mackenzie, which had chased away the shadow that had been between those two women.

" But at any rate," Carnton went on, seeing he had no answer, " I had to decide for myself, as everyone does, how I could best economize my strength, and how I could do the most for the mission, and I found I must sacrifice any romantic ideas I had."

" But how does Rokewood exasperate you?" per sisted Mrs. Clinton.

"Just because he takes the luxury of carrying out his early romantic ideas, even when they are not worth while. When he had charge of the Leper Asylum in Pithoragarh he lived among the lepers, when others thought he could do them as much or more good had he lived up on the hill a little way from them; but he thought not, and there was grandeur in this sacrifice because of its magnitude. To-day he is taking as great a risk, working all day in the sun without food, as he did when he carried out the dead Christian lepers in his arms and buried them with his own hands; as great a risk, but with this difference: then it was necessary, for even among those lepers caste still binds all, and there was need; but to-day there was no need. It is madness to go about the bazar without food, for cholera is waiting for any good subject."

"Is he the only one in danger?" asked Mrs. Clinton, quietly.

"No, and hence all the more need of great care. Not fear, but a steady, sensible care in keeping the system in good order lessens the chances. No one who is wise can wish one to take unnecessary risks; there are enough unavoidable ones to satisfy the most eager for accounts of missionary suffering."

At six that evening Rokewood drove into the compound just as Mackenzie was starting for the regular meeting of the Epworth League, and, much to Mackenzie's relief, looked well as usual and far more elated than he had seen him before.

"I have sold double the number of books to-day that I hoped—Bibles to Hindoos, stories of the Gospel to Mohammedans, and any number of medical hooks and of Murdock's moral publications. I've had a capital day, though I am tired out."

"You can thank me, for it is no doubt part due to the fact that you took my advice and did no walking, but saved your time and strength for your sales. Come on with me, if you are not too tired, to the Epworth League;" and, paying his gari wala, they were soon going over the road, which was being watered by water-carriers, as the break in the rain had made it necessary.

The Epworth League was quite in the hands of the young men and women of the native Church. Carnton seemed to have a good deal to do with it, but kept in the background and only appeared when necessary. It was his plan to let them learn to do all this alone. Mrs. Clinton, sitting quietly by the door, had a feeling of indescribable interest tempered with a humorous sensation that made it impossible not to laugh now and then as the familiar words, "Epworth League," "Committee Meeting," "Report," and a few others came out of the mass of unknown words as they read, talked, and discussed with the same eager interest found where the original society flourishes. She tried to think of what would be the effect on her Sunday school class of young ladies in America were they taken up bodily and suddenly put down in the midst of these olive-faced girls, draped in their white chuddars, and the dark-eyed young men in white. She amused herself with picturing the efforts of the young ladies to find out where they were, and to make themselves understood; but of one thing she was sure—they would be perfectly certain they were in a branch of their own society.

Rokewood was interested in it all and spoke strong words of encouragement, but he looked so pale and tired that Mackenzie took him away before the close, under the conviction that he had probably had no dinner even if he had had breakfast.

As they got into the gari Mackenzie said:

"We will go home to dinner. I thought from your appearance it would be better than staying longer."

"It is not really necessary on my account," said Rokewood, a little stiffly. "I do not wish to put you to unnecessary trouble, and, in fact, I would have stayed at the surai had I had my valise with me."

Mackenzie winced; he knew his words of the morning were not forgotten.

"Now, Rokewood, I call that very unfair of you, for in your heart you know I want you here, for my own sake as well as for yours. My wife is so much more contented in the hills when I have some one with me that it pays to invite people to come. But now own up, Rokewood, did you not have a luxurious breakfast?"

Rokewood laughed as he answered:

"I had the same as the people for whom I am laboring had, puris and parched grain."

"And for tiffin?"

"More puris and grain."

Mackenzie gave his pony a cut with the whip, but said nothing.

"You see," added Rokewood, apologetically, "I got so interested in my sales that I forgot all about breakfast until it was too late to come back to you. Besides, as I wish to go on to Allahabad to-night, I felt

I must not leave anything undone that I could do. I shall not have a chance to sell Bibles to these men in Lucknow again for a long time."

"Well," said Mackenzie, in despair, "I give it up. If you, knowing all you are risking, are willing to go the whole day with puris, which are about as wholesome as shoe-leather, and grain, which in connection with puris is as nourishing as gravel-stones, it is useless to try to teach you wisdom. You must do your own work in your own way, and may God care for you, for you will not care for yourself!"

"God does and will care for me; my part is only to obey him."

"Yes," said Mackenzie; "we each have only to do that, but I cannot think you have obeyed him to-day."

Then they talked of the different messages that come to different men, and each acknowledged that God's call to his servants must be different according to different natures and the varied forms of the work he required done in the world.

About ten Rokewood went off in Mackenzie's gari to the station, intending to sleep there in the waiting room and take the three o'clock train for Allahabad, and Mackenzie went to bed. About three o'clock Mackenzie was roused from the heavy, suffocating slumber that comes only at its worst in the rains when the punkah is stopped for a few moments and the blood settles in the brain and around the spinal cord with the effect of wishing to burst the veins and force itself to the surface. Gasping and struggling for breath he called out to the punkah cooly to know the reason of the stopping of his work.

"Preserver of the poor, a gari has come."

"Who is in it?"

"The Padri Sahib, and he sends his salaams to you, and he is very ill."

Jumping up and catching up the ever-burning lantern quickly, he cried impatiently as he ran out in his flannel sleeping suit:

"Why did you not say so at once? These fellows would take just as much time to tell one the news if the world were exploding! Come in quickly if you are ill, though I cannot see who you are."

"It is I—Rokewood," said a faint voice, "and I have cholera, just as you feared. Call the bearer and let him help me out."

A chill of horror kept Mackenzie still for a second; only a second, yet he had time to be thankful that his wife and Katie were safe in the mountains, and then he said:

"I can lift you; here, gariwan, help me; we are good for two of your size;" and a few minutes after the sick man was in Mackenzie's own bed, the gariwan was driving swiftly away for the doctor, and Mackenzie was applying the ever-ready cholera remedies.

As the pain eased, Rokewood spoke freely.

"How long had you been ill? You surely did not come as soon as you were ill?" asked Mackenzie, sorely distressed, and with the peculiar pain of having his worst fears confirmed—a sort of responsibility coming from foreknowledge.

"No; I waited, thinking I would be better; I did not think it serious; when I saw I was getting worse I came; I knew you would take care of me."

"Of course, but if you only had come at the first, the very first moment you felt ill!"

"Yes, yes; but it's all right; I'll pull through this time; I am already better; the pain is less."

Mackenzie made no reply; he did not need to see the set face of the doctor who soon came to tell him that there was grave doubt as to the possibility of the patient pulling through.

The morning broke with a whirl of dust and leaves and writhing of trees and long flashes of lightning from all sides, cutting sharply the thick, heavy clouds, and still the two men—the doctor and Mackenzie—worked steadily until they were joined by Carnton, who had listened to the messenger Mackenzie had sent to tell them of Rokewood's illness and of the doctor's order that no one·was to come, and drove over as quickly as though the doctor's order had been to come at once.

"I am come to help," he said, simply, in answer to the doctor's scowl.

Mackenzie was glad, for he himself was already beginning to show some of the symptoms of cholera, and felt strangely weak and exhausted, and was glad of a little respite and a chance to get some food and rest.

The messenger, after telling Carnton and seeing with pleasure that he disobeyed the doctor's order, went on to the Clintons, who had come out on to the veranda to watch the storm, which was traveling rapidly, leaving broken branches and even broken trees in its wake.

"The Padri Mackenzie Sahib sends salaam and an order that no one coming to hees house," said the man, enjoying the importance of his message and the chance to speak English.

"What!" said Mrs. Clinton, not understanding.

"Padri Sahib got collar, and Doctor Sahib say not coming to hees house."

The Bishop sprang to his feet.

"Mackenzie Sahib?"

"No, nuther sahib—the strange sahib who walks and sells books. And, your honor, Doctor Sahib says no one coming to house," the man added, as he saw the Bishop take his hat and stick.

"It does not matter"—in answer to the man—"the doctor cannot keep me from going. Of course we cannot leave Mackenzie alone in this calamity and danger. I shall take every care of myself," as he saw the white set look on his wife's face; "but, you see, I must go."

"Yes," she said, with difficulty, "you must go, but how can I have you go? O, how glad I am that Lillian is not here!" and she ended with a dry sob.

The man stood silent, quickly understanding the Bishop's intention and waiting for a chance for more words.

"The Doctor Sahib very zabberdust man, he let no one come. Carnton Sahib also zabberdust, and he gone running. He not 'fraid to the doctor;" and the man grinned with joy at the thought of one man not fearing the doctor.

Mrs. Clinton looked relieved.

"Wait, then; Mr. Carnton has gone; that is sufficient help now, and the chances are that the doctor may let one stay where he would order two off; and surely those who have lived here must know better what to do in such cases," she pleaded, weakly, feeling that it was ignoble to be glad that Carnton had gone, but unable to control the feeling. The Bishop looked undecided; the man, who was a chaprassi and proud of his English, suggested:

"Doctor Sahib very smart, very like obeying; he tell it, 'All come all get sick,' and then it make pretty-kettle-of-fish."

Even now, as ever, Mrs. Clinton felt inclined to laugh at the man's English, though it was a sort of hysterical wish.

The Bishop took two rapid strides across the veranda.

"I will at least write a note to Mackenzie and ask if I can be of any service;" and he went to his desk and came back quickly with a note telling the man to hurry and return with an answer.

They sat silent, waiting, and now the storm seemed also waiting, but there was a freshness in the air that told of rain somewhere—that in some more favored place the parched ground was soaked and the thirsty leaves of the trees washed clean—and a little of that freshness had extended to the weary people at Lucknow.

The man came back saying that the doctor would permit no one else to come, and that the sahib was no better.

"Will he die?" asked the Bishop.

"God knows," said the man, indifferently.

"We can at least pray for him," said the Bishop, and they knelt and he prayed for this soul which was battling for life; prayed earnestly that God would in his wisdom permit the restoration of life; but his words seemed to fall back, and would not ascend on the wings of faith. There was a heaviness that he could not account for in his petitions, though he continued long on his knees. Somehow he could only think of the many times he had encouraged Rokewood to continue in an experiment that others of long years in India believed to be fatal; of the fact that even while he had encouraged this poor young man in his theories he had thought them too full of risk for himself. True, Rokewood had no wife or children, yet it struck him all at once as a cowardly thing to urge another on in a course which he himself could not conscientiously take.

He had rather unconsciously felt that he was solving the problem by proxy; that he could report on Rokewood's experiment as well or perhaps better than though he went through it personally; for Rokewood knew the country and the ways and language of the native people and how to live cheaply, as he could bargain for things, and also knew how to protect himself; yet now it seemed another thing.

" But why," he asked himself in bitter self-reproach, " why does it appear so different now, now when it is too late, when poor Rokewood is dying? It is not at all certain that he might not have taken cholera had he been careful and wise; others have taken it, and why should I feel to blame in the matter ? "

But there was no answer, and the controversy with himself went on till another thought even more terrible came. He took his wife's hand in his and looked in her face. One thought was in both minds. Cholera was coming too near to be disregarded. At sunset one or both of them might be gone, aye, even under ground, for ceremony does not follow in the path of cholera, and then what of Lillian and the boys?

In other mission houses there was silence and waiting and prayer. For once the work stood still and also waited. It could not be long, for this dread visitor treads with no lagging footsteps, and while a life was passing who could do aught but wait in solemn silence? For it was all too true. Poor Rokewood's life was going out swiftly. Young, just beginning to work for God, eager and bold and ready for the hardest fight, the thickest of the fray, happiest when he had something difficult to do for the great Master whom he loved, and yet, before the morning had passed, before the dew was off the grass, before the freshness was gone from the trees, before the mists had fled, he was going, and hundreds in Lucknow, men who had only lived for self, for what the day might bring, were alive and going out for the day's work or pleasure, as the case might be.

It was hard; the Bishop must again settle himself to the idea that since God permitted it his servants must bow in acquiescence.

"Rokewood," said Mackenzie, as the dying man seemed easier and brighter, "you are very ill."

He turned his eyes quickly.

"Am I in danger? Will I not recover?"

"The doctor said it is always safe to make our final arrangements in case of—"

"But what did he say? Will I get well or not?" interrupted Rokewood, quietly.

"My dear Rokewood, we fear you may not recover, but we know you are in God's hands and not in ours. He knows, we do not; but we know you are ready either to live or die, as he wills."

"Yes, yes; but it is strange. I did not think I

would die until I was old; I am young, and I have done so little, so little. Do you think, Mackenzie"—with increasing feebleness—"He will count what I was ready to do—what I wanted to do for him?"

"Yes, yes, dear Rokewood," in a voice he strove to make steady. "Why not? It is our wills he wants, and surely you have given him yours."

"Our wills are thine," he murmured. "Yes; I gave my will up to him years ago, when I was on the farm, before I went to college; and mother, she was proud of her missionary son, prouder of him than of the others, with all their money;" and he rested, dreaming a little.

Mackenzie, after giving him medicine, again called his attention to any message or arrangements.

With an effort he brought his mind back from old days on the quiet farm.

"Tell mother and father that I had rather live as I have lived and die as I have died than to have been a king; it is glorious! What terror has death for me? None. It is only to be dying a moment and then eternity with Him who died for me." And a long pause.

"Rokewood, dear friend, I spoke sharply to you this morning; forgive me; I did it because I loved you and wanted to save you from this—" he caught himself; that was not just what he meant to say.

"Christ saved me," Rokewood said feebly. "Forgive? It was nothing, and you have stood by me nobly. You will find my mother's last letter with the address in my trunk, and all the accounts of the Leper Asylum and the subscriptions; they are all there; and—you will write."

Then gently as a child goes to sleep in its mother's arms his life went out, leaving the body straight and stiff and cold.

At sunset a lonely little procession passed out to the cemetery beside the river, and the body was placed in the unconsecrated ground outside, among the unbaptized, among all who are not of the Church sanctioned by the government.

Mackenzie, white and weak, looked as though it was with difficulty that he remained standing through the burial service. They had asked him not to come, but he had urged he would be better for going, and nothing more was said. Each one mourned genuinely for the great soul that had departed; not mourned for him personally—for him to die was infinite gain—but mourned that his familiar form would go no more out and in among them; mourned that the number seeking to plant the standard of the Cross was lessened by one; mourned that one so earnest, so true should miss opportunity to stamp his character on hundreds of others; mourned for those weak ones who might ever go unhelped by him.

Was his life wasted? Who shall say? The disciples objected to the breaking of the box of costly perfume. It might have been used, they said, to better advantage; but even though broken it has been passed down from century to century, shedding its fragrance all the way. So let us hope his life may ever be a memorial to be passed on down from father to son, for generation after generation.

In little homes in the mountains, away from the stir of the world, where the white topi of the sahib rarely comes, when the night-fire blazes before the hut, casting weird shadows in which lurk the jackal and leopard, the father may tell of a tall sahib who loved work and who loved the natives so that if any were tired he would do their work, and who said it was better to work than to have lacs of rupees; who said that the Greatest who had ever lived had been a mistri and held the hammer and chisel, and that this same Greatest would save them from transmigration if they only believed on him. And again on holidays, when the women have on their brightest jackets and chuddars, one will tell how on the mall which goes around the little lake away up in the mountain among the clouds, when all the great people were walking and riding and chatting, this same strange sahib had taken her son from her arms and carried him, because she was weak and tired and the boy was large, and all the sahib people looked at him and laughed and thought he was mad to carry a black baby among them. And other cooly women will tell of his helping them carry a piano down the mall, and how again all the people laughed and thought him mad, and that he came to be known among them as the mad sahib, who believed there could be work too hard for low caste women.

And they will then tell that he always told them it was because the God he worshiped and the Incarnation in which he believed told him to do these things; and because his God loved everyone, even under-caste women, who are nothing, as the whole world knows, he also must love all and help all; and when in trouble and sorrow, when the rains fail and the harvest is not, and there is nothing to eat, or when the son dies and the house is desolate, then may they not leave the

wooden images that cannot help them, and, imperfect
and feeble as the prayer may be, **shall He who heeds**
the **young ravens**—shall he not, even for this man's
sake, who died for them—shall he not **hear and an-**
swer?

CHAPTER XVIII.

CARNTON AND SIDNEY.

WHEN, after leaving the grave, the Bishop and his wife and Carnton were getting into their gari at the entrance of the cemetery, on their way home, they saw Sidney just about to drive off alone. Mrs. Clinton stopped her with a wave of her hand and went to her. The girl's white face made her heart ache, and as she held her hand a sudden thought came to her, and she said imperatively,

"Come with us; we will take you home."

Ordinarily Sidney's pride would have kept her from going where she would be brought into contact with Carnton, but she knew he had been helping to nurse Rokewood, and in the face of the fear that she might never see him again, that to-morrow at sunset they might again be in this cemetery to put under the white sand all that could make life dear to her, and all that was making it heavy for her, she could not keep up her pride. Her fear caused her to yield at once, and without the slightest hesitation she said, simply, "Yes, I will come." And she got out of her gari and came across. While the Bishop helped them in Carnton looked at her. Her face, with all the pretty color gone and drawn with fear, seemed to be the face of another, and not that of the woman he loved. His heart throbbed fiercely at the thought that possibly it

was because he had been in peril that she had that
stricken look.

Their eyes met, hers scanning his face anxiously to see
if there were any signs of coming illness; his with love
and longing plainly speaking—plainly to Mrs. Clinton, but not to Sidney, who had forgotten herself in
her anxiety for him. There was little said; some
quiet remark from the Bishop on the beauty of the
sunset showing brokenly through the trees, and soon
they were on the bridge that spans the Gumti. The
Bishop, with an exclamation of wonder, stopped the
horse. The river—flat, sluggish, bounded on either
side by wide stretches of level land, grass-covered, pool-
bestudded—was full of reflected glory. The sky up to
the zenith was spread with large lapis lazuli blue,
gold-lined, and bronze clouds, all gold-rimmed; and in
these masses of glory were little breaks through which
showed the sky a sea-green, pale and clear. At the
horizon, where the river disappeared in dim perspective, purple, soft, but strong against the gold, were
the domes and turrets of the Chutter Munzil palaces;
reflected perfectly in the water below was the same
—the domes and turrets on a background of gold, the
blue and bronze and gold of the sky, showing through
the whole long sweep of the river from bridge to
palace. At the sides, too, the pools had caught a
golden glow and gleamed like mammoth topazes in
the setting of bright emerald green grass. It had
been a dreary day, for the morning storm had, after
passing, returned and left the blessed rain, which
seemed to leave both blessings and beauty behind it.

The deep voice of the Bishop reverently said, as
though he were reading the psalm in a choired cathe-

dral: "The heavens declare the glory of God; and the firmament showeth his handiwork. Day unto day uttereth speech, and night unto night showeth knowledge."

Then as they drove on they talked of the life that had just gone out, of his work, of the possibility of his life having been saved had he taken proper food the day before, of the results of the work, and of Rokewood's parents, who had been so proud of their missionary boy.

"As far as men can see," said Carnton, finally, "he might have been alive had he taken proper care of himself, for in every case in this particular epidemic of cholera which has proved fatal there has been some irregularity of diet or exposure to wet and chill without proper after-precautions, so the doctor told me. But that is neither here nor there. God permitted it, and I had rather at this moment be in Rokewood's place than save my health at the expense of my work. We are here to care for ourselves in just so far as will further our work, and no further. We must be ready for whichever helps our work, whether life or death, and I, for one, am willing it should be either."

His face glowed as he said this, and the Bishop grasped his hand.

"My dear Carnton, I believe you, and I believe you are not alone. Every man I have met, excepting one or two I know, works on that principle. It is clear to me now to-day as it has not been before. It is for God and his work, and individuals must have liberty to live this out as best they can. Rokewood had his way.

> "'As man may, he fought his fight,
> Proved his truth by his endeavor,'"

he added, quoting from some old war poem he remembered imperfectly. Not since he left the old company of which he had been chaplain had he thought so much of battle and warlike valor and fields of glory and being buried with honor on the field of battle as he had since coming to India. There was the same valor, the same *esprit de corps*, the same grim determination to conquer or die, or willingness to conquer and die; and he had to confess, in face of all the difficulties, it certainly was as necessary as in those days of bloodshed, if victory was to be with them.

"Will you not go up with us, Sidney?" asked Mrs. Clinton.

"No!" said Carnton, authoritatively, "she must not go. With so much infection abroad she is better at home. Who knows where it will fasten next?" he added, in explanation of the surprised looks turned on him.

As they came up in front of the old palace he quickly helped her out and took both hands, and, with his eyes telling her at once of his love and devotion, he said good-bye softly, but tenderly and sadly.

And then Sidney was alone and must wait. She went up and sat on the roof in the dark, and held communion with herself. It was the first time she had wanted to be alone since the news had come at noon that Rokewood had died and Carnton had helped Mackenzie nurse him. Now she sat and thought of that hand-clasp and the look from his eyes. She sat and hugged the thought of these to her, and almost cried for pity of herself.

"It is a beggarly dole I shall have to keep with me and live on during the remainder of my life if he

goes. And I know he will go, for life seems to be
arranged that way—that what one most longs for is
snatched at the moment it is dearest. Perhaps even
the dear memory of that look may fail me. I may
forget the love that was in his eyes for an instant. I
may forget how it seems to have one's hands clasped
in love as though they would never be surrendered.
I shall go on in my work; thank God, there is work
that I love, and he will give me peace after a while.
The pain must lessen—must, or I cannot live."

The house was quiet at last, and still she sat and
thought. At midnight she said:

"He may now be ill; he may even be beyond help;"
and as these thoughts came she would rise and walk
up and down softly and quietly, for she wanted no one
to know the vigil she was keeping.

"If I were his sister, and though I cared little for
him, I might be in the house and watching for the
first symptom of illness, but I, who only love him
better than myself—I, who would give the whole world
to be near him, to know how he is—must not even ask.
I must wait. How hard life is for us women! how
hard!"

Was it strange that her fears never once reached
the other man, Mr. Mackenzie, who was in equal
danger? And was it strange that Mrs. Mackenzie,
when the news came to her, was torn with fear and
anxiety for her husband, but did not give Carnton's
danger one thought?

Then Sidney would sit quietly in a half-stupor for
an hour, and then again walk the floor. Finally, exhausted, she went into the house and threw herself on
her bed and fell into a heavy slumber, from which she

was awakened at a late hour in the morning by a voice outside the door :

"A letter has come, Miss Sahib."

"Where from?" she asked, her heart standing still at the answer :

"Clinton Mem Sahib."

She could only rush to the door and put out a shaking hand to take it, fearing news of the worst kind.

But it was only a note from Mrs. Clinton saying something of the station meeting—what, she could not understand. She was returning a book that Sidney had lent her, and was thankful to say that they were all well.

Sidney blessed her in her heart for her kindness. She knew well the station meeting and the book were only an excuse to let her know that Carnton had not suffered for his generous help to Rokewood. "It was sweet of her to do this," she said. "Had she not, I would have had to go there and find out how he is, but I am saved from that absurdity, at least."

The assistants and Bible women had gone out to work before Sidney was wakened by the arrival of the letter, and she went slowly after them. Her head was confused, and she felt stunned and numb, as though she had wakened from a bad dream; but when once with the women in the villages she forgot her own troubles, as she always did in the pleasure of greeting them, in answering their questions, and in teaching them.

Four days passed with only a lingering hand-shake from Carnton on Sunday at both morning and evening service in the English church; then came two notes one morning as Sidney was going to her work —one from Mrs. Clinton asking her to come over and spend the evening, and another which she opened with trembling fingers. She did not know the writing, but she well knew who had written it:

"My Dear Miss Mellen: Mrs. Clinton, at my request, has asked you to have tea and spend the evening here. I wish particularly to see you. If I were in America I would ask you to drive with me, but I have realized more than ever in the last few months that we are not in America and must yield to the customs and requirements of the land we are in in order that none may be offended. I have waited, hoping chance would favor me, but in vain. Will you come? Do not, I beg of you, say no, and please do not have another engagement.

"Yours sincerely,

"*Inyat Bay.* Sterndale Carnton."

A week ago Sidney might have had another engagement. She might have felt that something more was due to her than to acquiesce so easily, letting him feel that he could advance and retreat at his own pleasure. But that look of farewell as he stood and held her hands the night of poor Rokewood's burial was too true, too tender, too full of the pain of a possible long farewell for her to doubt him now. Even if, at first, he had felt he could not love a woman who had gone through so much publicity and made so many mistakes, still he was now conquered by his love whether he was willing to be conquered or not. All day she had a happy consciousness of the evening

to come. Not that she dared definitely to think of
what he wished to say to her or of what the evening
might bring. It was enough that she was to see him
because he wanted to see her. She had replied to
Mrs. Clinton's note, saying she would come, but could
not bring herself to reply to Carnton's. An unaccountable shyness overcame her when she thought of
doing so.

She never had found her work more interesting or
the women more interested. One woman, Piari,
asked her why her face was so glad—was she now,
at last, going to have her marriage arranged? The
native women can never understand how a single lady
can bear up under the disgrace of not being married,
for to them it is a heart-crushing thing, and denotes
something in themselves very unworthy.

Sidney laughed, though she was annoyed to feel
the color overspreading her face and to feel an inclination to hang her head, but she avoided giving an
answer.

Night at last came, and Sidney, in a plain soft
muslin, without ribbon or ornament, with the wood-
rose color blazing in her cheeks in a way she could
execrate, went.

Carnton met her at the door and helped her out of
the carriage in a proprietary way that was so nearly
a taking possession that she could hardly walk steadily
as she crossed the room to greet Mrs. Clinton, who
sat behind a teapot pouring out tea.

Mrs. Clinton chatted away, about what, Sidney
could not tell, and Carnton talked on to cover her
silence. He had been disappointed at her not answering his letter; but it was something that she was will-

ing to come; that she had not utterly refused to come, as he fully realized she might. Then Mrs. Clinton took the Bishop's cup of tea to the study, and he asked her to excuse him to Miss Mellen, as he was getting up a lecture on natural history for the boys in the high school.

Mrs. Clinton smiled quietly to herself and said she would soon come back and help him look up points and leave Mr. Carnton to entertain Sidney.

The Bishop looked up in surprise.

" You can hardly do that, can you, my dear?"

" O, yes, I think I can;" and, as he still looked doubtful, she added, " I will tell you why when I return."

She offered them more tea, but it was refused, and then she said:

" I know you will excuse me, as I wish to help my husband to-night. We often sit out on the veranda, for the lamp makes the room so very hot; you will find chairs out there," and vanished, seeming quite to forget to tell her husband why it had suddenly become proper to leave an invited guest for Mr. Carnton to entertain.

Carnton vowed in his heart never to forget her kindness, and said:

" Will you come? Let us walk a little on the veranda, if you are not tired. I have not had any exercise to-day"—and then, as she rose and moved with him toward the door—"and I think I can say what I have to say easier."

" Really," said Sidney, quietly, " I had never thought you found any great difficulty in talking."

" How unkind!" said Carnton, "and how unjust!

I often have the very greatest difficulty, and never more than when I talk with you."

" Ah, yes ; you find me dull and difficult of comprehension, perhaps."

Carnton was silent. This was not Sidney—this was not the kind, sweet woman who had scanned his face so anxiously the other day when she thought there was danger for him.

" Sidney," he said, firmly, " I have much to say, and yet when I begin I seem to have only one thing to say, and that is, ' I love you.' It sounds commonplace, but it means so much to me. It means that I loved you the very first time I saw you, and that I have loved you every minute since. There has not been a waking minute when I have not been conscious of you and of the possibility that perhaps I had at last met the one for whom I have been praying all these years. There have been experiences in my own early life that made me dread more than any other calamity an unhappy marriage. So for years I have prayed that if there was a possible one anywhere on the earth whom I might some day love with a love that I knew would make or mar my happiness—I prayed I might love worthily and well. I prayed that she might be such as would make me happy, and that I might be all that would make her happy, and that our purposes and our tastes might harmonize. From the first I have felt, in a way, though I would not acknowledge it to myself, that you were the one out of the whole world I would choose ; but I waited to test the matter, and I wished to test it as much for your sake as for mine. I am satisfied. It is the one love of my life. Whether you love me or not I shall continue to the end as I have begun. You will be the one woman in the whole world for me."

They still were walking, but when they again came to the corner where the chairs were Sidney sank down in the chair farthest from the light that streamed out across the stones on the veranda floor and out over the grass starred with fireflies, mingling with the white moonlight.

Then, as Sidney spoke no word, Carnton stood and waited before her, his face gleaming pale in the light —pale, but full of the eagerness of hope dashed with a little fear.

The crickets sang loudly, the fireflies shot back and forth, and the air was heavy with the scent of the white jasmine flowers gleaming in the moonlight. Away across the level tops of the houses were the familiar domes and minarets against the deep, dark blue sky of the oriental night, and the cry of a night bird rang out as it passed them.

" Sidney," he said, with great yearning in his voice, "Sidney, have you no answer for me ?"

" Did you ask me a question?" she murmured, her voice sounding strange and far away even to herself.

" Did I not? I have put my love at your feet. Will you take it up, or will you trample on it ?"

Again the silence and the sad cry of the crickets.

" I shall not trample on it," she finally said, slowly ; but when he took her hand it lay cold and passive in his close clasp.

" What is it, Sidney," he cried, passionately, " that has come between us? It ought not to be thus if your soul answers the call of my own."

With a visible effort Sidney spoke :

"We were very near each other once, just before the trouble over Sitara, but when I was full of burdens and anxiety and covered with shame at the publicity of the trial you drew away and left me to bear it all alone."

"O, my darling, did it seem that way to you? It was not true, it was not true." And then, low and quickly, "Do you not remember when Mrs. Clinton came down with me to invite you to go to Bibiapur, and she told you that it was my plan?" His lips were very close to her ear now, and he only breathed the words: "I knew—I knew then what would make or mar my happiness. I felt I was ready to ask and ready to receive, if I might, the benediction of your love; and I wished to take you away from all the noises of native life, away where we might feel free from interruption, away for a moment from all this life which has only work in its plan and has no time for love. I felt you would not be taken by surprise, that you, as well as I, had seen that we were sympathetic; that the attraction had from the first been mutual, and that I had been just to you as well as myself to give you a month or two to test the matter. I saw you were distant and even cool toward me, but I said to myself, 'The native people have been saying things to her as well as to me about our marriage, and she, like myself, wishes to avoid remark.'"

Sidney moved uneasily in her chair. She wished she dared to ask him what they had said.

"So when I was driven to give up the test; when I found I must have the right to see you now and then, to warn you to take care of yourself; when I began night and day to be filled with terror at the thought of evil befalling you, of accidents, of sudden disease, and at the thought I might never even tell you of the love I had in my heart for you, I went to you feeling you knew all that was in my heart, and would know why I came. Do you remember? You promised at first to come with us, and then when you knew that it was I who had planned it—that I was going—you drew back coldly and said the demands of your work would not allow you to go. It meant simply to me that love had no place in your plan—that you would not give up your work, that the liking I was persuaded you had for me was not strong enough to force you, as I had been forced, to doing what had not been in your plan. I went home with the same stunned feeling I had once after falling from a cliff and striking on my head. It did not leave me, and I hardly knew what was going on around me. A letter came from Marker, who has charge of the district while Thompson is away, asking me to go to Howali to look after some things there, and I was gone two or three days. After I came back I now and then heard some mention of Sitara and the trial, but I did not understand you had anything to do with it until I saw it in the papers. I was shocked and cut to the heart at what I knew you must have suffered, but when I tried to get near enough to show you my sympathy you would have naught of me; you kept me at arm's length and would not talk of your trouble. When, determined not to be put off, I asked you direct questions, you told less than you would have told a stranger."

"That was natural," said Sidney, simply, as he waited for a reply. She had found her own voice again, only there was a curious sound of elation and joy in it.

"I can see now that you thought I was avoiding you when I was so full of my own trouble that I hardly knew what I was doing. I suffered, I suffered, and I knew it was only a beginning of the long days and nights that must be lived through. When I saw poor Rokewood dying I envied him the short, sharp agony, and I would gladly have exchanged places with him."

Sidney put out her hand with a gesture of dissent.

"No, O, no!" she said, quickly.

Her hand was taken in that close, sweet clasp she remembered so well; and she thought dreamily that she had been mistaken—that it had not been the last.

"It was only the pity and anxiety in your face, and I almost thought something more than pity, that evening as we came from the cemetery that made me hope against reason. I could not help it. Was I wrong?"

Sidney's other hand, soft, clinging, and warm, crept into his, and her hot cheek was against his forehead, and he had his answer.

Later on, when she again found her voice, she said:

"When you came that night I had Sitara in the house, and I did not dare leave her. I was anxious and fearful, but I wanted so much, so very much, to go, especially as I had thought you unkind for a long time, and it must have been the effort I made to say no that made my answer seem cold; but that should not have been enough for any, except a very faint heart," she added, with a touch of the teasing spirit which lurks in all women.

"It was not all that. I had heard you say that a true woman would save a man the pain and humiliation of a refusal by letting him know in an indefinite way that she did not care for him. Your manner seemed plain enough, and I put the two together."

"Which," interrupted Sidney, with a happy laugh, "was very stupid. You should never, never put a woman's two and two together. They are made to be separate—ălăg, ălăg, as our Hindoostanee friends say."

"Very well, if you forgive me and make up the loss to me by marrying me at once I will not—at least I will try not to do it again."

"Ah, that is another thing," said Sidney, shyly; "there are too many things to be considered."

"Name them. I am ready, for during the last day or two I·have met and conquered every obstacle that you could possibly conjure up."

Sidney laughed at his earnestness and said, "Very well, if you know them so well, suppose you enumerate them?"

"First, then, your duty to your society; second, your duty to your society; third, your duty to your society, and so on *ad infinitum*, and that is all."

"Not all; in fact, only the beginning. My work is dear to me beyond expression. If I could only go on with it, and—and also do as you wish! How can I give it up? The women who stood by me in all my trouble; the schools that have not failed me; my assistants, especially the younger women, who need my help, and the Bible women—I have helped them all—I do not want to let them go."

"Why need you? You can superintend them from my—our—house as well, or nearly as well, as from the place where you are living."

24

Sidney looked at him with mingled affection and amusement and with a shadow of vexation.

"That shows just how much you understand our work, its difficulties, and its needs; and then you belong to another society. My fostering mother would hardly recognize me as her child after I had allied myself with a foreign power."

"Well, we will arrange it some way satisfactorily," he said, as Mrs. Clinton came into the drawing room.

He rose, saying under his voice, "I shall tell her; she has been so kind. Come—"

Sidney arose, and, taking the arm extended to her, went in happily to be presented to Mrs. Clinton, who, when she saw them enter thus, turned quickly and brought the Bishop, who, astonished and glad, gave them a blessing; and then, as Sidney said she wished to go at once, they had good-night prayers, as was the custom in the mission, and the Bishop craved a blessing from God on the two young lives which were to be united in love and in their devotion to the welfare of others.

Was there ever such a drive home as Sidney had that night?

"I think I may this night venture to drive home with her," he had said, smilingly, to Mrs. Clinton; "I can now defy the Hindoostanee Mrs. Grundy." And, Sidney's eyes giving consent, he went.

The white moonlight, pouring a silver flood over tamarind and mango, over dome and minaret and temple, over all in luxuriant splendor, seemed made for them. It was a night for love and sweet words and sweeter silences, and these two people knew it, and wasted neither time nor opportunity.

CHAPTER XIX.

SMALLPOX.

THE hot weather was beginning to lose its hold, and everybody was glad, though it was still too warm to be more than passively glad.

People who had got almost to the end of their strength kept up hope, thinking they would pull through if the cold weather came soon, and looked forward to the time when exhaustion and steamy heat and cholera and fever would give place to vigor and cold and smallpox and fever—to the time when fruit and vegetables would once more appear on the table and when it would be possible to think of meat without a qualm; when the troublesome, tiresome, ever-present white clothes might be exchanged for dark ones, even though they were far from fresh and had the charnel-house odor that all woolen clothes get, no matter how well put away in tin-lined boxes.

The cold weather was really coming, for the punkahs were being taken down, bungalows were receiving their annual whitewashing, and people were coming back from the hills with renewed strength. Lillian, among the number, had come down with Mrs. Mackenzie and Katie, both children wildly happy to be home again. This going to the hills was one of the points Bishop Clinton, as well as his wife, had objected to at the beginning of the hot weather, but before the middle of it the former was one of the strongest to urge men and women that were in danger of breaking down to take a few weeks out of the heat ere the doctor ordered it, saying that prevention was better and less expensive to the mission than cure. Perhaps he had been helped to see this by the fact that Lillian was obliged to go and that he knew his wife ought to have gone. It helps wonderfully toward a liberal view of things to have one's own in dire straits.

But Mrs. Clinton had pulled through, partly because she had determined to do so with a persistent obstinacy that was a surprise to her husband. She had kept up a little mission work, though much of the time it had been of a very passive kind; still even that had its influence. But she had often visited her *protégée*, Pulmoni, who was now going regularly to the Lady Dufferin School for Nurses, and now that the heat was abating she was again going out to the zenanas twice a week.

She had a Bible woman always with her who knew English, and who did much or nearly all of the teaching, and through her she was able to leave some word of truth with the women each time that was remembered perhaps better because of the fewness of her words, because of the novelty of having a great Mem Sahib come to see them, and still more because of her tact and of her loving heart and sympathetic ways. The women always asked about her children, and evidently felt much respect for her because she had two grown-up sons, and also showed much interest in Lillian Baba, whom many of them had seen on private visits to Mrs. Clinton and in the few times she had been to the zenanas with her mother.

Lillian liked going, and always said stoutly that she would be a missionary like Sidney, and that she ought to be allowed to go with her mother, because she was going to teach in the zenanas when she grew up. Mrs. Clinton had been advised not to take her, as there were many reasons why the zenanas were not a good place for a little girl. But one morning Mrs. Clinton was going to visit a particularly agreeable family that had often begged her to bring Lillian, and she yielded and took her.

They left the gari at a narrow street and passed on down by walls and shops and fat, shiny, brown children playing by huge wells, past mosques, and around square corners until the Bible woman rattled a loose door in a mud wall and called out, "Hăm awe!" which was answered by a shaky, shivery old man who led them at once into a courtyard and then through an arched gateway into another courtyard. The house on one side of this yard was two stories high; the side opposite to this was an arcade filled with various cooking-pots and housekeeping appliances of the most primitive order. The other and opposite sides of the square were arcades with double rows of arches and pillars and carpeted floors, arrived at by wide steps, being about four feet above the ground.

Here, sitting on the floor with their second-best gauze chuddars and silk gowns of all colors, were a dozen women. They were evidently expecting visitors, for these same women ordinarily wore cotton clothes of the simplest kind. They had on also their second-best jewels: their very best clothes and jewels always being kept like those of their sisters the world over for weddings and dinners of ceremony. Lillian loved these women as soon as she saw them. They were so pretty and so gentle, and their clothes flung such sweet odors about them as they moved; their rings and bangles and toe rings made such a delicious tinkle, softened by the swish of their silken garments, and she felt so obliged to them for making her nursery vision true, of the fair woman who, with "rings on her fingers and bells on her toes," has "music wherever she goes."

And, too, they each seemed as much little girls as she herself, and even more, for the one thing that delighted them more than an English child was an English doll. So Lillian had brought a doll to leave with them, though she herself was quite done with dolls. She and the doll both were seized by the younger women, who passed their babies to their nurses in order to take the doll to examine its hair, its eyes, its clothes, wild with delight as they found each garment would come off and could be put on again with wonderful buttons and buttonholes, unknown agencies with them. There is even no word for button in the Hindoostanee language, and no use for buttonholes; the Hindoo woman's dress being one garment draped artistically about the body and over the head, and the Mohammedan woman's clothes either draped or tied with strings.

After they had finished with the doll and overwhelmed Lillian with caresses for bringing it, they then came around Mrs. Clinton like a flock of gay, bright-colored birds, chirping questions. One exclaimed that the wonderful lady who had come to see them "had stockings on her hands," referring to the

MRS. CLINTON AND LILLIAN IN A ZENANA.

long Suede gloves she wore; another asked why the
Mem Sahibs did not cut holes in their ears and noses
for jewels.

Mrs. Clinton told them that many white women did
cut holes in their ears for jewels, but that they thought
it barbarous and unbecoming and unbeautiful to cut
holes in their noses.

At this there was a wondering silence and looks of
incredulity on their faces.

"But how can that be?" said one, finally. "Is the
nose an ugly feature, that it cannot be given a jewel?
Or is it more honor to the ear they wish to give?"

Mrs. Clinton had not a word to say. She had always herself thought it a very barbarous custom to
cut the flesh in any place, whether ear or nose, for
jewels, and therefore she had no excuse to offer. To
turn their attention she said her countrywomen, however, wore rings on their fingers.

"And on their toes, like us?"

"No, no; but they wear things like these," taking
the tiny perfect hand of the questioner in hers and
touching the heavy bangles.

"And like these?" putting out a perfect foot that
matched the hand, showing so many and such heavy
gold and silver anklets that the foot was raised with
difficulty.

"No, only on the wrists;" and again she could not
explain why it was nice and proper to wear metals on
wrists but not on ankles.

There was a little murmur of wonder, and then they
wandered to other subjects—"How many children
had she? and was it true that Mem Sahibs had men
to nurse them when they were ill, and that English

women did **not love** their babies and would **not give** them their own natural **food?** that as **soon** as the sons were married they were turned **out of** the house and obliged to find a house for themselves?"

She had to say it was the custom for the sons to have their own houses, and they preferred it; it was no cruelty. This, too, they could not understand, as in India every son brings his wife home to share his parents' house and be ruled over by his mother. She answered all their questions with patience, and sometimes amusement. There was a discussion among the women why Lillian was so white and their daughters so black, and one concluded it was because she used a particular kind of soap, but she was laughed to scorn by the more intelligent ones, who had had it explained years ago to their satisfaction—that is, that it was the Mem Sahib's caste to be white and theirs to be black.

Then a tray was brought, on which was a little silver dish of cardamom seeds, some pán, and two tinsel necklaces, or hárs, which were hung respectively around her own and Lillian's necks, and the cardamom seeds given them to eat and the pán to chew.

Lillian liked the latter, but Mrs. Clinton kept hers in her hand.

There was a little baby, that was kept rather in the background and nearly covered. The mother, a lovely child-woman, hardly larger than Lillian herself, had been much interested in the doll and Lillian, fondling both with affectionate delight.

Mrs. Clinton asked casually why that baby, too, had not been brought forward for inspection, like the others. The Bible woman looked grave at the answer.

and did not translate all the woman said, simply stating that the baby was ill.

"What kind of illness?" asked Mrs. Clinton.

"It is ill, but it will soon be better, and will it please your honor to go now?" she said, a little urgently.

"But first let us see if we cannot do something for the poor little baby. Bring it to me."

"Pardon me, your honor, but it is a sickness that English people do not like."

"Then tell me at once what it is."

"Smallpox. It will be better to go now. All Mem Sahibs do very much not like this disease."

Mrs. Clinton was silent with terror, not for herself, but for Lillian, for she remembered that the mother had had her sick baby in her lap just before she had put her arms around Lillian.

She took her leave without any apparent hurry and with her usual sweetness, but told Lillian not to embrace any of them or to even shake hands.

The visit had been long, and there was no thought among them that there was any precipitancy, but Mrs. Clinton was silent on the long drive, which seemed doubly long. The Bible woman was evidently troubled, though she tried to say that there was little danger and begged her not to be anxious.

When they were finally home Mrs. Clinton gave Lillian some disinfectant, and sent her to change all her clothes and have a bath. She herself went into her bath room for the same purpose, but when she was alone she sat down suddenly on her chair, unable to go any further. Time passed and still she sat as though stunned, her hands clasped tight in her lap and her face white and drawn. The hot season and the rains had told on her—told on her as she had not guessed, but as her friends were seeing with some apprehension. Now even a stranger might have been startled at the pale gray tone of her skin and the hollows under her eyes and the fixed look as though she saw some ghastly horror staring her in the face.

It was not the first time she had met this specter face to face, but now she not alone shivered under his gaze. Lillian, fair, dainty Lillian, had felt his breath on her face, though all unconscious of her danger, and because of this the full terribleness of life in India for the first time seized hold of her. And she felt she was not isolated in her agony. Nearly every missionary wife was a mother, and while fearless for themselves none could escape this deadly fear for their dear ones. They could give their own lives, they could risk the horror of infection for themselves, but what of risking lives that had been committed to them? They could pass in and out of the zenanas and schools, subject to contagion from loathsome and deadly diseases, with light hearts and clear, unfurrowed brows, but how could they go on as they had year after year, knowing that there was no likelihood whatever of all the dear little forms escaping and all the dear little feet walking straight and unharmed through the terrible ordeal? She seemed to see all the hundreds of men and women, brave and faithful, who had trod these paths of thorns with torn and bleeding feet, but without one murmur or even one thought of heroism. And she—she had been blind; but now with clear vision she saw that many a mother who could be brave and cheerful in daylight, in action, when faith could be upheld by the energy of work, dreaded the long hot nights when sleep was impossible, when she could only feel her empty arms, that ached more from their emptiness than ever they did with the weight of the dear burden, and could only see the pained, distorted face of her darling appealing to her through the darkness; and many a father who, as he went about his work, could rest in firm confidence on his call to help evangelize the world, at midnight could only turn on his bed with suppressed groans because of the bitter loss and because of a sense of the injustice done to the helpless, loving little things in exposing them to disease that had resulted in sudden and sharp or in lingering and painful death. There were little graves in Bareilly, in Shahjehanpoor, in Cawnpoor, in Lucknow, here and there all over India, whose little white stones she seemed to see gleaming through the distance with reproach. They seemed to be saying:

"We are a part of that easy, luxurious life that they have said our mothers have led. We are a part of the sacrifice of burnt offering. Our mothers gave themselves and us, that the poor people might learn of Christ; but was it not hard?"

Yes, but Lillian—she was not part of a life-sacrifice—she was part of a whim, a love of novelty, a wish to justify their own views, a dissatisfaction with the work of the toilers in this awful land.

It was horrible, horrible. Now that the terrors of heat, apoplexy, and cholera were hardly past, and while in the midst of the fever season, when people were dying right and left, there must come also this most loathsome of all diseases. Could she have taken her husband and Lillian and fled to her own home she would have gone at once; and yet the possibility of Lillian taking smallpox did not seem great, for she had been vaccinated, and never had been a child to contract disease of any kind. It was the general horror of living a life never one moment free from terror—smallpox, cholera, leprosy, fever, and sunstroke, always ready to snatch a dear one; never waking in the morning with the certainty that the sun's rays striking in one's eyes might not be intercepted before night by three feet of white sand. The thought came with startling force that even now one of those empty, yawning, ready-made graves kept in India might be waiting for herself or for one dearer than self to her. Only the day before had she seen them in the cemetery where she had gone with Miss Whitlow to put some flowers on Rokewood's grave, and the thought had hardly left her since, and this new danger seemed only a part of a ghastly life in a horrible country.

After five days—five days of harassing suspense, in spite of reason—Lillian was prostrate in her little bed, moaning with fever and raving in delirium.

When it was first known the doctor, a brusque man with a kind heart, ordered strict quarantine, and Carnton had sent a message to each mission house, telling of the calamity and of the doctor's orders.

It was a blow to all, for Lillian had from the first been taken into all hearts. And then, too, all the members of this great mission circle feel a blow to one as they would, in a less degree, to themselves; for it only shows them more clearly the dangers revolving around them. It is a circle that may be divided on plans and processes and polity, but in calamity it is

one, and there was not one of all that band that would
not have gone gladly to Mrs. Clinton and nursed
Lillian as though she were her own, had there been
need, or had they even been allowed.   But at once,
on hearing it, a much-sinned-against Eurasian girl
whom Miss Whitlow had sheltered in time of calamity direst of all that can fall to a woman, because of
the sin it represents, came forward and offered at
once to go and nurse Lillian.   This was especially
fortunate, for she had been two years in the Lady
Dufferin Nursing School, purposing to be a nurse;
and Pulmoni also, Mrs. Clinton's *protégée*, begged so
earnestly to go to the Mem Sahib who had done so
much for her that Dr. Milburn excused them both
from their attendance on their classes.   So the missionaries went on with their work, feeling that Lillian
was cared for better than they could have done it,
more than ever glad that these women, Ethel Lyon
and Pulmoni, had been saved, and praying much that
grace for every need should be given.

And then when Lillian grew worse, and there
was little hope of her being better, Sidney went to
Miss Whitlow, and they arranged to go and remain
alternately in the house, that Mrs. Clinton might
have the comfort of knowing some friend was with
her.

Sidney was to be the first, and went up to the
Clintons' bungalow after dinner to stay during the
night.   She entered quietly, having left her gari at
some distance.   It was so quiet that the house seemed
empty, but outside the blacksmith bird still beat the
air with his endless, never-quiet note.   The brain-
fever bird, however, was gone—dead perhaps of the

very disease with which he had been threatening the
world from the time he could form a note.

The vines over the veranda, the dense dark green
of the trees, and the rank grass in the compound were
soaked with the heavy night dew which caught the
white moonlight like a hoar-frost. Sidney saw Mrs.
Clinton for an instant, and her heart was wrung at
the sight of the careful composure with which she
spoke, the composure that comes only to one whose
nature, stretched to the uttermost, dares not give herself the luxury of one little thought of self-pity; or
dares not, even for a moment, take her eyes off the
beacon light of a duty in hand, fearing precipitation
in a hopeless abyss of helpless agony. Sidney could
only say to herself, as she sat quietly in a chair by
the door, that she was thankful that she had never
borne a child.

She looked vaguely at the corner of the veranda
where she had sat, not long before, on that ever-
blessed night with Carnton, but she could not go
there and sit, though the same chairs were there and
there was the same moonlight; that little spot belonged only to happiness, and had nothing to do with
the cruel bodily and mental suffering with which,
since she had seen Mrs. Clinton's face, and heard the
low murmur of Lillian's voice in delirium, the house
had seemed to be filled.

And here Carnton, coming in with quiet tread,
found her. He came swiftly toward her, and, taking
her hands, said sternly:

"What are you doing here? Why did you come?
O, my darling, why did you come? You know we
were in quarantine."

"Yes; but I told the doctor that I was coming to stay in the house; we could not let Mrs. Clinton be alone, and Miss Whitlow will take my place when I go. We will take every precaution, every care—"

"It is wrong, it is wrong," he said, in anxious pain.

"No, dear, it is right. Surely we can do for dear friends what we do for strangers every day. How could we let Mrs. Clinton think we had deserted her? I can see she is a little glad I am here, though she will not let me come into the room and help her."

"If you had asked me I should not have allowed you to come to the house, but now you are here—"

"Now I am here I will stay," she said, speaking quickly, to cover her mingled feeling of pleasure and surprise at his authoritative tone, but putting her hand on his face with a tender little gesture all her own.

"What did the doctor say to-night about Lillian?" he asked, presently.

"He would say nothing."

Tears came into Carnton's eyes. Lillian had been a pet of his, his "dearest little friend," he had sometimes said.

"Poor little lamb," he said, brokenly, and turned and went back to his own bungalow.

Sidney sat down by the door and listened to the unceasing murmur of the voice which had been so sweet and clear, but which was now changed and unrecognizable.

Mrs. Clinton came out and said, inquiringly,

"Perhaps I ought to send you away; I can hardly tell what is right."

25

"It is right for me to be here, I am sure. Certainly you will let me risk as much for Lillian, whom I love, as I do for strangers in the zenanas."

"But perhaps it would be better to wait until she is not so ill. There will be long weeks of nursing then, when my strength may give out. I shall surely want help then."

"But there are others who will only be too glad to come then. Do not think of me for an instant. I am here to give you comfort; not to add to your anxiety."

Then Mrs. Clinton turned and went back quickly as Lillian's voice grew louder. Sidney could hear it, an indistinct, hurried jumble of school in Naini Tal, of the lake around which she thought she was walking; then she thought she was in a dandi and being carried up from the railway station at Kothgadam, up the mountains, and talked of her fear that the coolies would slip and thus throw her over the precipice; then sometimes of her loneliness and homesickness. "Yes, Ally," she said, evidently to one of her girl friends, "yes, Ally, I am wanting my mother so, but you see she is having an experiment, and she cannot come; and she goes to the zenanas and the women love her, the pretty women with dear little hands and feet. Rings on her fingers and bells on her toes—one on each toe; but why put them in my head? She was to have them only on her toes. Why cut holes in my head for rings or bells. There is one big bell like the church bell, and it rings and it rings slowly, slowly—ring—ring, so it goes. But where is mother? I am going to the zenanas too, like Miss Mellen, but some way not now—not now, but when I can walk further—no, when I am bigger, but not now;" and

another time, "But why not now? It is only to tell
of Christ, how he died on the cross. I think his
head must have ached like mine; it does ache very
much, but I think I could go now; it is a long time
to wait, and thousands and thousands will die without
knowing about Christ—how they hung him on the
cross because he would tell them of a better way to
live; but they would be glad—" Then again, "I think
I would better go now;" and she would sit up in bed,
while her mother with breaking heart would persuade her to lie down again, or sometimes would have
to hold her down. Ethel and Pulmoni were ready
with loving devotion, as also was the Christian woman
who had been Lillian's ayah.

"But I want mother so much. The lake looks hot
to-day, or is it my head? Do you think it is cooler
down below? Perhaps if I put my head away down,
down below the shadows of the willows, down below
even where the goddess goes, it might be cool, but I
don't see why mother does not come. The teachers
are good, but I don't think they are mothers. I would
go to find her, but there are snakes on the floor, always cobras and cobras, and lizards, too, but I will go
when the light comes, so I can see to step over them.
It will be morning after a while, and then I will go;
when I find her I will hold her hard and never let go.
I will go when the light comes;" and the frantic,
maddened mother would take her hand and murmur
words of assurance and tender names which would
quiet her for a while.

The sting of it all was the experiment part of it.
Had they felt the call of God to come to this work
there would not have been this bitterness; but it was

their own experiment, and was God in thus rebuking them, was he not rebuking them in stern anger—yea, was he not chastising them? and how soon would he think their punishment heavy enough? And then there came a day when she heard a voice in her heart, "Be still, and know that I am God;" and she was still, and waited, leaving everything to him, even her own mistake in coming, her own mistake in staying—if it were a mistake—and her mistake in taking Lillian to the zenana.

Ever afterward the whole terrible time remained in her memory as one long day—a day wherein sometimes the lamps were lighted and sometimes there was daylight; a day in which the doctor seemed ever to come and go, but a day in which they all were helpless, cruel witnesses of pain and suffering so great that it seemed to fill the whole world; a day such as one might have in eternity, if eternity holds any agony so keen, so crushing, so terrible that it can take the life out of heart and brain and leave one simply an object that walks, hardly knowing how or why—that breathes, and can, by forcing itself to do so, say words of which it hardly knows the meaning; but an object that really belongs with that innumerable throng which had passed to the other side of the line that divides the living and the dead.

There were weeping and hushed voices in many a little home where dark-eyed mothers told their little ones that the beautiful-faced Miss Baba was going to die, and she was dying because one of their number —one of them—had not been honest and true, and warned her mother, the great Mem Sahib, that there was smallpox in her house.

Then, after a dreary while, the agony ended, and Ethel Lyon, who had so faithfully helped them, lifted the poor bloated, diseased little form, placed it in the box, and then the father closed and nailed it. As he did this the self-control which had come from his firm reliance on God gave way, and a cry so bitter, so full of agony, broke from him that Ethel fled, and his wife, forgetting her own sorrow, went to him and held his head in her arms, comforting him, stroking his hair, and saying tender words over him as though he were the child that had been hidden from sight.

After that they seemed to have reached the Nirvana of sorrow. Nothing could touch them or make them feel more acutely. The long drive to the cemetery, the dreary outlook across the plains from it, the lowering of the coffin into a grave that might be torn open by jackals or washed away by the rains, could not give them one added pang.

CHAPTER XX.

HOME AGAIN.

THE Bishop and Mrs. Clinton returned from the cemetery to Carnton's bungalow to stay while their own was being disinfected. Of course they were all in quarantine, but it was not very strictly kept, for in the matter of smallpox, as well as other things, familiarity breeds contempt. This is not a fortunate thing, for contempt has no disinfecting power, nor is it in any way a protection from contagion. Sidney and Miss Whitlow, especially, had been with them so much they did not think it necessary to stay away now, and messages, notes, and fruit and flowers, which were again beginning to appear in market, came pouring in on them at all times of the day from the various people they had become acquainted with in Lucknow. And from all over India, from Simla to Calcutta, from Naini Tal to Madras, came letters of sympathy to those sorely stricken parents— letters that the Bishop put away in a box for his wife to read some future day.

He had seen the effect on her of a few that she herself had opened and read, and thereafter he watched the mail, took the letters away and read them quietly, feeling that it was almost more than he himself, with all his composure, could bear. But there was a sweetness in them that, apart from the earnest sympathy expressed, or because of it, was precious to him, for it told of the universal brotherhood existing between all who were serving Christ in that dreary land; and there was a feeling of gladness that he had, even for so short a time, been one of a band bound together by a tie so strong and tender; and a new hope for India's millions entered his heart.

It was a quiet household, almost as quiet as when Carnton had been there alone. The Bishop was writing much, and Mrs. Clinton sat with a book in her hands, whose leaves she never turned, looking idly out on the ever-moving stream of native people passing and on the flocks of emerald-green parrots flying from one tree to another, screaming as they went.

Carnton came in rather excitedly one day as she was sitting thus, and told her that a new zenana missionary was on her way out from London, and that another, an old and experienced missionary lady from Calcutta, had written to say that she required a change of climate and would come and assist Miss Mellen for six months; which was so unusual a combination of circumstances that it must mean only one thing—that is, that it was best for him and Sidney to be married at once, though Sidney herself would not be convinced as yet; but he said it all joyfully, as though he did not really doubt the final result.

Mrs. Clinton smiled as she answered that she knew it would be as he wished. Carnton did not like her smile. There was a settled sadness in it that had no relation to natural, healthy grief. It was almost despair—not quite, but as near it as one having a hope of a glorious resurrection could experience. It was the smile that comes when there is a settled conviction that all one's days **will** hereafter **be** spent in a communion with pain ; **that** absolutely never in this world will a ray of pleasure permeate one's life, **and** that not the faintest thrill of joy can **again ever stir** one's heart. Such can smile, but cannot **weep.** Weeping means sorrow that will endure for a season, but that joy will come in the morning.

Mrs. Clinton knew there would no morning ever **come to** her grief. This passive grief and her pallid, **lifeless** face caused the doctor to give unasked advice to the Bishop. It was the good doctor, the kind, the patient, the never-failing friend of the missionary, who, meeting the Bishop one day, said to him:

" Why do you stay here ? If nothing urgent keeps you, you would better go at once."

" I do not think it can be managed," answered the Bishop, briefly. He was thinking **of his wife,** whom he feared could not be persuaded to give up the plan of staying a year. He had a strange feeling since Lillian's death that even her slightest wish must not be opposed. This silent, uncomplaining, changeless grief was appalling to him.

" But you must go ; you must arrange it," persisted the doctor.

The Bishop shook his head. He was recalling the time when **he** had once suggested it to his **wife** and she had refused, reminding him of his promise.

The doctor was getting impatient. He thought it was indifference in the Bishop.

" My dear sir, the first thing **I heard** of you was that you thought there should **be more** missionary graves **in** India. Surely you cannot wish to add another ! "

The Bishop turned white at this sharp thrust. He had forgotten his remark, and it almost seemed as though it were another man who had made it, so little could he recall the attitude of mind he had been in when he came to India; but he said, with grave patience, born of his great sorrow,

"No. Are you thinking of my wife?"

"I beg your pardon, Bishop," said the doctor, "I wished only to tell you that it is necessary that your wife be at once removed from all this, and I did it awkwardly, as usual, but she must go."

"In that case I will write to-day for a passage, and we can leave next week."

"That is right," was the hearty response; "this country is no place for any white man that is not obliged by his conscience or his finances to be here."

And the Bishop murmured a solemn and strong amen.

His wife said nothing when he told her their passage was engaged, but yielded passively, which made him more troubled than ever. Their quarantine was ended by the time they were packed up. Only once did Mrs. Clinton break down, and that was when packing up some of Lillian's books that her brothers had sent her; and she said, as she wrung her hands:

"How can we meet the boys without their sister? How can we live through the landing in New York alone?"

This made the Bishop ponder, and as a result he had the passage transferred two weeks later, and wrote his brother-bishops that he would do the work in Bulgaria and Italy and Norway and Sweden, if they

liked, instead of taking the full year of vacation they
had arranged for him.

He thought it might be well not only to let the
truth come to the boys gradually that Lillian, their
pet and pride, was really gone, but to have the terrible ordeal of seeing them be later, when his wife was
stronger physically, and when time had done what it
could for her.

The day before they started the pastor of the native
church had announced that the Bishop and also Mrs.
Clinton, if she was able, would be at the Sunday
afternoon service, as they would like from there to
bid their native friends good-bye.

The old church, the dear old church (since replaced
by a large new one) that had held so many farewell
meetings, was full, but the Bishop came alone, for
Mrs. Clinton had at the last seemed to feel it too much
of an ordeal, and was so white and trembling that he
led her back to the sitting room, and, kissing her
tenderly, said firmly that she must not go, and then
went away himself.

The Bishop sat inside the altar railing in front of
the pulpit and looked down over the audience, trying
to fix the whole scene as well as individual faces in
his memory. The young men and boys from the
Centennial School, the girls in their pretty white
chuddars, back of them the women from the Home,
and then the body of the church filled with clerks
from the railway or various offices, earnest, intelligent
men, sitting comfortably with wife and family at
their sides, and servants, teachers, and several pastors
who had work in different parts of the city. And
again was he struck with the different expression and

almost the different face Christianity gives to a human
being. He knew he was not mistaken, for here and
there in the audience were men whom he himself had
baptized and whom he had watched through the trans-
formation, and who now looked like different men,
simply because they *were* different men. The native
pastor, a fine, intelligent man, read an address in Urdu,
which was translated into English by the Sunday
school superintendent, dressed in English clothes, and
who spoke English well. Its purport was to the effect
that the whole Christian community had welcomed
with pleasure his visit to them, but the actual effect
of his visit had far exceeded their expectation ; that
one in his high position could leave all and labor like
one of themselves had taught them anew the beauty
of the sacrifice of Jesus Christ ; had taught them that
his followers could also, in some degree, really partake
of the spirit of their Master. But what could they
say when the thought of what this devotion had cost
was presented to their minds? They could say nothing, for no words would express what they felt. Their
hearts had been bowed down with grief, and they
could only say that they could never forget the beautiful child who had been so gentle and loving ; and
they realized with new force and sweetness what it
meant to have a hope of life after the grave, what it
meant to feel sure of seeing again the sweet face of
the dear child.

At first the Bishop could say nothing, and thought
it useless to try, but he commanded himself finally
and answered :

"If, as you say, you all will remember the dear little
face and the dear little form of one that loved you all

well, let each thought of her help you to a better life, to more love to God, to more love to those about you. She was ever loving, ever thoughtful of others, and the earnest resolve of her heart was to live to teach the people of this land of the love of God for his sinful children, that they might be saved through believing in our Lord Jesus Christ. Will you to-day resolve not to allow her life to have been in vain—to remember her, and always, always with the thought of carrying out her plans, to do what she would have done?" His eyes were on the girls from Miss Dillon's school, many of them not older than Lillian. "Take up the golden thread where it has been broken and weave a cord that shall bind many to the truth. Think of her sweetness, of her love for you, and make her resolution to lead many to know that there is salvation from sin, and from the consequences of sin, your resolution; make it the one motive of your life, and so our hearts may be comforted with the thought that she still lives in your hearts and in the lives of many won to the truth."

His voice broke at the last. Carnton had feared that the Bishop was beginning something which even he could not bear. Tears were in many eyes and rolling down many cheeks. Carnton himself could hardly sustain his composure. Lillian had been so much connected in his mind with Sidney, from the first, and then her little loving ways and her absolute friendliness with every living soul had made her very dear.

The address was placed in a silver box and given to the Bishop, and the hand-shakes given him were none the less hearty and affectionate because he had not been born under their flag and speaking their tongue.

The next morning there was a quiet departure from Lucknow for the North.

The Bishop felt it would not be just to the Church he served, nor to the brother-bishops who had taken his work during his absence, to leave India without seeing more of the work than was embraced in the limits of Lucknow, and, too, he hoped it might be a distraction to his wife. She had little packing to do, as now she had no interest in all the pretty Indian embroidery and bric-a-brac. Perhaps it was as well she had not, for the allowance she had planned had been overdrawn, and she did not like to think of the inroads that had been made on the bank account or that would be made by the extra tour; but she said nothing. It did not really matter—nothing really mattered. Life could never be aught but a continued pain, for a shadow had fallen on her which never would be dispersed until pierced by the glory of the Only-begotten of the Father which was before the world began.

So they went to Shahjehanpoor and saw the orphan boys learning trades by which to support themselves and their families; saw the girls' school, where the children of native Christians of the remote districts are gathered, then hurried on to Budaon and saw village work and the schools; then on to Bareilly to see the theological school, from which yearly many fully qualified preachers and teachers are sent out and scattered up and down India; saw the school for the wives of these same students where they are taught by the precept and example of the wife of the good

president to be fit helpmeets to their husbands, to
feel that they have a calling and a work no less sacred
and obligatory and precious than that of their husbands; saw the great girls' orphanage, moving in or-
derly systematic lines, from which will come women
for the future body of the Church; saw the medical
work and the dispensary where are given medicine for
the body and the word of life for the souls of the poor
women who throng the place daily; saw the native
church, the boys' day schools and the girls' day schools.
Then on to Moradabad, where perhaps all conditions
combine for a model mission—a city compact and
not too large; strong, faithful missionaries, who have
had twenty-five years of steady, hard, wise work, and
where the progress of the surrounding country has
kept in line with that of the central town; where
schools with pastor-teachers, founded by the wise gen-
erosity of one liberal man, have uplifted the peasant
population and made them ready to receive the direct
preaching when it could be given to them; with the
girls' and boys' high schools, and a church organized,
self-respectful and wide-awake, with its flourishing
Epworth League, its Woman's Missionary Society, its
Sunday school, its class and prayer meetings.

The Bishop gave up his last struggle for entire
evangelical work when he saw this. He saw that
while he and the other powers of the Church had
been thinking of mission work forever being mission
work—thinking of it as a jellyfish sort of thing—
a Church with frame and backbone and articulation
had been growing. When he found an enthusiastic
circle of young people looking forward to the Epworth League night and preparing for debates and

essays and recitations ; when he heard the reports of the
various committees on work, and all the regular routine of that wonderful organization; when he attended
the woman's missionary meeting and saw the president
in her chuddar presiding with the usual ease and grace
ever predicated of lady presidents—saw all the machinery of a Christian community moving on with a spirit
of earnestness and business, he said to himself : " I have
been dreaming. I thought Lucknow was an exceptional place, but I find in each place I visit the same
or even more exceptional qualities."

Mrs. Clinton saw a part of the work he was not allowed to see—the zenana and day school work ; but it
is all chronicled in the annual reports of the woman's
work ; all that they saw in the various stations, and there
also are many things told that they did not see.

Then he wished to go on to Agra and Delhi and
Jeypore, but the missionaries at Moradabad said they
were not done with him yet. He must go to the annual Christian fair, held at Chandausi. And again
Mrs. Clinton acquiesced. She was glad to find her
husband could be interested, glad that there was anything to lift his mind off the terrible visions of the
suffering child that never for a moment left her.
Sometimes she talked feverishly, hoping to forget it,
feeling that only by keeping her mind off of it, keeping the picture of her child's sufferings out of her
mind, would she be saved from madness. Other
times she gave up to it, finding the effort to fight it
too much, and yet in all this she did not murmur.
She felt that even though it might have been a mistake to take Lillian to the zenana God had allowed
it all to be done, and some way, some way that she

24

could not see, he could bring good out of it; but she had **this** terrible thought always before her, that the particular suffering Lillian had gone through would have been saved had she not proposed coming, or had she acquiesced when her husband had **in a** desperate moment proposed going back. It was an ever-haunting suggestion, a double-edged dagger, **ever** thrusting itself anew into her heart; **but** trying to bring a little good out of it all, trying to save the remnant of her life, she made an effort to be interested in all she saw, to remember everything, that she might tell them at home; tried to stamp on her mind the face and name, as well as the plans, thoughts, and devotion, of each zenana teacher, each school superintendent, each lady doctor, each missionary's wife, that she might, when stronger, when God would give her spiritual and mental and physical life again, tell all to the dear, hard-working ladies at home, no less hard-working and self-sacrificing than many who had come, **but** it was dreary, and almost, though not quite, hopeless work. She hardly seemed to notice the change from one station to another, and one day she found they were at a native Christian **fair, or** mela, which in character corresponds to the American camp meeting.

Think **of** long lines of straw tents, in front **of each** a little **fire, from** which the blue smoke curled **up** against the pale gold **of** the straw; on the fires shining **brass** vase-shaped cooking-pots; around the fires women **in** red or green or purple chuddars, white oxen grazing near, and **the air full of** the spicy smell **of** cooking **curry** powder; **beyond the straw** tents a few white tents, where the missionaries were encamped.

Here were gathered together **over two** thousand

Christians for the annual fair—Christians isolated from regular church services who had looked forward to this time for the acquiring of a deeper spiritual life.

And when Bishop Clinton stood on the platform at the first service—stood beside the missionary bishop, the little but mighty man, above whom he loomed like a giant—and looked out over the mass of people of another language and nationality, but of the same religion, other tints of complexion, but with the same heart of love for God and their fellow-men—saw this missionary bishop, who shoulders responsibilities enough for ten bishops, move these thousands as one man—he got still another up-lift in his hope for and belief in the India Mission.

When he heard him say that black would be white and the Ganges would flow backward and Christianity would become the national religion, both of Mohammedans and Hindoos; that even now the work of the Christian Church had become indigenous and would propagate itself, even if their efforts were put forth to stop it instead of to carry it forward; that while baptisms had numbered this year nineteen thousand —nearly three times those of any previous year— and he expected the following year the same ratio of increase if men and money were provided to justify the procedure—when Bishop Clinton heard all this and saw that great mass of Christians—Christians only because of sacrifice, first of Christ and afterward of his followers who were full enough of love to lay aside all minor considerations and determine to know only one thing, Jesus Christ, and to live and let that one thing show forth through all their lives—when he saw this mass of people rise and as with one voice sing the doxology, because of their leader's enthusiastic prophecy, in faith believing that things even greater than they hoped for would be done, he joined in that song of triumph without for a moment noticing that he sang the words in English and they sang them in Hindoostanee. After all, what are words but the expressions of our thoughts, and the thought was the same and expressed in the grand movement of the old tune that one expects to hear sung by angelic choirs when time shall be no more, when literally "every knee shall bow and every tongue confess."

While the glow of this enthusiasm was on their faces, and in the joyful hush that followed this outburst of praise, Carnton and Sidney emerged from the crowd, and in the Hindoostanee marriage service, which is only a translation of our own, were married. This was not unexpected to the missionaries.

Sidney had said the memory of all Lillian and her mother had suffered was too fresh and too much associated with everything in Lucknow to make her happy in being married there, and yet she wanted Mrs. Clinton to be present at her marriage, and so it had finally come about that, as she was coming to Chandausi to see Mrs. Clinton once more, that Carnton had persuaded her to let the ceremony be there.

She was in a fresh, simple dress and bonnet, and he in the ordinary dark morning suit usually worn by men in the cold weather.

One of the greatest difficulties in work among the Indian people is debt, and generally debt contracted for wedding expenses, which must always be on an extravagant scale, and handicaps many a family for years, and even for generations, the debts being

handed down. So for the sake of the influence of
example Sidney put aside the impulse to array herself in fair and shining raiment, and Carnton, well
pleased, was deeply thankful that his life was to be
spent with one so willing to give up everything for
the people they both loved.

That evening as they stood at the door of their
tent, watching the sun like a ball of fire through the
dust-covered mango trees, they saw an ox-cart full of
native people coming slowly into the camp-ground.
Some way their attention was attracted as it stopped
and the women and children began to scramble out.
"It is always a fresh surprise to me," said Carnton, "to
see how many people a native conveyance can hold."

Sidney did not hear. Her eyes were fixed on one
little woman in a red sari, who had left the group and
was coming swiftly toward them. In a moment she
was sobbing in Sidney's arms, and Sidney was crying,

"Do you not see? It is Sitara, my own little Sitara!"

Carnton, hardly less moved than Sidney, exclaimed,

"Sitara! Then she is still alive, and not gone to
her husband as we feared and hoped!"

Sitara it was, indeed, alive and well, though thin
and with an expression of patient resignation that was
not on her face when Sidney had known her before.

"Yes, my dear Miss Sahib," in answer to their
eager inquiries, "God is good to let me again see
your face, and he has cared for me as you said he
would. Waziran, the old woman who was with us,
fled with me that same night after we were in court,
and we went back to our own village and to the
mother of Shew Pershad's cousins. There was ever
an unkind feeling between the mother of Shew Per-

shad and the mother of his cousins, and she was well pleased that I came to her for refuge. She is getting old, and her sons are away, and it was so that I could make her food as she liked it, and I stayed on, but ever hoping to return to Lucknow when there might be an opportunity. There were some Christians, and when I could I talked with them, but not often. They always said, 'Wait for this mela, and then you will come with us and find your friend;' but my heart was always heavy, and I feared; but God is good, and notwithstanding my fears I am with you again. And never once did I forget to pray to him morning and night, and never once did I bow to those idiotic images which my people worship; and Waziran is also with me, and will be as I am, a Christian."

The world was full of songs of joy for Sidney. Never till this moment had she known just how heavy a burden had been the memory of Sitara and all thoughts of her. The sting of it all was fear, fear that had she herself been wiser or more capable it would have turned out better—that perhaps some one older or more experienced would have saved the girl from the dark fate which she always believed had overtaken the poor little thing. Now that burden was gone, and she began to feel that life was too full of joy, too bright to last—that it could hardly be right that she should be singled out for so much happiness; and she looked from Sitara to Carnton hardly less glad than she, as though she feared they might vanish from her sight while she was looking.

.   .   .   .

A few months later the Bishop, once more in his own native land, stood in a large hall, looking over

the eager audience that was packed nearly to the
ceiling.

Before he had left America on his tour of inspection he had said little of his purpose, thinking if he
found all that unkindly critics had said to be true it
would be well to have as little talk about his going
as possible; but some way the news had gone until
there was a general interest throughout the Church
in their expedition. He had written to no papers, he
had had no communications with the Board of Bishops
or of Missions; so there was even among them, though
boards are not expected to have curiosity, a good deal
of this vulgar quality, and it was very active as to the
discoveries he had made and the conclusions to which
he had come.

The report of Lillian's death by smallpox had come
and insensibly put a sterner aspect on his mission, a
graver interest in his proceedings, and when news went
around from church to church of the city where was
his home that the Bishop would answer the hundreds
of letters of inquiry he had received in public, at the
Monday meeting of preachers, there was no lack of
people early on hand, though the meeting had been
appointed in the largest audience room in the city.

Mrs. Clinton could not come. She said to him that
later on she would do her own share, and promised
many parlor talks and even addresses to small audi-
ences, but she could not bear it yet; she was not quite
recovered enough from the shock of meeting her sons
and of settling in her old home without Lillian.

The Bishop looked anxiously at her. Sometimes
there was a chill at his heart and he had a dread that
he had not yet paid the full price of his experiment.

"No, dear," she said, answering his look, "I am well, and I shall be better now that we are settled here, and then the boys are such comforts. They seem to have grown into men since we left them. And do you know what Fred said to me last night? We were talking of Lillian and her love for the people of India, and he said, ' Mother, I have always thought of going as a missionary, and more than ever now I mean to do so. I will do what Lillian would have done.'" This coming from Fred, the incorrigible, the one of the three who was fullest of fun and life, the one about whom they had had misgivings, was something of a surprise to his father, and, perhaps, not altogether a pleasant surprise. He was prepared to urge young men, other people's sons, to go out to this great work—even prepared to urge middle-aged men to go; but when it came to his own sons, in whom he had much pride and hope, he felt it to be a severe test of the new interest in and love for missions that he had acquired.

He said impatiently to himself that it seemed that they were never to be done with the consequences of their trip to India; that it would pursue them to the end of their days in one shape or another. And he was right. Who thinks he can take a year out of his life and give it to one thing, whether a worthy cause or not, and then return, untrammeled by any thing the year has builded, to his old routine, to his old life, has not yet learned the first principles of living—has yet to learn that his life is a sacred thing with which he cannot trifle, and that each important break or plan is fraught with consequences from which he cannot escape, try as he may.

One other consequence, and one which he did not

regret, was his power to shape public opinion, for he
was a just, true man, and he felt he could use this as
a lever to move the Church to a true estimate of its
responsibility. But when he stood before this great,
eager, self-satisfied, comfortable audience a revulsion
came over him for a moment, and there is not one of
all that number that will ever forget that moment.
They were so well dressed—the women in fresh spring
costumes, with dainty gloves and pleasant smiles, the
men in well-fitting, stylish suits—all so eager for something interesting, something thrilling, and so little
comprehending the seriousness of the message he had
for them, that he was stirred to anger and almost
contempt, and he felt he could turn and rend them.
An audience is like a dog—it likes you better if you
whip it, provided you do not whip it too hard; and
the Bishop stopped short of making his castigation
too hard, though some began to fear he would not.

They were all there that he wanted to see and
wanted to reach—all the people who had been
to India as well as those who had not been to
India: the tourist architectural, who saw more in a
Saracenic tomb than in a mud mission schoolhouse;
the sightseer, who had not time when in India to see
missions, but who now would be glad to listen to anything of that strange, interesting country; there, also,
was the traveler whose mental eyes had double convex
lenses and could see around corners; the critical
personage who considered green pease in February a
sin, but who could not wait to see what he would have
paid for them in June; the one who thought the first
duty of missions was to clothe the people; and there
was also the optimist, who saw good in everything, and

who breathed hope and encouragement wherever he went. They had all seen India in the short three months of cool weather, and the missionaries remained in their minds as people to be envied if they themselves only could see the advantages of their surroundings. Of course, they knew that there was another side to the question, nine months in the year, but it was indefinite in their minds, and apt to be forgotten.

Besides these there was the gentleman who had sent the circular letter to the missionaries asking for photographs of their houses, and another person in authority who would give missionaries the best of everything going, and then say it was not good enough. There, too, were the hard-working "ladies at home," devoted, earnest women, going with their hearts in their mouths, fearful of hearing something derogatory to a work as dear to their hearts as though they, too, had given up for its sake home and friends. And there were their daughters, and there were their nieces, coming on to take the elder ladies' places on committees and as presidents and secretaries.

As the Bishop eyed them a moment before he began an ironical smile was on his face, for like a flash, after taking them all in, his mind went back to those exiles in that far-off land which at that moment was being swept by scorching, sand-laden winds, to darkened houses where men and women were working with the odds of life and health against them: languid, homesick women, whose hearts were aching for a sight of the old home-land, and the sound of running streams and familiar voices; palefaced little children, whose brain must ever be dulled by the fact of their birth in that weary land; men fearing each

week and each month might be the last they could
have to work for God, and still toiling bravely on.
And the absurdity of these comfortable, happy,
well-dressed people, who were enjoying a free government and a Christian civilization, sitting in judgment
on those others, pointed the arrows he let fly.

Just what he said can never be told, but he put the
two phases of life before them, the two pictures as
they were presented to his mind, showing them the
contrast, and then he turned the vials of his wrath
upon them for daring to criticise people who had
given up what they would not give up—people who
were living lives that they would not be willing to live.

Then he went down and fished up their motives and
showed them that the fact of their giving one dollar a
year, or subscribing to a missionary journal, or going
to a missionary prayer meeting when it did not rain,
or when they had no other engagement, did not
entitle them to demand their pound of flesh in the
sufferings and cruel experiences of people whose wild-
est dissipation was a missionary conference once in
three months and a garden party once in three years.

He told them that as they had come to hear criticism
they should hear it, not where they expected, but it
should be on themselves; on them because he knew
where they stood, knew what was in their minds, for
only a little over a year ago he had been where they
were, thought as they thought, and felt as they felt;
and he knew they would forgive him for saying it
because he had himself in mind more than them, and
he was lashing himself over their shoulders.

"I repeat," he said, "I have had myself in my
mind more than you, while speaking—I, myself, as I

was—and that I am glad of the opportunity of holding myself up to myself. A little more than a year ago, and yet ages seem to have passed; or perhaps more truly I might say that I am another man; for I can never go on in the old selfish round again, bound up in the temporal Church, bound up in my own success, living for the worldly advancement of my own interests. Perhaps those of you who have known me best may be kind enough to say that I have not been eminent in the pursuit of my own interests; perhaps you may see no great difference; but I know what it means to be emptied of self, since I have seen it among these people I went to criticise. I know what it is, and I know that it is possible in this our land, as well as in that deadly place. Do not think that I found there, and mean to hold up to you, any 'perfect men sublime,' or 'women winged before their time.' They may live somewhere, but perhaps they are no more common in India than other places. Great natures have great faults, so the man who is great enough to put aside all ambition and everything that is commonly believed to make life attractive, and live for people who are unconscious of the sacrifice made in their favor, may have great imperfections. But that has nothing to do with the work one way or another. I shall now tell you a little of what I have seen. If any of you know how to put the experiences of one year into a half-hour I will sit at his feet and learn."

But perhaps he knew, though the half-hour lengthened to one hour and a half, and still his hearers were not weary. He plainly told them of the doubt of the wisdom and good faith and courage of those in the field that led to his going; of the difficulty he had at first of making his methods coincide with those of the missionaries; of his surprise at the size and extent of the mission; of his criticism of methods; of the absorbing interest of a work where so many doors were open that the only difficulty was to choose which one should be entered; of the deadly climate, emphasized by constant and never-failing contagion and infection; of the rushing on of the evangelical work, bearing fruit in a night like Jonah's gourd; of the slower and more permanent school and literary and other organic work; of his objections to many things, and of his gradual swinging round to believing that, after all, though not perfect, perhaps the whole plan was as nearly so as could be expected in a mission a little over thirty years old. Then he told them of their own part in it all; that because of their prayers and their money and their interest and love for missions this had all come about; that it was their own work, and, as such, they were responsible for the salvation of the thousands who were so ready to be taught.

"There is," he said, "a policy or plan in the minds of the far-seeing ones that is widespread and comprehensive. They understand the tremendous responsibility we have as a Church, and that it is an absolute command 'to go into all the world.' We as a Church dare not shrink from the responsibility of taking India for Christ. It is ready to be taken as soon as the Church understands her obligation and ceases to regard it as a matter of inclination, or as a side issue, or something that depends on impulse. She must call on those that have trumpets, at their peril, to give no uncertain sound, for the time has passed when she can say, 'I will or I will not plant a mission in that land.' She has planted and Apollos has watered, and now that the increase is so great that she finds trouble in caring for it she must not falter and quibble about trifles.

"One superintendent of one district alone reports ten thousand inquirers—that is, ten thousand men who have found paganism inadequate for their needs, ten thousand men who have heard of a God, just and pure, who can save them from their sins; and friends, dear friends, what shall we answer in that great and solemn day when they say, 'We would have served God and not Rām, only there was no one to lead us or even to point the way?'

"What shall we say when it is said to us that had we not failed in our duty, those suffering, dying thousands would have gone joyfully to meet a loving Father? This, dear friends, is the point, this is the thing we must think of, and not whether missionaries suffer more or less. Their heroism, their sufferings, their exposure to dangers, their isolation, have nothing to do with it. There is this side of the question, and, perhaps unfortunately, people wanting money for missions have found that it is easier to appeal to your sympathy than to your responsibility as servants of the living God and as coworkers with him. There is this side of the question, and God forbid that their dangers or sufferings be any greater.

"Let me forever set you at rest on this. Perhaps it was meant that I should be fully qualified to speak on this point;" his voice wavered and friends in the audience feared he had begun something he would find difficulty in finishing; but he rallied and went on. "And yet I have only known the everyday life of the ordinary missionary, and in some respects I was mercifully spared. My wife and myself escaped" —again he faltered—"and are left to care together for our boys. Others have been less fortunate. Even since I left, a mother, as well as her child, has been stricken and three little children are left without her tender care. Another, comparatively young, forever isolated from her friends, will labor among lepers, because through the exigencies of mission work that dread disease has come to her; and Mackenzie and Miller, the men I worked with and who were the first to greet me, have gone down. First, Mackenzie, doing two men's work without the bodily strength of one, after a few hours' illness, was snatched away by cholera. When I heard that the light had gone from his genial eyes, that the kindly, generous hand was forever still, a picture was presented to my mind of him as he stood one morning in the church, describing the device on a missionary paper, of an ox standing with a plow at his right, an altar at his left, and of Mackenzie's saying, 'This device represents my thought in being here in this work. I am ready for either work or sacrifice. If it be the former only I shall be glad; if it be the latter, as I sometimes have felt it will be, I am content and can say, God's will be done.'

"And Miller, when urged to leave his work and try the effect of the home climate in prolonging his life, said, with the gentle heroism ever characteristic of him, 'No, it is better to die in the harness.'

"And, friends, the bitter thought to me is that while my own short service in India cost me so dear, yet I did not see what the core of the trial of mission life was until it came home to me in the loss of my own dear little lamb. Not till then did I understand the sacrifice they make who live in that terrible land —in that sweet land: terrible because it has bereaved me of my friends and my child; sweet because it has become their last resting-place.

"And I say to you, do not dare, as I did, to deny the heroism of the lives of those who still live and toil there, nor of those who have died to prove it.

"O, wild hot winds, sweeping over those brave ones who have died for a cause they loved better than long life, touch lightly, we pray you, the sacred sand that lies above them, and had you a known voice and language I would pray you ever through all the coming years to tell all men, not only in that far, sad land, but throughout the whole world, of the love they had for humanity, of their brave, unfaltering work, of their unwavering trust in God and in his Son, our Lord Jesus Christ. I would pray you tell them how, unmurmuring, they went down in the strife, how courageously they died in the harness, and I would have you beg others to keep their lives before them as beacon lights to lighten their way when it seems darkest, and I would beg you to tell those people for whom they died to remember that a double responsibility rests on them to emulate their work and their sacrifice, and to believe, as I have come to believe:

> "'Alike are life and death,
> When life in death survives,
> And the uninterrupted breath
> Inspires a thousand lives.'"

THE END.

www.ingramcontent.com/pod-product-compliance
Lightning Source LLC
Chambersburg PA
CBHW030822110726
47900CB00006B/1709